Wearing th.

"This is such a solid book that I have difficulty believing it is Mr. Harmon's first novel. The story is polished, well edited, tightly plotted, and stocked with interesting characters. Like Peter Clines' debut novel, Ex-Humans, this sets the bar so high for follow-up work that I'm sure Mr. Harmon is feeling the pressure."

Michael of Dover, Delaware

Villains Inc.

"A riveting follow-up to Wearing the Cape, *Harmon's sophomore novel continues to satisfy those of us who need a fix of well-written superhero fiction. Fans of the first book will not find its sequel lacking, and while it might be more of an adjustment to readers who haven't picked up the first book, it stands well enough on its own."*

Avander Promontory

On the *Wearing the Cape* series.

"The Wearing the Cape *series is the gold standard that all other superhero novels should aspire to."*

Hero Sandwich

Small Town Heroes

Mr. Harmon knocks the ball out of the park once again in Small Town Heroes. *His realistic take on an absurd reality is, as always, an extremely interesting read and his characters continue to be deep and immersive.*

Amazon Reviewer

Ronin Games

As always, the Wearing the Cape *series delights and entertains, with some solid twists and further exploration of the nature of superhuman in the very well thought setting of the series.*

Tim Kirk

Books by M.G.Harmon
Wearing the Cape
Villains Inc.
Bite Me: Big Easy Nights
Young Sentinels
Small Town Heroes
Ronin Games
Team-Ups and Crossovers

Short Stories by M.G.Harmon
Omega Night

Team-Ups and Crossovers

Marion G. Harmon

Copyright © 2016 Marion G. Harmon

Astra Gets Grrl Power by M.G. Harmon and Dave Barrack.

Historical Accuracy by K.F. Lim

Velveteen, Jacqueline Claus, Polychrome, Victory Anna, and The Princess owned by Seanan McGuire

Cover art by Kasia Slupecka

All rights reserved.

ISBN-10: 1540417441
ISBN-13: 978-1540417442

DEDICATION

To my fellow-travelers in the young and growing genre of superhero fiction.

CONTENTS

Author Foreword
p.ix
Dating Games
p.1
Killing Sleeping Beauty
p.11
Velveteen vs. The Crossover
p.46
The Oz Job
p.68
Through a Bright Mirror
p.93
The Traveler's Tale
p.111
Grimworld
p.121
Wargames
p.217
Astra Gets Grrl Power
p.225
Everybody vs. The Team-Up
p.277
Historical Accuracy
p.301

ACKNOWLEDGMENTS

Special thanks to Seanan McGuire and Dave Barrack for letting me play in their worlds.

Author Foreword

I've never written a foreword before, but this book just screams for it. *Team-Ups and Crossovers* is a huge departure from my usual style of writing for the Wearing the Cape series. The book is a series of short-stories ranging from 5,000 to 40,000 words, each story covering one piece of the overarching plot. Why? It is the only way to tell this kind of story.

Two seemingly universal tropes of superhero comics are the team-up (two or more heroes from different comic titles getting together for an adventure) and the crossover (two or more heroes from different comic *universes* getting together for an adventure). Detective Comics (DC) first became famous for it, with team-ups between Superman and Batman becoming so regular that they spawned their own comic—*World's Finest Comics*—a tradition carried on with Superman, Batman, and Wonder Woman in today's *Trinity* comic title. DC also featured crossovers between its own two superhero universes (Universe A, where Superman and the others first appeared in the 60s and Universe B, where they appeared before World War Two), and DC and Marvel led the way in publisher-universe crossovers, with Spiderman and the Hulk meeting Superman, and later the Justice League of America meeting the Avengers. And of course today crossovers of every conceivable type are a favorite subject of fanfiction.

After *Ronin Games* I decided it was about time for Astra to experience her own crossovers, and here they are. Since true team-ups and crossovers require partners, I was fortunate to gain the invaluable cooperation of three fellow writers:

Seanan McGuire: author of the October Daye, InCryptid, and Indexing series, plus sundry other marvelous stories, not least of which are the Velveteen Vs. books. As prolific a writer as Seanan is (as near as I can tell she is always working on at least three books) she could not contribute directly to this anthology (again, working on at least three new books). However, she graciously allowed me to use her wonderful Velveteen Vs. superhero world and characters for two linked crossover stories. Note: these two stories—*Velveteen vs. The Crossover* and *Everybody vs. The Team Up*, are non-canonical for Ms. McGuire's Velveteen Vs. stories and characters, but canon for mine. Purists may consider that Astra visits a close parallel to the world of the canon Velveteen Vs. stories.

Dave Barrack: artist/writer of the wonderfully hilarious *Grrl Power* webcomic (grrlpowercomic.com). Dave co-wrote *Astra Gets Girl Power* with me, and Halo, Maxima, and everyone else in the story except Astra belong to Dave. As do most of the jokes and pretty much all the insanity. Dave's world is one of the most imaginative and funny superhero worlds out there today, and Halo is certainly one of the most original superheroines I have met.

K.F. Lim: a practicing (and harassed) attorney in family law, jewelry designer, voice-actor, and writer. *Historical Accuracy* is her first published short story. An unconnected epilogue to the anthology's main plot arc, it is a wonderful tale of Astra's team-up with a…different kind of Crisis Aid and Intervention team.

A final note: readers will notice that the narrative style in this collection shifts from story to story. Some stories are told in first-person narrative, others in third-person, and not all of them from Hope's point of view. One story, *The Traveler's Tale*, is told in almost a play-script style! (If you don't like it don't worry—it's short.) Mostly this is due to my desire to stick to the narrative style used by the other authors, but it's all also an experiment; I had tremendous fun writing it.

But enough of this, on to the stories. Enjoy!

Marion G. Harmon

Dating Games

by Marion G. Harmon

"In Hollywood everything is about the image. But how is that different than life as a celebrity cape? Answer: it's not, and there are good people there, too—you've just got to remember that the pretty wrapping is never the package."

The Hope Corrigan Interviews.

Kitsune was *stalking* me. Actually he was stalking my *dates*, which was worse. Tonight "she" was our beautiful Asian waitress, Mei. I almost tucked my hands beneath me in an effort not to jump up and go find our real one, who was almost certainly peacefully sleeping in a closet somewhere. She'd wake up later to find she'd made the most amazing tips tonight, but—

I blinked. "Sorry?" My date had just asked…what? Had I seen his latest movie? Had I *been* to the movies lately? What did I think of movies? Super-duper hearing did no good if I wasn't paying attention.

But it was my super-duper nose that had distracted me. I wasn't quite a bloodhound, but ever since the Thing in Tokyo We Never Ever Mention I'd been able to recognize Kitsune by his smell; it was the same undertone of musky, furry something no matter what form he wore.

I'd learned to dread it, and with "Mei" standing by our table, I'd lost the tenuous thread of our limping conversation again.

Tony kept his smile up—probably second nature in public where there might be paparazzi or anyone willing to sell a tidbit of observation to a tabloid.

"I said, 'how's the mushu?'"

"Oh." I looked down at my plate. LA's Silk Road served the *authentic* mu xu: sliced pork tenderloin, cucumber, and scrambled eggs together with thinly sliced wood ear and velvet foot mushrooms, all stir fried in peanut oil and seasoned with minced ginger and garlic. I could taste the bite of the rice wine under the flavors.

I bit my tongue before I said all that; being reduced to talking about the food was a Bad Sign.

And this was going to end epically badly.

It was all Quin's fault. After Jacky, Ozma, and I had arrived back from That Place We Do Not Speak Of I'd been benched for physical therapy. And after everything we'd been doing lately to give poor Quin public-relations fits, I'd felt I'd owed her and made the mistake of telling her so.

She'd collected.

Tony was date number five, latest in my string of "celebrity dates" and the highest on the scale of celebrity stardom so far. He did *action* movies and had the kind of long face that didn't look handsome until he smiled and then your breath would catch. Quin wanted me to be seen doing "adult socializing" while I was in LA to re-train and work back up with Rook. It was all part of her campaign against my Wholesome Teen Sweetheart brand, which had never completely died despite my rumored "romantic relationship" with Atlas during my sidekick tour. It didn't help that I still *looked* like a wholesome teen sweetheart despite being just a couple months shy of twenty-one, and that these dates were the *most* I'd agreed to do to "mature" my image.

Quin's other suggestion had been a costume makeover that would have made me look like a Victoria's Secret model in a catwalk costume, so here I was out on a date with Tony.

Looking at his handsome-homely face as he took another bite of his fish, I wondered if *he* was regretting *me*.

His agent had agreed because Tony's next movie was a superhero flick; Tony was playing a "super-normal" vigilante out after the supervillains who killed his family. There were rumors that the script was vaguely anti-cape, so the idea was that being seen with me would buff his pro-cape credentials. Celebrity actors shaped their public images even more carefully than capes did. *Tony* had agreed because the singer *he'd* been dating had dumped him after a drunken fight the tabloids were still telling conflicting stories about. *I was beginning to think she should have maimed him on her way out.* Sure the guy had come off a long day on a sound stage, but he was putting as much energy into our conversation as a flat battery.

Now he blinked slowly at me and I realized I should be talking. Even Kitsune was looking at me a little funny.

"The mu xu's good." I smiled at *Mei* because if she'd been her I would have. "And your fish?" Tony had ordered the Sichuan fish, poached in hot chili oil.

"I've had better." His face said *from the food-truck on the set.*

I barely kept from rolling my eyes; my nose told me the oil was pure and fresh, the fish practically teleported from its salt-water tank into the poaching pan before it had known it was dead—my father the foodie would have had nothing to complain about except maybe the dish's "mouthfeel."

I bit my lip and didn't suggest he change his micro-brew beer. The original Mei hadn't recommended it with the fish, and it was probably swamping his taste buds. Kitsune didn't twitch even though it had been her question—*And how is everything?*—that had sparked Tony's question to me (and obviously the word "movie" had come out of his mouth enough times before he'd gone quiet for me to swap it for "mu xu").

She smiled widely instead. "Is there anything else I can get you, perhaps?"

I didn't close my eyes, groan, drop my head onto the table, or run screaming, although all of that sounded good.

Because Tony was a Dead Man Walking.

Mei departed with a smile when neither of us said we wanted anything, but it was only a matter of time; Tony was probably *safer* when she was standing right here.

It had started with Date Number Three. One and Two hadn't been teeth-achingly bad although my opinion of actors as Dateable Human Beings had suffered a little. Hopefully I wasn't getting top-draw in the Hollywood dating circuit. Possibly the fact that I still looked like a before-the-makeover Disney Princess scared them off. Regardless, numbers Three and Four had been...bad. So bad I'd hoped that a supervillain attack would end the date since I couldn't stick a fork in my own eye.

The dates *had* ended, and technically Kitsune was a supervillain...

Number Three had taken a bathroom break and then suddenly and urgently had to leave—face-planting into another couple's table on the way out; I'd *carried* him out to the town car while our driver held the door, and the paparazzi had of course caught it. The opinion of the emergency room doctor (leaked to the tabloids, of course) had been *too much coke during the bathroom break*, and Number Three was now in rehab.

Number Four had *caught on fire*. Kitsune had attended the Hollywood house party as a minor celebrity (I no idea where the real one had been), but he'd been standing nowhere near when it happened. The spilled alcohol fire hadn't hurt Four but it had destroyed his suit and his dignity; he'd absolutely panicked instead of doing anything constructive, and I'd had to toss him in the mansion's pool. Again caught on camera, this time another party guest's phone, and I still didn't know how Kitsune had done it.

So part of me was waiting in sick fascination to see what doom would befall Tony and wondering if I could keep it out of the tabloids—who had realized something was happening and started placing *bets*. The other part of me was determined to grab Kitsune and make him explain how he was finding out about my dates—which were hardly publicized beforehand—and why he was destroying the *bad ones*.

I picked at my mu xu without tasting it.

After all, in a weird sort of way we were *betrothed*. (And didn't that word just make me giggle half-hysterically.) I'd agreed to marry him at some unspecified future date—the same day that he carried out his promise to swear himself to the service of my family like an old-style samurai retainer, so that was never going to happen. So why the stalking? And if he was staking some kind of sneaky claim, why end the bad dates?

You'd think he'd shut down the good *ones*. Not that any of them had been exactly great— "Sorry?"

I'd ignored Tony again.

And he was just watching me, looking for *what* I didn't know. Then a half-smile crept across his face.

"This is terrible, isn't it?" His lips twitched and his eyes, which really were tired, invited me to share the joke.

My face went hot. I hadn't been the most conversationally engaged date either, not since sniffing Kitsune. "A little? I'm sor—"

He *snorted* and leaned in, elbows on the table and hands clasped under his chin. "Don't say it. This is my fault. I never should have agreed to a night when I'm not firing on all cylinders. And this can't be you—I talked to Seven before telling my agent to go ahead and set it up. So both of us are failing to prop up this thing, though you gave it a great shot in the beginning. Yeah?"

I deflated. "Okay, yeah. This is pretty bad."

"Then how about this. We doggy-bag our dinner."

"We— Really?"

"They know me here and I'm usually much better than this, trust me. They'll box our entrees, slip some tasty dessert into the bag, even include the linen and silver—they know I'm good for it."

His half-smile went full bore, much more real than the earlier photo-op one. "I know a nice little park in the Hills not far away, it's a warm night, I can take off this hangman's tie and jacket. And if we can't start a better conversation in five minutes out there, you can ditch your excuse of a date. What do you say? There are ducks."

"Well, if there are *ducks*." That twisty grin had talked a lot of girls into bigger things than ducks, I was sure of it. But—it sounded fun. And away from our audience. I was suddenly hyper-aware of the clink of cutlery on china, the low rumble and susurration of a dozen dinner conversations around us.

Everybody at the Silk Road, guests and staff, had been super-great about ignoring us. It was one of the high end establishment's best selling points I supposed, but it wouldn't continue when doom befell.

If I could get Tony out of here intact, away from *Kitsune*...

I nodded hard, a matching grin splitting my face. "I'm in. Let me tell Mei." An un-doomed date. The thought made me almost giddy.

"TIME TO PAY YOUR DUES, OPPRESSORS!"

You have got to be kidding me.

The guys in the black bandanas and hoodies fanning out from the kitchen weren't staff and the guns and bags they carried weren't aperitifs. The dinner conversations turned into dismayed shouts and screams, but nobody got stupid as the intruders pushed through the dining room. They wore black armbands decorated with broken red "A"s—the anarchists' favored symbol—on their right arms.

Eight of them. All armed. How was I supposed to stop them without someone getting hurt?

"Shell?" I whispered, and got nothing. She stayed out of my head on these dates (her commentary was monumentally distracting), but a shout through our quantum-neural link should have gotten her attention. So either one of the wannabe anarchist redistributors was a superhuman somehow jamming me, or they'd bought a universal blocker off of a black-lab Verne and it was working even better than they knew. And if they had Verne tech jammers, what else did they have?

Moving very slowly, I slipped fingers into my purse and withdrew the pair of Anonymity Specs Ozma had let me bring to LA. With her sense of humor, she'd made these look exactly like the kinds of big, dark shades Hollywood stars tended to wear with baseball caps when trying to avoid notice. Mine worked.

"Thanks for giving!" The hooded thug looming by our table grabbed my bag and the specs in one big gloved fist, stuffed them into his sack. Then he shoved the gun in my face, eyes on Tony. "And calm down, action-hero—there's no retakes on this scene, hate to end it with your little slut's brains spread over your entrée. Phone. Watch. Ring. Wallet. Money-clip. Now." He raised his gun like he was going to pistol-whip me with it.

"Okay! Okay!" Tony held up both hands. "Don't do anything!" He carefully reached into his jacket and pulled out his wallet, phone, and cash, pulled off his ring and unlatched his watch, dropping everything in the sack.

His hands were steady and his breathing deep, like he was gathering oxygen for extra energy. His heart was racing but not with the tripping speed of panic; he was ready to *do* something. "Please, nobody needs to get hurt," I whispered, keeping my eyes on him.

"Effing-right, girl." Our robber purred at me, looking me over.

I'd raided Beverly Hills' Rodeo Drive shops for tonight, and was wearing a bustier-dress with glittery top and a skirt almost short and poofy enough for a ballerina. With tights, of course. The miracle had been that it was in my elfin size, but I'd picked it mostly because back-crossing straps supported the bustier—if I got in a fight wearing this confection there would be zero wardrobe accidents. Now I felt like I was wearing too little. His pistol dropped and I shivered as he used its tip to push the ends of my bobbed hair off my shoulders.

"Please," I repeated, thinking faster than I ever had.

There could easily be one superhuman in this hooded gang—first rule of being a professional supervillain: unless you're *trying* to make a point, don't identify yourself with a flashy costume when you're actually on the job—you just give someone like me a target and a chance of knowing exactly what you can do if you have any real rep. You saved the costume for hanging with your minions and peeps.

He let my hair drop without a flicker—or panicked freakout—of recognition and I slumped with relief. Of course he misread it. "Maybe we'll get acquainted later," he tossed off as he moved to the next table.

Nobody else looked at us, and that was getting *weird*; the dining room's lights were kind of dim, but it wasn't like the tabloids hadn't been spreading my unmasked face around recently. But none—*none*—of the guests or staff were giving me a *Save us!* look either, and that was just against human nature. I'd put being ignored before down to LA-society politeness; now it was freaky.

Which didn't mean it wasn't *good*, since I didn't want these social-justice redistributionists to panic and spring into hostage mode; there were too many to protect and I could all-too-easily picture someone else's brains spread over the white tablecloths.

And I didn't even want to see *theirs* there, no matter how rude they got.

Our robber moved on from our neighbor's table, leaving the nice older couple there more than a little shaky. I really hoped it wasn't their anniversary or something, and worried about the lady; she looked unhealthily pale and wasn't breathing well.

But this was okay. It would be okay if everyone just kept ignoring me—our robbers could sweep the room and switch to getaway mode and *then* I could pursue with nobody to get hurt. I wasn't a local cape, but it was legal so long as I didn't lose contact; I'd get somebody even if they dispersed on the streets, turn him over to the LAPD if they just—

"No! No!" The panicked cry came from the man eating alone three tables away and our personal robber clubbed him with the pistol he'd waved at me. Screams spread as the man, halfway to his feet when the heavy weight met his head, crashed to the dining-room floor and his attacker pointed his gun. And *still* nobody looked at me until I launched myself with no time even for a prayer.

"*Everybody down everybody down everybody down!*"

And the lights went out—which didn't slow me down at all. I hit the would-be shooter hard, carrying him over the table and into the next-closest—dropped him but not before crushing his gun hand while disarming him. At least he still had his fingers.

Silk Road's patrons and staff followed my screamed instructions, but the anarchists didn't—they stayed on their feet, nice glowing targets in the black illuminated by their body heat in my super-duper vision. I collected and scattered guns, calling on them to surrender every time I bobbed up to give them something to focus on and shoot at in their blindness. The smart ones tried to run—also stupid since they couldn't see—but none of them shot *down*.

Even so, my heart stayed in my throat the entire time and I didn't breathe except to keep shouting for their attention over the bangs and screams until the last of the seven were down and the crashing chaos died. And the lights came back.

It was a wreckage but not—*thank God*—a bloody one. The seven had joined everyone else on the floor—I'd dropped each hard when I emptied their hands and left them broken wrists or crushed hands for good measure, and I didn't see any injured patrons. I settled to an upright table in the center of the dining room, feeling light headed.

"Everybody wearing a hoody will stay on the floor, and if you move I'll hang you from the ceiling. Would everyone else please move to the walls? I'm sorry for the fright you've been given."

Tony rose from where he'd obviously, with care and foresight, gotten our neighboring couple to the floor and then crouched over them. Now he helped them up and away as staff began remembering themselves and doing the same. Some of the less shaken ones even picked up dropped guns as they moved away from my targets.

I couldn't see "Mei," but then I didn't expect to; she would be somewhere with the lights if she wasn't gone now, and I forgot about her and tried to look menacing—not easy to do standing on a table in my kicky shoes and sparkly dress, but I'd just inflicted serious pain on all of them and their monkey hindbrains wouldn't forget that soon.

And I could hear sirens.

Minutes later the dining room flooded with half a dozen blue-boys and I climbed down. Tony helped me, a totally pointless and very nice gesture. "Excuse me?" I called to our maître d'. A bit pale himself, he did seem to at least be tracking things. "Have you seen Mei?"

He stopped giving the staff quiet orders and drew breath, looking around the dining room. "No. Not since these men arrived."

I sighed. "Look in your supply closets, but I'm sure she's fine."

"Thank you." He nodded and dismissed my bizarre suggestion, but he'd remember it as soon as he had a moment, I was sure of that.

Tony chuckled beside me. "Do I want to know?"

"Not really." I recognized the expression on the officer headed towards me, and sighed again. Debriefing time. Turning to Tony, I looked him over. His jacket was rumpled and he'd loosened his "hangman's noose," but he was still in better shape than numbers Three and Four. And he'd acquitted himself surprisingly well back there...

"I can't believe I'm going to ask this, but— Would you like another date? A do-over?"

His half-smile spread to full, without a trace of irony or sarcasm as he looked around at the trashed room and back at me.

"I'll need to check my insurance, but sure."

He could be Number Six.

Document 43.5284, recovered text file.

To Blackstone:

I'm sure you've received the official police report. I'll write it up tomorrow and explain whatever doesn't make sense in the debriefing when I get back. After searching all of the "anarchists" turned up no Verne-Tech, I discreetly spoke to the maître d' about signals-jamming and mental manipulation and he privately confessed that the Silk Road employs a high priced witch to maintain anti-eavesdropping and anonymity charms to shield the restaurant's patrons from unwanted surveillance or attention. I don't think he knows how powerful they are, but they explained my weird anonymity and Shell's silence, and they're harmless enough that I promised not to tell anyone official. I do recommend Ozma look at them and write up the basic technique of the anonymity charm for the DSA to know about without telling them where it came from. Banking some favors with Veritas and his people may pay dividends later.
Speaking of Veritas and favors, he's called and asked me to join a special DSA-CAI task force trying to trap a superhuman serial killer. I said yes and am leaving LA tonight, so Quin's celebrity-dating scheme will have to wait. Please tell her that I've let Tony know and that I look forward to seeing the ducks when I return.

Sincerely, Hope.

Killing Sleeping Beauty

by Marion G. Harmon

"The problem with making yourself the sword of justice is knowing when to stop chopping."

Jacky Bouchard, aka Artemis.

He was trouble in a cop suit. Looking up at the ringing of the shop's silver bell and seeing him push his way into Beantown made me reconsider my open door policy. Not that I didn't like Detective Paul Negri, but since I'd slipped from being on the side of the angels—or at least the law—the New Orleans Police Department and I didn't have much to do with each other. I'd fallen from grace when I became the completely deniable enforcer for the Midnight Ball—New Orleans' completely deniable vampire *familia* headed by the Master of Ceremonies—and Paul was too much of a straight-arrow to not take my defection personally.

Not that I'd had any real choice.

At three in the afternoon, tourists and locals packed the small coffeehouse. I'd been up for two hours, and sat at my "office" table where I could watch over things while working on the shop's books on my epad and sampling our latest delivery of Ethiopian shade-bean. He ignored the serving counter to push through the close-packed little tables to my corner.

"Paul." I lowered my cup, careful to set it on its Beantown coaster (I hadn't named the place *Beantown* for Boston, but tourists from New England loved to buy them). Edwardo appeared at Paul's elbow with a Peeler's Cup, the special house blend we complimented to any officers of the law who crossed our door. Half of the uniforms on night patrol in the French Quarter dropped by at least once a night for theirs.

"How are you, *chère*?" he asked as soon as Edwardo left.

"Emerson send you?"

He winced. My accusing him of being here on orders from his boss was probably unfair, but he hadn't exactly earned fairness. "It's good to see you, Jacky."

"You too. Emerson send you?" I put an impatient edge in my voice, but looked past his head. I wasn't being rude; eye-contact magnified a vampire's influence and I wasn't going to push him, even accidentally.

He sipped his Peeler's Cup, grimaced. The stuff was bitter and strong, meant to shock the half-asleep mind awake and set the drinker's nerves dancing. It wasn't drunk for pleasure, though a lot of uniforms had told me there wasn't anything else like it once they'd gotten used to it. Kind of like fang-addicts.

"I need your help." Putting the cup down, he reached into his blazer jacket and slid his cellphone across the table. Its screen showed a raven-haired, fresh faced young girl, fifteen or sixteen. She looked happy.

I studied her. "A case?"

"I wish." He crossed himself, something he always did when saying a prayer in his head. A prayer for her, I assumed. Which saint had he invoked? "Her name is Sabrina Garnette."

"I'm just a PI these days, Paul. I do security, bodyguarding, private investigations. Which of those do you want?"

"All three, *chère*. But it can't be a job." He managed to look both annoyed and shamed, quite a trick and the conversation lost what little pleasure it had.

"Midnight Ball business." The words tasted sour. If Lieutenant Emerson and his team were going to lock me out, sending Paul to negotiate a favor was just shitty. "Dammit, Paul—"

He held up his hand. "Please, *chère*. The boss didn't send me. If he knew I was talking to you, it would be worth my badge."

I didn't believe that for a second. The ruthless bastard probably knew right where Paul was, just not officially. Which meant if whatever this was came to light officially and in a bad way, then Paul would be the one to take it in the teeth instead of his rat boss.

Realizing I was showing fang, I got a grip. Lieutenant Emerson was a rat and a lot of other things, but he was a *good* rat—he did what he thought he had to do to protect the people in his precinct, and most of the time he was right. "Okay, Paul. Tell me what your boss can't tell me."

He accepted that. "The girl's got a friend who's got her back. Her parents sure don't—they're a business couple, out of town half the time. The girl practically raises herself."

Great, the perfect target for the kind of trouble I usually got called by the Master of Ceremonies to straighten out. The cops making the call was new. "Seems lively. So her friend thinks she's in trouble, but can't prove it?"

He nodded. "She's smart, spotted all the signs. 'Course, Miss Garnette could just be getting into drugs—just about the same social cues—but she's gotten into goth, too."

Shit. "And what have you done?"

"We interviewed her. But we've got no proof she went anywhere she shouldn't, and without it we can't get a warrant for a physical or psychological examination."

One that might show evidence of bites or repeated enthrallment. I looked at her picture again. "Behavior changes?"

"Plenty according, to her friend. She reported her anonymously."

I was beginning to like her friend; most girls that age wouldn't be observant enough, thoughtful enough, and then strong enough to figure out something was seriously wrong and take steps that amounted to "narking"—the unpardonable teen sin. If that's what this was.

If it was, then she'd probably tried to intervene herself, first. Depending on Sabrina's degree of enthrallment—if that's what it was— the results could have been scary as hell.

"We put a watch on her place for a couple of weeks," Paul went on. "But she's not sneaking out and we don't have the manpower to keep it up. With nothing to use…"

With nothing concrete, they couldn't go in to look for more. Glancing up from the phone, I caught Paul's expression before he smoothed it out. He was resentful, worried, tired, obviously the two weeks' watchman. I handed the phone back.

"I'll talk to some people, Paul. That's all I can do."

I didn't wink, but I nodded. He met my eyes—a stupid thing to do with a vampire, even in the day—and unwound just a little, letting a little more of his fatigue show. If the Peelers Cup wasn't doing anything for him, he needed days of downtime. Standing, he drained it, gagged a bit.

"God, *chère*. That stuff's horrible."

"If I'd made it for you I'd have spit in it. Go get some sleep. Or go out to the bayou where you can get furry and chase something." I mimicked howling at the Moon. He actually laughed.

"I just might. Be careful, *chère*."

"Because just talking is dangerous? Go away, Paul. And next time come back after dark. Acacia misses you."

The first "person" I talked to was a ghost; not like Casper, the ghost who lived in my coffee shop, apartment, and PI office (Acacia called him Charley) but a cyber-ghost. I didn't even need to leave my table. I could have gone to the Department of Superhuman Affairs for this (I *was* their civilian consultant here in the Big Easy), but Gray and I cordially detested each other. At least I detested my sometime-DSA handler; I had no idea what he thought of me—the man had the polar opposite of charm, and he used it knowingly.

Shell answered as soon as I inserted the earbud and slid on the special shades she'd sent me just a month ago. The "reality plus" projector in the shades painted her virtual image directly on my eyeballs so that it looked to me like she'd taken the chair emptied by Paul.

"Hey Jacky! What can I do for you?"

I snorted. Shell usually presented virtually as an older teen—which she chronologically was, having lost three years while she was "dead" and then a few more months because she was actually a backup—but lately she'd been presenting a bit more mature. I didn't see many personalized t-shirts anymore, and her red hair was cut shorter in a shoulder length doo. She wore a military-style blue and white jumpsuit with a Chicago Sentinels patch on it.

"I need to know everything about somebody fast."

"And you can't get your DSA contacts to do it for you?"

"No." I didn't elaborate.

"Gotcha. Who?"

"Sabrina Garnette. Local teen."

"Okay... Sabrina Eleanor Garnette, seventeen." She projected an image of the girl's yearbook picture and I nodded.

"That's her. What can you tell me?"

"Nice Garden District address, good school grades until recently, no juvie record, no electronic footprint you wouldn't expect. She's not on any sensitive lists."

So she wasn't a known or suspected breakthrough. That had been the first thing I'd thought of checking off; it could also account for the behavior changes and Paul's people wouldn't have known if the DSA hadn't seen fit to tell them. And they wouldn't have; if Sabrina had appeared on the DSA's radar as a quiet breakthrough, the only way they'd share was if someone with her suspected power-set became active.

If I'd asked Gray, he'd have asked why I wanted to know.

"Good to hear. Can you send me her address, electronic receipts, and your best maps of her neighborhood and home?" Her financials (and I'd bet her parents had given her a personal account and debit card) were the first thing to check; Paul couldn't without the warrant.

"In your super-secure mailbox as we speak. Anything else?"

"No, that's—yes. How's Hope?"

"Doing a job for the DSA right now." Shell's whole body said she wasn't very happy about it, and I kept myself from smiling. She probably didn't think that Hope should be on active *anything* yet, still working up her arm after the hit she'd taken in Tokyo. "Oh! I'll send you the news report of her latest date."

"I could use a laugh. Want to run a surveillance job with me?"

Her eyes lit up. "Midnight Ball business?" Ever since she'd had a chance to meet the Master of Ceremonies, Leróy, and Darren during our Littleton adventure, she'd been deeply fascinated by what I did down here. It wouldn't hurt to show her something that was at most PG-13.

"Maybe. You in?"

"Yes!"

"Then I'll call you tonight. Later." I removed and stashed the shades and earbud, opened my Shell-secured epad mailbox to study what she'd sent me while finishing my drink. Sabrina did have a debit card, and lucky me, she used it on a regular taxi service. Some of those debits had been made after dark, and a follow-up note to Shell got me a record of those fares from the cab company. (Hope hated it when Shell used her 22nd Century quantum-computer powers to hack any system she needed to loot for information, but I'd always figured that when you knew a Cyberspace Goddess it was stupid not to ask for divine favors.)

One taxi fare put Sabrina at Angels three months ago.

Shit.

If I was the enforcer for the Midnight Ballroom that Paul and his boss thought I was, I'd have gone right to the Master of Ceremonies. Of course they also thought I was a loyal minion of the DSA (which made them just as unhappy—cops hate feds). Paul asked once how I kept my loyalties straight, one of our more heated conversations. The easy answer was I didn't. I had zero loyalty to any organization—government, criminal, or otherwise. What I did have were *personal* loyalties, and I could number them on one hand. I liked MC, sort of, but he wasn't on that hand and he knew it. It served his purpose that the rest of the Midnight Ball didn't know it.

So I wasn't checking in with the Master of Ceremonies on this. Not unless I needed to mobilize Midnight Ball assets or do something I simply couldn't get done without his approval. But it also meant that any solution I came to would need to fit his definition of acceptable.

Sometimes a staked, decapitated, and cremated vampire was acceptable. This might be one of those times, but I wasn't going to be hasty.

I had plenty to do before sunset. Finishing up the Beantown books took another hour and then I walked to Leróy's fencing school, the Salle d'Armes. Everything was close, in the French Quarter. Leróy's salle taught competition fencing and cane fighting (*La Canne de Combat*). After I'd nearly gotten killed by machete-swinging vampires during my first visit to New Orleans, Leróy had offered me serious saber lessons and I'd accepted; bullets could slow vamps down, especially high caliber headshots, but nothing stopped them like decapitation.

He also helped me train my Vamp-Fu. (He called it Will and Balance, I called it Vamp-Fu to annoy him.) Today was saber work, with Rafe since Leróy wouldn't be up until sunset. An ordinary human, Rafe couldn't give my supernatural strength or will a workout, but he was an Olympic-level trainer and worked me hard on speed and style.

Afterwards I headed over to Esplanade for dinner with Grams; I didn't live with Mama Marie anymore, but the town's reigning Voodoo Queen expected her granddaughter to see her at least two or three times a week. She was proud of the family *le vampire*, more so since I'd become the Daywalker. Since being a breather rather than an undead animated corpse meant I could eat and get something resembling a suntan, I was happy about that myself.

(Bonus, the fact that now I could sally forth to hunt out any other vamp in his lair *in the daytime* had turned me into a bogyman with the rest of the vamp community.)

I crossed Beantown's threshold just before sunset. Acacia had joined Edwardo behind the counter, and she bounced around the end to hand me a card.

"Morning, boss! This got dropped for you." It was a black card with the silver razor crescent of the Midnight Ball. Because MC didn't know how to text. Or call. I stuck it in my pocket.

"Thanks, Steph. You need to go out, tonight?"

She blushed, shaking her head. "Officer Blake dropped by for coffee last night, and we…"

God save me from shy vampires. "You necked in the stockroom?"

"It's not like that! …um, yeah, we did. He's sweet."

"He's crazy." Officer Blake was playing with fire just stepping out with a vamp; Acacia, sweet Stephanie Dupree, looked like Barbie, dressed in bright pastels, and loved kitten videos, but she had more issues than a *Psychiatrist Monthly* subscription. "I'm taking the Cadi, may be out all night. Can you handle it?"

She nodded uncertainly. The crowd hadn't thinned much, and wouldn't until the small hours, but what really worried her was other vamps dropping by when I wasn't here. But she had my cell number, and Edwardo was an ex-con with a shotgun full of blessed silvershot and a seltzer bottle full of carbonated holy water. He also knew how to swing a machete, not that he'd need any of it; MC had declared Acacia off-limits for any vampy dominance games, and everyone knew I'd rip their heads off if they laid a finger on her.

But she still went to stay with Leróy when I was out of town.

I grabbed my keys and cases from the back office, and packed the Cadi; the NOPD never had reclaimed the old Cadillac Paul had found for me (impounded in a drug-cartel bust), and its trunk had room for a body or a vamp needing shade during daylight hours. On the drive to the Garden District, I texted Paul to suggest he spin by for another coffee if he hadn't skipped town. He'd gotten real protective of Acacia, before my final divorce from the police, and if she was going to be stepping out with a cop I'd rather it was him; at minimum I trusted him to treat her right—and trusted him to go all *Benandanti* wolf-man on anyone who gave her the least little grief when I wasn't there.

Yeah, I'm a romantic.

I put on Shell's VR shades after texting Paul, slipped the earbud on. Shell appeared in the passenger seat beside me, ignoring the aluminum case where her butt would be. "So you want to know more about the Garnettes?"

"Hit me."

"They drive an electric car, donate to Greenpeace and the Sierra Club, back every environmentalist super-PAC with an office in

Washington, and Dad and Mom Garnette are currently away at a spiritual green retreat. They probably decided against another child because having more than one is 'unsustainable' or something."

I didn't comment. Since they were leaving their only progeny to raise herself, reproductive restraint could only be a good thing.

Turning us onto Sabrina's street, I took us past her home. It proved as nice as it looked from the pictures; smack in the middle of the Garden District, a new house styled to look older rather than an older house recently renovated, it screamed *business money*. The last of the blue faded from the sky as I parked us down the street to study the house and neighborhood. This block of the Garden District held big tree-edged lots, which cut down the amount of street-lamp light that reached into the yards, and most of the homes didn't have exterior lights anywhere but their doors. Good.

"You ready?" When Shell nodded eagerly, I opened the case she'd been sitting in. "Then go, girl."

Shell disappeared and the tiny drones I'd foam-packed into the case whirred to life. Cracking the driver side window, I leaned back as the three drones rose and ghosted away into the deepening night. I rose into mist behind them.

TV gets it wrong: vamps don't come with a special vamp radar. We can *smell* each other up close. We've got the noses of bloodhounds, which means that we can pick up that slight hint of cellular necrosis (being undead means vampire bodies are *dead*). Cadaver dogs can smell us, too, but as the Daywalker (the only *living* vampire) I can hide from both vamp and dog noses.

We can also smell vamps who'd recently fed (blood-breath), and we can feel a vamp's projected influence if it touched us. Since in mist-form we are pretty much nothing more than a spread out cloud of water vapor and influence, that means that we are most detectable when floating as mist.

So mist spread my senses, but also made me more vulnerable; I floated over the Garnette house to come down on the roof of the next home west of it. Sunset had cast its east side into shadow, and the corner of an upper window gave me cover from the street. Back in flesh, I spotted one of the drones covering this side of the property.

Vulcan had made the handy things for me, and he hadn't even had to resort to Verne-tech to do it. After my nearly getting stupidly killed on my first visit to the Big Easy, I'd put a lot of thought into how to detect and track other vamps without being detected myself. The answer was laser. A low-power laser can tell a sensor all sorts of things about the medium through which the beam travels—like the humidity of the air. Thinking that way, the answer is a no-brainer; as humid as the Louisiana coast could get, a misting vamp was still a significantly more humid pocket of air. With my Shell-piloted drone vamp detectors pointed in the right direction I could spot a floater from blocks away.

Shell appeared beside me. "I'm in position. Got a three-sixty coverage going, settled in trees and gutters to save batteries."

I smiled. "It's probably overkill—no vamp would enter a donor's home through the *kitchen*." Because adherence to the role makes most vamps stupid.

"So we wait?"

"Yes. Might not get anything tonight. We're fishing."

She frowned, obviously dissatisfied. "Seems kind of boring."

"It is. Got anything to make it more interesting?"

"Well...I looked into her debit card transactions some more? Guess what I found before she went to Angels."

"Not a clue."

"She attended a Barnabas Cross concert last Halloween."

I leaned back against the roof. "Shit." My favorite word today.

The first "real" vampire to show up post-Event, Barnabas still toured with his goth-punk band and of course the limey bastard made New Orleans an annual stop. I'd never met him, but Barnabas Cross was one of the vamps I hated just on general principle. Had she gone with some friends for kicks? Had she been one of the girls he regularly picked out of the audience to take backstage?

"Yeah, and after that I found a series of purchases at clothing shops catering to goth couture. From the receipts I'd say she's assembled a complete goth-punk and loligoth wardrobe. Her parents have to be *blind*."

"They'd have to be here to see it. I'll bet if you check you'll find she went to Angels while they were out of town. She probably only dresses up when they're not here."

Ghost-girl nodded, worrying her lower lip. I didn't really know that much about Hope's BF—I didn't share, so Shell didn't either—but I knew from comments Hope had dropped here and there that Mrs. Boyar had raised her alone and been the opposite of a negligent parent. Between her own mom and her experience with Hope's family, she probably couldn't imagine a pair like the elder Garnettes, but I'd had several girlfriends in high school who could real easily.

Would we see anything tonight? I'd figured we had a one in three chance of getting a hit. Paul had said that Sabrina wasn't leaving home after dark, which meant if anything was going on, then the vamp was visiting her. And vamps who sipped only shallowly could drink from the same donor about every third day for a long time before they became seriously anemic. Why do it that way? Because a situation like this, if it was happening, wasn't about thirst; it was about sex and dominance.

Or as they liked to call it, *Dark Romance*.

I was right, or we were lucky; just after twelve Shell called out a hit on her nearest drone. From my distant vantage I couldn't see anything at Sabrina's bedroom window, but Shell assured me the misting vamp had dropped down from above the house and then vanished. I imagined the girl had left her window open a crack.

"Now what?" Shell whispered needlessly.

I didn't say anything. *Now* I had to make a decision. This might be cause for a warrant. I could call the precinct, report it, and send an email attachment with Shell's dated readings. Except that I'd never told the police about my handy vamp-sensors; they'd be easy enough to make, didn't *need* a cyber-ghost pilot, and would give them one more way to watch *me*. So since there was no procedure here, would a judge accept mist-at-a-window readings as sufficient cause?

I couldn't be sure, and on top of that, bringing the police in *was* sure to piss MC off. Every public arrest and prosecution of a vamp was bad publicity, and he'd far rather administer justice in-house. Any vamp who pulled this kind of shit and got caught at it would rather be arrested.

"We wait. Can you listen?"

"I can bounce a laser off the window, sure. But why aren't we *doing* anything?"

"Because I don't know who it is. And if he's been taking advantage of Sabrina for any length of time, she'll be enthralled and on his side. Or hers. I'm not going to start a fight on ground I don't know and where the girl can be hurt, so we wait."

That didn't go over well; ghost-girl pouted, positively mulish. "*Fine.*"

Less than an hour later, the Shell's sensor caught mist again as our vamp lothario left the house.

"Do we follow?" Shell asked.

"How far can the battery take the drone?" There was practically no chance that whoever it was would be unobservant enough not to notice *me* tailing him on the night air. If I could sense him, he could sense me. The drones...

"Five minutes, tops. Depends on the wind." Shell looked crestfallen. "I'll work on that."

"Do. And don't feel bad—I never expected you to. Now it's my turn." Being what I was, I was one of only two vamps I knew of who didn't need an invitation to enter a home. "You be quiet till I'm done."

"Gotcha. I'll just wait out here."

I smiled at the sarcasm. Taking off ghost-girl's shades I turned to mist myself, rising to drift across the property.

I'd come prepared to commit a little B&E—the Garnette's home security system was laughably basic—but Sabrina had left the window cracked and I drifted into her teen sanctum. Her frilly four-poster princess bed, matched to the rest of the pastel room, almost made me rethink my decision not to call in the police.

The teen years are years of trying on different selves, I remembered that. *I'd* gone the it-girl, cheerleader route in high school; it had meant biting my tongue a lot when classmates in my circle did or said stupid shit, and I'd shed that skin in college, but I'd been as fake as the rest of them. But I hadn't been stupid about it, and Sabrina had obviously completely embraced the stupid. She might dress goth out on the street but in here she'd gone completely pastel Lolita, turned herself into a total Mina for someone. There wasn't a hint of goth in the room; in this *relationship* the vampire was goth, not the pure and innocent mortal victim.

But this might not be all her; just how much of it was *her* choice was one of the things I'd come in to find out.

"Sabrina? Wake up now." I made it a whisper, but sent influence with it. The girl in the bed stirred.

"Gareth?" She sat up, only half-awake but pushing her covers away to show me her white Victorian nightgown as she brushed tumbled black locks out of her eyes.

And now I really wanted to set someone on fire. *Gareth*. That had been easy.

"Not Gareth, but you don't need to be afraid." I used only the tiniest bit of influence and it was enough to leave her breath shallow, her eyes wide and dilated.

She nodded sleepily. Seeing a strange woman in black jeans, black top, black leather jacket, looking like a pissed-off Mina after Dracula had his full way with her, standing by her bed with murder in her eyes should have triggered a much more energetic response. The girl was so enthralled that any vamp could have told her to take a walk off her roof and she'd do it without thought.

I sat down beside her, close enough to brush aside her high collar and check her arms to see that he hadn't bitten her neck or wrists. She didn't flinch, and I didn't search the rest of her body to find out where he had; I could guess, and confirmation needed an intimacy I wasn't going to force on her.

"I need to ask you a few questions. Is that alright?"

Yes would have taken too much energy and she just nodded again. It was like playing Twenty Questions, but I asked until I was satisfied. Finally I leaned in, kissed her forehead. "Thank you Sabrina. Now forget that I awoke you and you spoke to me. Go back to sleep."

Still so enthralled that I could have given her complete amnesia with a suggestion, she fell back so bonelessly I had to catch her. Tucking her in, I checked her pulse and looked for signs of serious anemia, then went to mist.

Gareth and I were going to do more than *talk*. But first I had to get rid of Shell.

I met Shell back at the car as she brought the drones home, putting the shades back on to do the courtesy of seeing her when I told her she was done for the night. That didn't help a lot—the kid had heard Sabrina's interview and was all ready to help me find and stake Gareth—but she accepted it. Ungracefully.

She'd have still been useful, but I wasn't going to involve Hope's BF in murder and that was what it might come to. We said our goodbyes and I put away the earbud and shades before getting on the road. The silent drive gave me time to think.

I'd never met Gareth, or at least I hadn't been introduced. That wasn't strange; since Sable's attempt at taking over the Midnight Ball, MC had instituted stricter rules about feeding. Now, vampires could only feed from a court or a harem. Courts were basically open parties like Sable used to throw, but could only be held in specific public places like Angels or the rebuilt Lalaurie House. Harems were a string of arranged partners the vamp could visit every three or so nights (with breaks for their recovery), and MC had to know of and approve all of them.

Most vamps used the courts. Since I rarely showed up to socialize and never fed at court, everybody assumed I had a harem; only MC knew that I hunted to drink, wiping the memory of the experience with each donor. I would not create or sustain fang-addicts. Hypocritical? Hell yes—especially since MC sent me to visit our harem-keeper's donors occasionally, to check on their health and continued willingness. One night he'd laughingly let me know that my "visits" were occasions of terror (I didn't do friendly very well). Being the only vamp in the Big Easy free to hunt was the price I asked for being MC's boogeyman.

So I knew Gareth didn't keep a harem (and even if he did, there was no way in hell that MC would have approved an underage teen), and even if I'd known him personally (and I didn't recognize Sabrina's description of him), I might not have known where he slept. Lots of vamps were cagy about that, unless they kept an establishment with enough minions to protect them during the day.

Of course *MC* knew where to find everybody—another of the new rules. Driving back through the French Quarter, I called MC and told him I'd gotten his card and would need to see him tomorrow night. And I asked for Gareth's address.

"*Jacqueline, is this business I would want to know about?*" His deep, velvety voice was practically phone-sex.

"Yes. And I might tell you later." I smiled when he sighed. He projected the cultured gentleman, but I'd been able to make him slip from perfect tone and diction quite often in the couple of years I'd known him. It was an ongoing project, one I didn't have time for tonight.

"*Would it be too much, to ask you to fear me a little?*"

Okay, I had a little time. "Yes. Yes, it would. Because you looove me. You want to maaaarry me. You want to—"

"*Jacqueline!*" I heard the sound of a door closing, hard, and laughed.

"So, address?"

Vampires (other than me) don't need to breath except to talk. I could hear him breathing to calm down and get his voice straight. "*When you have finished your business, you will come?*"

"I'll be there with bells on. Vessy will deliver me to your chambers with your evening paper."

He sighed again, gave up the address, and hung up without saying goodnight. Rude. Anyone seeing me through the Cadi's windows would have caught me smiling, whistling, and tapping on the steering wheel.

The bats have left the bell tower/ The victims have been bled/ Red velvet lines the black box/ Bela Lugosi's dead. Undead undead undead.

The happy tune carried me all the way back home. Pulling into the garage and letting the door close, I unpacked everything and put the cases back in the office. I didn't go up front; I wasn't staying. Five minutes later I was armed for a visit: needle-stakes in my sleeves, saber sheathed down my back, and my hunting bag slung over my shoulder. And my guns, of course, loaded for vampire.

Back in the garage, I misted away through the bottom of the door.

Gareth—and what kind of name was that?—rented a back bedroom in an old home on Royal Street not far east of Esplanade. It had once been servants' quarters, and was accessible only through the alley into the back. The front of the house was currently unoccupied, which suited me just fine.

The Midnight Ball owned the property through a dummy corporation, and had put the coffin under the floor while renovating; only vamps who could afford guards and serious room security slept in coffins sitting out where anyone could get to them.

Gareth could just mist through the vent by the wall to get down to his coffin, but if you weren't a vamp then even if you knew it was there you had to tear up the floor and then torch your way through a massive iron plate to get at it directly—and the iron plate was bolted into a concrete box surrounding the coffin. Finally, if someone tried to get at him during the day, Gareth could either mist away through the vent network to a secondary buried chamber, or seal the box from the inside and wait for help. And his coffin came with a landline.

Fiendishly clever, almost impossible to break into. Except I wasn't going to.

Being brought all the way back to life by a divine Word of Power meant I couldn't be as *still* as I could once; a living body is always in motion, with a hundred little twitches and adjustments every moment. Undead vamps could imitate, well, *corpses* if necessary, not moving so much as a tiny muscle for hours, but I didn't need to be that quiet; I was where I couldn't be—inside Gareth's *home*, without invitation. I took the corner by the window, and settled in to wait patiently.

Gareth didn't disappoint. Half an hour before dawn he misted through the window. Mist-form spreads your physical senses but also makes them much less sharp; I held my breath, needle stake ready, and when he came together into flesh I struck.

The African Blackwood stake, barely as thick as a drumstick and steel cored, slid in past his ribs and pierced his heart before he had a chance to react to the pain. He dropped like a puppet whose strings had been cut, and I got to work. Five minutes later, I pulled the stake out and watched the life come back into his eyes.

"Hello, Gareth," I said.

He blinked stupidly, tried to sit up, and only slowly realized that I'd mummified him in duct tape up to his neck. He wasn't strong enough to break it, supernatural strength or not, and he couldn't mist away since I'd shackled his feet to the old-style radiator by the wall.

I gave him a moment to figure it out, then straddled him and sat on his chest. "I've checked the house and the neighbors. Gareth. With all the brick, nobody's going to hear you scream." And I smiled.

Vamps can't go paler than they are, and if he was alive he'd have pissed himself. He did lose control of his voice for most of a minute; I might not have been introduced to him, but he'd obviously had me pointed out. Or he'd heard the stories.

"That's right," I whispered in his ear. "I'm Death, Gareth. I'd *love* to see every wayward bloodsucker in the world ashes in the wind, and you've royally pissed me off. You've been a very bad boy." Patting his cheek, I sat back and waited for him to find his voice.

"Y-you can't do that!"

So stupid. I rolled my eyes. "I've talked to Sabrina, Gareth. She told me about meeting you at Sables. She told me about your following and *charming* her afterward. She told me about her inviting you in, about your visits and your wardrobe and decorating suggestions. She *loves* you, you little molesting creep, because you've got her so addicted and enthralled that she can hardly think of anything else."

I ran a finger down his nose, tapped his cheek and watched him flinch like I'd burned him. "And that's bad enough, Gareth, but she's a *minor*. That makes it all not just mind control but statutory rape."

That finally shocked him into more coherent speech. "I love her!"

"I'll bet you do, in your twisty little black heart. Do you think that a jury will care when they learn how you made her your Mina, your adoring little blood doll? Of course they're not going to hear any of that, because there isn't going to be a jury. That would be bad for our community. No, I'm going to take care of you, and then the Master of Ceremonies is going to let the rest of the Midnight Ball hear just how stupid you were. Your ashes will look very nice in their urn on his mantle. Or he may want to keep your fate quiet. His choice, rumors can be good, too. You learned the rules when you came to town. You know the penalties. You. Knew. About. *Me*."

And there went his voice again. Really, this wasn't any fun.

Sable and his vamp thugs had nearly killed me, before I'd learned that some vamps could actually *fight*. But most of us were no more fighters than most living were. MC, Leróy, a couple of others I knew of actually *practiced* to train their Vamp-Fu, but I was to the average vamp what a special-ops soldier was to the average citizen. And even if he'd been a fighter, this didn't do it for me; going up against a monster out to take my head in return was therapy—terrorizing a scrub of a vamp like this, with no steel in his spine and no chance to fight back, was just sickening.

The worm was *crying*. Yes, we could. Dead or not, we stayed hydrated. In life he'd been a skinny, Ichabod Crane kind of dweeb and undeath hadn't improved him. Maybe that's why he'd gone vampire-goth; without some kind of glamour or mystery, most girls wouldn't look at him twice. Maybe his actual vamp breakthrough had given him delusions of entitlement; with the power to influence and enthrall, it could be easy. Maybe he'd learned his lesson now. Well he still had to be a lesson to others.

Time to get it over with.

"So here's what we're going to do. First—"

"I know something you need!" He screamed it, gulped for air. "I know something you need."

Well that was new.

"And what do you know?"

"There's some people in town. They're looking for a—a vampire they say has to be here. They want her."

"Hunters?" Shit, that was something I'd know about if MC did. And he'd have known if they were any of the usual suspect groups.

"I don't think so. They're not interested in anyone but her. I think they want to take her."

"And how do they know *you*?"

He licked his lips, swallowed convulsively. "They're paying me. To listen. They don't— They don't want a war."

Which meant they wouldn't go around randomly or even specifically grabbing vamps to question forcefully; the Midnight Ball kept close track of everyone, and only partly for policing and politicking in-house. We watched for hunter activity.

Grabbing his chin, I looked into his wide wet eyes. "I didn't think it was possible for you to sink lower on my maggot scale, but it looks like you've managed. Who are they looking for?"

"No! I'll tell you if you promise to let me go!"

"No deal. I promise not to kill you. That's all you get, and if you don't take it, well." I smiled again. "I'll make it slow and get what I need somewhere in the middle. What's her name?"

He told me. I asked more questions and he babbled like I'd hit him with truth-serum, detail after detail. He finally wound down, eyes darting like he was *looking* for more information to give me, anything to make himself more valuable.

I sighed, patted his cheek again.

"Congratulations. You get to live. I'll decide the state you get to live in later." I ran the stake back into his heart, watched the light go out of his eyes.

Then I called MC. Actually I called Vessy; it was dawn, and MC would be in his jammies and dead to the world. Vessy would be, too, but being the boss's number one meant that you got to take his daytime calls.

He answered on the tenth ring. This number wouldn't go to voicemail. *"What do you want?"*

"Always the charmer. I need a daytime pickup for Gareth, Vess, nice and quiet and right now. And I need you to wake up your boss."

"Not going to happen."

"It is. You know why? Because if I show up tonight when he does wake up, and tell him what you didn't wake him up for, you are going to be sleeping for a long, long time. Wake him up and send the freaking car. Now."

I hung up and prepared Gareth.

"Were you going to kill him?"

The library at Lalaurie House had a fully stocked bar, and MC poured himself a drink. Bourbon. He'd had time to feed before his delivery boys brought Gareth and me back to Lalaurie House. That didn't make him one-hundred percent—no vampire not me was one hundred percent in the daylight hours—but he was functional. Built like a husky pro-wrestler, he looked ridiculous in his dressing gown but I managed not to smile. He needed to keep some dignity in front of his people, even if right now that was only Vessy.

I lounged in my deep leather armchair. "I was going to leave him staked, wrapped, and stored away for a decade or two." Long enough for Sabrina to forget him after I'd gone back and used my own dark vampy powers to deprogram her of his manipulations has much as possible. "I'd have told you where he was, and you could have stolen some ashes from somewhere to display on your mantle."

"And now?"

"He changed my mind. We need to take him out of circulation without it looking like we've taken him out of circulation. So I'm going to give everything to Lieutenant Emerson and the NOPD is going to arrest his ass for rape and mind control."

He surprised me with a nod. "Clever. And I think it is time for the city to see justice done in the day." He waved away Vessy's protest. "So vampire-haters will get some ammunition. Our turning one of our own over, voluntarily, will go a long way to building community trust."

The words were right but his expression said something else. However the Midnight Ball spun it, Gareth's public trial was going to be an absolute public relations nightmare for the vampire community. It was going to be hell for Sabrina, too. We were not being kind.

He swirled the dark liquid in his glass before looking at his right hand man. "Vessy, wake and clean up Gareth. I'll be down shortly to explain what he will tell the police when they arrive." He waited until the door to the library shut, dropped into the leather chair beside mine.

"And now, dear Jacqueline, who are these not-hunters looking for?"

"Claire. Leróy's Claire. Our very own Sleeping Beauty."

He nodded, completely unshocked. If it had been anybody else, I wouldn't have woken him in the morning for it. I'd have arrived with his evening paper, after I'd gotten Gareth to tell me how to directly contact the not-hunters and visited them myself.

"So someone knows." He took another sip.

"Gareth gave a perfect description of her, too—these people showed him pictures."

"If they think Gareth is still useful, they will try and get to him in jail."

"I'm counting on it." I knew I was wearing my evil smile. "Gareth told me that they contact him through a burner phone regularly—they think Claire's buried deep in our little society here, supported by a secret harem."

"Why?"

"They didn't explain anything to Gareth—he's their tool, why would they? But I'd guess it's because both she and Leróy disappeared after the attack on her in Canada, and she's never surfaced anywhere while he's here under an assumed name. They know she was a new vampire, and *young*. Because of her illness she'd never been self-supporting, never really been on her own—she'd depend on Leróy or someone else to keep her safe and hidden."

"So," MC set his drink on the end table between us. "They learned of Claire, but why would they know she's special? These are obviously not the spirited but unprofessional hunters who attacked her in Canada."

"But when she disappeared up north Leróy did, too. So what if the original hunters found Leróy, here? His fencing school makes him pretty visible. They'd be shocked to learn he'd been turned, but might have decided to steer clear of New Orleans. Only somebody learned about their hunts, and understood what Claire actually turning Leróy meant."

"That she is very likely a master vampire."

"Exactly." I slumped a little in my chair. "I might not have helped, either. I showed up here, with no real history, and turned out to be as much an odd vampire as Leróy." Also not hung up on the lifestyle or vulnerable to the usual vamp phobias and compulsions, Leróy was just like me other than not being a daywalker. "That's *two* super-vamps in one place, obviously not the result of traditional vampire breakthroughs."

He nodded. I'd never asked why he had decided to help hide Claire. Altruism? Maybe. MC liked to be on the side of the angels when the situation let him. Which wasn't as often as either of us would like; vamps tended to be as self-centeredly amoral as cats, and keeping a couple of dozen vamps in line made it tough. Or he could be keeping Claire as a secret weapon; if anyone *really* came gunning for the vamp community, an attempt at extermination, he could wake Claire and use her to turn dozens or hundreds of new vampires.

And that was what made Claire so dangerous; Claire Rideau was a potential weapon of mass-destruction, the seed of a vampire apocalypse. MC didn't even need to ask—he knew that these new hunters were almost certainly some government's agents. Or they could just be mercenaries who wanted to capture innocent Claire and sell her to the highest bidder. She'd be worth billions; whoever controlled her could make a nearly unstoppable army or make any terrorist group too terrifying for words.

Which would probably get out of control and eat everybody.

"So, Jacqueline." MC stood and straightened his dressing gown. "You already have plans for Gareth. What do you intend to do about Claire?"

"The only thing we can do. We're going to have to kill her."

I made sure that MC knew what Gareth would need to say if Claire's hunters got to him in jail (I was *counting* on that), and left Lalaurie House. Scarhead—Raphael, MC's big, bald, scarred, and tatted omnipresent punk-vamp bodyguard—showed me out. Feet on the street, I walked. It gave me time to think.

The only way to stop Gareth's owners from hunting Claire was to make it so that they believed she was dead. That would take some doing; being undead meant we could take a *lot* of damage and get better pretty quickly. Stake us through the heart, and we were up and coming for you the second the stake came out. Decapitate us, and we'd heal and wake up given a few quiet hours of reattachment; minutes once, in my case—but I'd had help. (Being a *living* vampire, I didn't know what would happen if someone staked or decapitated *me* and let necrosis set in before reviving me. I'd probably come back undead again.)

For any of us, the only way to make sure we were *dead*-dead was to cremate us. Well, possibly dissolving us in lye, or mincing us up and feeding us to bears, or something else that extreme would do it. But fire was the traditional and easy way, so why experiment?

The biggest problem was that we couldn't simply move Claire, bury her somewhere nobody else knew about. She was low-maintenance, but her hunters would eventually get less subtle and try and come directly at the one person they were sure knew where she was. Leróy. They'd take him and torture the shit out of him if they could. Even if they didn't succeed, eventually their efforts were bound to draw the attention of the DSA, and the agency would want to know what the hell they were looking for.

The DSA *would* find her. And they'd probably kill her. It was the sanest thing anyone could do.

Wait. Could we move her? I almost walked into a curbside tree pot. It would solve the question of how to get the hunters to go the right direction; to attract attention, you break cover. The possibility opened the next step beyond the one I'd planted with Gareth.

But first things first. Stepping through my front door I nodded to Kimi and Dave, my Beantown morning staff, and locked myself in the office. The call to Paul wasn't fun, but the drone contact records Shell had left me, added to my over-the-phone recorded testimony of my conversation with Sabrina, was all he needed.

Gareth waiting and gift-wrapped for him (supposedly I'd gone and had a conversation with him, convinced him to turn himself in and taken him to Lalaurie House to await the police), tied up that loose end. Paul would get the warrant, nobody would ask me if my favor had involved any crimes, Paul would get me what *I* needed, everyone would be happy except Gareth. Well, Sabrina and her parents wouldn't be happy either, but her age would give her some shield from the media-circus and with Gareth pleading guilty the trial wouldn't take long. And Sabrina had made the initial bad choices that ended with this; at least she'd survive her stupidity.

But stupid wasn't bad, and she deserved better.

That done, I connected with Shell again. It didn't take much to sooth her mad over my cutting her out of the action last night, especially once I explained what was going down and told her who I needed to get on board.

"Yeah, he can do it. He's free and, knowing him, he'll love it. He doesn't get nearly enough opportunity to do this kind of thing, he'd do it just for the *art*." She lounged virtually by my desk, and this time she wore a t-shirt. It said *I'm with stupid*. I pretended it didn't exist just to bug her.

"We'd need him here *tonight*," I cautioned. "This could go pretty fast."

"I gotcha. No worries—I'll book him ultra-luxury class to New Orleans, even charter a jet if I have to. We need to get one anyway." She gave me a mock-salute and vanished.

I wasn't sure if unleashing ghost-girl on this was a good idea, but that was one genie that wasn't going back in the bottle. I called MC and told him about stage two of the plan so he could be ready. He told me he was on the other line with my "travel agent." Shell worked fast.

And I needed to sleep. At least a few hours, then I'd be good to go.

Our shared "crypt" was as secure as Gareth's, with the added bonus that it connected by the vent system to every room and all of the wall-sharing shops on my street—MC had bought all of them. Going to mist I floated down into it to sleep beside Acacia. Settling in, I decided to make a day of it. She'd be surprised to find me there when she woke.

"So you didn't kill Gareth. I saw the police report. That was nice." Tonight Shell wore a black t-shirt that read *I'd rather be breathing*.

"I'm not nice. I wasn't even nice before."

Acacia looked around. "Um, who are you talking to?" Her eyes widened and she whispered "You can't hear *Charley*, can you?"

I sighed. Breakfast—orange juice for Acacia (she got no nutritional value from it, she just liked the taste) and an omelet and juice for me—was turning out awkward with one of the girls at the table unable to see or hear the third. I tapped Shell's earbud as explanation, but Acacia's frown remained.

"But you are nice."

"Only to you."

"Before what?"

"What?"

Acacia actually rolled her eyes. "You said you weren't even nice before."

"Before I died." I ignored Shell, who was laughing at her end of the table. Our little kitchen would have been pretty tight if she were really here.

"Oh. Well, I'm glad you got better."

This was how a lot of conversations with Acacia went; I wasn't sure I wanted to know what she meant.

Acacia wasn't stupid; in fact, she was rather smart. She'd been dumb in the way that too many fang-fans were, and it had gotten her months of horror at the hands of Sable, a serial killer turned vampire who'd made her his little torture pet. Undead, she'd been recyclable. That much trauma, even erased from her brain, had left her fragile and scattered and not at all interested in the Children of the Night vampire scene anymore. She was even a little phobic of other vamps, with the exception of me, Leróy, and strangely, MC.

And with everything going on, I wanted her close to home. "About new inventory—" My cell chimed. It was Paul.

"*Karl Notts.*"

Gotcha. "Whose Karl Notts?"

"*A local public defender. One of the slimier ones. He arrived to see Mr. Minns—your Gareth—twenty minutes ago. Chère, am I going to know about this one?*"

"Nope. Did he come alone to offer his services?"

"*Yes. This isn't part of something, is it? A setup?*"

"The arrest is legit, Paul. It's exactly what you and Emerson wanted." But almost certainly what they hadn't *expected*. "The evidence is solid and he confessed. He's your guy. We just need to know who he talks to, there's someone he knows who we need to get to know. Nothing to do with the case."

"*Okay. Is it— Be careful, Jacky.*" He hung up.

I closed the phone. "Got to go. New inventory?"

Acacia nodded. "I'll take care of it. Paul's coming round when he finishes his shift. Is that alright?"

"Sure, you can take him and throw a Frisbee in the park if he doesn't chase the rabbits."

She scowled. "That's not nice."

"Told you I wasn't. Don't wait up."

Shell let me get myself dressed and us out on the street before she opened her mouth again. I'd decided to walk to Leróy's school after calling MC and telling him who they needed to follow. And since it had been a while, I dressed as bait. Bright skimpy club wear, junk in my hair, Shell's shades, I looked like I'd wandered away from the Bourbon Street clubs.

"So, Gareth?" she started.

"What about him?"

"You gave him to the cops because of this thing? What were you going to do? If this hadn't come up?"

I looked her over. She'd swapped to a matching club outfit and was trying on a swagger. She looked like a teen who'd crawled out her bedroom window to find some grownup fun; if she really had been I'd have scared the shit out of her and sent her screaming home. "You were pretty hot to do something extreme about him last night."

"Yeah, well..." She looked...guilty. I stopped on the sidewalk, focused my eyes on her. Yeah, yeah, she wasn't really here; I could tell myself that all night, but she had the whole reality-plus interaction down so cold it didn't make a difference.

And it didn't make a difference from her end, either; someday I was going to need to find out just how "real" her reality-emulator interface made this for her. Right now she wouldn't meet my eyes. Guilty. And worried?

Ghost-girl was scared. I'd scared her. When had I—

I'd kept her shades and earbud on me last night. I hadn't put them back on, but I'd kept them with me.

She'd turned them back on.

"How much did you listen to last night?"

"I—I shut it down when you went to Lalaurie House."

Where MC's electronic security might have spotted an active signal. Right. So she'd heard my whole interaction with Gareth. She'd been pretty good about not letting on when I'd called her late this morning, but her laughter tonight at the breakfast table had been nervous and I'd missed that.

Hands in my jacket, I bunched my fists. "You want to know what I'd have done to him, if not for this business. You want to know what I do down here, where Hope's not—where the Sentinels aren't watching. I'm being *me*."

"But what does that *mean*? Are you a *supervillain*?" It was almost a wail.

"Am I— Shell, I swear to *God*—" A big hand came down on my shoulder, spun me around and almost to the ground. I snarled "*What?*" before seeing the snub-nosed revolver being shoved in my face.

The guy behind it almost stepped back at my look before rallying. "Give me your purse, bitch! We're going to have some fun!"

"Oh, for—" I snatched his gun away, breaking his trigger finger in the process. It went off, shooting Shell to no effect. "I'll be right back." Like she could actually stay on the sidewalk when I half pulled, half carried my mugger and would-be rapist into the bushes.

I didn't ask his name and when I was done I took his pistol and wallet, leaving his cash. Putting influence behind my words, I let him know that I'd give his ID to *friends*. If any of them saw his face in New Orleans again, they'd be the last ones to see him before Judgement Day.

Then I let him go. He'd pissed himself, but that didn't slow him down.

I wiped my lips. "So what were we talking about?"

Shell's eyes were wide as saucers. "You just— You—"

I sighed. "Yeah, I just. I don't feed the addicts, Shell. I take donations from guys like *him*." And others too, but I didn't let them remember it and didn't want to complicate the explanation. "To answer the question you're trying to ask, kid, I wasn't going to kill Gareth. I've killed only two vampires, both lots worse monsters than him. I haven't killed anyone else who wasn't trying to kill me, but Shell, *I'm not nice*. I *wanted* to kill him. I *could* have killed him and lost zero sleep over it."

Looking up and down the street, I started walking again. "I can pass for a superhero if you squint, but not down here. I'm what I need to be for this patch of darkness, and if you have a problem with that—"

"No! No." Ghost-girl took a breath, kept pace with me. "I was just— I'm sorry, I just, I didn't want you to be what I thought you..."

She tapered off, but I got it. She didn't want me to be a killer. Too late for that, but I made myself smile. "It's okay. It's okay, and I can take it from here if you don't want to sidekick for this."

"No! We're helping someone, right? I want to help."

"Yeah, we're helping someone." We kept walking.

The Salle d'Arms remained open after dark, but the nature of its students changed a bit. Leróy taught a few nights a week, drilling MC's boys and girls in Vamp-Fu. He and Vessy danced across the floor of the *salle*, trading saber cuts and parries as they danced in and out of mist. Everyone else watched.

Since the point of Vamp-Fu was to incapacitate the other vamp and we could take stabby wounds anywhere but the heart (and even that unless it was wood), legitimate scoring meant slices to the arms and neck. Take a vamp's sword-hand off, and you were halfway there, take his head off and you were home; you could reattach everything later if you wanted, but he was out of the fight.

(Leróy also taught stake fighting—basically knife fighting that cut to the heart of the matter—but stake vs. saber was mostly a losing proposition. The needle stakes I kept up my sleeves were a vampire's ninja-weapons, good for targets you either surprised or found asleep.)

When the flurry of mist-flesh-mist-flesh exchanges and cuts ended with Vessy dropping his point and stepping back, a line of red at his neck, they exchanged salutes with their blades and Leróy handed him a handkerchief to keep the blood off his shirt. Most vamps played to the whole aristocratic and sexy vampire cliché, with varying degrees of success. MC played it more aristocratic and scary, playfully aristocratic, effortlessly scary. Marc Leróy didn't play—he *breathed* aristocratic sensibility. And boredom. Or disdain. He was the only black vampire I knew (fixation with pasty undead bloodsuckers apparently being pretty much a white thing), and he managed to communicate his feelings about most of vampire society around us without so much as a single snark or insult. I was jealous.

Also a little in lust; the guy was seriously hot. When we first met he'd thought me just another silly child-of-the-night vamp and aimed his disdain at me. To be fair, I'd been dressed totally loligoth. I'd *so* wanted to express my opinion of him with a stake at the time, and I'd still wanted to jump him.

"Jacqueline." He dismissed Vessy from his focus, eyes raking my club-slash-hooker outfit. "No practice tonight? Or do you intend to use improvised weapons?"

Vessy and I exchanged glances. "Sorry, Marc, business tonight. Midnight Ball business."

He nodded slowly. "My office?"

When Leróy closed his office door, shutting out the ring and shouts and stomping thuds of the salle, I introduced Shell by simply turning on my cell and setting it to speaker.

Shell did her usual good job of introducing herself; the kid wasn't the quite as earnest and determined as Hope, but she made up for it in cheerful enthusiasm. Then I explained what was happening—it was the first time both of them had heard all of it. Leróy was grinding his teeth by the end.

"So they've come."

"Not the ones that attacked you and Claire in Canada. At least we don't think so."

"Nope," Shell said. "I checked. Those guys were part of a bunch of weekend-warrior hunters, Order of St. George guys. Bunch of religious bigots, seriously unorganized. The Catholic Church kept trying to reign them in, finally threatened the entire bunch with excommunication and they disbanded."

I stared at the phone. Shell had disappeared so as not to split my focus. "When did you find that out?"

"Soon as you said Claire's name just now. I checked the police reports in Canada, did a search of related incidents, you know, research. And you've got trouble."

Leróy looked ready to break things. "There is more?"

"Yup. A couple of the Georges didn't give up—just made lateral career moves. They joined *Spezielle Ressourcen*. That's Special Resources, a European outfit."

The name rang a bell, somewhere in my memory. "And what does Special Resources do?"

"They're like Special Solutions—they match superhumans to jobs. But they're not superhumans themselves, they recruit them."

"We're worried about recruiters?"

"When I say recruit, I really mean *acquire*. There are lots of buyers willing to pay big bucks for superhuman assets they can control. They mostly operate in Europe, Africa, and Asia so you might not have heard of them. And they're bad news—if they're here then they might not want a war but they can fight one."

"They'll bring superhuman assets."

"Whatever they think they'll need to deal with any vampy opposition."

Despite the situation Leróy choked a bit, grimace twisting into a smile. "'Vampy opposition?'"

I shrugged, pulling out my epad. "She's hung around me too long. Show us, Shell."

She linked with me and started scrolling faces and numbers across my screen. A multimillion-dollar company, it was privately owned (and didn't Kurt Leitner, majority owner and CEO, look like a real piece of work). It had wide reach, deep assets they could draw on, and Leitner was willing to burn assets to get more. Just the kind of people who would be interested in the worst possible uses for a master vampire.

Shit. So they might have gone looking for Claire, thinking to pick up a handy vampire-assassin or something. Leróy had disappeared with her, so they'd probably expected to find him playing Renfield to Claire's Lady Dracula. They'd have been shocked as hell to find he'd turned, and that would have tipped them to Claire's nature. They couldn't *know* that Claire was a master vampire, but the odds of Leróy—her childhood friend—*also* going vamp were miniscule. Nonexistent once they researched his background and interests.

And they had a market for monster-makers.

Leróy took the pad from me to look at the Interpol reports. Murder, kidnapping, extortion, human trafficking, the list of crimes imputed to them read like an FBI Most Wanted List. Of course their lawyers maintained it was all lies or rogue actors. "So we leave. Now. I wake Claire and we go. We have prepared for this."

I chose my words carefully. "You can't just run, Marc. They know about Claire now, you'll always be looking over your shoulder and someday they'll be there. Them or someone like them."

"You think I should—" He bit the rest off, but his eyes promised murder. He knew how I'd been made, what I'd done to my maker, and what I thought the only rational choice was.

But meeting Claire had introduced me to one line I couldn't cross. I couldn't kill Sleeping Beauty, even if waking her might trigger a vampire apocalypse. But *waking* Claire...

"No, Marc. I don't. But I don't think you should wake her up. Better to run with her as she is. I can—"

"We do not need your help. As I said, we are prepared. And you should go, now."

"Marc, please—"

He pushed my pad at me, turned away. "No. Go, Jacqueline. And thank you. You have been a good friend."

I stared at his back. I had an eight-inch needle stake in my sleeve. *Damn you, Leróy.* I could stake him. MC could order Vessy and the rest to lock down the salle while we took Claire and Leróy out of here as *freight*. We could find every Special Resources employee in New Orleans and send them home in their own boxes. We could—

I left.

"So, what are we going to do?"

Shell had reappeared before I hit the street, but kept quiet for the first two blocks. As fast as I was walking, that wasn't long.

I didn't look at her. She asked again a block later, ignoring the night crowd as we turned down Royal Street.

The only idiot drunk enough to touch me ran when I looked at him.

I got control of myself only when I realized I was walking in a widening circle of empty street. Partiers and strollers were ducking into bars and cafés, stepping into the street, going the other direction, whatever they had to do to get clear of the oppressive weight of my ice-cold influence.

"Is he coming?" It was almost a growl, but Shell understood me.

"He just landed. Just needs to know where to go—we'll never even see him till it's time. But it won't work now, will it?"

I finally stopped. With no useful destination, I stepped aside to let foot-traffic pass, put my back against the cool wall of the fine establishment I'd stopped beside.

"No. Maybe. No."

"So what are we going to do?"

My cell chimed and I looked at it. Well who knew? MC could use a phone. *"You guessed right, Jacqueline. Mister Knotts passed a message from Gareth. They contacted Raphael with their proposition."*

I kept my voice level. "And he knew what to tell them?"

"He did."

"Leróy won't cooperate."

"I know."

I closed my eyes. "Jacob, do you trust me?"

"I trust you to do what needs to be done."

He couldn't see me wince. "Then you need to help Leróy. The rest—the rest goes as planned, tonight. Call when it's time." I hung up, looked at Shell. "What are we going to do? Something immediate and extreme."

Five hours later, Shell and I watched the black van pull up to the front of the Salle d'Armes. Real inconspicuous; it might as well have been a hearse. The driver didn't turn off the engine and Scarhead came out first (I really was going to need to start calling him Rafael), and looked up and down the street.

When nobody started shooting, or even paid attention, he gave the all-clear on his radio and two more stepped out. Even in shadow I recognized Leróy. Although I'd only seen her once, sleeping, the young woman on his arm was unmistakably Claire.

And here we go.

Beside me, ghost-girl wore a t-shirt that read *You want to do what?* "Yeah, this isn't at all risky. You know this is crazy. Right?"

I shrugged. "One way or another, they're not getting their master vampire."

"Well, at least it'll be epic."

"Last stands usually are."

"Ha, ha. Let's go, Spartacus." She vanished, and as the van pulled away I followed suit, rising into mist.

When you have to run, the key to making sure nobody chases you is to make sure you leave nobody behind able to chase you. Sure, sneaking out works, but then you'll never know when they pick up your trail or from what direction they'll come. So I'd told Gareth to tell them that he'd spilled his guts to me (he had), we knew they were coming (we did), and that we'd try and get Claire out of town (duh). I'd also told Gareth to tell them that Raphael wasn't happy with his boss, and would tell anyone who paid him enough what the Big Plan was. That was sort of a lie, but the skeevy lawyer they'd paid to defend Garth delivered the message, and they got hold of Raphael not long after sundown.

The Midnight Ballroom was now richer for one offshore bank account stuffed with several million dollars, and we had a tail.

Several, probably.

Not that I was looking for them; I trusted they'd be there as I rode the mist fifty feet above the road. I couldn't float fast enough to keep up with a car on the open road, but the van drove through Marigny and Bywater before heading north on surface streets and this meant plenty of stop signs and lights. I got ahead to drop back into flesh at intervals so I could touch base with Shell, but she reported nothing exciting. Yet. I could feel the others around me as I flew through the night, their edges touching mine, and found myself humming Mussorgsky's *Night on Bald Mountain*. We were demons riding on the night wind, bound for a very, very bloody sabbat.

The hunters could have kicked off early, but distance from the center of town meant time; they didn't want New Orleans' own capes breaking up whatever they had planned too early, and in the wee hours they'd have fewer witnesses and an open road. Their own extraction plan would be safer.

Besides, they knew where we were going. The airport.

Lakefront Airport had been built in the mid-30s, on an artificial peninsula thrust out into Lake Pontchartrain on the north side of the city. It used to be the major airport, but with Louis Armstrong International Airport built further out to handle modern capacity, it was reduced to operating locally and serving private and business flights. Tonight, it made the perfect battleground.

When I dropped into flesh about halfway there, Shell popped in. "Okay, night drones make five tails, up to eighteen unfriendlies. The faces I've been able to identify belong to a mercenary black-ops group, soldiers recruited out of a couple of failed states."

"Any sign of breakthroughs?"

"Nope, but I couldn't ID half of them, so assume they're there."

"Damn right." This was looking more and more chancy; sure we were *vampires*, fiends of the night, but a properly trained and equipped normal could handle your average vamp—and even our better-trained bloodsuckers trained mostly to fight other vampires. Eighteen. Shit. "You're ready to clear the airport?"

Not that there would be many civilians there at this time of night.

"Yup—the second the balloon goes up I'm set to hit all the alarms. And I've disconnected the link to emergency dispatch so local fire and police won't hear about it too soon. That should buy you some minutes."

"Thanks." I went back into mist.

The last stretch of road was long and uninterrupted, opening the distance between us and the van. Fortunately, it ran along the south side of the airport before turning in, letting us cut the angle and even arrive at the arranged spot before the van did.

Two armed vamps dropped into flesh in their prearranged posts at the stairs to the waiting private jet. The rest of us hung back and above, letting the van pass beneath us. It came to a stop fifty feet from the jet, and Leróy handed Claire out, supporting her by her elbow as they headed for the stairs. The five following cars turned onto the runway before they'd gone twenty feet, fanning out to the right and left as their doors opened.

"Run!" Leróy shouted, pushing Claire forward and turning back. She stumbled, recovered, and followed instructions. Three shots hit her in the back and head right in front of the stairs, throwing her to the foot of the tarmac as the two vamp sentries went to mist. At least a dozen black-clad shooters advanced on the jet as Leróy screamed and launched himself as well.

And I and the others dropped into flesh behind them.

Bang-bang. Bang-bang. Bang-bang. They had to be using blessed rounds to drop a vampire like that—but since ours weren't blessed a stray round of friendly fire would just slow one of us down. We didn't need to worry about accidentally shooting our own. They were wearing helmets and body armor, but I still dropped two before most of them turned to face us.

Which didn't do them much good; Leróy and his two came out of mist right into them and the fog of war descended. "Shell! Tell me what they've got!" I danced in and out of mist, taking shots and *moving*. Something burned a lava-hot trail across my thigh.

"AR-15s, no full-autos!" I could hear that much, there being a *big* difference between staccato bangs and ripping zipper-sounds. "They've got grenades!" A *whomp* to my left and screams with a vapor-wave of water told me they'd brought high-tech water-bombs. Holy water, of course.

Then a vamp lit up like a torch. They'd brought a *pyrotechnic* to the party and his victim screamed, flailing in agony until he managed to focus enough to flee into mist. A second lit up as I spun about wildly, desperate to locate the source.

"There!" Shell screamed, lighting a soldier up with a bright red icon. I leaped back to mist and came down on him, driving a needle-stake into his neck. I heard fewer shots and screams already; it was a gun battle with no cover and total surprise and we were winning this.

"They're going for her!" Shell pointed and I turned again to see the furthest car, a suburban van, peel rubber to close on the jet. Claire hadn't risen—we were out of time.

"Now Shell, now!"

The jet exploded into a fireball that ended the fight.

Later examination would show that stray shots had hit the fuel tank, letting fuel out and air in. After that the first spark in the wrong place finished the job; the force of the fuel-air blast turned the jet into slivers of metal that vaporized both Claire and the pilot. Half of *Spezielle Ressourcen's* still-standing soldiers lived through it because of their armor.

Their rides turned out to be armored, too, saving the driver and passengers of the van that had gone for Claire, but the fight was gone from all of them as vengeful vamps took them down, *not* killing them on strict pre-fight orders from MC (though I couldn't claim that one or two already injured weren't helped to finish dying before the ambulances arrived). I didn't see Kurt Leitner, but then I hadn't expected him to lead his paid kidnappers—a good thing since Leróy would have killed him.

I certainly wanted to.

Only the coming dawn forced the NOPD to finish their questioning and let us go. There'd be more questions later of course, *lots* of them and we'd had to leave our weapons for the crime-scene analysts; they'd find every shell casing, match every bullet to a gun. That quite a few of the mercenary's wounds were inflicted from *behind* wouldn't help, but fire had been coming from everywhere and I was confident the scene would back up our story and the fact that *Spezielle Ressourcen* had been equipped to perpetrate a vampire massacre would close any possibility of a case against *us*; they'd come to snatch one of ours, we'd tried to get her out of town, they'd followed and attacked, and we'd won. Sort of. The DSA might learn about Claire from all this, but she'd been flash-burned and vaporized—an extreme enough final death even for a vampire.

We dragged our own injured back to Lalaurie House before dawn, and between the pyrokinetic (who survived with extreme blood loss), the blessed bullets and holy water, and the fireball, we looked more like fresh-mangled zombies than vampires. MC met us there with a full staff of donors and a waiting "secure crypt" for everyone. We waited until the rest of the team had taken him up on it, leaving the library to the three of us.

MC poured four drinks, handing a tumbler to Leróy first, then to me, and the three of us sat.

Leróy had taken five blessed bullets (and somebody's stray), and if he hadn't been a supervamp like me he'd have been carried back as well. The bullet hole through the meaty part of my thigh had leaked a bit, too, and one of the staff had thrown cloths over the chairs since neither of us had had time to clean up.

He sipped his bourbon with a grimace. His mask was good; he'd been holding the rage behind it for hours, and now he let it out. "I want Leitner."

MC looked at me and I shook my head. Shelly had briefed me on this. "You won't get him. He's not even in the country. But Interpol might now, and the US government." This disaster was too big for the mercenary businessman to distance himself from. Even if prosecution didn't work he could easily find himself bleeding patrons and backers, and then there was Europe's vamp-community. When *they* heard of this... I really didn't have it in me to feel sorry for the man. I'm no bigot; some monsters are human, and I'd happily stake them all.

And that was the problem.

But there was no time for me; Leróy wasn't accepting it. "For Claire—"

The study door to the library opened, and a white-haired man with a cane stepped through. "Ah, the fourth is for me?"

"Jacob," I said to MC, "I'd like you to meet my other boss. Blackstone, meet the Master of Ceremonies, the completely deniable godfather of New Orleans' vampires."

"A pleasure." Blackstone accepted his tumbler from MC's hand, sat in the fourth chair. He'd been where we'd been, but he'd never left the van; his tuxedo wasn't even creased although he did smell a bit of burning jet fuel.

Leróy nodded to him. "Thank you, sir. Claire and I owe you an unpayable debt."

"All debts are payable, young man. But how was my performance?"

Leróy shivered. "When I saw Claire fall—I knew it was your illusion and yet—I could have killed them all."

"You sold it, boss." I saluted with my tumbler. "And Shell has already changed the records, so the DNA results from what little the crime scene guys recover will match hers and the poor pilot's." The *pilot* had been a John Doe body diverted in his trip from the city morgue to a medical research firm, and Shell had given him a brand new and ironclad history. "The illusion is complete."

"And the best kind," Blackstone concluded. "An illusion that nobody will see through, because nobody suspects to even look. Mister Leitner's own men will tell him, through their lawyers of course, that their hoped-for master vampire is so much ash." He sipped his drink. "Jacob, this is excellent."

"Thank you. And thank you for convincing Marc here to let us attempt a diversion before moving Claire. Who may now continue to sleep in peace."

Blackstone set his drink down, resting both hands on his cane. "But not here. I am calling in your incalculable debt now, I'm afraid."

The self-congratulatory vibe of the room fled and I became hyper-aware of exactly where my guns were—which was not on me. I still had a needle stake up my left sleeve—the other one was also back at the airport—but I couldn't draw it faster than MC or Leróy could act. Could I take them both? Could Blackstone teleport to safety quickly enough?

"I assume you will explain?" MC's voice didn't change its pitch but I could feel his influence rising, not directed yet but a storm of cold anger.

"To be perfectly blunt, I have been aware of the danger that Jacky colorfully calls a *vampire apocalypse* for some time, through the dealings of a…time traveler who left records of various potential futures as a warning. We had thought that Jacky here was the only progeny of a true master vampire, and that that one was unique. You can imagine my dismay when I was informed that my help was needed to secure the safety of another one."

He leaned forward, ignoring MC to address Marc in gentle tones. "Mister Leróy, you have done a commendable job of keeping your friend safe. And perhaps together we have succeeded completely. Perhaps. Nonetheless, you remain her vulnerability. You cannot hide yourself easily, and should someone else follow the same trail, come to the same conclusions, the potential richness of the reward could inspire another attempt—if only to verify that she is, indeed, gone. And it would start with you, wherever you go. As I understand it, you were unbelievably fortunate to see this attempt coming. You are not likely to be so fortunate again."

Leróy could have been carved from ice. "Marc," I whispered. "Don't—" He held up a hand, eyes fixed on Blackstone. Someone living would have blinked. He didn't for long seconds, and when he moved it was only to put his own tumbler down.

"What would you do with her?"

Blackstone stroked his elegantly short beard. "I have in mind a fallout shelter, long-forgotten and easily convertible into a nigh-impenetrable crypt accessible only by those with the appropriate codes and abilities. Maintained by the Sentinels, through enough layers and cutouts that God himself won't know about it. I work with the DSA at times, but I am less its agent than Jacky here is. Of the Sentinels, only Jacky, myself, and one other would know of her existence. Sleeping Beauty will continue to sleep. Not a permanent solution, I'll grant you, but in our adventures our team encounters all kinds of things and of course research is ongoing. Perhaps one day we will stumble upon a cure for vampirism—I know that Jacky would devoutly wish that, despite her rather special status among you.

"If not—" He sighed. "Undoubtedly, in the future we will be better able to deal with the dark possibility that Claire represents."

"I'll go with her, Marc," I interjected before he could say anything. "Do you trust me enough for that?"

MC straightened in his chair. "Jacqueline—"

"I'm leaving anyway, Jacob. You had enough bogeymen to keep the others in line before I came down here. And I can always return if I'm needed. But..." Now *I* sighed. "I can't stay. It's too much."

"This is about Gareth?"

"No. Yes. The list of people I could kill without a second thought just keeps getting longer. It's not good for me, it's too easy for me to...get dark, doing this." Well, get *darker*. I'd have to thank Shell for shocking me into realizing it. "I need something that isn't here."

"And what about your responsibilities?"

"Acacia? I'll leave her Beantown, if she wants it. Marc? Could you take care of her? She really doesn't belong in Lalaurie House—most other vamps give her the willies."

"Yes, I can do that." The look on his face was...odd. He'd spent years being Clair's protector. Now, what was he thinking? "I can do that," he repeated.

"Thank you. Blackstone, if you'll go back and make arrangements, I can follow in a few weeks with—" My cell buzzed. It was Shell. "Excuse me." I opened my phone. "Yes?"

"*You should keep that earbud in! I'm texting Blackstone, you two need to get your asses back up here now—Hope vanished in the middle of her DSA op!*"

Blackstone had read his own text, and now he stood. "Gentlemen, it was a pleasure. Now Jacky and I must go."

I beat him to the door.

Velveteen vs. The Crossover

by Marion G. Harmon (with permission of Seanan McGuire)

"Superheroes are crisis-magnets. Yeah, sure, a lot of the time we get called or dispatched to deal with whatever mess some supervillain is making, but other times we're just there when it hits the fan. On my road trip to Oregon I just happened to stop where an old teammate led a crustacean uprising against the Isley Crawfish Festival (really), and then got a temp-job at Andy's Coffee Palace to fix my old beater of a car. Andy's Coffee Palace's perky manager Cyndi (yes, with an 'i') led the Midnight Bean Society, a cult powered by black coffee from the Sacred Bean cultivated in natural caverns beneath an Aztec temple and burial ground. Yeah, they tried to use it to ascend to a higher plane and rule as gods, and yeah Andy's got sucked into another dimension. My point is that superheroes go looking for trouble in self-defense; at least then we see it coming."

Velma "Velveteen" Martinez

Velveteen heard the explosion from five blocks away and was down on the ground and skating her Tony Trains up the empty street in under a minute. She'd found the sturdy little anthropomorphized engines at the local Good Will on her last foray into the donated toys section; it was like riding two skateboards at once, but the game little trains cooperated to stay under her feet and sped her along fast enough that she beat anyone else to the scene. That it was the middle of the night helped.

This part of Portland had been hit hard by the recession. A lot of the shops and warehouses were closed up, and the one that had exploded was a failed glass distributor. The small warehouse full of mirrors and window-glass and custom frames had been boarded up for months, now it looked like an air-bomb had exploded inside—no flames, but overpressure had blown out the boards and the windows behind them.

Velveteen called it in just in case an ambulance was needed, hopped off the wheezing trains and crunched through glass to carefully climb inside. "Hello?" she called into the dim interior. Against all odds, some security lights had stayed intact and Vel made more light by pulling a Miner Joe from her utility belt. The action-figure ran ahead of her, helmet-lamp lighting up an impossibly wide field for his size. For good measure, she sent a handful of plastic doodlebugs scampering into the shattered spaces to look for injured.

When nobody answered she shrugged and ducked her head so her bunny ears cleared the edges of drooping glass, and stepped over the window frame.

Glass crackled in front of her, and she pulled up short. "Hello?"

"Yes?" someone answered. The voice sounded shaky and young, but *unhurt*, which seemed impossible.

"Where are you?" Velveteen peered around, waved Joe in what she thought was the right direction. "Don't move, it's not safe."

"Okay." *Not safe* didn't sound like a big deal to the voice, and Vel wondered if its owner was in shock. Or drugged. It beat freaking out, anyway. Following Joe, she stepped around a concrete pillar and froze.

The girl on the other side of the pillar shouldn't have been shaky—she should have been screaming. She was covered in so much blood that Vel couldn't be sure of her hair color or what the shredded tank-top she wore had printed on it. The bare legs below her spandex shorts were just as red-splashed and dripping as her upper body, and shock wouldn't protect *anyone* from that much pain.

The girl held a steady hand up to shield her eyes from Joe's light. "Is that a toy?"

"Are you okay?" Velveteen asked stupidly. "*How* are you—" Then she spotted what seeing the horrifyingly blood-soaked girl had made her miss. The shredded corpse at her feet.

The blood covering the girl was all *splatter*.

Vel was back-pedaling over the glass-covered floor, emptying toys of every kind out of her utility belt pockets as she went, before another thought registered. Both the girl and the way-too-dead corpse had been here for the explosion. Which meant the blood-covered girl was a superhuman of some kind.

"Stay right where you are! You're under arrest until I figure this shit out! Did you do this?"

"Maybe?"

Fucked up times a thousand. "Don't move!"

"Toys? You're arresting me with *toys?*"

Bare feet crunched over glass and Vel's army of plastic green soldiers opened fire. Granted even the bazooka-soldier couldn't fire that big a plastic round, but they *stung*. At least they stung *normal* targets—the freaky-scary girl didn't flinch. "Hey," she said, hands raised "It's okay, I'm—" Vel threw a tangle of rubber monkeys in her face. They wrapped around the girl's head, cutting off whatever she'd been going to say and Vel managed to get some distance. Hitting the window frame, she almost tripped backwards into the street—which would not have been good for her admittedly reinforced crushed-velvet bodysuit.

"Now that's just—" Nightmare Girl stopped where she was, carefully peeling the clinging monkeys away from her face so she could see. "—rude." She tossed them away one by one, frowning as she tried not to rip any rubber arms off while pulling them apart.

"I'm trying to tell you," she said, voice getting stronger. "I'm *Astra*. Whatever happened I didn't *intend* to do it. Where's here? It's not my bathroom." Coming to the window, she looked down at her hands in the light of the street lamp. Then she looked back into the shadows. And then she threw up.

"So, where am I?"

The paramedics had arrived with the police, and while Portland's finest were keeping their distance and letting their resident superhero sort out the superhuman stuff, the EMTs had provided Astra with an emergency blanket after rinsing and wiping her down to make sure that, under the blood and shredded nightclothes, she really was unhurt. She'd patiently let them do it, and didn't that just say volumes about her experience with paramedics. Now she sat on the back of the emergency vehicle watching the police move through the taped-off wrecked building.

"Portland." Vel watched her blink. "How did you get here?"

"Portland? I know the Portland Guardians, and they don't have a bunny-girl."

"Oh, come *on*." Vel rolled her eyes. As famous—infamous—as she was with the Super Patriots and by extension pretty much the entire superhero community, the blonde girl had to be lying. "And who are the Portland Guardians? There is no licensed team in Oregon."

"Licensed? Not certified?" The girl's brow wrinkled. It was cute. Under the blood everything about her was cute, from her diminutive size (Vel was actually taller, a rarity), to her bobbed blonde locks and fresh faced and sweet sixteen, girl-next-door looks. She looked like the peppy high school or even junior-high school cheerleader from every teen movie. Or possibly the good-natured but slightly dim supporting friend.

"Of course I was certified. The *Super Patriots* don't let anyone on one of their teams without it. But they're not here."

Astra shaped the words, "Super Patriots," with her mouth, again cocking her head. She'd been doing that a lot, like she was trying to listen for something. Whatever it was she didn't hear, she closed her eyes and took a deep breath. "Super Patriots. Okay. They formed when after The Event?"

"The what now?" Vel blinked. Was the girl going into shock or something?

"The Event. How about the Big One?" Astra looked at the EMT on her right. "Ted? Anything?"

Ted shook his head. "Sorry, girlfriend. I know a lot of big, but no Big One. And the biggest event around here recently was the Oregon Truffle Festival. That's probably not what you mean?"

"That's—" She put her hands to her face for a moment, sighed and rubbed her eyes. "Can I borrow your cell phone?"

"Uh, sure." Vel handed it over and watched as Astra punched in a number. A bad one. Her shoulders slumped.

"Got a couch I can crash on?"

It wasn't that simple of course. Vel had to fill out the usual forms—the fact that she hadn't been there until after the explosion made things easier, but the police were reluctant to "release" Astra officially until the crime-scene analyst guys gave a preliminary judgement that whatever had caused the explosion hadn't been an apparently invulnerable teen.

When asked who the body was, Astra had looked green and said "We only just met before the boom, and he tried to gut me."

Since the obvious cause of death was a million shards of flying glass, the police took Astra's name (just Astra—she refused to give up a civilian name), remanded her to Vel's custody "pending resolution of her status," and left them alone.

"My status?" Astra asked as they walked away from the scene. The cool night air and colder sidewalk wasn't bothering the girl at all.

"You're not a registered superhuman, are you?" Velveteen looked at her sidelong, wondering how the night had ended with her getting a problematic houseguest. "And you're not confused anymore, so mind telling me why?" She was tired and the adrenaline rush from getting the absolute shit scared out of her by a blood-dripping girl had long worn off.

"I'm not from around here?" Astra's laugh was bitter. "Which is so *cosmically* messed up, considering what I went through last year to make sure this wouldn't happen." It was the first crack in her careful calm, and Vel recognized the sound. The girl had hit the end of her personal rope, and the next step would be to lose her shit.

Spotting a taxi, Vel waved frantically. Amazingly, it pulled up and she practically shoved Astra into the back seat before the driver could realize just how not-normal his fare was. "Thank you, George," Astra said automatically, squinting slightly to read the cab license dangling from the mirror without straightening from where she'd flopped against the opposite door—a nice trick. Enhanced vision, too?

"Yeah, thanks," Vel seconded, giving him her address.

"I don't want any—" the driver started, but whatever he saw in his mirror made him stop. He grunted weakly. "Let's get you home."

"I don't think you'll go that far," Astra laughed with an edge, covered her mouth. "Sorry."

And that was it from her for the rest of the ride.

Velveteen—a name that perfectly fit a toy-animating, bunny-suited superheroine—let Hope stew quietly until George pulled up in front of her place; a kindness for which she was desperately grateful. She almost as silently pulled Hope inside, showed her where the bathroom was, and left her with a fresh fluffy towel and a pair of sweats to change into.

Most of Hope's jitters swirled down the drain with the blood—the wash and wipes the EMTs had used hadn't *cleaned* her, just cleaned her enough for them to know she wasn't the source of any of it. She turned the water up to scalding (not for her, of course) and washed and rinsed her hair three times before it felt sufficiently un-yucky, scrubbing hard enough to half-destroy Velveteen's loofa.

Opening the bathroom window to let the cloud of steam out, she blow-dried her hair and pulled on the sweats. They were too big for her, but not by very much and her University of Chicago tank top and sleep shorts were beyond recovery.

Closing the window, she hung the towel, opened the bathroom door, and stopped.

A love-worn teddy bear waited for her in the hallway.

They looked at each other. He wore a Build-A-Bear tux, and had one eye. Since nothing else about him was piratical, Velveteen had obviously taken the time to give the little guy his dashing eyepatch. What was toy etiquette?

"Hello? Can you take me to your person, Mister Bear?"

He nodded and turned to lead her back downstairs. Hope smothered a half-hysterical laugh.

Yeah, like you haven't seen weirder. With only silence where Shell's voice should be—a constant and crushing reminder that *she* wasn't where she was supposed to be—Hope found herself supplying her own. And her inner-Shell was right; hanging with Ozma, and therefore Nox and Nix, gave her no room to complain about strange. She followed Butler Bear. Beartler?

She stopped again on the stairs.

"No," Velveteen was saying, using a telephone-voice that told Hope she was holding her cell phone between her shoulder and ear while rifling through the kitchen. "She doesn't look like an analogue of anybody I know, even trying to picture a mask. Of course I— What should I have— The kid was freaking out, and I couldn't just leave her with— One wrong step, and Legal would eat her alive!"

Seeing Beartler looking up at her, Hope realized she was eavesdropping. Thumping loudly down the last few steps and across the hallway and through the swinging door to the kitchen, she found Velveteen closing her cell.

"Feeling better?" her host asked.

"Yes, thanks. I think I used up all your hot water."

"S'okay." Velveteen had changed too. Gone were the rabbit ears, domino mask, burgundy velvet leotard and brown tights with the utility belt that had held way more toys than its pockets had room for. Out of her high-heeled boots, Vel wasn't much taller than Hope, and her dark brown hair wasn't cut much longer than Hope's bob. She looked tired. "I've got decaf. We should talk and I've made up the couch."

"Thank you. Really. I could hear you."

The older girl winced. "Of course you could. What are your powers besides not being sliceable?"

"I'm super strong and can fly. And I've got super-duper senses."

"So you're a flying brick, that's pretty common. How strong?" She poured two cups while talking, set them on the kitchen table.

"I can punch out a tank. I can't throw it." Hope sat and Beartler stayed beside her. After a moment she reached down and lifted him into her lap, where he settled in.

Velveteen eyed her Butler Bear, her hard smile smoothing out. "So, maybe level four."

"And what are you?"

"I'm an animus. Officially, level two, and officially my power enables a 'Semi-autonomous animation of totemic representations of persons and animals, most specifically cloth figures, including minor transformation to grant access to species-appropriate weaponry.' *Unofficially*, that official stuff is a little out of date."

"Wow that's a mouthful. What did you mean when you said 'Legal would eat me alive?'"

Velveteen gave her a long look, put down her cup. "You gave me a superhero name. Astra."

"Yes?"

"I don't know how it is where you come from, but here it's illegal to be an unlicensed superhero, and against federal laws to harbor one. If The Super Patriots got wind of you, their legal division would notify the Superhuman Affairs Commission and get a warrant to bring you in as a hazard to public safety. You *don't* want them to get their hands on you."

"Oh. You mentioned The Super Patriots before. Who are they?"

Velveteen told her. It took a while.

"They use *children*?" Hope knew she'd gone pale. Her eyes had to be wide as saucers, but she didn't care about looking tough and On Top Of It just that second. "Child *soldiers*?"

"Child *heroes*," Velveteen corrected, her voice dripping her opinion of that. "I was one of them, but I thought you were the same. You can't be what, sixteen? They don't send you out to fight?"

"No! I mean— Yes, I fight, but no I'm not sixteen, I didn't gain my powers until I was almost nineteen, and— *No*, we don't do that back home!" She felt sick again, blinked tears. So much for thinking this extrareality couldn't be too different from— "Just, no."

"Okay, okay." Velveteen made soothing motions, her voice gone *careful* again, and Hope tried to pull herself together. "So you're nineteen?"

"Almost twenty-one, actually. I've been a cape for two years, but since my breakthrough I'm not aging anymore..."

"Got it. That's got to suck."

"I'll be carded for*ever*." That was actually worth a sad laugh, and laughing helped. The warmth of the coffee cup and the bear in her lap helped.

"So, how did you get here?"

"I wish I knew." *Shell* would be all over it with hypothetical explanations. Shell wasn't here.

"Okay..." Velveteen worried her lip, looking tired and thoughtful. "So what were you doing when it happened?"

"I was bait."

"Huh?"

Hope closed her eyes, hugged Beartler. "I got a call from the DSA— that's the federal Department of Superhuman Affairs back home. They were after a superhuman serial killer they'd named Red Jack. He only attacked *sorority girls*. Of a certain physical type."

"Blondes cute as buttons?"

"Um, yeah. He'd come out of mirrors at them. Only at night, when they were alone in a dark room—like a bathroom or bedroom with the main lights off. And he'd slice them to bits with his razor fingers. In seconds."

Velveteen choked on her coffee. "That—sounds like a bad grade B slasher movie."

"Yeah, which makes you wonder how twisted the guy had to be to make him *that* kind of breakthrough. Anyway he'd killed two girls, in different sororities, different states and a month apart, each on the night of the thirteenth. That was enough for the DSA's incredible search and pattern-matching systems to figure it out. They couldn't track him, but since they knew what he wanted they decided to give it to him."

"You?" Now Velveteen was looking at her like she was wondering just how dumb the girl sitting across the table from her could possibly be. Hope shrugged defensively.

"Pretty invulnerable, remember? And not just me—a good half-dozen capes who fit the general description or could be made to with dye jobs. And since we couldn't tell if he was picking them by location, or psychically homing in on targets that met the metaphysical qualifications too, we also all got crash-pledged."

Just thinking about *that* still made her smile. She'd long reconciled herself to the destruction of her original college plans, but the Bees had been *thrilled* to pledge her into Phi Mu with them. *Love in our bond. Yay!*

"So then it was just a matter of spending the night of the thirteenth in the sorority house, dressing for bed and stepping into the bathroom after lights-out." She stopped.

"And?" The older girl gripped her mug tight.

"Red Jack," Hope said carefully, "Was an evil clown—talk about horror-movie clichés. He chose me, came right through the mirror and tried to slice me up." She kept her breathing even. She'd had the smallest concern that his razor-fingers or whatever he used would be supernatural—that her normal toughness wouldn't protect her. It had. "And I grabbed him. Your medical examiner will probably find a crushed wrist. When he couldn't get away he reached back and— Everything went weird and then there was exploding glass. We were here." All her smiles were gone. "Which makes no sense. At all."

There was silence in the kitchen for a long moment. Hope pushed back a sniff and squeezed Beartler harder. Sleep. She needed sleep and then she'd be able to woman up.

Velveteen sighed and Hope made herself refocus. "Call me Vel. It's short for Velma, but I haven't really been Velma Martinez for years."

"Okay. Why?"

"Because you could be here awhile. I was hoping you'd tell me you'd fallen asleep or gotten knocked out or something, which would have meant that going to sleep *here* might have been enough to send you back. I'd wake up to an empty couch."

"Yeah," Hope laughed wetly. "Been there, done that. Was trying not to do it again."

Coffee sloshed as Vel straightened up. "Really? Then I may know what happened."

"What?"

"Slippage. You've traveled to alternate realities before?"
"We call them extrarealities, but yes."
"Not just parallel timelines?"
Hope blinked. "Um, no. Those exist?"
"All over the place, potentially. Where did *you* go?"
"Well, a town-sized extrareality pocket. And a Japanese spirit realm. Um, two of those."

"Got it. One of the documented problems of traveling is that, the more you do it, the less glued you are to your proper place in the multiverse. You said Red Jack moved through mirrors? That usually means using mirrors as *gates*—which means an in-between place of whatever size that's probably not solidly fixed in your reality. Like a wormhole. So if he tried to get away, dragged you back in with him..."

Hope felt light-headed. "His in-between place couldn't hold onto me. And he wasn't going back to the world, and I wouldn't let go of him..."

"You went spinning under huge metaphysical pressure, popped out in the 'closest' spot to a real-world analogue to his special place—"

"A glass and mirror warehouse. Which reacted badly. Oh. That's, that's awful."

Vel nodded. "Kind of poetic, actually—a mirror-jumping slicer getting terminally sliced by mirrors. But the multiverse does have a sense of humor. A bad one."

Hope used one of Chakra's controlled breathing techniques until she didn't feel like she was going to float away anymore, made a mental note to *never* use Ozma's mirror-travel magic that Grendel had told her about. And yawned. And made another mental note to tell the DSA case-team to look for an abandoned mirror and glass warehouse in Portland when she got home. If she got home.

Vel scooted back from the table. "And that's it for tonight. Let's get you to the couch." Hope nodded like a marionette and followed her, still holding Beartler. And there was a couch.

In the cold spring night outside Vel's kitchen window a deeper shadow detached from the darkness lying across the yard, flowing silently until it reached the dark of the neighboring address. There it thrust up and grew three-dimensional and then human. Diffuse, the best sneak-and-peek superhuman in The Super Patriots Inc.'s security department, pulled her cellphone from her cloak and speed-dialed.

"Sir?" she said to the voice that answered. *"Diffuse, assigned to Rabbit Watch. I need to report an opportunity."*

Vel's bedroom mirror frosted over and stopped reflecting her room just before dawn, and Jackie Frost stepped out of it. "What?" she said at Vel's look. "You knew I was coming."

Vel shrugged. "Just thinking about what else can come out of mirrors."

"Hey, at least I'm not *Alice*. So, is she still here?"

"Where would she go? I asked if she wanted to check on analogue family here—she's from Chicago—and she looked like I'd suggested mailing them a bomb. After what I told her about The Super Patriots, I can't blame her."

"So what is the law about alternate superheroes dropping by?"

Vel laughed. "About what you'd expect. They're illegal aliens, of course. The Super Patriots takes them into *protective custody* when they're discovered."

"Well, I've got the clothes. So what's your plan?"

"Celia."

"The Iron Lady? Yeah, good plan."

Jackie didn't seem to faze Hope at all. She accepted the bag of clothes from the white-haired girl with the pastel blue skin with a polite "Thank you," and went upstairs to change. After a breakfast provided by Vel's house toys, they climbed into Vel's compact car and hit the road. Both Vel and Jackie were in their hero uniforms—Vel in her most formal and Jackie in one of her less abbreviated blue-and-white "skating costumes."

Hope wasn't. Jackie's choices made her Christmas-themed—white shorts with snowflake fringe, blue sparkly t-shirt, and matching white sneakers—but she still looked like a fresh-faced teen ready to hang for the weekend. She was also a lot steadier this morning; Vel explained the plan on the way, and she nodded solemn approval.

"Yes, please. The thing to do when lost is to wait to be found, so if you don't know someone who can just twinkle me home then the best thing would be to leave a message and contact number back at the warehouse, and not leave the area."

She didn't sound like she was whistling in the dark, giving Vel hope that she really did know people who could come looking for her.

Since Vel's house sat in Portland's southern suburbs, the drive to Salem didn't take long. This early, Salem traffic was light and they made it to the Capitol Building with only a brief stop at a Starbucks for a jolt. Vel showed her official superhero ID to capitol security and got visitors tags for them all, then left Hope to admire the rotunda's architecture while she and Jackie went upstairs to see the Governor of Oregon.

And talk fast.

Celia Morgan met her guests in the formal office. It wasn't her normal practice when meeting with Velveteen, Oregon's official state superhero, but the young woman's text had indicated she was bringing Jacqueline Frost, the daughter of Jack Frost and the Snow Queen and an official representative of Winter.

While not Alaska, Oregon was far north enough that keeping on the good side of that particular Season was good politics.

Her appointment secretary showed them in, and Celia didn't stand on ceremony with Velveteen. She'd given the young hero refuge in Oregon to piss off The Super Patriots, but the girl had proven an able protector of Portland—sometimes with the help of Jackie Frost and The Princess, true, but the governor was beginning to suspect that her toy-wielding hero was stronger than her old Super Patriot tests and evaluations had reported. Which didn't surprise Celia, since The Super Patriots Inc. would lie if asked the direction of sunrise. Or recuse itself.

"So what can I do for you, Velveteen? You're not ready to renegotiate your contract already, I hope?"

"No, ma'am. Actually, have you heard about last night?"

Celia frowned, smoothed her face. "No." And if she should have, somebody was going to learn their boss was seriously displeased. Velveteen filled her in, and Celia found herself sitting although habit kept her from leaning into the high-backed chair. "A multiverse traveler? And a superhero?"

"You can see the problem?" Velveteen's question was utterly rhetorical; Celia knew her state's laws well, and the federal laws that constrained them—especially regarding superheroes.

"So what do you suggest?"

Velveteen took a deep breath. "The first thing is to quietly make her a legal resident, even if we have to send her to Vancouver while we do it. Once that's done, the state can issue a superhero license and make her fully legal for as long as she stays."

This time Celia didn't frown, not with her face, but she tapped a knee.

"I understand why you want to help, Velveteen. Hell, so do I and we can probably swing the residency. But as for a job, we took a chance with you because, before you dropped out, you'd been fully vetted and trained by The Super Patriots even if they trashed your reputation after—and as little as I like to say anything good about them, they turn out competent heroes. You've known her for one day. Can you vouch for her character?"

"Benny likes her," Velveteen answered. When Celia raised an eyebrow she explained. "He's my teddy bear butler. He glued himself to her like her personal bear, and he's *my* toy."

"Mmm. An interesting recommendation. Anything else?"

Jacqueline Frost spoke up for the first time since introductions. "She appeared on the big guy's Nice List. I don't know *how* good she is, but you can trust her."

Celia nodded, both in respect of the source and confirmation of why Winter's representative was here.

"Well, let's see her."

It took only a minute for Celia's secretary to call down and retrieve the girl from the rotunda. A perfunctory knock on the door by the guard, and then it opened to admit her.

Oh, hell no. There was no way that Celia Morgan was going to let this young woman fall into the clutches of The Super Patriots. The tiny blonde who advanced across the carpet with a hopeful smile looked like she should be here on a school fieldtrip instead of seeking asylum, and Celia's fingers itched to start signing legal documents. She was going to wrap this girl in every legal protection her position allowed.

"So, Astra?"

The girl nodded. "I guess I've got a real live secret identity again. I don't want any family I have here involved in any way." The look she gave Celia said that was non-negotiable, but since Celia knew The Super Patriots wouldn't think twice about using any analogues of the girl's family as leverage, she wasn't about to negotiate that point.

"That will not be a problem. Here's what we're going to—" The *thump* that shook the floor cut her off.

The scene outside the room's floor-to ceiling windows ended the meeting.

"What is *that*?" The question came from Astra, remarkably the first of the four able to vocalize although Celia would later wonder if she'd heard Velveteen mutter *Faked up times tin bullion*. The early morning sun shown on the Capitol Mall, and on the utterly fake looking Tyrannosaurus Rex—at least twice the size of any actual T-Rex that had ever roamed the Earth—lumbering towards them across the road at the open mall's end. On either side, cars veered to crunching stops before crossing its path and pedestrians scattered.

"It's flickering," Astra added, as if that was the only problem she had with the impossible thing. "Can you tell me anything about it?"

"Flickering?" Velveteen blinked. "Shit! Someone let Cinemaniac get his hands on decent projection equipment!"

Astra glared at her. "Okay, what does that *mean*?"

"It means that thing's unkillable! We've got to find the projector and shut it down!"

Celia grabbed her cell and hit speed dial, but Astra was already in motion.

"Then find it! I'll hold it in place until you do! Clear the building!" She opened the window with a sharp *pop* of the security lock and pushed out the screen before stepping to the window ledge and heading out and *up*.

"Wait!" Celia cried, grabbing for her. But she was too late—the girl was gone.

This was where Shell was normally feeding her aggregate pictures of the situation, from street-cams, police radio, whatever source was useful, and Hope forced herself to pay more attention to her environment than to the target. The thing hadn't crushed anybody crossing the busy street, but even at its slow speed it wouldn't take long to hit the Capitol Building behind her. It ignored her popping up to fly above it, focused on its obvious goal.

From the window Hope had exited, Jackie Frost threw out an ice ramp and skated down it to begin turning the mall grounds closer to the building into a very uneven ice-rink. A swarm of what Hope's super-duper vision showed her were tiny plastic fairies fanned out from the open window to scatter in every direction.

Recon was being handled, obstacles created, so it was time to be direct.

With no idea how dense the T-Rex really was, Hope picked a joint—the knee of one of its hind limbs—as her target and dove, ignoring the laughing screaming man standing on the thing's head. It didn't look like he was directing it at all.

Hitting the joint was like hitting dense rubber and Hope took the shock of the foot-first impact in her knees, felt the joint *bend*. And then it wasn't. Between one flicker and the next, the joint was undamaged. The T-Rex wobbled and roared, but stayed upright and took another crunching step.

"What do you think you're doing!" the man perched above her screamed. Screaming seemed to be his natural volume.

"Stopping you!" Hope circled high, came down on the T-Rex's nose. It bent, pushing its head down and nearly unseating the man, but flickered back to its pre-hit shape.

"You can't! Ha ha ha! Finally the world will know the wrath of the Cinemaniac! First Salem, then Portland! Then the world! Ha ha ha ha!"

"You're *monologuing*? This place is *insane*!"

And it was getting to *her*—why hadn't she thought to take him down first? He was just a wild-eyed bald guy in mechanic's clothes who hadn't shaved in a week. Hope swung around, sweeping low over the T-Rex's head to gather him up—and did, until he flickered and was back on his perch.

"Ha ha ha! You are fools! Do you think I would expose myself? Risk my genius? I'm being taped and projected with my beautiful creation!" The T-Rex took its first step onto Jackie's ice-rink, slipped—and then didn't. It lumbered on.

They weren't going to evacuate the Capitol Building fast enough. Astra hit it again, in front to at least stagger the thing back a half-step—again the flicker kept it upright.

She landed beside Jackie. "Ice isn't going to stop it. Freezing?" Frozen rubber was brittle.

Jackie shook her head. "It goes back to its original condition, even if I could freeze more than a foot that fast. Nice hits though, kid." The blue and white girl's fingers twitched like she was going to try it anyway.

Hope forced herself to be still and *think*. "The Cinemaniac talked about his projection like it's an ongoing process. Velveteen is after the source?" Jackie nodded and watched the thing lurch closer. Really, the thing kept moving so far off its center of gravity that it should be toppling on its own, kept upright by movie-magic. The power of the cinema—

"Wait, projections—it's a movie projection!"

"Say something not obvious."

"I don't know how it's using the air as a projection screen, but it has to have an unobstructed range to the source! Maybe we can't find it fast enough, but can you—" She didn't need to say more.

"Snow globe! Yessss!" Jackie lifted her hands and the world went white. The T-Rex flickered and disappeared a second before the rising vortex of snow got too thick to see more than ten feet from Hope's face.

Velveteen started swearing nonstop when Astra went out the window, but kept control of her Disney-fairy scouts. Beside her Celia talked *intensely* into her phone, directing the capitol police to evacuate and then search. She didn't move from the window even as she sent her secretary and guard away.

"Can they stop it?" she asked Vel once she'd given all the orders she could.

"This is *so*— I don't know, they're slowing it down a little." Her little scouts zoomed over the landscape, excited to be hunting and communicating their glee through that part of Velveteen's power that touched and animated them. "The Cinemaniac is crazy, but he isn't *stupid.* He won't have the projector set up in plain sight on a roof somewhere." If he had, she could send Astra a fairy-guide and the girl could take it out before you could yell *Cut! That's a wrap!*

Celia nodded, eyes on the action as they watched Astra and Jackie fail to really slow the thing. Vel tried once more to catch it with her mind; it should have been hers, except that it wasn't *there*. There was nothing real for her animus' gift to hold onto.

Then the girl landed beside Jackie and the two put their heads together for a long moment, stepping apart as Jackie raised her hands.

Jackie Frost wasn't the Queen of Winter, not yet, but as the daughter of the Snow Queen and Jack Frost she had a double-helping of mythic juju flowing blue through her veins. Winter was a memory in Salem, but not yet a distant one and the earth and air remembered the last freeze. More, Jackie had primed the pump when she laid down her rink; now she called to the wet and cold that returned year after year and was already half there.

Vel had the foresight to grab Celia before the arctic wind hit, knocking them off their feet as it filled the room. It was less gentle outside, and as the world beyond the window disappeared in a wall of white she felt her fairies still in the now-emptied mall freeze and crack. The fairies *beyond* the mall and the great globe of white fluttered, righted themselves, and kept to their mission.

"Yes!" Beside her, Jackie did a dance on the ice that should have planted her on her face. "Suck it, you nut-job! That's *it*—you've been *owned*!" She slapped Hope on the shoulder. "Get up there!" Hope headed straight up.

Jackie hadn't been kidding about the snow globe; her winter storm covered the mall in a radius centered on the frost girl, but that was it—it ended about twenty feet up, about where the T-Rex's head had been, and didn't reach the city street.

And, crucially, the T-Rex hadn't reformed at the edge of the obscuring storm; it was trying too—Hope could see flickering green light at the white vortex's edge, but the swirling snow kept breaking it up. Now if only...

She caught the convergence of darting fairies across the street, and dove. The swarm of Tinkerbell merchandizing beat her to the high office window, but not by much as they darted vengefully through the open window to open a toy box of plastic-pinching torment on the room's occupants. Hope ignored the screams and wild shooting to unplug the big movie projection machine and snap off its points. Smashing things was for amateurs.

Cinemaniac was shorter in person.

She stayed in the wrecked office space until the police cuffed Cinemaniac and the last of his moaning minions. Covered in angry red spots, they looked like they'd been attacked by army ants. Shaking hands with the arresting officers, she flew back to the governor's office over a now flooded mall; a localized and quickly draining flood—they'd managed to save the day with minimal property damage.

She found Velveteen toweling off while the governor talked loudly into her phone. The woman obviously didn't like what she was hearing. Vel looked like she knew what it was about and agreed with the governor.

The woman closed her phone and looked at her, eyes full of rage and despair, and Hope realized that as much as this was about her it was also personal. "That was the US Attorney General's office," the governor said. "A friend owed me a favor. The Super Patriots have a warrant, and they're coming."

Hope blinked. "How— Too many cellphone cameras, right? Someone posted it to ViewTube and there I am? Big as day in front of the Oregon State Capitol Building?"

"That's right. And now we have no time."

Hope nodded slowly. "So they get me. Will they be able to do anything to me, with everything out in the open now?"

"You're not going anywhere." The woman practically bit off the words. "I won't let them—" Her phone rang and she put it to her ear. "What!"

A hand on Hope's elbow made her jump. Jackie Frost had come back upstairs and slipped in the door behind her. "C'mon kid, let's go freshen up." Beside the governor, Velveteen nodded.

"Okay..." Hope let Jackie drag her out into the empty hallway. The frost girl stepped up to one of the ranked hall mirrors and touched it, frosting it over. "This is our exit."

Hope stood rooted to the floor. "But—"

"Trust me kid, *this* mirror isn't going to get nasty on you. And this is why Vel brought me, really. Look. If you stay, Vel and Celia are going to fight for you. And Governor Morgan is probably going to lose her office and then Vel will lose her nice new home. *Don't* let them do that."

That was enough to move Hope forward and she took Jackie's hand. The frost girl pulled her into the mirror and they were gone, leaving an empty hallway and a faint scent of peppermint and pine needles.

Hope hit the snowdrift and tumbled butt over blonde bob, but the snow was soft and she could have fallen a lot further without injury. The snow was also barely cold enough to announce the sensation and tasted like spun carnival sugar on her tongue.

"Watch that step," Jackie snarked, helping her to her feet. She stood *on* the snow, her quality leather boots not sinking more than a quarter-inch into the drift, but that was a trivial note in the symphony of impossible that stretched out in front of Hope.

Curtains of blue and green fire lit the night sky above them, the Northern Lights in extravagant, glorious performance. Nothing less would have matched the scene below. Down the slope from the girls awaited a collection of buildings half-buried in new snow, a village painted by Thomas Kincaid or some other artist capable of painting sentiment and warmth into every brick and cross-paned window. People smaller than the size the buildings called for moved from shop to shop in the cobblestone square, around the huge striped pole that marked the center of the impossible town.

Hope started to laugh.

"The North Pole? Really? Jackie *Frost*?"

Jackie grinned. "Now you're getting it, kid. C'mon."

Breathless and dizzy, Hope lifted to glide down the hill rather than flounder along beside Jackie, and they hit the cobblestones and strolled through town without the scurrying elves paying a bit of attention to them. Jackie led her through the square and to the building on its other end, half a toyshop and half city hall.

Hope stopped at the steps.

"I'm going to meet..."

"The Easter Bunny? Yeah, right through those doors." She laughed at the tongue Hope showed her. "You know who. Scared?"

"No," Hope whispered, forgetting Jackie's teasing. "*No.*" She ran up the steps.

The front hall smelled of pine and cider and cocoa and sugar cookies, every smell Hope had ever associated with Christmas. Jackie led her past open shops where elves spun wishes into reality, and through a small door at the back of the hall. Out of the bright hall, Hope blinked as her eyes adjusted to the dimmer lamp and fire-lit room. It was a smaller office, with wall-to-wall shelves stuffed with account books, an old carved roll-top desk, and a big chair in front of the fireplace.

Santa Claus sat at the desk, shirt collar open and sleeves rolled up, a pencil behind his ear. He stood as Jackie closed the door on them.

"Hello, Hope."

He opened his arms, and Hope barely remembered not to crush him. His beard smelled like winter forests, but she forced herself to let go before hugging a huge man to whom she hadn't been introduced got *awkward*.

"Thanks for that, child." He twinkled at her. "Sit down." A second chair had appeared by the fire, with a hot-chocolate laden table.

Hope sat. "I'm in a coma, right? I've been dreaming since the sorority house?" She knew it wasn't so, but had to check off the boxes anyway, and Santa smiled to acknowledge the hidden question.

"Would that it were so simple. But given your own experiences, you know that it isn't."

Hope found a mug of cocoa in her hands, her feet up in front of the fire. "Would it be rude of me to ask? How real this really is?"

"On a line with God on one end and the idlest post-cookie dream on the other, this place falls only slightly to the right of your waking life, my dear. Dear Vel asked if you could have sanctuary here if it came to it, and although I knew nothing about you until your name appeared on the Nice List last night, it is my absolute pleasure. If only you could stay."

And the cocoa didn't taste quite so perfect. "Home."

"Yes, I assume that is where you eventually wish to go. In some ways this place is but a reflection of the magic of your home."

Hope nodded, the sudden wave of absolute longing nearly crushed her, until the wood in the fireplace popped, throwing out a spark and bringing her back to herself.

"My domain is Christmas," Santa gently explained. "It is the holiday that anchors Winter, and my borders reach only as far as the reality you just came from. That's why your name only now appeared on my list."

Hope chased Santa's hint to its conclusion. "Which means nobody will be able to find me, here."

"No. You have 'broken your trail,' so to speak." He pushed his spectacles down his nose, regarded Hope over them. "You are a good girl, Hope. One of the best. And you are welcome here for as long as you wish to stay—indeed Christmas could use you. Hope is one of its greatest gifts, after all. But home... That you will have to look for."

"Then I have to go." Hope swallowed the growing lump in her throat, the song playing in her head. *Childhood joyland, mystical merry Toyland. Once you pass its borders, you can never return again.*

"Not true," Santa said sternly. "Christmas is ever a return to this place. Adults visit it with their children every December the twenty-fifth—indeed you don't *really* know Christmas until you've watched it with grown up eyes."

Hope nodded again, blinking. "But I still need to go."

"Not today, or even tomorrow. The elves are still preparing a few things you'll need. But when you're ready, there is this." Santa held a snow globe in his hand, appearing like one of Blackstone's tricks. Hope gingerly accepted it. In clearest crystal on a gold filigree base, wrapped in gently swirling snow, lay Chicago's skyline. It wasn't a model.

"I cannot take you home," Santa said regretfully when she looked up. "As I said, your home lies beyond my boundaries. But this can send you on your way. It has twelve turns in it, one for each day of Christmas, and then it must wait for the next turning of the year to fully recharge its power. We can hope that twelve is all you need." Then he smiled, and despite everything that waited outside of this moment, Hope laughed. It was his magic, and it wrapped her up in its warm embrace.

Three days later, properly dressed in an Astra-suit that he promised would weather her travels and more, the magic followed her when she turned the globe and disappeared in a rush of Christmas snow.

Vel looked up when Jackie came through the mirror.

"She's gone?"

"On her way. She's a tough kid. She'll make it."

Vel scowled. "She shouldn't have to 'make it.' She should have been able to sit right here till her people came for her."

"Yeah well, *should*—" Jackie shrugged. "You know it was The Super Patriots, right?"

"Duh. Cinemaniac pops over to *Salem*? Just on time to out her?"

"They were hoping you and Celia would fight for her. That woman is one tough bitch, and she's got the power of a state behind her. But only when the law's on her side, and Legal would have crushed you both."

"Yea, well." Vel mimicked her friend. "So they won't leave me alone—I knew that already. I feel like punching bad guys until dawn. Want to patrol?"

"Can we invite Princess? And then shots!"

Vel laughed and it felt good. "And then shots. After the punching. A bunny has to have her priorities."

"Damn straight! And maybe we'll see the kid in another crossover. When The Super Patriots aren't hounding your fluffy tail anymore."

"I'll put it on my wish list. Call Clarabelle, and I'll change."

The Oz Job

by Marion G. Harmon

Grendel

"It is almost always true that the more titles one has, the less happy one is. The greater the title, the heavier its weight."

Her Most Excellent Majesty Princess Ozma the Sixth, Defender of the Emerald City and Empress of Oz.

"Grendel, you are good to go. Go, go, go."
   I wanted to tell Dispatch I'd heard them the first time, but Watchman heard too and dropped me. Flying five hundred feet up had kept us clear of the cloud of superheated steam rising above the Braidwood Nuclear Station as Tsuris pushed it away from town, but I was down in it in seconds. The membranes I'd grown over my eyes cut visibility, but saved my vision—it would have grown back, but temporary blindness right now would be inconvenient. The cork-textured thermal armor layer of skin, grown on the way up, left me feeling like I'd stepped into a spa instead of dropped into Hell. My outermost layer of nerveless leathery skin was already ablating away.
   I barely saw the ground through the fog before it hit me, but I'd come down loose and ready. The broken pavement shattered a bit more, and I stood to look around.
   The Braidwood Reactor was a pressurized water reactor, which they said meant it used water as both coolant and a neutron moderator in the plant core. Or it should have been; someone—probably the Ring—had decided to see what would happen if the plant's pressure was compromised while its control-mechanisms were disabled. A bomb

and a cyberattack had done the trick and now the Sentinels were trying to save the day.

We couldn't save the plant; it was done for.

"You need to move to the reactor vessel, Grendel. Temperature readings give us less than ten minutes to meltdown." Meltdown—when the rods got hot enough to melt their cladding and contaminate the already superheated water in the core now depressurizing and boiling into steam. They'd told me ten times; if I couldn't get the rods out, fuel-coolant interaction had a fantastic opportunity to generate enough H2 to spark a massive hydrogen explosion totally shredding the plant's already compromised containment. The contaminated coolant would be into the air and groundwater, creating a Chernobyl Event. Fun times for *everybody*.

Following the ping of my GPS navigator, I punched where it marked the spot. A minute's work removed the shielding above the core, and now I could feel the heat. I thickened my skin as much as I could without losing grip function, and started hand-cranking the rods back into their graphite-cladding travel housings.

And this was going too slow.

With oxygen-saturated blood, I could hold my breath for maybe eight minutes—letting superheated steam into my lungs wouldn't kill me right away, but it would be a start and then I'd be helpless to keep myself from dying. "Dispatch, I need a bath. *Now*."

"Understood, Grendel. Stand by."

I pulled two more fuel rods and then had to stop and grab hold as Riptide dumped Lake Michigan on me.

"Temperature still rising," Dispatch informed me redundantly.

Yeah, yeah. Riptide wasn't close enough to command the water *inside* the core, but I could take a chance on breathing now. I didn't die.

Five minutes later they announced temperature leveling, and eight minutes later I ripped the whole upper plate from the core barrel and carried it out of there to where suited plant workers could remove and store the rods.

"Crisis averted, Grendel," Lei Zi said in my ear. *"Good job."*

"Anytime." I headed for the decontamination tent. The sun wasn't even up yet, and already I wanted to call it a day.

Of course I couldn't; my earbud chirped while I was in the chemical shower. *"Grendel, we're leaving cleanup to the Crew,"* Lei Zi informed me. *"I, Variforce, Riptide, and Tsuris are remaining to handle short-term containment and security. Watchman is flying you back to the Dome and then returning.*"

I shook water out of my dreads. "What's going on?"

"*When you need to know, which you won't until you're back there. Go.*"

Well that was fine; it wasn't like the day could get any more exciting than stopping a nuclear meltdown, right?

Ozma

I had come to know Hope's closest friend well. The girl had been through a respectable number of transformations: a human girl, a quantum-ghost copy of the deceased girl, a robot girl, and now a quantum-ghost and flesh and blood pairing referred to as Shell and Shelly respectively. They might be two people now (I was hardly certain of that, but willing to leave such questions to philosophers), but they still acted in concert to the point of ending each other's thoughts when they were in sync. To live through so many fundamental transformations was a rare experience, even in Oz, and I found the two of them fascinating.

This morning I found them worrying. "You cannot find Hope anywhere?"

"No!" Shell confirmed. She'd burst into my lab wearing her civilian "gynoid dronebot" body. "And there are only a couple of ways that's possible. Someone could be using a—"

"—quantum-interdiction field," Shelly continued from the screen she'd commandeered to speak through. "But that's Verne-tech stuff and—"

"—this mission didn't have anything to do with that kind of thing. We think."

"Very well." I turned off the Bunsen burner I had lit to heat a distillation of cloud salts. "And what have you done so far?"

Both of them looked back at me helplessly.

"We can't *do* anything," Shell finally admitted. "She's been gone for hours, but the mission she's on is a classified Department of Superhuman Affairs operation. The DSA team she was with—"

"—and the investigation team they called in won't let her disappearance out. We've been watching them, hoping—"

"—that they'll figure out what happened. They haven't."

"They don't even know if she's alive," Shelly finished

I took off my lab coat. "And so you've called everyone in, I presume."

They both nodded. "Even Jacky—she'll be here by tonight."

"I see." I considered the girls for a moment. "Then it would be best if our meeting takes place here." One of the first things I'd done when I moved in was set up protections to ensure privacy, and when those in authority believe a problem is their responsibility, they frown on others taking an independent interest. "While the rest are on their way, I can begin my own investigation. Nix? Will you please assist me?"

By the time Mal and Jamal arrived, I had consulted my mirrors and learned, to my carefully hidden relief, that I could not find Hope either. Whatever Hope's physical state, she was beyond the reach of my magic as well as the quantum-twins' ability to hear her through their link—a negative result that left open the possibility of a positive outcome.

And while there was a possibility, I would be positive.

Brian was the last to arrive, looking slightly cooked. He smelled of unnatural chemicals and I didn't doubt he had an interesting story to tell, when an opportune moment arrived.

Seeing all of us together didn't improve his mood. "What's going on?"

I smiled fondly, pointing to a seat. I would never tell him that I had started my lab work early today to keep from spying on his mission. Or simply fretting. Princesses didn't fret. "Perhaps now that you're here, Shell will tell us."

"Hope's vanished!"

"Again?" Grendel sat. "She's about due."

I frowned at his flippancy, but had to allow that was true. Shell didn't receive Grendel's unconcern well. "*We* can't find her! Nobody can."

"Perhaps," I suggested, "now that we are present you should take it from the top?"

"Right. Okay." She visibly got a grip on herself. "The details are *classified*. The whole op is, but the DSA recruited Hope to be *bait*. Some breakthrough serial killer is targeting victims close to her description, under a very specific set of circumstances. So Hope and a basket of others with powers that pretty much guaranteed their safety were put in those circumstances. He picked Hope. Now she's vanished."

A wave of protest went around the lab table. Jamal raised a hand. "Hey, you said 'killer' and 'victims.' Did the previous victims vanish, too?"

"Nope. He just made them horribly dead."

I put a hand on Brian's arm; his claws were out and making chalkboard noises on my steel lab table. We had never discussed the matter, but I was certain that in our first months here Hope could have made Brian her boyfriend with the slightest expression of interest. Fortunately she didn't play those sorts of games, and he had settled into a kind of older brother protectiveness towards the girl. "I assume that there was good cause to assume that our Hope would not be treated likewise?"

"Nearly invulnerable, duh. The others got—never mind, it's not what happened to *her*."

"Can you show us what happened to her?"

"Yes! Here it is, what she saw." She pointed at the lab's main screen, which lit up to show a bedroom. The camera motion told us this was the scene through Hope's eyes, translated to digital through her connection with Shell. Hope closed the bedroom door and turned out the lights, then walked into the connected bathroom, flipping on the bulb over the vanity mirror. In the mirror we could see the pink University of Chicago tank top and white sleep shorts she wore, and the circus clown standing right behind her. Hope didn't have time to turn before he came out of the mirror at her.

Then it got confusing, but after the first scream the rest weren't hers—they were his as she grappled with him. He obviously couldn't make her let go, and— I blinked. "I believe that the mirror swallowed them?"

Shell replayed the last couple of seconds in slow motion, and yes, when the clown's flailing hand touched the mirror it seemed to jump right at us before the image froze. Nobody in the lab took this well and, pitching my voice evenly to try and inject a tone of calm, I summed up. "So, the killer succeeded in escaping back into the mirror." It didn't work, but it seldom did with Shell.

"With Hope! Wherever she's gone I can't *find* her, and the DSA agents on this have got nothing! Zip. Zilch. Zero. Nada. *Nothing*."

I saw Brian open his mouth to protest, shook my head. "Is there anything else?"

"Only that the mirror exploded into a zillion pieces, completely stripped the paint off the opposite wall. Anyone else standing in the room would have been bleeding hamburger."

"And what does the DSA make of that?" I didn't ask how she knew what the DSA was doing, with Hope no longer there.

She threw up her hands. "They don't know? They don't know *what* happened. They couldn't track this monster's mirror-jumps before, they can't now."

"Wait a sec." Jamal frowned. "The whole mirror breaking bit wasn't normal?"

She shook her head glumly. "No, it wasn't. They've spent *hours* at the scene, and they still don't know why it was different this time."

I nodded thoughtfully. "Shell, would you be a dear and review the news? Please look for any reports of mirrors violently breaking anywhere."

"What will that— Sure." Her eyes unfocused and a series of data-points scrolled down on the main screen. "I assume you mean incidents not simply written off as property damage associated with a documented incident? We've got…hey! One that looks weird. And pretty spectacular." An image of a generic box-shaped outlet warehouse popped up. All of its windows were shattered.

"Freemont Glass, Portland Oregon, does windows and mirrors. Late last night it exploded. Initial police report is some kind of high pressure explosion, but they can't find traces of the container or even the center point of the blast yet. Nobody else was on site or in the street, which is good because every sheet of glass in the place including the windows got turned into slivers."

"And the time of the explosion?"

"It was reported at the same time as Hope's disappearance!"

"Well then. The form of mirror travel we have just seen usually requires a mirror at each terminus. If something catastrophic eventuated, it will have likely occurred at both termini." I gave a sharp clap, making everyone jump. "We are going to Oregon."

"Hold on," Mal protested. "Won't we be interfering in a DSA investigation?"

"Nonsense. I have an interest in mirrors myself, and we are merely going to observe an interesting spectacle. Come along."

Her witchy majesty insisted I get a real shower and change into civvies before we left. Fair enough, I smelled like a chemical spill. A shower and change later I found out that, by *we*, Ozma had meant just the royal we plus one; she took only her army (with Hope gone, currently me), and we went by Travel Dust.

I *hated* Travel Dust. When it cleared and I decided I wasn't going to throw up, I looked around the alley it had dropped us in. Blowing in out of nowhere in the street would have made it tough to be unnoticeable, even with the Anonymity Specs she'd insisted I wear.

After being spun about topsy-turvy and dropped onto her feet again Ozma looked a bit pale. Putting a hand on my shoulder, she took a bracing breath.

"Well!" she said brightly. "The Portland police are admirably efficient."

Both entrances to the service alley were sealed by yellow crime-scene tape, ensuring our privacy. When we took a step bits of glass crunched beneath our feet—even the thick and heavy-framed windows facing into the alley had been blown out by whatever had happened inside.

The alley door was steel, but Ozma made quick use of Thieves' Powder on the lock to defeat any alarm and I opened it with a single sharp tug. Shell had already assured us that the place should be empty. Budget constraints; once the Portland Police Department had determined it hadn't been a bomb, they'd just taped off the site. Nobody had been hurt, so at worst it was a weird kind of arson or vandalism; they might look into the owner, but if they found nothing suspicious then the investigation would be closed.

The inside was one large warehouse and showroom space, with a small office and staff rooms on one side taking up less than a tenth of the square footage. Every step we took crunched on glass. Every surface was covered in it and there wasn't an intact freestanding mirror or window in the showroom. There should have been; a lot of the frames were at right angles to each other, and some stood on the other side of mirror-hung gallery walls.

Ozma agreed. "This was not an explosion, Brian. Or rather, this was many explosions. Every mirror exploded at once. The windows were destroyed by the mirrors."

"What blew out all the mirrors?"

"That is what we are here to find out." She set her case down. For the trip she'd worn a pair of green coveralls with lots of stuffed pockets, but apparently that wasn't enough; the case opened out into a witch's kit of wands, crystals, vials, and weird stuff. Donning a pair of multi-lensed gold specs, she unrolled a set of tuning forks and began striking them against the empty frame of the freestanding mirror in front of her.

As she patiently worked her way from the high to low range, I looked around. Nothing to see here, *except for the steam-punk robot wavering into existence out of empty air.* Shouting a warning, I lunged just as its metal feet crunched down on the floor and it grabbed for Ozma. She turned and screamed, falling against the mirror frame to narrowly avoid the buzzing, sparking claw that reached for her. When the robot lurched forward to reach again, I ripped its head off before kicking the body halfway across the showroom.

Spiking the clicking head like a football in the end zone, I put myself between Ozma and the rest of the showroom. I was so hair-trigger focused I jumped when her hand touched my back.

"No, Brian. We're safe."

Looking down I saw that my claws were out. I'd also grown fang and started growling, and I forced myself to pull everything in. "What is that?" I asked as soon as I could talk around my teeth again. Riding on adrenalin, I looked for something else to tear into. The crushed head clicked unevenly, the robot body lay twitching, and nothing else moved.

She knelt to touch the head, eyes wide. Her voice shook. "It's a tick-tock. It's from Oz."

Ⓩ

Oz. It was from Oz. Of course I'd known the instant I'd seen it, and yet it was beyond all things astonishing. I'd quickly gathered up packets of mirror shards to take with us while Brian had collected the tick-tock's body and head, and we had left in another whirl of Travel Dust before the crashes of the brief fight could be reported and perhaps summon an investigating officer.

Why was it here? I was rather peremptory in clearing the lab even of Brian—the man wanted to break off a few more bits of the thing to make sure it was "safe" and I couldn't allow that. Before the morning gave way to afternoon I considered that perhaps I should have kept him to help me unbolt and unhinge the automaton; my gloved hands ached and the clear oil that smoothed the functioning of its moving parts liberally coated parts of my face and hair. I rested my head on my folded arms, knowing I was getting more oil from my sleeves on my forehead. It stank.

I considered the brass automaton.

It had no windup gears for voice. Separate gears wound up its clockwork brains and motivational train. It was wholly recognizable as an evolution of the magic-mechanical concepts that had driven poor Tik-Tok. In the attack on the palace, Tik-Tok had held the doors to the Crown Treasury against the Mombi-armored nome hoard while I had sent away my magical treasures with the aid of the Magic Belt, the Magic Belt last of all so that it could find me. I still had nightmares about it.

And I'd thought Tik-Tok destroyed. Had he instead been disassembled and studied for duplication? Neither the Nome King nor Mombi had the skill. Only the Wizard, with his rather mechanical approach to magic, had shown an interest in Tik-Tok before, and he—

My head shot up. "Nox! Fetch me a vial of sundrops, quickly!"

My tiny courtier and bodyguard leapt from the table where he'd been suspiciously watching the thing's completely harmless head, and returned with a box. Opening it, I removed the shining bottle. I'd filled it weeks ago, the last time I'd been able to catch rain falling through the light of a sunset, and in the box it had not yet been able to release its golden store. Now it glowed joyfully.

"The lights, Nix, please." The artificial lights turned off, the room lit only by the warm yellow light, I began my examination. And there it was, inscribed on the thing's windup motivational train: *O.D., Tick-Tock Works, The Cascades, YF,* in bright gold sunscript.

Where the thing had been assembled, doubtless inside a factory, no direct sunlight would ever have touched its inner works to illuminate the letters. They were for me.

And that solved the mystery of the tick-tock. My hands shook, but I reboxed the sundrops and then retrieved the samples I had taken from the site. Now for the mirrors.

"Think she's found anything?"

I shot another sniping enemy. "No. She'll tell us when she does."

Jamal smirked, shot his own five targets. "Yeah, right, like she tells us everything ever. I *still* don't know why she wanted my shoes."

"Ingredients. Don't ask, you'll get a headache." We finished off the challenge and I saved the game. Playing with Jamal always made me feel slow, but the waiting was getting on my nerves. The only updates we'd gotten were from Braidwood, letting us know that everything was good, there'd been no radiation-contaminated leaks, and the DSA and Department of Energy was securing the site; soon the rest of the team would be home.

"Besides—"

"*Everyone to the lab!*" Shell called out. "*Ozma's got a show-and-tell!*"

"Never mind." I put down the controller, stretched and cracked my neck. Jamal was already gone.

Shell and Shelly were back in the lab, by dronebot and screen. Mal and Jamal circled the lab table, geeking over the disassembled robot. "How did it work?" Jamal was asking. "It's gears and springs!"

"It uses a..." Ozma stopped and smiled. "Magic. It's clockwork magic."

"Cool!"

"Slowpoke," Shell shot at me before turning to Ozma. "So, what's going on?"

What was going on was we were going to do something exciting and dangerous. Ozma had cleaned up and changed into her "field costume," a white flowing shoulderless gown over an equally white bodysuit, with her gold-wire circlet crown. She'd dressed for authority, which meant her witchy majesty was going to try and talk us into something.

"I have determined what happened to Hope," she announced, "and what we may do to find her." She looked around, satisfying herself as to our complete attention. "The killer Hope faced used the factory warehouse as his base. Shell has confirmed that a man matching the biometrics of the mirror jumping clown we saw works there as a night-shift maintenance man and security guard. His current whereabouts are unknown. The *mirrors* appear to have been destroyed by proximate discharge of— Of a bad jump with a worse result.

She indicated a petri dish of glass shards floating in a bell jar on the counter beside her.

"I believe that when the killer attempted to flee back through the mirror his power could not carry him and Hope, to whom he remained attached. They stuck, between mirrors, until the bottled force discharged uncontrollably and catastrophically. It created an open *rift*, a weak spot in reality. And they fell through it. They are not in our reality anymore."

"So where did she go?" Shelly on the lab screen looked heaps more calm than her twin.

"I don't know. Somewhere else. But I believe I have a way to find her." She gracefully waved at the dead steampunk robot, now just a spread out collection of copper parts. "This tick-tock interrupted our investigation, attempting to capture me and return me to Oz. I have determined that this was its sole function—its lightning weapon would have rendered me quite helpless had it not been for Brian."

"She's in *Oz*?"

"I do not think so. Rifts of this nature are like junctions or crossroads, allowing travel to and from a great many places where local rifts harmonically— Where they match. I believe that this tick-tock was planted in a corresponding rift in Oz, waiting as patiently as only such a thing can for me to appear on this side. If Mombi has been able to observe me at all, she knows that I am free and myself, preparing to return."

Mal nodded. "Got it. It's a gate guardian."

Shell gave the thing an unfriendly look. "More like a trapdoor spider."

"Yes it was. I was very nearly captured by a trap similar to the one our Hope took part in. My presence triggered its response, and it came through the rift for me. Please look here." She directed our attention to a silver ball just above what I guessed was the thing's wind-up heart. It looked like it was made out of concentric silver bands—a fancy version of the old rubber-band balls I'd sometimes made for kicks at school. The silver had a milky, translucent quality almost like crystal, and the ultra-fine inscriptions etched into it made my eyes hurt but I could see that it was made of two halves that snugged together.

"This is what allowed it to travel here. It has two settings, with the capacity for more. The first setting is for Oz, to return it. The second setting is presumably for me, triggered by my presence at the rift. It sought me, although if set later it might have been able to also seek out my trail from the rift."

"Oh!" Shell lit up. "You think that you can set it to find Hope?"

"No." Ozma smiled sadly. "I don't know how it was set to find me, and I do not dare to disassemble it to see if I can work it out. But its creator might, and fortunately I know him. I propose to go and ask him."

"You *know* him?"

Ozma's laugh was the tinkle of silver bells. "Of course I do. He is my wizard, Oscar Diggs. And his current address, or his address when he built the tick-tock, is the Tick-Tock Works, somewhere upon the Cascades. It is the best news I have had in quite some time."

"Wait." I poked the robot with a claw. "You're saying the *Wizard* of *Oz* built this. To catch you? And that's *good* news?"

"Yes, Brian. I believed that he was dead, but it is obvious that he is too valuable to Mombi and the Nome King. They forced him to build this, but he signed his name. Here." And she showed us.

"YF?"

"'Yours, faithfully.' I believe that he hoped that I would be able to defeat the tick-tock, and he knew I would study it."

"So he told you where to find him?" I barked a laugh. "We're off to see the wizard?"

"The wonderful wizard of Oz," she deadpanned with the barest hint a smile.

"Yay!" That was Nix—everyone else groaned or face-palmed as I wondered if I should write the date in my calendar; the day her serene highness told a joke.

Naturally it wasn't that simple. First, not all of us could go; we'd gone haring off before, following our idealistic team leader into messes that weren't our business, and nearly gotten shut down over it. Jamal and Mal weren't eighteen yet, and we were talking about a recon and retrieval mission into enemy-held territory. *Extrareality* territory. And Shell couldn't keep a link with her robodrones across reality boundaries without preparations Ozma didn't have time to make.

We also had to report the Portland site to the DSA investigating Hope's disappearance or pure shit would rain down on us when they found out we'd known about it, so we had to go now since we couldn't risk them working the site and then deciding to close the rift or ban us from it. So it was going to be just Ozma and me again, with Shell letting the DSA know about it after we'd gone in; they probably wouldn't close the gate with us on the other side.

And we were going incognito, which meant Nix was going to dress me like her personal doll.

It was getting more and more difficult to resist playing with Brian's hair, and it shouldn't have been an obsession of the moment since I was *home*. We were far from the Emerald City, but the red rock and soil of Quadling Country brought tears to my eyes.

Twisting the ball to its home setting had brought us to a place I'd only read about but recognized; the Ruby Cave behind the Great Waterfall. The rift debouched into the cave's roiling cauldron pool, and we had arrived with quite a splash. Querying the Question Box before our departure had told me that we would arrive safe and free and this time I had managed to quell my spontaneous scream (empresses don't scream, and neither do superheroes), but I had been silently concerned of other waiting guards. There had been none. After drying us and our belongings with a simple chanted cantrip, I had found the exit to the cave and now we stood beside the Great Waterfall, breathing the mist-filled air and looking out over the rolling hills and redstone ridges of Quadling Country.

And I couldn't stop thinking about Brian's tight woven night-black locks.

Fudge.

Perhaps it was that he looked so at home here. In his loose black trousers, tucked into rugged boots, and red leather vest over an embroidered white tunic, he looked the image of a Quadling troll. Even his hair didn't look out of place, since trolls were known for their extravagant attention to their locks and sported mohawks, braids, weaves, and wings of eye-popping styles and colors. A troll master hairdresser made as much coin as the fanciest chef. The great iron staff he carried, with the huge pack upon his back, announced his strength to anyone who looked. Strength and hair—a troll's great pride.

Fudge, fudge, fudge.

"Are we going to stand here admiring the scenery?"

I made myself laugh. It wasn't hard; we were on an *adventure*. "Don't be a gooch. Is your pack sitting right?"

Nix had dressed us both; Brian as a Quadling boy, me as a Quadling girl. My vest and tunic matched his, though my short white embroidered bloomers and high gartered socks had made him comment about wearing my underwear on the outside (I'd ignored him—the linen and cotton clothing was *not* lingerie). Our identical embroidery designs announced to anyone we might meet that we were married; I was a traveling hedge witch, my profession proclaimed by my wide-brimmed pointed red hat, and my husband carried my pack of herbs, ointments, potions, pastels, and witchy tools as Brian called them. And bashed anyone I couldn't hex.

"And what was my name, again?"

I rolled my eyes at his grumbling—a bad habit I had picked up from Hope. "Benagain. BEN-again. Now say mine."

"Pennigal."

"PEN-ee-gal."

"That's what I said, Pennigal."

"Ben means strong in ancient Ozian. Pen means wise, but you're an unlettered troll so you don't know that."

He laughed, looking down at me. I'm not small, but he could. "And what does Ozma mean?"

I raised my nose in the air. "*Oz* means 'Great and Good,' you peasant. Nearly every reigning king and queen of Lurline's line since Ozma the First has taken a derivative reign name. Ozmund, Ozanus, Ozi. And you won't use it here." I pointed a finger at him, waved it. "Pennigal."

He grabbed my finger, my whole hand disappearing into his. "Who are you, and what have you done with she-who-will-not-be-named?"

"We're on an *adventure*. Come on."

We could have descended the precipitous switchbacks to the floor of the falls, where the roaring water filled the great pool and descended to the underground rivers that watered the springs and aquifers of Quadling Country, but instead we climbed. We needed to go up, up, up, above the falls and north, to the cascades that fed it from Green Lake and the central lands ruled directly by the Emerald City.

Brian could have put me on top of the pack and sprinted up the switchbacks, but even trolls weren't supposed to be *that* strong and my legs started to burn long before we'd reached the top.

"So why are we going to see the Wizard again?" Brian asked about halfway up. "Didn't he sort of, *kidnap* you as a child or something?"

"The Wizard came to Oz after my father was already dead and I'd disappeared," I explained as we climbed. "But there were rumors that he did away with me, spread to undermine his rule of the Emerald City. Of course when I was found the rumors changed to say that he'd given me to Mombi. There was no truth in them, she kidnapped me herself and turned me into Tip."

"And why are you having so much fun?"

I'd have laughed if I'd had breath from the climb. "I liked being Tip, after I got away from Mombi. I *liked* adventures. No protocol, no courtiers, no responsibility for anything except my friends—I don't care what Baum wrote, ruling Oz took a *lot* more work than a freaking hour or two a day."

"Freaking?"

I turned around. "I *won't* say the real f-word! My language is cleaner than Hope's. One hundred years of habit, by golly. As *Tip*, I swore like a sailor. Mombi was a terrible role model."

Below me, Grendel looked stunned. "*That* didn't get into the books."

"It wouldn't, would it?"

He was quiet for another two switchbacks.

"So, they did it to you again?"

"When they conquered Oz? Oh, yes. They can't kill me because I have no heirs and the magic of Oz is tied to the fairy blood of the royal family, so this time I was *Kip*. Kip Nelson, a boy in foster care until the Magic Belt found me and woke me. I liked being Kip, too. Foster care was nowhere near as bad as Mombi."

All I'd had to worry about as Kip was schoolwork, chores, and the occasional bully foster kid. I hadn't been a big boy.

We stopped talking again, though I was very conscious of him stomping along behind me. With all the noise he was making, my boots made no sound as I dug into the trail.

I supposed that Brian had never really taken it all seriously. The real world that Mombi had exiled me to was full of superhuman breakthroughs who often made big claims about themselves and the sources of their powers. In Hillwood Academy we'd known a couple of avatars and demigods, and Brian was nominally Christian so he hadn't exactly believed *them*. But now we were in Oz, and either I was really Ozma or I'd created the whole place from breakthrough-fueled delusions. *Poor baby...* I hoped this didn't make him take me more seriously as a princess and empress; he was my dearest friend, not a soldier or courtier.

And he wasn't going to be just a soldier or courtier when I sat on the Emerald Throne again either. I didn't look back. "Benagain? I have not seen Kindrake recently. Are the two of you still stepping out together?"

The stomping stopped, resumed. "She's busy. And dating in LA."

He couldn't see my smile.

The switchbacks ended atop the cliff, and we finally stood on flat ground beside the terminal end of the Great River.

"Now that's a big waterfall."

"Larger than Niagara Falls," I said proudly. "And much higher. We've got an easy walk now—there are a lot of them, but the Cascades aren't very high." I turned away from the beautiful view to look north. "But we may have a fight now. Put down the pack, dear. Remember, do not change. Trolls don't do that."

The pack of silver wolves raced down upon us almost silently. The smallest of them outweighed me, and they bared silver teeth and let loose their barking howls when they saw us turn to stand ready. The closest wolf gathered itself and leapt, Brian's iron staff cutting through the air with a vibrating hum to batter it aside. My willow wand out, I shouted "*Lim Tin Tak!*" and the two lunging for me yipped as their bodies lifted and drifted, suddenly as light as leaves on the breeze which blew them out over the cliff edge.

Brian stepped in front of me before the others reached us and simply roared at the remaining four. They weren't talking animals, with sapient wisdom, but they were smart enough to see that he was too tough for lunch and their barks turned to yipping howls as they fled.

I took a few breaths before my heart stopped racing and I trusted myself to be steady. Stepping to the edge, I looked down to see the two silver wolves I had charmed bobbing and bouncing lightly down the rocks below us; they would arrive at the bottom before the magic wore off and they'd be able to stand against the wind blowing them about. Brian laughed at the sight, and I could imagine how it might look to anyone below as two very confused wolves drifted down like half-deflated balloons.

"Easier than turning them into hats, right?"

"Changing their mass is much easier than changing their form." I gripped my willow wand and gave Brian a tight smile. They shouldn't have been here at all. During my nearly centenary reign, the reunited lands of Oz had rendered a wolf attack as likely here as a wolf attack in England. Silver wolves roaming this close to the City Lands, the territory under the direct administration of the Emerald City, was a bad sign indeed. Straightening, I returned my wand to its sheath at my hip. "Well, let us be off. We can reach the first cascade before sunset."

Something was upsetting her witchy majesty. She'd been chatty, even exuberant, on the way to the top of the falls. The attack? Maybe. She wasn't a fighting cape, really, and most of her work was support or civil emergency, but the wolves hadn't shaken her so what was going on? I adjusted the pack, watching her stride along. The girl never looked less than sure of herself, ever. I figured that was from being Dictator for Life of Oz but I'd learned her tells; when she was unsure she got on her best imperial behavior. More proper than proper. She also liked to stand practically right on top of me, and right now we were practically shoulder to shoulder as we followed the river upstream. She was worrying.

So talk about something. "So the Tick-Tock Works sounds important, right? Why would it be clear out here, in Quadling Country?"

"Factory works are waterwheel driven." She didn't look up. "With its sequence of falls, the Cascades are the best source of water power in Oz. Also, Quadling Country's most valuable resource is radium. It's a vital piece of clockwork magic, used in the winding springs to multiply motivational power."

"The thing you took apart was *radioactive*? What the fu—"

She patted my arm. "No, Brian. Radium in Oz isn't like radium on Earth. It's not radioactive. You've seen it. The Travel Sphere we used to get here is made of it. It magnifies anentropic forces to— It enhances magic. Many believe it has healthful properties and wear amulets of it on necklaces or bracelets. You know, the way some people swear by the powers of magnets. My crown and scepter is made of it, and radium thread is woven into my Magic Belt. Wizards and witches love the stuff." She laughed. "It's fortunate that the Quadlings were not a scholarly people, before unification. They were militarily aggressive enough that had they known how to use it they might have conquered Oz."

"So instead you guys did?"

"We did, but not with radium."

"Why?" That was something I'd never been able to figure out, and it had always seemed sort of a touchy subject.

She was willing to talk about it now. "The Emerald City is surrounded, and the crossroads to everywhere in Oz. Emerils eventually tired of being attacked by everyone else. If it wasn't the Kingdom of Quada in alliance with the Kingdom of Munch, it was Quada and Wink. To be fair, they fought each other more often than they fought us, but the final straw was the Quadruple Alliance, when even Gilli joined in to take their share of the City Lands."

"Holy—cow. How did you survive?"

"Thick city walls and deep granaries. They couldn't break the walls and couldn't out starve us. Also the Quadling king died, and when his children started fighting for the throne the Quadling army had to go home. After that, Ozamund the First launched the Unification Wars. We conquered and incorporated Gilli first, then Munch and Winki, and by the time Ozamund's daughter invaded Quada it wasn't a contest since we had the armies of all the others with us. We united the lands into the Imperial Realm of Oz, spread Emeril learning and law, and made everyone Ozian."

She waved at the low hills around us. "Even the names of the old kingdoms are gone, and now it's just the City Lands, Gillikin Country, Winkie Country, Munchkin Country, and Quadling Country, all equally represented and administered under the Emerald Throne. Or it used to be. It fell apart for a while under the Witches, and now, well now it looks like it might all be gone again. These were *tame* lands." She glared at the grass and flower covered hills like they'd personally offended her.

Gotcha. Ozma was scared. Not by the wolves but what they meant. The girl had sat on that throne for nearly a hundred years (and now I was getting the idea she hadn't always liked it), worked hard to patch everything up, and now it was all broken again? So she was worrying herself into a mess.

We couldn't have that, right?

"So..." I poked the girl's shoulder, making her stumble. "The Emerald City is like, what, Rome? Marching legions, burning cities, all that stuff? Did you have gladiators? Dynastic struggles? Assassinations? Riots? Wild animal fights?"

"No!" she laughed. "You watch too much cable, Brian." She put her nose in the air and put some distance between us, but she started humming. Probably some Oz composer, because I sure didn't recognize it. I didn't complain—Ozma had a sweet voice and whatever it was she stayed on key. Her steps bounced her red hair (she'd magically dyed it for our adventure), and all was right with the world.

At least it was until we saw the first cascade.

Ozma said it wasn't a fort. Its walls were brick and too low, its gate too wide and unprotected. Tall smokestacks and tiles roofs of big blocky buildings rose above the walls, and the tops of the walls looked like they were covered by their own peaked roofs, with peaked towers at each corner. The cascade thundered over rocks within a hundred feet of its western wall.

"It's the Tick-Tock Works," she decided. "We are close to the northern radium mines, and not far downriver from Southford." We found the dirt road that led from the hills to the gates, and trudged on. The guards at the gate carried ax-bladed pikes, and dressed in dirty green uniforms with lots of brass buttons under breastplates that looked like they hadn't been polished in years.

"Halt! Stand in the name of the Crowns!" The more active of the three guards had waited until we were practically standing in the gate. Now he leveled his pike at my chest. I stopped, no problem.

"State your business!"

I glanced down at Ozma, who didn't look at all impressed. She pointed to her hat. "We are on our way to Southford, and decided to see if there was any need of my simples and cures at the works."

"And why do you travel on this side of the river?"

She shrugged inelegantly. "We come from the mines, and Southford is on this side of the river. Here." Fishing in her vest, she brought out a bundle of folded papers, handed them to the guard. I tried not to look curious as he opened them. They were blank.

He studied the blank papers carefully, handed them back with a sneer. "Everything is in order, perhaps the nursery can use you." Fishing in his own pocket, he tossed each of us a chip. "Don't lose them, and return to this gate tomorrow." He looked up at me. "Leave the pole."

I let go and he scrambled to grab it before it fell to the ground, straining to juggle it with his pike. "Careful, troll. You may be more useful than your woman around here."

He didn't like my smile, but they let us pass. The wall wasn't thick at all, just enough to support a wooden walkway under the eaves around the top, and the inner yard was dirt and badly laid stones, full of wagons. We could see all of the buildings now, the big block buildings with their chimneys and rows of long low buildings beside them. Obvious guardhouses hugged the inside of the walls and I was starting to get a bad feeling about this place.

It wasn't the smoke or the rhythmic ground shaking thumps and clangs, it was everyone I saw. The sloppy guards were the best-dressed people in the works; everyone else wore close to rags, and nobody not in a uniform looked at a guard as they went wherever they were going. There were a lot of guards, and they weren't guarding the walls.

Nobody in the yard seemed at all curious about us until a white-haired man spotted Ozma's pointy hat and hustled over to bow. His clothes weren't as ragged as the others.

"Excuse me, mistress..."

Ozma nodded. "Mistress Pennigal, sir. And this is my husband. We have been directed to the nursery?"

"Well that is *most* splendid! Your pardon, I am Diomedus and I can take you there directly. There is a fever in the works, and with the poor diet here... We are most happy to see you." He led us quickly to the long low building closest to the east wall. This one had its own guardhouse, and they didn't let me pass. Instead, Ozma had me put my pack down against the wall and sit with it while she took several packets from our gear and went inside.

I watched the guards in the prison yard, because the Tick Tock Works was a prison. A whistle blew and I saw a work-party transfer, a file of workers marched out of the closest factory building under guard and into one of the long ones. They weren't in chains but all of them were ragged and thin, and none looked up from their feet as they marched.

Ozma stayed in the nursery for an hour, and when she emerged past the guards and sat down beside me her eyes were red. Her fingers moved and she whispered a rhyme I couldn't catch, before looking at me.

"It's a prison camp for rebels, Brian." She kept her voice low, but didn't look at the guards. They were lazy, but close enough to hear us so she must have witched them somehow. Or witched us. "When someone is taken for rebellion they take his family too. The children are held hostage in the nursery." Her voice shook. "It's awful in there, but I'm told it's not as bad as the rest of the camp."

"Is the Wizard here?"

"They say he is, under lock and key in the factory where he directs production and crafts the finer gears and pieces they need. They're building a tick-tock army."

"Got it. What do we do?"

"We are going to break the works, Brian. The Army of Oz will march and not one brick will stand on another brick before we are through. Wait here and be ready." She rose and took more packets inside. I didn't see what they were; I was busy counting guards.

The sun set, more work parties leaving the factory before Ozma came out again, so I was pretending to doze when she touched my shoulder.

"Brain. The factory is yours. Tear it down. There will only be guards inside it now, except for the Wizard, and I know my Wizard. He will be ready."

I shook myself and stood. "Okay. And where will you start?"

"Here. I will start here. *LUX!*"

The explosion of light blinded me, and then Ozma stood tall in her white sheath and gown, silver crown on her head, Magic Belt at her waist, and scepter in her hand. She glowed and the light was a wind, sweeping between the buildings and sparking flares off every pike and lamp.

"I am Ozma! Daughter of King Pastoria, Princess of the Emerald City and Empress of Oz the Great and the Good! For crimes against my subjects your lives are forfeit, your names forgotten, your lineages cursed! All within these walls are mine by right of ancient law!"

Shouts and cries of alarm filled the works. Ozma shown bright while behind her vines sprang out of the nursery gate to choke the entry and climb its walls as white blossoms opened to bathe in her light. I laughed and charged, my boots bursting as I bulked while I ran. Halfway across the yard, I felt a push at my back as power poured into me and fire lit my skin to sink to my bones. I'd burst if I tried to hold it in, but that wasn't what she wanted at all and I *grew*, bigger than I'd ever been. When I hit the factory doors they shattered and I had to bend to enter. Dark cavernous halls lit by only a few lamps stretched the length of the building, full of belts and forges and tanks and machinery I didn't even try to identify.

It would all be wreckage anyway, and the few night guards scattered and ran as I got to work.

Half-finished tick-tocks made handy projectiles, support beams made great clubs, and banked forges made great fire starters. I punctuated swings and stomps with roars of "Magician! Magician!" Halfway through the hall I found him waiting by an open cell, an old man with thinning hair and sagging skin on a face that used to be fuller.

He bowed, smiling savagely. "I am the Wizard, and it is a pleasure. Shall we be off? Ozma is here?"

"She's outside, and I'm bringing it all down."

"Right-oh, then. Don't take too long, young man, and may I suggest lighting more fires and then breaking the pillars? Burst the water pumps at the back when you're through, and you can flood out what doesn't burn." He practically skipped for the doors, carrying a dusty tool bag with him and moving a lot faster than I'd have thought possible for his age.

I found the pumps and wrecked them, but stayed to make sure the ceiling came down. Then it was easy enough to punch my way out, knocking the few standing walls in as I made my way out of the mess.

Stepping out of the rubble, I expected to enjoy a fight. I should have known better—I couldn't see a single guard, past a handful without weapons beside some prisoners who put themselves in front of them when I stomped up.

"Sir Brian," the oldest prisoner managed to say. "These helped us, before today, and her majesty has extended clemency. She wishes you to attend her."

"Right. Thank you." I looked down at my claws, realized that the heat in my bones was fading, and decided it was time to scale down anyway. By the time I'd stomped back to the nursery I was my normal self again, or at least as normal as I got. The Magician was with her, along with the children now that the protecting vines had been cleared away.

"Did you have fun, Sir Brian?"

"It was alright."

"Good. The guards have fled through the south and north gates, and my subjects have armed themselves. They are gathering provisions for our march, and while they do so I would be very grateful if you would also break down the walls."

The walls actually gave me a workout, but only a half-decent one.

Oz

The Wizard, a man who liked his large breakfasts and desserts, was as thin and worn as I had ever seen him. And as charmingly confident as ever. It had been his *plan*, so of course I'd come and he even chastised me for being late with a twinkle in his eyes. And I of course was my imperious best, except with the children for whom I could smile and even cry. We both had our parts to play.

Here I was the princess. And empress.

The elders among the prisoners quickly organized things, reuniting children with their parents, arranging stretchers for prisoners who now needed to be carried. We left nobody behind as we marched out through what had been the south gate, a long, strung out line on foot and pulling wagons. Once we left the road and climbed the first low hill, I turned to look at the wreck of the works.

"Well that looks like a good job done," Brian decided.

"Indeed," my wizard said. "I am glad to see the last of the place."

I smiled. "And now you will see my place, Oscar. My court in exile is humble, and you'll find that America has changed a great deal since you came to Oz, but I am happy to have you with me again."

He humphed, a sly smile showing a glimmer of his old humor. "I know it has, my dear. I kept my eyes on it over the years. But I am not going back with you, princess. I'm sorry."

"I— Wizard, I command it."

His smile turned sad. "Young lady I am Oscar Zoroaster Phadrig Isaac Norman Henkel Emmanuel Ambrose Diggs, a Yankee boy from Omaha. My father was a Nebraska Senator, and in my day I have worn many hats. Flim-flam artist. Politician, which is the same thing. Carny barker. Magician. A fake wizard, and then a real one. Your advisor and humble servant. What I have never been is your subject.

"Ozma." He touched my hand, the twinkle gone from his eye. "Only the City Lands are truly held by Mombi and the Nome King now. Quadling Country is in quiet revolt, so we will have help on our way to Jinxland. That old and only independent kingdom in Oz has become a refuge and center of Quadling resistance, and I have been stocking my bag of tricks, enchantments, clockwork magic, and humbug. I will see your Quadlings to safety, and offer my services. There is much to do before you can return for good."

"Oscar, *please*—" I closed my eyes, opened them and nodded. He was right, I knew he was right, but I had so wanted my dear old friend beside me. "I will speak to the elders, and you will go with my blessing."

"Thank you. Oh, and I will be able to show you how to reset the Traveling Ball before we part ways. I hope you will be able to find your friend." He gave me a tired nod, stepping away to proceed towards the front of the march. Brian looked at me.

"So what now, your witchy majesty?"

Water pricked my eyes and I hid my smile. *Please love, don't ever change.* I raised my scepter, laying a hand upon my Magic Belt and whispering to the land. *My* land. With a great crack and a ground-shaking roar, the river rose to sweep away the remains of the works.

"Now let's go home."

DSA Field Report: Agent Smith.

Boss, we've secured the site. Per previous report, elements of the Chicago Sentinels have conducted an independent investigation and determined the identity and base of Red Jack. Got to tell you, it really makes us look bad; we spend hundreds of man-hours, and a fictional magic princess and a cyber-ghost we're not supposed to acknowledge Nancy-Drewed the case and told us everything there is to know about our serial-killer. They've also presented us with a method whereby following Red Jack and Astra may be possible—and of course it requires them. My recommendation: lock down the determined location but allow "monitored" Sentinel access.

Boss, they can't do worse than we have so far.

Red Jack Case File 1-B634 D.

Through a Bright Mirror

by Marion G. Harmon

"Of course we don't live in the best of all possible worlds. We're human, we mess up, we could have always done better. Which doesn't mean that we can't *do better. We can do worse, but we can always do better, too."*

Hope Corrigan

I opened my eyes and looked at the ceiling of my room. *Huh.*

Graymalkin vibrated with silent cat-snores against my side, his tail twitching against my hand where it had wandered out from under the blankets sometime during the night. I usually woke up this way at home, bumped out of deeper sleep by Gray jumping up and settling himself; half the time he'd open an eye when I got up, then get back to chasing dream mice or whatever made his tail sweep the covers.

But I didn't remember coming home.

What was the last thing I remembered?

Put that way, with nothing connecting *then* to *now*, it was tough. Especially since, still half-asleep, I couldn't be sure which were memories and which were dreams. Memories of dreams.

Okay, there was dinner with Tony. And Kitsune. Did I see the ducks? No.

Red Jack. And mirrors. Velveteen and Jackie Frost. *Santa Claus.*

My fingers twitched in Graymalkin's fur as my whole body froze. Not a dream.

"Shell?"

There was only silence in my head.

Checking under the blankets revealed my favorite sleep tee and shorts. But my last North Pole memory was of me all kitted out in an elf-spun Astra uniform, turning the snow globe over and making the magically real snow inside swirl around Chicago's skyline. Pushing up on my elbows, I looked around my room.

No uniform. No snow globe.

"Shell?"

Graymalkin complained and settled when I pushed the covers aside and swung my legs out of bed, trying not to panic. A quick check in my closet let me breathe easier. None of the Astra suits were my made-by-elves outfit—all but one was a form-fitting bodysuit and cape—but while they weren't *my* styles, for some bizarre reason I'd been afraid I wouldn't find *any*. I refused to think about that weird conviction, or Shell's continued silence, and instead pulled on a pair of sweats.

"Good morning, sleepyhead," Dad greeted me as I padded down the stairs to the kitchen. A stack of Belgian waffles waited for me on the table. "Your mother had to leave early—hey."

I ninja-hugged him in his chair, careful not to squeeze. "Love you."

"Love you too, bug. Are you going in today?" Since I wasn't dressed for the day yet, that was a valid question. I swallowed all my questions; I couldn't think of a single one that wouldn't start him wondering what was going on. Worrying.

"Yes. There's always stuff to catch up on." That felt safe to say.

"Okay, but don't forget lunch with your sister. She told me that the next time you leave her waiting in the Walnut Room she's going to strip naked and go streaking until Macy's security takes her down. Hope? Is everything alright?"

I sat down. "I'm fine. Just wobbly for a second."

He frowned. "Have Doctor Beth check you out."

"Yes, Dad." I managed to roll my eyes, the expected response to parental concern. The rest of breakfast passed without more existential ambushes and I was able to stay involved in the conversation—mostly about Mom's Foundation schedule and my plans. And Faith's science studies.

Faith's. Science. Studies.

Somehow I got away without triggering Dad's parental "Something's Wrong" radar again. Dressing, I chose the single skirted outfit—it most closely matched the made-by-elves design—and flew out. Coming down over Grant Park, I couldn't see any sign of the post-Green Man redesign but the normal crowds were there. Landing, I did my usual wave-to-tourists entry and nodded to the armored Bobs, settling into a headspace of *same, same, different, same, same, really different*, not thinking about it yet.

I should have gone straight to my Dome apartment—instead, on autopilot, I found myself passing through Dispatch to say hi to David; even standing down, it was good to let the Dispatch watch know when I was present and in uniform.

David was at his station. So was Shell, and for one heart-stopping moment everything was *right*. Then it wasn't Shell.

"Hey! What are you doing in today?" The too old not-Shell wore a blue and white bodysuit with what looked like data-line attachments and had her flame-red hair up in a tail, suit and hair framing a more mature and narrow face and figure than I'd ever seen on her. "Hey, what's going on?"

"I'm just— I'm here for— Hi, David. Going downstairs now." I turned and fast-walked out, not speeding up when Shell's quick steps sounded behind me. She closed the gap and made it into the elevator right after me, to burst out laughing when I turned around and carefully poked her in the shoulder.

"Okay, really. What's going on? You looked like you'd seen a ghost—"

I didn't even try to not hug her. "Quite the opposite. It's good to see you."

"And now you're totally freaking me out."

My Shell would have never let me sit her on my bed to patiently wait while I opened file after file on my desk screen, checking the team roster, doing multiple news searches, occasionally giggling but gasping just as often. She texted on her cell a bit, but otherwise just sat and watched me.

No news items anywhere referred to the Green Man. Shelly was on the roster as the team's Galatea drone-pilot. Atlas was *alive*. And Ajax and Nimbus. No mention of Artemis anywhere, but there was a news article about Chicago's youngest female detective, Jacky Siggler. They'd taken her picture outside her precinct at high noon.

There were no Young Sentinels. Also, no Megaton—or Mal Scott when I accessed Hillwood Academy's records. No Grendel, either, although Ozma was listed as a graduate.

A hand settled on my shaking shoulders. The manicured and painted nails on it didn't belong to Shelly and, looking up, for a moment I thought she'd called Mom. She hadn't, but the dark hair was Mom's.

"F-Faith?"

"No, the Tooth Fairy. What's happening, Ace? You're scaring Shell."

I didn't crush her, but it was a close thing. It was turning into a morning for hugging people, and then I had to stop laughing and crying. Eventually I was sitting on my couch between them. I couldn't stop touching them, and they let me.

"Have either of you heard of the Teatime Anarchist?" He hadn't been mentioned anywhere, either, but I had to check. My breathy question drew two blank stares. "Okay. How did I become Astra?"

"Riiiight." Shell stood up. "I'm getting Doctor Beth."

"No!" I pulled her back down. "I'm okay. Please?"

She rolled her eyes, for one second totally my Shell. "Fine. The day I was stupid enough to try and chase my own breakthrough. And you were smart enough to get to the apartment building for your own breakthrough when I jumped? You caught me on the way down, and I wouldn't speak to you for weeks until Faith here yelled at me for being a dumbass?"

"I was *fifteen*? They made me Astra at fifteen? Tell me I didn't have a total crush on Atlas?"

Faith laughed, capturing all my attention. "Hardly. No, you did, but the parentals shipped you off to Hillwood. By the time you came back here to do the whole sidekick thing you'd got over it. At risk of repeating myself, what's going on?"

I closed my eyes in sympathetic mortification for my younger self, opened them and turned back to Shell. "And how did you become...Galatea?"

"Duh. Graduated early, enlisted in the Marines, didn't get a boot-camp breakthrough. I became a drone pilot and helped test Vulcan's Galatea Program. Went civilian last year when the military dropped the program, signed on with the Sentinels to help the idiot keep field-testing his hardware. Plus, Awesome Girl and Power Chick together again—how could I not?"

I nodded. "Faith? When did Mom start her foundation?"

"After I nearly died. Ace, much fun as this is, I'm going to repeat myself."

So I told them. It took a while, with lots of exclamations from Shell—"The Bees? Really? We made so much fun of them!"—and careful questions from Faith. I stopped with the Red Jack thing, but somehow Faith knew I was holding something back and made me finish the story with Velveteen, Jackie Frost, and Santa Claus. Shell was snickering by the end. Faith wasn't.

"So, Shelly and I are dead," she summed up. "Though Shell has a twin? And half the senior Sentinels are gone?"

I nodded.

"And you got here because of a gift from Saint Nicholas, but you don't remember arriving. And the magical snow globe is gone."

I nodded again.

"Ace, that's all kinds of messed up. You know that, right?"

"I know!" I put my head in my hands. "But it's true! I remember every awful bit!"

Faith one-arm hugged my shoulders. "It must have been horrible. But you're here now, and we'll figure it out."

"What's to figure out?" Shell asked. "Somebody's messed with our girl's head. Chakra will get her straightened out."

"Ace?"

I raised my head. It wasn't like I had any choice; if *I* was the problem, if somebody had *messed with my head*, then I couldn't be relied on until we figured it out. After all, if I'd forgotten my real history, who knew what other important details—gaps in my training, nemesis I should know about, whatever—had gotten buried. People could die because of something I should have known.

But Faith was watching me thoughtfully, like she wasn't sure my head was the problem.

It's never that easy. If I'd not been distracted, I would have asked why only Shell had been in Dispatch—instead I got the shock of learning that the only Sentinels in Chicago at the moment were me, Rush, and The Harlequin. The rest were away with Heroes without Borders seeing to a disaster. A tsunami in Indonesia.

It wasn't as crazy as it sounded; Nimbus could be back in the blink of an eye, we had the Guardians teams to help out, and Dispatch's criminal intelligence people saw no big threats on our near horizon. I let the fact that Blackstone had a whole intelligence department now distract me again, but only for a minute.

Then I reviewed the Day Brief; fortunately all the Sentinels protocols I remembered seemed to be correct. To my huge relief, SaFire had the Atlas Watch today. A B Class Atlas-Type, she could handle anything but an A Level problem, and was better than me at the more normal emergency stuff. I breathed a little easier when I saw that.

They didn't call it Atlas Watch, though; they called it Overflight Watch.

Shell had been able to pull Faith in so quickly because Faith had been in the Loop on errands of her own before our lunch date, and we decided to head out early. I made Shell check me out on my Dispatch link doctrine before deciding it was okay for us to leave, but everything was the same there too.

The Walnut Room had recently undergone a change of management—I knew about it because they got Mom to host a foundation dinner there after they'd finished retraining the staff—and Faith confirmed that, yep, it had really happened. They gave us a table by the windows (which also put us out of sight from the open Macy's floor above us), and I ordered their signature pot pie. Faith got their crusted chicken.

"So," she said after our waitress had filled our lemon-freshened water glasses and departed. "On a scale of one to ten, how freaked out are you right now?"

I managed to keep from laughing hysterically. "Eleven? This feels like a bad *Sentinels* episode. I don't think the writers ever did something this weird to me."

"Yet. Give them time. Remember the evil Mirror Universe twin of Atlas last seas—oh, you wouldn't."

"No." The show writers at least *tried* to keep to the obvious Real World facts. When Atlas died, *Sentinels* had gone on a half-year hiatus while the studio salvaged what they could of the episodes already in the can and worked up a huge Final Atlas Story arc to cover the events of the Big One and the Fort Whittier Attack. None of which had really happened.

Faith frowned, watching me until I couldn't ignore it.

"What?"

She shook her head. "Don't freak out more, but I don't think the problem is your memory. Part of my studies is the *weird* stuff—the extrareality stuff. I think you really *did* jump. And when you did, you made a Candide Selection."

The world wobbled and I couldn't breathe. "A what?"

"I think you're an extrareality intrusion into this reality. There are one of two ways intrusions work. The direct way is physical translocation. The indirect way, which happens a lot with extrarealities that are 'close' enough to have local analogues, is mental translocation. The intruding mind highjacks the body of the local analogue for the duration of the stay. Count Ace, and breathe."

I looked down and realized that she'd reached across the table to take my hand

"All the stories we have of mental intrusions go the other way— from here to an extrareality. But I'm one of those who think that we aren't Reality Prime, so I don't see any reason why it can't happen like this."

"You think I'm not— I'm not me?" Until now, with Faith *believing* me, I hadn't realized how much I wanted it to be a memory problem.

"I think you're not *my* Hope, though I'm really glad to meet you and I'm sorry it has to be this hard. It's more than memory." She stopped to look for words. "What you've said, everything in your world seems harder. Atlas, Ajax, and Nimbus dead. Me. Shelly. Lots of high-fatality superhuman attacks. And, back there at the Dome? The second you realized half the team was gone, you shifted into leader-mode. Made sure the situation was okay and someone was on watch, and then pretty much benched yourself because of—" She tapped her head. "Those are just the most obvious moments."

That made *no* sense. "I wouldn't have done that?"

"Nope. Don't get me wrong, I *love* my sister. But she's not exactly...proactive. She's strong. She's determined to do the right thing whenever she knows what it is. But back there? The *first* thing she'd have done would be to call Blackstone, spill everything, and get instructions."

"But there's nothing he can do about it from Indonesia! They've got a mission to focus on."

"Bingo. Also, you hate SaFire, here. You're nice about it, because you are, but you hate her. *You* don't, and I can't imagine why someone rewriting your memories would flip the script on that."

I almost put my face in my hands again before remembering we were in public. It helped, a little, that Faith wasn't loudly denouncing me as a bodysnatching intrusion who'd stolen her sister.

"Why would I hate— No, never mind. Okay, so, Reality Prime? Candide Selection?"

That won me a smile. "That's it—you deal, you learn what you need to know to keep moving forward. She's not as good at that either, not yet." She was obviously trying to make me feel better, but it worked; it looked like I'd do anything for a smile from the big sister I'd never known.

"So. Reality Prime. That's the theory that this is the Real World, and all the extrareality worlds are breakthrough-created. They're only real subjectively, for a given value of 'real.' We're Reality Prime, and we make them."

"But you said you don't believe that?"

"Nope. Nobody's been able to prove it experimentally or observationally. Nobody can *disprove* it, either, but to me it feels waaaay too egocentric." She flashed another smile. "And now that I've met you I'm glad I don't believe it, 'cause if we're not equally real then one of us would be the other person's figment, and I don't want you to be a figment, Ace."

My big sister was *so* cool.

But she didn't give me much chance to sit and luxuriate in that. "So forgetting about Reality Prime and who's real and who's not, you were given an enabling device that should get you home. It's 'magic', which means no technobabble and red button, and magic is *intentional*—it either works or it doesn't. No extrareality is really 'closer' than any other, so if it could jump you at all, why didn't it jump you home?" She gestured grandly with the hand holding her water glass, plunged on.

"Since it's *magic*, I'd guess that we're talking about something spiritual or karmic. Santa Claus is only nominally a Christian figure anymore, but since it's *that* holiday it gets even weirder. His magic's going to be Christmas Magic. So, twelve jumps? The Twelve Days of Christmas end with Epiphany, the day the searching magi found what they were looking for. See? Twelve days for you to wander, the final day being the day you get home."

"Um, he didn't sound as certain as that."

"Would he be? He's a secularized saint, not God."

I nodded. He had talked about his *domain*, and it hadn't been infinite.

"Or he might have known exactly what was going to happen, but couldn't tell you. These iconic types don't so much live by rules as *exist* because of them."

"Okaaay, I can sort of see that. But where are you going? I mean, other than saying I should expect to use up every turn of the globe?"

She put her glass down, leaned onto her elbows.

"Well, if the point is the journey as much as the destination, then it's not going to be random, is it? It's going to be guided by what you need—which might not be what you want. This first one..." Her brow furrowed as she thought. "This first one, I think, was a grace? To give you something you need before you go on. So *I* think it was your own Candide Selection." She looked at me expectantly.

"I'm going to start shaking you until an explanation falls out."

Faith laughed. "*That's* my sister. A Candide Selection is a search constraint. The current explanation for the apparently infinite number of alternate worlds out there that aren't fictional worlds—you know, like Barsoom or Middle Earth—is that the moment of creation birthed the whole infinite array of primary realities at once. They all started as perfect copies, but over time small divergences make them more and more different. Got it?"

Crap, this was going to be like listening to the Teatime Anarchist explain the "obvious."

"No."

She deflated a little, and I could practically see her mentally rewinding.

"Imagine that there are two realities right now, okay? This one, and that one. Until ten minutes ago, they were absolutely identical. Then in this one you ordered the pot pie, and in that one you ordered the crusted chicken. Which is so much better, FYI. Also, *five* minutes ago in that one a mailman across town tripped over a cat he avoided in this one. He took a really nasty fall, but it was nothing to do with us. Got it?"

"Um." I sat and worked through it. "I think so? You're saying that divergences don't create new realities—they're just different paths taken in realities that looked identical before? And multiplying divergences within realities don't have to be related to each other?"

"Right! And similarities don't need to have the same cause, either. Say that a year from now the lucky mailman in our reality gets sideswiped by a bad driver. In both this reality and that one, he finds himself in the ER for relatively similar impact injuries, and in both he takes a recovery vacation to Bora Bora where he meets the love of his life. At least two roads get him to Bora Bora. An infinite number don't. Still with me?"

"But if divergences are happening all the time, wouldn't all of the realities look completely different from each other by now? After a few billion years?"

"What part of infinity are you missing? There's an *infinitude* of realities, thus the name—plenty of room for smaller infinite sets to still look identical or nearly. At least that's the theory. I think that the reason we're not finding a lot more really extreme divergences is a higher power may be narrowing the phase space of possible outcomes. The mailman might be destined for Bora Bora and True Love unless he really messes up, but let's leave the providence vs. randomness can of worms closed. It's a really big can."

"You think the road to Bora Bora may be greased? No, ew, bad metaphor and, anyway, nevermind. Okay, I think I've got the Infinitude. So, a Candide Selection in the Infinitude is selecting the 'best of all possible worlds' from the infinite set? *My* best of all possible worlds?"

She nodded sharply. "Got it in one! At least it selects from the array of choices for what is the best of all possible worlds in your heart of hearts. What's wrong?"

Our waitress arrived with lunch, giving me a moment to process that. It didn't make me feel any better.

"That doesn't say much about me," I sighed when we were private again. "Shouldn't I have selected for a reality where the Caliphate and China wars hadn't happened?" I stared at my pot pie. "Where millions of people hadn't— Hey!"

Faith had leaned over her plate to rap my hand with her fork. Now she pointed it at me. "No wallowing. Don't!" She kept it aimed between my half-crossed eyes until I snorted. "Better. In your head you know *that* would be a better world, but you didn't *make* this reality—you just selected this one to visit 'cause it's the Best of All Possible Worlds *for you*. Got it?" A grin split her face.

"And may I say how awesomely self-affirming that is for me? You didn't just select any world from the set where both Shell and I survived. You selected the world where Shell and I are the best, most amazing Best Friend and Big Sister we can be—that's what a Candide Selection *means*. Of all the set of Faiths, I win the Worlds' Best Big Sister competition because that's what you'd want. Score!"

I was laughing before she finished. "Do you want a trophy?"

"Yes!"

I settled back, took a few bites of pot pie before moving on.

"So, why a Candide Selection? Why didn't I just jump home? And how do I jump now? I can't— I can't stay."

"Of course you can't. You couldn't even if you'd arrived physically and weren't displacing my own little sis. Mom and Dad are waiting back there."

"Right. Well, maybe. I've only been gone a couple of days now, they might not know. Or my whole trip might not take any time at all back there. At least if I make it home on my own."

"True, that. Synchronicity between realities isn't required as long as you return after you left. Let's hope that's it."

"So how do I jump, without the globe?"

She shrugged over her chicken, cutting up more slices. "Well, in theory you still *have* the globe. You just didn't bring it along directly. Unless your physical body is sitting back in Christmastown, which seems unlikely."

"You mean, I'm carrying it along in spirit?"

"Sounds right. Try picturing it in your hands, and turning it."

I suddenly had no desire to try it. Big surprise. Looking across the table at Faith, I fixed her face in my memory just in case and closed my eyes to imagine the globe, flipping and spinning it to make the snow swirl.

I opened my eyes to find Faith watching me solemnly.

"Still like the pot pie? 'Cause my Hope doesn't."

Dessert arrived before a solution did, but the cheesecake was to die for and brainstorming quickly gave way to "what happened to—" questions about people and events in our respective realities. I didn't ask the *big* questions; I'd been too young to remember Faith at all, and had no idea why she'd lived here and died in my own reality. It seemed arbitrary and horribly unfair. But Faith didn't ask either, and the last thing I wanted to do was trigger some sort of weird "survivor's guilt" in my sister.

She laughed, watching me pick up the last crumbs of cheesecake crust with my fingertips. "That's—"

My earbud chimed. *"Astra. Potential A Class Nightmare Breakthrough, corner of 33rd and South Prairie. Rush is clearing, do not allow breakthrough to move north."*

I paled. *Nightmare Breakthrough* didn't mean a thing to me, but A Class meant that SaFire could not take point and I couldn't sit it out. 33rd and South Prairie was in spitting range of two schools and Mercy Hospital.

"On it! Recall Nimbus! Advise, what is 'Nightmare Breakthrough?'" I stood to make for the Walnut Room's entrance and Faith cleared her throat, pointing at the window beside us. It had a red-painted catch.

Obviously the reason they'd given us this table.

Pulling the catch popped the window and I dropped out and away from Macy's. A last look behind gave me a glimpse of Faith, securing the window. How many lunches had ended that way?

"*Astra.*" This time it was David. "*Please confirm readiness.*" My question might be worrying, but you couldn't hear it in his voice.

"I am able, Dispatch. Galatea can confirm."

He didn't hesitate more than a heartbeat. "*Understood, Astra. Nightmare Breakthrough is a drug-triggered category, most often from bad trips on strong psychedelics. NBs are likely to experience triggering and possibly permanent psychotic breaks, and their breakthrough manifestations are likely to be nightmare fuel. Unverified, but the target presents all characteristics of NB.*"

Crap crap crap crap crap. Back home we just called them Psychotic Breakthroughs, and this was going to *suck*. "Understood, Dispatch. Will contain the NB by any means necessary."

Arcing over the Loop, I spotted the flare of Galatea's boot-jets and dove to grab her before pulling onto a hard push south. "Need a lift?"

"*Always nice. Pass me the situation lead?*"

Right—I had no idea what pieces of field protocol were different here. "It's yours. Let me focus on sticking him to the ground?"

"*That works. This'll be easy.*"

I missed Shell's virtual HUD tactical display, but could spot 33rd and Prairie on my own. For one thing, it had a police helicopter over it. And a *thing* that filled the empty lot just north of the intersection.

"Now that's just *wrong.*"

"*You think? Drop me and go see if it's open to talking. Probably not, but hey, first steps.*"

I let go of Galatea and dropped down to land near the edge of the thing. If it was going to get aggressive, I wanted to be the closest and most obvious target.

It was definitely nightmare fuel. Covering most of the empty lot like a tangled mat, it only loomed up into more or less human shape in the center. There it looked like a gangly man covered in shrouds—except the shrouds were eruptions of bone-white fleshy roots. It wasn't hair; each root branched into tangles of finer root systems, and they *moved*. Halfway to its edge, the mat of weaving roots bulged over three smaller shapes. There the white roots had flushed a sickly *pink*.

I felt sick. To my super-duper vision, the three shapes glowed with fading heat as the covering roots absorbed them. I couldn't hear heartbeats, but they were human sized.

The smell was hideous, like rotting meat, and I swallowed twice before I could control my gag reflex.

"Hello? If you understand me, nod."

It didn't. Instead the fringe of the root mat crawled towards me. The thing's circumference didn't seem to be growing, but the whole thing was slithering out into the intersection and it did not belong in the sane and waking world at all.

"Please nod."

Not a twitch from the shrouded figure, and when I took a step back its near fringe thickened and lunged, wrapping me tight. "Nimbus! On me!"

She flashed out of the sky, glorious, and the beam she fired into the mat shriveled and blackened tendrils around me. The looming shroud screamed and lurched as its roots smoked.

The stinging on my skin where roots reached above my collar migrated to my nose and mouth. "Stop! The smoke is dangerous!" I tried to fly, felt rootlets clinging to the street pop and separate as I strained upward.

"*Not that important!*" Nimbus stopped, but Shelly-Galatea flushed a rack of explosive mini-missiles into the mat growing around me. The tough roots resisted her bursts, but enough gave that I ripped free of the thing. Darting upward, I watched it fill in the burned and shredded patch below me.

"Galatea, material analysis?" I prayed that this Galatea had the environmental analysis mods of the one back home.

"*It's organic, secretions are a deadly neurotoxin. Continued burn will put lethal concentrations into the air, neutralization rate unknown.*"

"Aerokinetics? Force-field projectors?" I had no idea of the full Guardian roster here.

"*None locally available. We'd have to call them from other municipalities and arrival time is too long.*" David didn't ask why I was asking—why I had to ask—and I made a mental note to ask about Veriforce later.

But all that would come later; below me, the thing turned to slither up the street. North. Of course. "Evacuation?"

"*The schools will be empty at its current rate of progress. Mercy Hospital will not have fully evacuated all movable patients, even with Rush and SaFire's help.*"

I listened to the beat of the police helicopter above us, the only sound in the empty street besides the distant sirens the wash of Galatea's jets. And the hiss of creeping nightmare-roots.

"Dispatch, its reaction shows it still has a central nervous system but I don't think it's even got bones left, the way it's moving now." It was getting less and less human-shaped by the minute. Sadly, that made my decision easier.

Nimbus' pure energy-transfer laser attack could burn the root network to ash, but with the toxic smoke a simple Green Man solution was not happening. Which left only one option that I could see.

I stripped off my cape. "Dispatch, is Jack Frost available?"

"*Affirmative, Astra.*"

"Have Rush deliver him now! He is to freeze the perimeter of the growth once I have removed the central body. Galatea, stand by to core the apple. Dispatch, ensure that the flight bay is clear and sealable."

"*Deliver Jack Frost, clear and prep flight bay. Understood, Astra.*"

"Galatea?"

"*Got it, go!*"

I dove, sweeping down to wrap the bulging top of our breakthrough's shrouded form in my cape before grabbing hold and pulling *hard*. It didn't budge, but then Galatea's micro-missile salvo arrived and I closed my eyes tight as fragments of burning root flew around me. Severed from its wider anchoring net, the screaming and writhing thing ripped free of the ground as I took us *up*.

It was *not* fun; my wrapped cape protected my face from direct contact with the thing, but its lower body still hung with root shrouds that brushed and stung my bare legs above my boots. I ignored it. "Nimbus! Please follow, be prepared to burn!"

"*Roger dodger!*" She chirped cheerfully in my ear and I almost dropped my armful; obviously they'd figured out a way around Nimbus' incorporeal muteness here. Good for them.

The short, arcing flight to the Dome with Nimbus alongside gave me a few seconds to plan—and to worry about the roots winding themselves around my legs. In descent, I aimed for the flight bay doors without slowing; the bay floor had been built for crashes.

"Sealthebaynow!" I shouted in one breath as I hit the bay floor and dropped the still-struggling mass. I could barely feel my legs, not even the sting, and it was scaring me. They rumbled shut as I tried to peel the thing away.

TEAM-UPS AND CROSSOVERS

"I've got this!" Metal hands joined mine. Shelly had obviously switched operation to one of the Galatea backups in the bay. A second Galatea stood ready beside an open high-impact plastic crate.

The rootlets came free with sucking pops, and I realized that finer root fibers had actually managed to burrow into my skin. I dropped the nightmare thing into the crate, and the second Galatea promptly filled it with freeze-foam before dropping the lid on it and punching a couple of holes.

I breathed a sigh of relief. My plan had been to seal it in with us, then have Nimbus burn it to ash if I couldn't get control of it; this was *much* better.

"Vulcan's on his way up," the Galatea said. "He's going to treat it as an aggressive hazmat situation until we know for sure what will contain it. You need to get to the infirmary."

"You think?" I laughed as Nimbus nodded.

"Well, yeah. Why did you wear that outfit, anyway? I thought Hope had got rid of all of them when she switched to the bodysuits last year."

I blinked, sucked in a breath. "Oh. *Oh.*" They both looked at me funny and I shook my head. "Infirmary, right." I headed for the elevator. Doctor Beth would have something for my red perforated legs, but both the numbness and the stinging was already passing, which told me it hadn't been major and my body was healing. I tried not to think about the pinkish mounds in the root carpet back at the site—it hadn't been major for *me*.

A few words with a slightly puzzled Vulcan confirmed that procedures for psychotic breakthroughs were the same here; they'd find a way to communicate with it—bringing in telepaths if necessary—find out if there was any real mind left. If there was, they'd do their best for it. But that was something I wouldn't stay to see.

Before I let Doctor Beth lay a single probe on me, I called Faith and told her I knew where the snow globe was.

"So, where is it?" Faith asked, looking not at all patient.

We all stood in my—Hope's—room. Now that I wasn't half-freaked out by it all, I stood turning in a circle, spotting all the little differences. Some, like the Hillwood Academy sports banner, were not at all little.

Shelly had come back with me, Faith meeting us here with a bag she had yet to explain.

I stopped turning. "You explained that I'd sort of 'displaced' your Hope, sort of overlapping her. It didn't occur to me that my *stuff* might be linked to analogous things here, too, until Shelly commented on my uniform."

Faith looked even less patient.

"I was wearing a *skirted* costume when I jumped," I explained. "I wasn't when I woke up, but there was one hanging in the closet."

Her eyes widened. "Oh. *Oh.*"

"My words exactly. Remember the snow globe I got when I was eleven?" Stepping into the closet, I rummaged through the boxes on the top shelf. *Gotcha.* Pulling it down, I stepped back out to open it. "I think that, just like I displaced your Hope, my costume displaced one here. Sort of. And if that's true, then *this* is it."

I handed the box lid to Faith to reveal my gold-filigree nested snow globe—gold plated, high quality crystal, exquisitely hand-painted sculpt of Chicago's Miracle Mile inside. Not the magic one Santa had given me—just like the now half-ruined outfit I'd worn wasn't quite the one made by elves—but close enough for metaphysical equivalence. I hoped.

"This should do it. If the rules for all this are consistent, anyway."

She nodded. "Impressive, Ace."

"Maybe. And—" I swallowed the hard lump that rose in my throat. "And if it is, I've really got to go. *Your* Hope—"

Faith nodded solemnly. Much as I wanted to stay and get to know my sister better, she wasn't *my* sister and I needed to let her Hope come back from whatever mental limbo she was in. Would this be a dream to her? Would she remember it at all?

I reached into the box to extract the globe, but Faith's hand shot out to cover mine.

"Stop!"

"Yeah, not so fast." Shelly chuckled. "She's been getting ready for this while you were in with Doctor Beth, so give the girl her moment."

Faith frowned at her. "Right. I've been getting some things together—just in case you can take them with you." She held up the designer handbag she'd brought with her—many pocketed and big enough that it would barely qualify as an airline carry-on. "Road trip stuff, mostly."

I traded the box for the loaded bag.

She grinned as I opened it. "Since you've obviously not booked a direct flight, I got you a few things for the layovers." The bag contained some changes of underwear, civilian clothes, basic toiletries, an epad, and a roll of money. It also held a small gift box. Opening it, I found a crystal hologram cube—the kind carved with lasers. It held a frozen image of me and Faith, heads together and laughing at the camera as she held a hand up behind my head to flash a "victory" sign.

"I don't know if you'll be able to take any of this with you when you jump out of here," she explained while I carefully put it back in the bag. "But I thought..."

I swallowed. "I know. Thank you."

"Give everyone my love?"

"I will." I hung the bag off my shoulder by its strap and hugged my sister tight, eyes closed as I breathed in to remember her smell. Drawing back, I blinked until I could see clearly. "Any advice for me?"

"Sure, Ace." With one last squeeze, she dropped the snow globe in my hand. "When you give this story to the show writers, make sure you leave out Santa Claus. Nobody's going to buy that one."

I laughed helplessly, and spun the globe.

DSA Field Report: Agent Smith.

Ozma has proven that, using the site, she can transfer herself and others to the extrareality into which she believes both Red Jack and Astra have been dropped. We have designated the new extrareality SP1. Unfortunately, her method of travel is not a gateway through which we can send probes; she or someone else must translate there with her device. (She says it's clockwork-magic, boss, whatever that means.) Needless to say, neither Astra nor Red Jack were found at the SP1 end of the rift, and early information about SP1 indicates extreme caution. The Sentinels are preparing to establish a base of operations there, from which Ozma can attempt to track Astra, whom she says is "wandering." Note: Ozma is of the opinion that Red Jack is dead. Since the SP1 terminus of the rift appears to have been cleaned after experiencing the same explosive result as our own, I'd say it's a good bet. One less thing to worry about, but I'm asking them to find confirmation if at all possible. I am also opening a new case file, *Odysseus*, to designate the operation from here out.

Red Jack Case File 1-B634 F.

The Traveler's Tale

A play in one act, by Marion G. Harmon

Scene 1: a clearing in a twilight woods.

Enter Hope.

"Shell? Hello?" She puts down her bag, sits upon a fallen tree, and taps her earbud to make sure she's recording. "Three turns of the globe since meeting Faith, and I'm beginning to wonder if the thing has any more sense of direction than a compass at the North Pole—an ironic thought considering where I began. And Unplugged Syndrome has me making an audiolog just to talk, go figure. So…"

She looks around her.

"I cannot seem to fly here, wherever here is. And it's been twilight for three hours, so best guess is I'm in a pocket-extrareality with its own rules. It's not *that* strange, really. The trees are mostly oak and ash, and I've recognized blooming witch hazel and purple crocuses. There are so many flowering plants the place reminds me of a wild English garden, if someone planted one in the middle of a woods. Mom would love it. There are birds, but I'm not an ornithologist. The most ferocious animal I've gotten a good look at is an incurious hedgehog."

She yawns and stretches. "Grounded or not I'm clearly the toughest thing around here unless the Jabberwock shows up, and since the flowers aren't talking I don't think there's much chance of that. But besides not flying I'm also talking funny, which is passing strange—I mean *very weird*. So I'm going to sleep a few winks and then go back to the brook if I can find it and take a bath, and then I'm out of this flowered greenwood."

Taking off her cape, she lies down under it. "I wonder if anyone at home knows I'm gone yet?"

She falls asleep.

Enter Titania, queen of the fairies, with her court.

"It is long past enough! Ever my lord and husband brangles, never ceasing to disturb the idylls of our wood with his demands. Fairies, stand watch and mayhap we will yet enjoy an hour or two of undisturbed pleasures—what *is* it, Cobweb?"

"We are not alone, my queen! Look here, a sleeping mortal lies beneath near moss-grown tree!"

"A mortal!" She sweeps close to bend over Hope. "And such a pretty child. How does she come to lie sleeping here? No matter—should arrogant sovereign Oberon see this treasure, will she or nil she, he will surely claim her for his entourage."

"He cannot, mistress!" Peasblossom daintily sniffs the air. "From her scent, she is fairy-touched and claimed by some other spirit. Should our lord press ownership, he will certainly be contested."

"Yes, and with this maiden trapped between. Mustardseed, learn this scent and fly! Seek out the spirit that has bound itself to her, that it may find her before our lord!"

"I go, mistress! As swift as sleep, shot from Diane's silver bow!"

Exit Mustardseed.

"And we, my gentle fairies, will remove our revels far from here, that she may rest undisturbed as we draw the king's greedy eyes away."

Exit Titania and her court. The woods are silent except for the birds' evensong. Enter Oberon, king of the fairies, and Puck.

"You swore they came this way, jester! Do you lead me about with a jest of your own?"

"Never, lord king! Puck is your true servant, and with the hatred your queen bears him, would be banished from the wood if you liked not his merry company!"

"Indeed hobgoblin, but I do not smile now. You have misled me!"

"Not by my will, lord! We are poor hounds tonight, and the fox has slipped away."

"Then we shall let them be, and make our own entertainment this eve. Bye and bye my queen will return and tender her submission, for more than fighting she most hates to be ignored. What shall we—wait!"

Oberon spies Hope asleep. "And what is *this*?"

Puck stalks close.

"A mortal maiden, majesty! A young and fair one!"

"Both young and fair, and all alone in our woods with naught for bed but her own cloak. Does she flee or does she pursue? Has she lost herself?"

"I have seen no other mortals in the green since midsummer last, my lord."

"Then lost, certainly—and surely affrighted, with only her poor female strength to rely upon. But by my eyes she is a lovely flower, skin smooth as whitest samite, hair like sunlight spilled upon her mossy bower. She would make the prettiest of my lady's fairies jealous, dimming their own much-treasured beauties in compare."

"Surely she must be in flight then, lord. For no man with eyes would flee from her!"

"Only a bedlamite, surely." Oberon gazes down at her. "Hobgoblin, attend me! I would have this lost treasure for my own court, a jewel to match any of my queen's. What, goblin? You do not second your king's will?"

"All in the woods are your majesties, to claim or to dispose. Yet..."

"Speak!"

"Surely the queen, in loyalty of her sex, will seek to pluck such a tender maiden from the rough company of your court."

"Aye. And never cease to rage until I bend, though I be sovereign. I do think... Yes, an old trick will suit my present purpose. Hobgoblin!"

"Yours to command, sire!"

"Trip swiftly now, goblin, ere she awakes. From that distant blossomed field fetch me the flower, love-in-idleness, whose petals, pierced by Cupid's wayward shot, do drop the nectar of love's sight upon sleeper's eyes—infecting them with lover's fevered imaginations, such that the first face they see upon awakening, be it ever so foul or beastly, they fall into irresistible enchantment with its wearer. I shall stand by as she awakes, and thus enamored of me, she will resist all my queen's efforts to tear her from my court!"

"Excellent device! I go, oh king! Watch how I go!"

Exit Puck.

"And I shall hide her beneath nodding green, myself withdrawing until my hobgoblin's return."

Oberon looks sternly at the tree above Hope. They lower their bottom-most branches, largely concealing Astra's sleeping form.

Exit Oberon.

Scene 2: elsewhere in the woods.

Enter Mustardseed with Kitsune.

"Make haste, fox! We are almost to her sleeping place, and mayhap will come to her before any think to rob you of your mortal maid."

"Hope is hardly mine, good fairy, except with mutual promised contracts. But thank you for bringing me here, and what is she *thinking*, wandering these woods? She's gone through more trouble than I can ever say, just trying to remain at home!"

"I think you have a pretty tale to tell! But can you take her there?"

"Not on the roads I follow, but I'll help her out of here!"

"Then— Hist! Hide! I hear familiar mischief-making feet—Oberon's own some-time companion and jester approaches and you must not be found!"

They hide, watching. Enter Puck.

"So am I become my king's delivery boy, no more than a page though seldom one in his book. Run here. Go there. I would not mind so much, if he left the tricks to me. At least, methinks, there promises to be some humor in this one. For the queen knows my king well, and will surely suspect foul play no matter how the pretty maiden pleads. None are so ridiculous as when my lord and lady drop their dignity and brawl like the commonest plowman and aggrieved goodwife!"

Exit Puck. Kitsune and Mustardseed emerge.

"Pretty maiden? Oh woe, I fear my lady's stratagems have failed and *your* lady has been discovered! Come, fox—that we may make timely arrival before they steal your hen!"

Exit all.

Scene 3: the clearing in the woods.

Enter Oberon and Puck, finding Hope still sleeping.

"The maiden dreams yet undisturbed—my plan is well laid! Quickly, hobgoblin, the flower! And now take yourself about, make certain that we remain sequestered here until all is ripened!"

Exit Puck.

Oberon bends over Hope, who turns over to sigh in her sleep.

"How beautiful, innocent, fair she sleeps! I would enchant her to such sleep a thousand years to ornament this emerald glen. Yet no, my queen would not abide it. Well then."

He gently touches the purple flower to her eyes.

"Now patience. Soon enough I'll know the color of my new treasure's eyes."

He waits.

Enter Kitsune and Mustardseed, unseen.

"I am amazed, Master Fox! Lord Oberon's watchful Puck is a very Cerberus, and yet you took us by him as if he'd been some drowsing owl or day-blinded mole."

"The mole is meat for the fox, but who is this varicolored knave who watches over Hope?"

"Alas, Lord Oberon himself has found your maiden and waits to claim her! You will never take her from him now!"

"Wait, Mustardseed! Is it true, what you said of your lord and mistress' turns and quarrels? Then fly to her and bring her hence—but I'll stay and fox this one!" He stands, his shape flowing into a perfect likeness of Puck's.

"Oh, but this is a trick I long to stay and see! Yet I'll to my lady!

Exit Mustardseed.

"Now little woodland king, let's see if you are ready for a bit of domestic strife."

He steps into the clearing.

"Milord! We are undone, for your lady comes swiftly! Surely someone has told her of your plans!

"Damn and blast! Branches, hide her once more! Goblin! Work your art! So shroud the greenwood and maze my lady's court that she cannot find this little glen though she had visited it a thousand times. I shall act as bait to lead her away, and then return!

Exit Oberon.

"Well, that was easy, but no-one who thinks they're clever knows when the joke's on them. And now—" He bends over Hope. "Wake up, Hope. And tell me how you managed to wander off into a piece of English comedy!"

He touches Hopes shoulder. She opens her eyes.

"What— My love!"

"My—what? How can you know me, when—"

"I *don't* know you—except as my love!" She reaches for Kitsune. He dances back.

"Wait—no! This is not my true face!"

"Why should I care? I love whatever face is yours! If your face and form are as changing as the wind, my heart is constant!"

Kitsune dodges Hope's attempted embrace.

"Wait! Stay!"

Enter Mustardseed.

"My lady comes! But—ha! What is this?"

"Hope has gone mad! She does not know me—but dotes on me!"

"Yes, I do—and beyond all reason or wish to reason otherwise! I burn for you—do you not feel the same?" Hope lunges again, Kitsune ducks aside.

"She is enchanted, fox! Tis one of my lord's old tricks, and now you are your lady's prey! But why run, if she be your lady?"

Kitsune skips away from another lunge.

"Neither of us belongs to the other, yet! Not in her heart, though *I* grow fond of—hey! Hands!"

Hope laughs. "Your fondness is enough, whoever you are! Stand still!"

"Hardly! I can't believe I say this—you would not respect me in the morning!"

Exit Kitsune, fleeing.

"Wait! Come back! Stay and I will give you all!"

There is no sound but crickets. Hope slumps.

"Isn't that just—"

"Like a man?"

"Yes! But, what are you? And what is he?"

"I am a humble fairy maid, mistress, lady-in-waiting in my lady's court. *He* is not what he seems, which is your fortune, for he wears the face and goatish form of my king's self-loving clown and jester, Puck."

"Well whomever he is, he is mine and I'll not stay to let him get away!"

Exit Hope, pursuing Kitsune. Mustardseed watches her go.

"So the rabbit chases after the fox, the god flees the pursuing nymph! All turns and the hunter becomes the hunted! Well that's a merry sight—but this trick, even misplayed, will not please my lady when reported."

Exit Mustardseed.

Scene 4: elsewhere in the woods.
Enter Puck, complaining.

"Fly here, hobgoblin, and take this unwelcome message! Go there, goblin, and fetch me what I have just now wished for. Keep watch lackey, so that my sport is undisturbed! And so I am Oberon's fetch-and-carry boy, his mute sentry when I could carry all the jest myself! Was there ever anything so tedious as this pointless standing watch?"

Enter Hope.

"I have found you, my love! Why did you fly from me?"

"Fly from you? I? Why, I have never before seen you but as a snoring lump upon the forest moss!"

"Not so, for you did wake me—the leaf-green wonder of your eyes the first that my eyes saw! First you run, and now you dissemble? Why, when you are all my world and all my thought?"

"Woke you— What trick is this?"

"No trick but love! And now I *have* my love!" Hope embraces a stunned Puck.

"Wait— No— Madwoman you are enchanted from your mind and not for me! Gods but your arms are vises, a very serpent's winding embrace—but I am not your prey! Stop kissing me, woman!"

"Never!"

Enter Oberon

"Foul treason! So the lackey would be the lord and take the prize for himself? Most foul deceit, to warn me away and open her bespelled eyes to look upon you first. Be sure I'll pay thee back for this—uk!"

Hope impatiently pushes him back, one arm still around Puck. Oberon flies backward, rebounding from an ancient oak to land in the moss.

"'Beware, sire! She could teach the martial amazon to strike, and her strength rivals mighty Hercules!"

"And I will strike again, if you threaten my dearest love again!"

"I am not— No, sire! I stood faithful watch, and none passed by me while you waited for the maid to wake! She lies to claim I captured her first sight!" Puck wrests his arm away from a shocked and tearful Hope.

Enter Kitsune, still in form of Puck.

"*My* lady would never lie, but surely can be deceived. I shook you from your dreams, Hope, but wore this face to put to flight this quondam king, this petty monarch of whims and fancies."

Hope turns about, amazed. "Two? And one who knows me?"

"Hardly two, for I am very singular. And although my face and form are indeed as changeable as the wind, you know me also. I am your fox."

Kitsune transforms.

"Yoshi! My love is my affianced?" Hope steps forward, Kitsune retreats.

"Affianced, yes. Love, mayhap—but not by whatever base enchantment holds you! Think, Hope! When did you first love me?"

"When I awoke to find you!"

"And did you ever think so fondly of me before waking in these woods?"

"I—I—love comes suddenly, between one breath and the next!"

"Fascination, yes. *Enchantment*, yes, but not love, which grows upon a thousand thoughts, a myriad of looks, acts, and evidences until it blooms. Love can grow where fascination first draws the eye, if the object of your attention be worthy, but so quickly and untended to? No."

"Then I loved you not knowing!"

"And yet loved not knowing it was *me*, till now?"

"I— But I burn! And—know not what to think! If this hot desire is compelled—and I see that it must be—then from whence did it come?"

Enter Titania and her court upon the end of Hope's speech.

"Who lit this fire in your brain? *That* intelligence I can provide. Who else but my lord and husband, who stands convicted by his wrath at his knave's perceived betrayal? A pair of clownish jesters, butted by their own jest to make you drunk upon false love. What do you say, husband? Speak."

"Be silent, shrew—and do not question your lord's will!"

"So this broil is your will, then?" Titania sits, arranging her robes. "I wait to see how you will unwind it. Good fox! What is your claim, here?"

Kitsune bows.

"My claim here is but to see that my lady leaves these woods as freely as she entered them, her mind her own again."

"A worthy claim, plainly stated. My lord, what would you recommend?"

"Claim! From a petty fox-spirit who so insults me! I'll make his pelt my, my..."

Hope steps in front of Kitsune.

"Some item of apparel? No doubt you could, husband, but then what of his kin? For a fox has many kin, and I am minded to consider that this fox is the sometime-servant of much more powerful spirits besides, the member of another court in a wider realm than ours. And since *my* summons brought him here, responsibility for what e're befalls him is surely mine."

"Then—to repay the insult, I'll have whatever claim he holds in the lady!"

"Fox? Do you relinquish your claim?"

"I'll tear his—! Gracious queen, I cannot. My claim is part and parcel with my lady's claim on me."

"And the nature of these claims?"

"A promised marriage for promised service, majesty."

"My Lord Oberon? Would you take the maiden's claim of service with the fox's claim upon her? A sovereign spirit in service to a mortal maid?"

"Sovereign Oberon to serve a mortal? Nay—not before the day's golden orb shines at midnight and the lunar sphere marks the heated noontime hour!"

"Then I think that you are quits, his words to you just recompense for the wrenches his lady has been given here, in *our* woods, *our* sovereign responsibility. Do you both agree? And I will undo what has been done—I am sure that my lord carries the poison which is its own timely remedy?"

Titania rises, holding out her hand, and Oberon sourly deposits the purple flower in her palm.

"Come here, child. You can trust me."

Kitsune nods, and Hope steps forward. Titania bends, touching the flower to her blinking eyes, and chants.

"Fancy bound, turned around. Now be free, again see—be as you were wont to be. Well, child? Are you well?"

"I— Oh, no! No! Did I— Did I really chase—?"

"Sparing your modesty, yes you did. The juice of love-in-idleness intoxicates as it does deceive, therefore blame it and ease your maiden blushes. And now, fairies! Skip hence! My lord, let us leave these two to find their own ways home. You and I have much to discuss, prively."

Exit Titania, Oberon, Puck, and all the fairy court.

"Well, my dear." Kitsune takes Hope's hand. "Are you going to tell me how you came to be lost in these woods?"

"Yes, when I do know myself! But how did you come here? And can you take us home?"

"Alas, you cannot travel the worlds as I do, though now that I know you wander I will certainly seek your friends—who I am certain seek for you."

"Then do but show me—I mean *just* show me—where I slept, and I'll take myself away from—*get out of*—these woods!"

Exit Hope and Kitsune together.

DSA Field Report: Agent Smith.

Boss, I hope you know what you're doing. Per your instructions, I allowed the Japanese National who is *not* a person-of-interest access to the site. He walked off into thin air. The site security detail is reporting hot-spots and isolated breezes all over the warehouse floor at intermittent times. They've also found a spot where you get a hell of a fine echo on any loud noise, for no apparent reason. They're starting to call the site Spook Watch.

    Also, the Young Sentinels team on the other side is sending us back reports, news and library downloads, stuff like that. Boss, SP1 is one freaky place, and since I began working for Uncle Sam before The Event, that's saying something. I remember what normal was like, and SP1 makes our world normal by comparison. To give you just one example, over there, if you leave out milk and cookies for Santa Claus *he'll show up* and leave you a present if you've been good or coal if you've been bad. He's far from the only Omega Class-level personification over there, and they recently had a superhero civil war in which some of the participants displayed Ultra Class-level powers. Boss, I don't think we should be sending anyone else into that weirdness. I think we should pull everyone back and seal and bury the site before something comes crawling out of it at us.

Odysseus Case File 1-D265 B.

Grimworld

by Marion G. Harmon

"Once, just once, I'd like to be able to do it the easy way. Would that be cheating or something?"

Hope Corrigan

I came out of the whirling flurry of snow high over nighttime Chicago.

"Shell?" No virtual quantum-ghost popped up to berate me, and my heady excitement chilled. For one wild moment, I'd hoped this was it.

So I'm not home yet. Pull it together, this is a lot better than it could have been and at least I'm in Chicago again.

But why Chicago, this time? When I started jumping I'd imagined that even an artifact powered by whimsical *Christmas* magic would at least have the decency to jump me to the same topographical point in the new reality as in the old, the same latitude and longitude (I'd fully expected to be flying back from the North Pole on my first jump). But no, so far travel by magic snow globe had turned out to be disturbingly *intentional*. It kept sending me where the action was—rather like a fictional Time Lord's time-traveling police call box (and if I ever saw that blue box I was absolutely knocking on the door and asking for a ride).

So until I jumped home, every jump was going to be "interesting." This time I'd spun the globe to leave a shattered and burned San Francisco and jumped halfway across the country.

I whispered prayerful thanks that at least this Chicago wasn't a burned-out ruin. But if I wasn't home, and my jumps weren't random, then why was I here?

And why was I me?

I'd finished this jump still in costume and carrying my stuff, so I hadn't "jumped into" a this-reality version of myself again. I didn't exist here. But far below me the Dome shone pearly white in the middle of its landscaped park—which meant I'd jumped into a close enough parallel that the *Sentinels* did. And that was...worrying. If the Sentinels were here, *some* version of me should be too, but if that were true then I wouldn't be *me* now.

Think it through, Hope. That was Blackstone's voice in my head. *No steps until you know what's under your feet.*

I hung in the sky and reviewed what I knew.

And I knew a *lot* more than I had when I'd started jumping. My second snow globe jump had been pretty quiet, at least once I'd finished helping a New York homicide detective and her tag-along writer friend with their investigation (it hadn't worried me that the writer had figured out I was a superhero—since super-powered types didn't exist there nobody'd believe him). Before turning the globe again, I'd sat down in a private carrel in the New York Public Library to read everything about extrarealities that Faith had dumped into the epad she'd given me.

Which had been a lot. Some of it seriously weird.

Either extrareality science was more advanced in Faith's reality or I hadn't been paying enough attention to it in mine, but they'd divided all realities into two classifications: Stage I Realities and Stage II Realities. Stage I Realities were the parallels rising from the original creation of the universe—the ones like Faith's that were just like mine but with divergent histories in the recent or distant past. Stage II Realities were "contingent realities," and *in theory* their existence was dependent on the existence of the Stage I Realities. They got *weird*.

Stage II Realities seemed to derive from and get shaped by Stage I Realities, but nobody was willing to bet that it might not be the other way around—their existence might be inspiring their *fictionalization* by people in Stage I Realities instead. Whichever, the only example I'd known before had been Oz, but now I had personal experience with two—the Santa's Village at the North Pole and the pocket reality inhabited by the fairy folk of Will Shakespeare's most popular play. (And the only reason I'd gotten out of that one safely was having a Japanese fairy tale of my own on my side.)

Don't think about Yoshi—Kitsune— Whatever. Don't!

If all that wasn't weird enough, the *truly* weird part was the most accepted explanation of why I couldn't jump physically into realities where I had analogues of myself already. Where I *merged*.

The theory was that I wasn't just *me*, the pale blonde pixie I saw in the mirror every morning when I brushed my teeth. Nope, I was an iteration of an *omnisoul*, co-existent across who knew how many realities, brushing my teeth in lots of places. The bit that I thought of as me was just one "instantiation of awareness" in the bigger Me.

All Hopes were Hope, separate in thought and action, one in existence—like the Holy Trinity but without the absolute awareness and omnipresence, and two instantiations of the same omnisoul couldn't exist coequally in the same reality. So when I jumped into a reality that I already existed in my resident instantiation went to sleep while we "overlapped." If I'd stayed long enough in Faith's reality, maybe the *me* there would have "woken up" and we'd have merged into one Hope that had both sets of memories.

Maybe.

It all felt vaguely blasphemous; it was pretty easy to wrap my mind around the idea of many Hopes, but the idea that all of us were one big HOPE was just bizarre. I also didn't understand why we had to merge—I personally knew breakthroughs that had one mind and an overabundance of bodies—but apparently it explained the observed phenomena better than any other theory.

So let's find out what that means for me here.

Staying up in the sky thinking about it wasn't going to tell me anything I needed to know. I'd popped in below the thin cloud layer, and since the moonlit night showed no capes in the sky to explain myself to, I just dropped. There were plenty of dark rooftops to land and change on.

Super-duper hearing saved my life—the rocket that rose to meet me wasn't supersonic and its climbing roar gave me enough warning to go into twisting evasion even before I spotted its flaring burn below and behind me. It followed as I punched into a hard spiral climb, which meant that it had to be laser guided from a launcher. Radio controlled? Or wire? Flipping over into an arcing dive showed me where the rocket's initial back-blast had cooked a few feet of rooftop into glowing visibility in my infrared sight, and two body temperature human lightbulbs told me it was a two-man fire team.

Cutting the angle, I put the rocket behind me and dropped hard for their roof as I counted.

One...two...three— The rocket detonated harmlessly thirty feet behind my boots—they weren't going to let it follow me back to them—and I cut away and *down* to drop below my shooter's rooftop level. Leveling off, I turned hard and punched the speed to race through Chicago's canyons to put four blocks of taller buildings between me and them.

What the *heck*?

Really—what the heck was *that*? I ignored my hammering heartbeat, tried to tune out the traffic below as I searched for a lower and overshadowed building to drop my bag on. Finding one, an older brownstone between two newer and much higher business towers, I dropped into the deeper shadows of the building's big air conditioning units. Under the cover of the heat-exhausts, I'd be invisible even to another Atlas-Type.

So, what *was* that? Catching movement, I looked up in time to see Watchman cutting fast across the sky towards the tower from which I'd been shot at, Variforce tethered to him by his glowing fields. Okay, it looked like my Sentinels were here. Had that been Paladins on the roof? Had they been lying in wait for just any unsuspecting flyer?

The beating of helicopter props split the night as a CPD bird followed in Watchman and Variforce' wake, and then another. I had to move; they might be prepping to cast a wide search net over Chicago's rooftops, and while I felt better that my team was here I still had *way* too many questions to pop up and say hi yet.

I changed fast. The skirted body of my costume, rolled tightly and wrapped in my cape, fit snuggly into my bag with my mask, gloves, and boots. My white costume tights worked with the fashionable black and white skirt and button-down top that Faith had picked for me. Slipping on the matching street loafers, I was ready to walk down Michigan Avenue without attracting friendly or hostile attention.

Dropping into building's service alley, I got to the ground and out onto the safely lit street without trouble. Putting another block of shuttered businesses between me and the widening aerial dragnet, I turned to head down Miracle Mile in the evening pedestrian crowd.

Where I began spotting differences.

The crowd was thinner than it should have been for the warm night. Walking south, I saw way too few cars on the street—most of them models at least five years old. Channeling the Bees' fashionista radar and looking at the crowd around me, I didn't see much of this year's fashion modes, either—even pedestrians obviously dressed up for clubbing and high-end dining mostly wore stuff a couple of years out of date. And there were a lot fewer of those than there should have been, too.

There were a lot of strolling foot-police, though, and— I stopped right there in the street until I remembered to *blend* as I looked again. Maybe a fifth of the men in the evening crowd seemed to be armed, a lot of them carrying their weapons of choice in belt holsters designed to minimize their profile without really concealing them.

What? Seriously, what?

And...yes, the women too; a couple of happy ladies lurched into me outside Club Nocte and my super-duper sense of smell picked up the unmistakable whiff of gun oil. Their club dresses were too short for thigh holsters, so I guessed they were packing in their little shoulder-slung handbags.

My Chicago didn't allow much concealed carry, *didn't* allow public carry, and this was *not* home—maybe not even close to it.

More spooked than I'd ever admit to anyone, I clutched my bag tighter and picked up my pace. Two more intersections brought me to Millennium Park, where I could cross to the Atlas Memorial and the Dome. Except it wasn't the *Atlas* Memorial; people-watching had distracted me so badly that I didn't notice the change until I'd crossed the street to the memorial plaza and saw *IT*. It was—

Oh God. Oh God. God wasn't here. He couldn't be, not where this abomination was.

"Miss? Are you alright?" The man beside me touched my elbow, one dip of my sway away from grabbing on to hold me up where I stood on the curb edge of the plaza.

No. No, I'll never be alright. "Yes, I— Thank you."

He nodded doubtfully, but accepted it and stepped away as I lowered my hands from my mouth and tried to breathe in a normal and non-worrying way. And not run.

It was the Heroes Memorial, and I couldn't look away.

There I was, in *bronze*, kneeling slumped over bronze Atlas. Even before I forced myself to turn, scanning the explanatory plaques in the half-circle of low wall around the plaza and us, I knew what the scene was—what it *had* to be.

The Whittier Base attack. This was Atlas and I as Seven and the army medics found us after our fight with Seif-al-Din. Except here they hadn't found us—found *me*—in time. I'd *died*, here and now I couldn't breathe. Mom. Dad. Aaron, Josh, Toby, the Bees, *everyone*. They'd had to *bury* me. I couldn't *not* see them walking behind my casket as the drums beat and pipes played on a bright cold morning. Not screaming made me dizzy.

The memorial changed all my plans. I couldn't have taken one step closer, but super-duper vision let me read the plaques behind that obscene monument just fine from where I was, and the center plaque listed the current roster of serving Sentinels: Lei Zi, Watchman, Sifu, The Harlequin, Variforce, Platoon, Psimon, and *Iron Jack*.

Dad had buried me, here, and he was probably at the Dome *right now*.

I nearly stepped into traffic backing out of the plaza, and when a cab honked at me I turned and ran.

I didn't run very far; running drew *attention*, and my brain started working again before I'd gone half a block. And where was I running *to*? I crossed at the next intersection and found a drugstore, one of the all-night ones that served the local hotels, and bought some hair-ties and a pair of shades with some of Faith's cash. They looked a little odd at night, but were the kind that darkened or lightened in response to sunlight or lack of it and they could pass for prescription glasses.

Would I need anything else? Probably not; it wasn't like anyone was looking for me and I was pretty sure that most of my posthumous news coverage would have stuck to my in-costume shots. Just a pair of glasses and my hair pulled into a messy tail should be enough to fool anyone who didn't know me. Hair up and shades firmly on, I took advantage of the sanctuary of a bus stop bench while I tried to think.

So now what? Where could I stay? I really had no idea how long I was here for; while the globe's destinations had been less than random, it showed a distressing tendency to "recharge" at its own speed. Until it was ready—and I had no idea when that would be—all the snow stuck to the bottom of the globe like it was glued there and I couldn't shake it up and jump again until it drifted free. My...interesting night in Shakespeare's fairy wood and my adventures with Jolly Man and Davy

Jones under the Blue Moon never would have happened if I'd been able to just leave within a few hours after popping in.

I'd been stuck in a pirate movie for *days*.

What, then? A hotel was out; all the good ones would require ID, and I'd stand out like nobody's business in the ones that would let me pay for anonymity with cash. Home? Just the thought of what that would mean made me edge on panic again. Call the Bees? Putting them through that would hardly be better. So, where? I waved away two busses and the evening crowd thinned out a lot more before it came to me. Jumping up I hailed the next available taxi I saw.

"Nineteen Lexington Street, please!"

"Yes, ma'am." My Middle-Eastern driver didn't blink at my instructions, repeating it to his car to get the best route as he pulled away from the curb. *This* cab was shiny and new—which was good since my super-senses made taxies a bit chancy sometimes despite their cleaning services.

He wasn't chatty, a blessing I was very thankful for as we left the Loop behind and the streets got darker and overhung with older trees. Lexington Street sat in the part of Chicago where many of the wealthier families of the Gilded Age had made their homes. A lot of the neighborhood had faded into shabby-genteel, grand old Victorian homes remodeled into apartments or even torn down and replaced, but Lexington Street had survived mostly intact and even been renewed by the interest of the Chicago Historical Society and our 21st Century crop of multi-millionaires.

And Grey House had seen it all.

I got out at the gate, paying the fare with a couple of twenties and not asking for change, and waited until the cab's lights disappeared around the turn of the road before opening the box to ring the house on the gate phone.

"*Hello?*" Henry answered on the third ring.

"Good evening, Henry. Is Mrs. Lori at home tonight?" I held my breath.

"*And whom would she be at-home for?*" Who is that knocking on my door so late?

"It's Hope, Henry." Looking up, I took off my shades and made sure that the gate-camera got a good look at me. "Is it too late to ask for some of your famous cocoa?"

"*...I see. One moment, Miss Corrigan.*"

The line went dead and I counted the seconds until the gate clanked and opened. Walking up the lawn-light illuminated drive, I looked for changes. The Grey House gardens looked as they should, but somebody had trimmed back the trees closest to the property wall. The stone property wall now had an inner security system wired to detect anyone coming over it, making me wonder what I'd find on top of the wall if I looked.

Armed partiers on the street tonight, and now extra home security. *Maybe this isn't a good idea.*

Henry met me at the steps to the front doors. *He* looked the same as always: a butler right out of any British period show, complete with silver hair, stern face, and waistcoat. He'd opened his collar and rolled up his sleeves for the night, but had obviously taken a moment to button up the coat.

"Miss Corrigan. It is a...surprise to see you."

"I'm surprised to be here too, Henry. Is it too late?"

He smiled. "Never, for you. Mrs. Lori has not yet retired, and I have informed her that you are here. She is waiting in the library."

I blinked back tears, and just managed to keep from hugging him. "Thank you, Henry. I'll go right in."

He held out a hand for my bag, and I gave it to him. "And *I* will see about that cocoa."

Henry had left the library door open and I took a breath before stepping through, bracing myself against the rush of memory. The roomful of shelves with their leather bound books had been the scene of many pre-debutante visits, a few times just me and Mrs. Lori, most of the time with half a dozen daughters of Chicago and their moms. Post-debut I'd learned the rest of the house over the course of many dinners and society parties, but I liked the library best.

"Well." Mrs. Lori regarded me from her chair by the fireplace. "You look very well, dear. Although hardly dressed to visit." She was dressed for receiving, in a lace trimmed long-sleeved shirt and a narrow gray skirt with hemline decorously below the knee, gray hair pulled back and gathered in a tight bun to frame her almost unlined face. Did she *ever* let her hair down? "Come, let me look at you."

When I obediently advanced across the carpet to stand before her, she regarded me silently before pointing to a close chair angled towards the fire. I sat, back straight and hands folded—I couldn't sit any other way, not in this house and under the eyes of the Grande Dame of Chicago.

"I will say that this is a surprise, dear," she said finally. "Not an unpleasant one!" A thin smile—the only kind I'd ever seen her make—softened her face a little. Anyone listening would have thought I'd just unexpectedly dropped by after seeing her at Mom's last fundraiser, but her voice shook just a little and her eyes were bright in the light of the reading lamps.

I made myself match her manner; the rules required it and I fell back on them naturally. "You don't seem *that* surprised."

"I have failed to be utterly surprised by anything since the day I witnessed a flying man catching a plane, dear. Nothing is impossible anymore, merely improbable or rare. May I ask why you are...here?"

Cutting off a laugh, I had to swallow a couple of times before I could control my own voice. "Why I'm not dead? I'm sorry but I am—I mean, I'm dead here. I've come a long way."

And the story spilled out. The whole story, jumbled and confused, ending in my horror at seeing my own memorial. Henry brought a tray of his cocoa before I'd finished, giving me something to do with my hands, and through it all Mrs. Lori asked almost no questions. When I finished she sat without moving for more than a minute, cup in hand as she looked at me.

"Of course you can't go home. Good Lord."

I nodded, vision blurring. "How— How are they?"

"As well as can be expected for parents who have had to bury both of their beloved daughters, which is to say not at all well. But time has passed, and is a healer. It has not broken them, dear, but I am glad you came to me."

"I have prepared a room, ma'am," Henry informed her. He hadn't left us after bringing the tray.

"Thank you, Henry. I believe that you should retire Hope. Grey House is yours for as long as you need, we can talk more in the morning."

When I nodded again and rose, Mrs. Lori shocked me by rising as well. Before I realized she stepped in and pulled me into a brief, tight embrace. "It *will* be alright, dear." It almost broke me down, but I was able to nod and thank her before following Henry.

Henry had turned on the lights, turned down the sheets, and left my bag on the dresser. I knew without looking that he'd have put out towels in the attached bathroom. Putting everything away, I flopped back on the bed and out a long breath.

Sanctuary achieved, for as long as I needed it. Now what? My mind churned, thoughts chasing each other in useless circles. Mrs. Lori was a determined luddite, but her social assistant and Henry both used computers and the internet—I was sure that Henry would let me use his office system tomorrow to research this reality to my heart's content. Then I could decide what to do next. But the one thing that kept me from changing for bed and crawling between the sheets was *Shelly*.

I'd become Astra in this reality, so the Teatime Anarchist and his evil twin had existed here too. Obviously. The Big One and Whittier Base Attack had happened, so their time war hadn't resolved itself before then; that meant I could count on their actions being the same in this reality at least until that awful day. Probably.

But that meant the Anarchist should have "twinned" Shelly, intending a quantum-ghost Shell to be my interface with his Big Book of Contingent Prophecy if he took himself and the Dark Anarchist out of the picture. So why wasn't she in my head now?

A horrible thought jerked me upright. What if the Teatime Anarchist had *lost*? The awful possibility stole my breath until I remembered the armed civilians I'd seen tonight. The Dark Anarchist had wanted the US government to go fascist, thinking it the best protection from actual *anarchy* (I really had named him badly). If he'd won then the government wouldn't be letting its citizens run around armed, would it? That at least hinted at a Teatime Anarchist win, right?

Okay. I fell back on the bed to stare at the ceiling. Back to Shell. Where was she? She'd been *awake* before the Whittier Base Attack, a quantum-ghost waiting to reach out and touch me through our neural link.

What do you do when you lose connection? You hang up. I'd died. Our neural link—the one I hadn't known about then—had been cut from *my* side. She'd have hung up, maybe re-tasked her end of the link to someone else?

I swallowed thickly around the sudden lump in my throat. The Anarchist had brought her back for me, her Best Friend Forever—and then I'd died before she'd been able to let me know she was even here. It was like a horrible joke, two people calling and missing each other. Souls passing in the night.

Calling each other. I jackknifed upright again, staring at the guest phone on the bedside table.

Could it be that easy?

I tried to imagine Shell. Her back, me *gone*. Assuming one of the Anarchist's *other* endgame traps had taken his twin and probably him out of the picture, then she'd have been left alone. She'd have had to reach out. With her contingent future-knowledge of the Sentinels she'd have probably reached out to them—I desperately wanted to think so—but she'd have kept other lines of communication. Knowing her sense of humor, she'd have arranged *one* line of communication she'd had before, and even six years after she'd died I remembered her cell number.

Could I just *call* her? It would be almost as bad as contacting my parents here. So why didn't it feel that way?

She died first.

As juvenile as it was, I realized I was grinning ear-to-ear. Shell's first grand reappearance in my Whittier Base hospital room was forever burned into memory. *Hi!* If I was right, then it was *my* turn.

I punched the number with a shaking finger, nearly dropping the receiver.

It rang. *Pickup, pickup, pickup...* Twice. Three times, she was probably tracing the number to see who was calling and—

"Hello? Who is *this*?"

My vision went spotty and I swallowed until I could open my mouth without breaking into hysterical laughter. "Hi, Shell. It's me."

"...Hope? Hope!"

"Yeah. Could you check our neural link? 'Cause I've been *calling*—"

"Hope!" And there she stood in virtual presence beside the bed, wide-eyed and gripping her hair and looking at me like I was the most beautiful thing she'd ever seen and I'd pop like a soap bubble if she took her eyes off me.

I laughed. "One of me, anyway."

"You can't be— I can *hear* you, but—"

"But I can't be here?" And just like that it wasn't funny anymore. "I'm a copy like you. Sort of. I just got here sideways." And I told her. Not *everything*, and more organized than I'd managed with Mrs. Lori, but enough about the two of us that she understood. She plopped down on the chair beside the bed before I finished.

"*Wow*, that's— Hope— I'm *alive*? Living with Mom?"

"Back home yeah. One of you. Both, I suppose—it's complicated."

"You *think*?" She scrubbed her cheeks. "You'd think I'd know all about extrareality crossovers—I do—it's just—"

"You never thought of this?"

"No—I mean yes, I never ever did!"

"I'm sorry it took me so long to get here."

"You should be!" She laughed giddily. "But I guess it took me three years to come back so bygones, right? This is just— But—" She sobered fast. "You can't stay, can you?"

I winced. "You know I can't. You're waiting for me back there, too. With everyone else." I *couldn't* stay, but the thought of leaving her here, where I'd died and left her alone, made me physically ache. She could come—she could move herself onto some kind of 22nd Century storage device and I could take her in my bag, give her to Shell to actualize when I got home. Except *her* mom was here, her fight, her responsibilities. "I—"

"I get it," she agreed with a seriousness that surprised me. "I'm probably pulling the world apart figuring out how to find you right now. If this Kitsune person hasn't already told me. He sounds *hot*."

And that was the Shell I knew. "He is when he's a he."

For whatever reason, she missed my rising flush. "But you're getting back on your own. Cool. What can I do to help?"

I honestly had no idea; the adrenaline of the missile-race and the shock of the memorial had long worn away, and my brain was finally shutting down. Shell assured me that she'd be there when I called in the morning and she'd keep an eye on me. The only thing she'd say about the current situation was that the team—*this* team—had caught the Paladins who'd fired at me and were "helping the police with their investigation into the identity of the target." And that I *really* didn't want to talk them. The Sentinels, not the police. Both, actually.

She didn't "leave" until I'd turned out the lights, and I felt her virtual fingers in my hair as I drifted off. Comfort-touching.

In the morning I checked the snow globe (still dead) and after feeding me breakfast Henry let me use his office computer to research. The first thing I learned was Jacky was in New Orleans. She wasn't on the Sentinel's public roster anymore, but she hadn't opened Bouchard Investigations in the Big Easy, either—instead *Artemis* was a huge CAI hero down there. That she was *alive* (or still undead) was really the only good news; Jacky had gone big because she'd had to.

Because neither Blackstone nor Chakra were anywhere on the roster, either. And they hadn't been since not long after...

The Pulse.

Omega Night had still happened. Because Shell, Seven and I hadn't been there to work together, they hadn't been here to stop it.

I almost heaved up Henry's excellent scrambled eggs.

Without us there to shoot it down, the Overlord's Verne altered Trident II missile had climbed to optimal distance and then detonated. The generated electromagnetic pulse had covered most of North America, dropping planes out of the sky like the day of The Event, burning out power grids and telecommunications systems, crippling industrial and transportation infrastructure across the US, even frying the engine-monitoring chips of most newer car models. The power went away and all hell broke loose.

I forced myself to read on. The death-toll had started in the thousands and then climbed from there as life-saving drugs spoiled without refrigeration and our smashed distribution system stopped bringing food to the supermarket shelves. Sanitation systems went down in too many places, and hunger and disease spread *fast*. FEMA hadn't stood a chance of staying ahead of the disaster, even with every Crisis Aid and Intervention cape helping and relief supplies and personnel pouring in from the other League nations and from Heroes Without Borders.

It was too awful to be believed. Starvation, infection, and sickness had kicked off rioting as gangs turned most of the biggest cities into war zones. Seeing their chance, The Ring had hit us over and over again, targeting more critical infrastructure as whole urban centers burned or became just unsustainable. Displacement camps sprang up everywhere, and for months it had looked like it was all going to come apart as we clawed our way back from the edge of total collapse.

We only lost twelve million. Twelve *million*. That had been wildly optimistic in the Omega briefing I remembered, back before I'd taken my near death-ride to make sure it *didn't* happen. Here they'd named it The Pulse, and hadn't begun to really recover yet.

I read until I couldn't read any more. All the deadly numbers, the images of looted and burned cities, massive tent and trailer camps, and mass graves of unnamed dead blurred into one long gallery of awfulness and horror. Tears pooled on my cheeks to run between my fingers as I tried to hold my grief inside with shaking hands

"I couldn't tell you," Shelly said beside me. I barely jumped. Normally her popping up in my peripheral vision would have sent me halfway to the ceiling, but I was already practically vibrating in my chair with the absolute need to *do something* or fly apart into a million pieces.

But what? It was like looking at the aftermath of a tidal wave or meteor strike; where would I even *begin*? And— "Mom? Dad? Mrs. H? Everyone?"

"Everyone's fine! They're all fine, I made sure of it."

I scrubbed my cheeks. "We stopped it. Back home. We stopped it together. You, me, Seven."

Her mouth dropped. "Us? So I'm— Nope, not talking about any of this, we've got to *go*. *Now*."

Shelly's Business Voice had me up and moving without thinking about it. "What's going on?"

"Downtown cameras caught you getting down to the street. The police have linked you to the missile last night—no, nobody got a good look and the cameras didn't catch you till you'd changed!"

"But they can trace me here? Why are they after me?" I stepped into the hall, stopped and turned. Where first?

"From street-cam to car-cam, you bet. I've played with it a little so face recognition screening isn't going to be cluing anyone in that you're you, but you broke city ordinances and state law with your night flight. Illinois passed the Public Safety and Security Act last year—publicly using superhuman powers without being registered and monitored is against the law, and they're coming with a warrant to ask you lots of questions any minute now. They've got a watcher in a car parked on the street, but I've taken care of that and now we need to get you gone."

"They'd arrest me for *flying*?"

"Arrest?" The way she laughed said it wasn't funny. "They don't *arrest* breakthroughs who haven't committed crimes. They detain you to ascertain your identity, check for outstanding warrants, hold you for psychiatric evaluation till they're sure that you're safe to be let out in public. And since you're..."

"Right." I swallowed panic—Shelly wasn't screaming *Fly! Fly like the wind!* so I had to have time. Mrs. Lori first. I found her in the breakfast room, Henry only just setting down her morning meal. They stopped talking when I entered the room.

"Good morning, Mrs. Lori—"

"Good morning, Hope. I believe that since you are now hiding in my house, a degree of familiarity is appropriate. You may call me Elizabeth."

I blinked, laughed in spite of everything. "Oh no, Mrs. Lori. I really, really can't."

"I see." She smiled back in fond understanding. "And what puts you in a rush?"

Tell her, Shelly mouthed beside me.

"The police and maybe the Sentinels are on their way here to ask me questions about last night. And there's a law? I can get my things and fly—"

"Certainly not. Henry will drive you wherever you need to go."

Henry nodded. "Of course, ma'am. Miss Hope, if you would quickly pack, I will meet you in the front hall." He finished laying out Mrs. Lori's breakfast and then left, walking quickly.

Shell agreed invisibly, and I turned to Mrs. Lori. "I'm sorry, I—"

She sighed, looking old, and smiled softly.

"Do not be, dear. I watched your coming outs—both into society and as a hero—and couldn't have been more proud if you were mine. I knew your grandmother, you know. Indeed we were old school friends, and despite your family's initial disapproval of your father I attended your mother's wedding and helped her launch her philanthropic career after— Well. Come here."

She reached out and took my hands as I stared in shock. "I have missed you a great deal and hoped that we would have a few more days."

"Really?" I squeaked, flushed. "I mean—"

"I do know what you mean." She squeezed, and when she let me go I hugged myself. "Now run along. Certainly dallying now would be folly. I will remain and speak with the authorities."

"You won't be in any trouble?"

"Not unless you are still here. Shoo. Off with you. And be safe, dear."

"I—thank you." I bent to hug her carefully, and ran.

To the discerning eye (and after three years of in-the-field training, my eye was pretty discerning), Mrs. Lori's town car was bulletproof. It also hadn't been washed in a while, which had to be intentional; Henry would never have allowed Mrs. Lori to be seen in anything not flawless and pristine.

Shelly disappeared before I met Henry in the hall, saying she had to take care of some stuff. Henry settled me and my bag in the back seat, opened the garage door, and then listened on his blue-tooth earpiece for a few minutes before driving us out.

The car windows had been tinted, but I still wore my shades. I also sat, bag in my lap and hand on the door latch, ready to get out and *fly*. Shelly had said she'd "taken care of it," but if anyone was waiting for us then I was going to put distance between me and anyone who could be collateral damage when I resisted arrest. We passed only a single car parked on the street, about fifty feet from the gate. Its two occupants slumped down as we went by, but I could see their body heat and I started scanning the sky; if the CPD had put the car on Grey House to keep watch until the Sentinels got the warrant, then they'd just called it in and I could expect Watchman and Variforce to make this a short ride.

My fingers felt slick on the door handle, and neither of us talked. Still listening on his earpiece, Henry stopped for longer than he needed to at a couple of stop signs, and ran a few more without even slowing down as we kept to the surface streets. Was Shelly spotting for him, somehow? I tried not to feel helpless, a package Shelly and Henry were delivering who knew where.

Henry drove us west, avoiding the freeway and still taking surface streets. We pulled into the parking lot of a boarded up strip mall and parked, but Henry stopped me from getting out. Then we drove again, and I stopped worrying about what might be coming up behind us; what we were driving into looked worse.

I hadn't noticed anything off about downtown Chicago until I'd gotten on the street and seen the people, but now the further west we drove the worse things looked. A *lot* of homes were boarded up or gutted, and whole streets had been abandoned. Some of them sported rough pavement patches—the kind of first-stage repair job you might slap over the results of a high powered breakthrough fight. A few abandoned homes showed fire damage and a couple of blocks we passed were completely burned out, blackened skeletons of wood frame and brick all that remained. It all reminded me of LA after the Big One.

The streets weren't *completely* empty; some cars moved on them. We drove by government food-distribution centers, a couple of them in taken-over grocery stores, more in big trucks and mobile offices arranged in parking lots. Here and there, groups of residents watched us pass and the look in a lot of their eyes was calculating enough that I understood why Henry hadn't washed the town car; I was willing to bet that the heavy police presence I'd seen downtown didn't extend out here—at least not beyond the food centers.

A few miles past the last distribution center I had only a second's warning as the sounds of the car engine and tires on pavement muted almost to nothing like my ears had been suddenly stuffed with cotton. The *bang* that lifted the front of the car sounded like a popped balloon. The airbags deployed, the driver's bag flattening Henry into his seat—saving him from worse as the car slammed back down with barely a sound.

"Henry!" I hardly heard myself and he certainly didn't hear me, but he didn't go limp as the airbag deflated. Instead he reached for the gun under his seat. "No!" I shouted uselessly. Ignoring the gun in my face, I pulled gently on his arm and mimed that he should stay. When he nodded I unbuckled, turned in my seat to put my feet up, spot-checked the view outside, and kicked my door out of its bent frame hard enough to rip it away and send it skipping across the road and into the boarded-up window of an abandoned house. I followed it out.

They shot me, pissing me off. Faith had given me that shirt.

Five flankers, guys wearing black ski masks, at angles where our opened doors would provide no cover. Two of them fired AR-15s *pop-pop-pop* as I charged, drawing all of their fire to my side of the car. One not shooting stepped up to swing at me and I ducked under his wild haymaker to clip him with my shoulder on my way to the shooters.

Shooter One dropped his AR and I stomped on the muzzle before lunging for Shooter Two. He didn't let go, and screamed silently as my yank broke fingers and I swung the rifle by the barrel, smashing the stock on the still-standing bare knuckle fighter's raised arm.

The rifle broke instead of his arm, raising his hypothetical rating another notch, but I danced back anyway to bring the other two unarmed guys into view.

Atlas Rule # 9: When you've got multiple opponents, don't spend more than a beat on anyone.

Unknown Two held some kind of gadget—I guessed a sound suppressor. Unknown Three...stumbled back and ran for it. Smart boy. Then my world lit up as Bare Knuckle hard-blocked me and I hit the street. It *hurt* but I made myself come up, keeping my feet on the ground.

Okay, at least a C Class, possibly B. I hadn't been braced so I couldn't be sure, but the others stayed back so now I could focus.

I wiped the gravel off my face, put my fists up.

He laughed silently and charged.

Henry shot him.

Yes, *Henry*. Mrs. Lori's butler. Sometime between my kicking the door out and kissing the pavement, he'd exited the car with the biggest short-rifle I'd ever seen and where had *that* been hidden? I actually heard a dull *crack* leading the muffled *thud* when its solid and probably armor-piercing slug hit Bare Knuckle in the back. He went down hard, but no blood confirmed his probable Class and I kicked him in the head without a thought. He stayed down.

I turned around. Shooter One and Two were sprinting away now, but the gadget-holder stood in shock. I pointed to the gadget.

He turned it off and the sound came back.

"Good boy," I said. "Henry?"

"Fine, ma'am. And the Sentinels are on their way."

"Yes they are," Shelly whispered in my ear. "ETA three minutes for Watchman, Variforce, Iron Jack."

I froze for only a second, didn't take my eyes off my guy. "Henry, would you please open the trunk?"

"Yes, ma'am."

When I pointed at the ground my guy dropped his little box. I frisked him fast and, grabbing his arm, frog-marched him over and tossed him in the trunk. "Stay." I shut the trunk on him. "Henry, I've got to—"

"Of course, miss." he nodded. "Go."

I pointed. "The house, until it's clear." With flyers in the air, I wasn't going to try and do anything but hide.

"Understood. Phone."

"Right." I'd wait for his call? Had he packed a cell phone for me? I grabbed my bag and *ran*.

It was hot and stuffy in the abandoned house, perfect for masking my own body heat from Watchman. Going in through the shattered plywood that had been nailed over the front window, I crouched in shadow as I watched the street—I couldn't leave Henry completely alone with Bare Knuckle until the guys arrived. If he stirred...

Henry kept his elephant gun on him but he didn't, not before Watchman touched down with Dad, Variforce right behind them. They exchanged only five words with Henry before Dad clumped over to check Bare Knuckle, who finally started to move. Watchman went back up to scout the area for our runners while Variforce and Dad secured the scene in anticipation of the special police wagons. Mostly he stood there like an iron statue, arms folded and scanning the local environment. And I tried to breathe.

When Shelly popped in beside me I didn't twitch. *"That was...holy shit, Hope. That was amazing."*

I mimed zipping my lips.

"Right. Watchman."

I really doubted he could hear street-level whispers from up there, but I was happy for the excuse; I had no idea what would come out of my mouth, but Shelly provided a running virtual-monologue while the police did their job.

"It was an IED—there's so many road patches around here it's easy to hide them. You just stopped a carjacker kidnap-gang that's been operating for weeks. I'd bet their strong guy buries the IED in the road overnight—it's a shaped charge under a steel plate that knocks the car on its ass instead of blowing it up. Then they rob the occupants and kidnap anyone who looks worth anything. Three jobs in three weeks, nobody could catch them because the sound-dampening field let them get it done and get out before anyone could know what was happening. Just awesome chance they picked you."

I muffled a hysterical giggle behind my hand. Yeah, awesome.

"FYI, the arresting detective just offered gadget-guy immunity from the death penalty if he'd give up the location of their hideout and kidnap victims. He took it."

And that explained Watchman's return and their fast departure.

Closing my eyes, I shook my head. Now that the opportunity was past I was shaking, partly from dropping off my fighting adrenalin high but mostly from keeping from running out there, straight to Dad. I wasn't sure if I'd ever wanted anything so badly in my life as I wanted my father to hug me and make this all better.

But Shelly had said I did *not* want to talk to my team, and my morning's research hadn't told me why.

With the team gone, the police moved fast. They didn't even bother with the street, beyond taking pictures of everything and collecting the weapons, before pulling out with two special wagons and a convoy of cars to take their prisoners to the hard cells. They took Henry, of course.

And my bag rang.

"*Hi!*" Shelly chirped when I fished out the cell I hadn't known was there. *"Henry doesn't know about our neural link thing, but he just texted me to call and tell you that he'd send another car with a shirt for you. Two blocks north in an hour. Bye!*" She hung up.

I rolled my eyes at her. "Funny, Casper. Ha ha." But I was smiling again, sort of. "How did he explain away me happening to the car-jack gang?"

"He told the detectives that you came out of nowhere and Good-Samaritaned him."

And now I laughed for real. Like anybody'd believe *that*. "And they're not looking for the Samaritan?"

"Nope—'cause if they found him they'd have to 'detain' him. Any licensed CAI hero has to hold an unregistered breakthrough for processing when he finds one."

"And the cops?"

"They came out for the arrest—no way they're going to go looking for superhuman trouble without backup."

It made stomach-churning sense; the government was issuing laws and procedures that the capes and cops were ignoring whenever possible. *State law? Who cares—if mystery-girl doesn't drop bodies or destroy real estate, we sure don't.* Something like that, and that was disturbing in a whole new and different way. Old Me wouldn't have thought twice about it, but after nearly three years of sometimes mind numbing and always bewildering political education from Blackstone, New Me wondered just how bad the breakdown between government and law enforcement was getting.

Because that was a Bad Sign.

When it came time to leave my hiding place I went out the back and kept watching the sky. Shell disappeared so as not to distract me, but the short walk proved uneventful; two streets away I found Henry waiting for me in an almost identical town car. This one was cleaner.

Henry assured me that he was fine and I had to accept that. Considering his age and how he'd gotten slammed around, I wasn't willing to bet that he wasn't secretly a D Class Ajax, or maybe a Paragon. Breakthrough-boosted specimens of physical perfection, Paragons didn't have any obvious powers but they tended to have incredible stamina and bounce back nearly as fast as Ajax and Atlas-Types.

If he was, he was smart to keep it quiet.

Henry didn't say much and neither did I—after everything that had just happened I wasn't in the mood—but the rest of the ride to wherever stayed blessedly uneventful. We did get stopped at a US Army checkpoint; Henry explained that most of the troops were home protecting the food and fuel and helping reestablish order under a suspension of the Posse Comitatus Act and declaration of quasi-martial law in large parts of the country.

The soldiers checked Henry's ID—and mine, which I hadn't known I now had to make sure that we didn't have records or warrants on us before they let us continue. They did suggest we not go much further south than we were; apparently "Southcamp's gang fringe" had gotten pretty wide. Southcamp was run by the state, not the Army, and from what the soldiers said it sounded like Springfield was doing a less than wonderful job with Illinois's displaced. Looking at the streets we were driving through, my only thought was *It's worse than here?* Henry thanked them politely and they waved us along.

And half the country was like this? Or worse?

Then I saw the white towers.

They weren't high towers—none of them could be more than twenty stories and they were wide enough to look pretty squat—but they stood out against the empty fields and the single-story homes closest to them. From here it looked like they were made entirely out of shipping containers and steel scaffolding, bright white-painted exteriors broken only by rooftops and platforms covered with green and flowering plants. Steel-scaffolding walkways, festooned with more hanging plants, connected all of the towers on their lower levels so that it looked like they melded together to form almost a single structure.

"What is *that*?"

"West camp free hold."

I blinked. "Okay so, I understand all those words *individually*..."

Henry laughed. "Westcamp Freehold," he enunciated carefully. "It's...complicated. It's on private property, Miss Hope, and it doesn't recognize the authority of the local city or state government. You'll be safe, there."

"It's a *camp*?"

"It's not like Southcamp. You'll see."

I considered asking what *Southcamp* was like, but kept quiet and watched as we got closer.

At the entrance to a gated parking lot, men in white uniforms with orange helmets and vests labeled Westcamp Public Safety checked my ID and a return pass Henry showed them. Henry paid a fee and they took my picture and thumbprint, entered them, and gave me a day pass with my picture and print on it. They politely cautioned us against losing our passes—we could be asked to show them by any Public Safety officer.

"What did they check?" I asked Henry as soon as we'd pulled away from the booth.

"Their private system and the National Criminal Database. Westcamp Freehold is private property; no one with a criminal record gets in, and no one who they've ejected gets back in."

When we parked Henry tried to take my bag—I slung it over my shoulder—and we walked through an open street gate into the camp. The place didn't look like private property to me.

Outside of Chicagoland the streets had emptied and we'd driven past whole neighborhoods that looked like ghost towns. *This* street was bustling, full of people going places. It was a pedestrian street—no vehicle traffic other than slow moving electric carts—made of some sort of rubber-coated metal grill system instead of poured asphalt and with wide green-planted medians down the center around and between molded benches and busy kiosks. I stopped in the middle of the street and stared. Just like in downtown Chicago, everyone and their dog was packing—actually more of them, here—but it was the towers that captured my attention.

The entire "camp" wasn't really constructed from steel shipping containers; someone had fabricated modular boxes that had the same dimensions. For transport? Quick assembly? Each tower was up to twenty stories of stacked and connected boxes, every other story above the second wrapped with wide balconies most of the way up. The lower wrap-around balconies of each tower were linked to the adjacent towers by broad steel-scaffolding walkways, and every tower gleamed brilliant white under the green and flowering plant boxes and baskets and trellises that had been strung up literally everywhere, like the place was one big garden nursery. With the shadows cast by the towers I imagined that most of the species were shade plants, and why was I even thinking about that?

I stared around as we walked. The first two stories of each tower were given over to businesses, shops, and what looked like community centers and dining halls. Everything was clean. *Theme park* clean, like they had professionals come out every night and hose the streets down. I spotted two paint crews further down the street touching up tower exteriors and another crew working on newly hung planters. There wasn't a graffiti-tag or piece of loose litter in sight.

"Good morning, ma'am." As I'd been taking everything in, a helmeted and orange-vested PS officer had walked right up to us. He smiled, nodded politely. "May I see your passes?" When we presented them he passed a reading pad over both, then looked at my large handbag. "Are we staying with a resident, ma'am?"

"Miss Evans is," Henry said. "Her host couldn't meet us at the entrance."

"Residence number?"

"Four-Seventeen A."

He entered the information in his pad. "Very good. We'll expect a notice from your host and will deliver a guest card once he has done so if he does not check in. Is there anything I can do for you?" When I shook my head he nodded again before strolling off.

I watched him go, looked at Henry. "His visor has a camera in it?"

"Yes."

"Facial recognition system?"

"Oh yes."

"So...the officers at the booth don't search vehicles, and just issued me a day pass. But my bag says I might be staying, and any safety officer who sees me will know from the entry just now that I am but haven't secured a guest card yet. Right?"

"Correct. You won't be bothered again but you will see another officer tonight, who will either give you a new card or escort you from the camp."

"What about people who work here?"

"If you work here, you live here."

I nodded, still not getting it. So Westcamp really was private property? But it sported public business like a mall, and private residences like a gated community? What kind of camp was it—and how did it get away with its own security and *no* cops? How could Westcamp not recognize city and state authority? And—most important—if anyone tracked me here, how could Westcamp keep the State of Illinois from issuing a warrant and forcibly collecting me? Forget about fleeing to Canada; I already felt like I'd crossed the border into another country. This was completely messed up. What had happened?

Henry got me moving again.

We walked to the center of the "camp." A huge open plaza with a fountain, a tiered arena and stage of grass and concrete, and tree-flanked walks with more benches and kiosks, it was all so professionally laid out and landscaped that I wanted to call time out. Who built *this* in the middle of a national crisis?

Just beyond the plaza, Henry took us into the lobby of one of the towers—as clean as everything outside—and we caught an elevator to the tenth floor and stopped outside the door to apartment A. He knocked.

"Come iiiiin!" I knew that voice and Henry chuckled when I glared at him accusingly.

Shelly greeted us, standing proudly in the middle of the apartment's main room. She gave Henry a playful kiss on the cheek. "Any trouble getting here?"

"As if you don't know, young lady. Miss Hope, I hope we will see you again." And he was gone. Shelly tackle-hugged me. I braced and didn't go down. Dropping my bag, I hugged her back.

"Let me guess. Galatea?"

"Yup! Fully humanform gynoid drone-bot. Vulcan's best work! What do you think?" She jumped back and twirled. Her hair was black and cut in a short bob that matched mine but otherwise it was Shelly, maybe eighteen or nineteen—I had to look close to see that her skin was too perfect and smooth to be real.

"So you're not actually *in* there?"

Her eyes rolled. "That would be stupid, moving myself into a vulnerable shell."

I nodded weakly. "Yeah, it sounds a little dumb. So who knows about you?" *Why aren't you with the Sentinels?*

"Vulcan of course—but he thinks I'm a cyberspace-phantom breakthrough named Cypher. Come on—let me show you around!"

Shelly's home—and I supposed all of the apartments in the tower—was made out of two joined eight-by-forty boxes. The interiors were probably completely modular; hers had an office-bed-bath suite (made bigger with a workstation and bed that folded into the walls), a common kitchen and living space, and an armory.

That was different.

"As Galatea I'm a member of Westcamp Freehold's CAI team," she explained. "So I've got extra armor, racks of non-lethal loadouts—gluetape, freezefoam, flashbangs, that kind of stuff. I'm great for riot control and non-lethal force."

My first mental picture was Shelly—Galatea—loading up and then taking the stairs or elevator down. Then she tapped the outside wall and it turned into a door onto her small private balcony. It had hanging plants on it, of course.

"Got a green thumb?"

"Westcamp law. If you have a balcony you grow stuff on it; if you can't or won't then you pay with Westcamp Bucks for a service that does. Same for cleaning—they're big on cleanliness and hygiene here after the sickness of the first post-Pulse year."

"Strict homeowner's association?"

"You have *no* idea."

She handed me a black wig to match my shades and took me to Charlies' Wok for lunch. It turned out that not all of the businesses and shops were down on the street; her tower had a couple of eateries open to the pedestrian balconies—again packed into the double-wide spaces. Mostly they cooked for delivery, but there were adjacent public spaces with tables for eating at.

Charlie's Wok did Chinese food, rice with wok-fried or steamed sides in returnable bowls. Charlie wasn't Chinese (he looked like a truck driver and wore a Harley Davidson cowboy hat) but he spoke it. His army-unit and mission tats explained where he'd picked up the skills.

Shelly traded Chinese with him when she ordered and with a couple of fellow eaters before bringing our tray of bowls to our table. I watched her tuck in, and realized that for some reason our half of the public dining space had emptied of everyone but us.

"We can talk," Shell said. "Trust Charlie."

I nodded, picked up my sticks. This was Shelly's territory and she wasn't *my* Shell but I'd trust her with my life. "So, does everyone here besides Vulcan think that you're, you know, a meat-person?"

"Everyone here thinks I'm a burn victim who got a Second Skin treatment, and they're always asking if it 'feels real'. FYI, they also think I'm a D Class Ajax-Type and my silver-blue Galatea armor is a Verne-tech powersuit. If you're here long I'll introduce you to the rest of the local CAI team."

"Is that safe? I mean—"

"I know. Trust me, you won't be you. And you're safe in the freehold, even if Chicago or Springfield figures out where you disappeared to."

And now I *had* to know.

"I keep hearing that. Freehold. Doesn't that just mean your land isn't owned by the bank?"

"Nope. Well, yeah, but a lot more than that now." And over the excellent mushroom chicken, she told me.

I couldn't believe it.

The way she said it, the federal and state governments were mostly smashed. Just overwhelmed. The Pulse and everything that happened after had wrecked things to the point where, with *all* the federal agencies, with most of the Army brought home and all the National Guard and state militias called up, they'd barely been able to hang on—*hadn't* been able to keep things going in a lot of cities in the face of the mass flight and food riots. All over the place people had had to do for themselves, forget about the government. Focused on keeping the marginal zones from also descending into hellholes, the governments let them. At first.

After the initial crisis had passed—which took *months*—the state agencies tried to move back in and administer centralized policies to places surviving on their own. And a lot of those places said *no*. Camps with barely enough food where the government wanted them to take more refugees. Counties holding onto the food they had to stockpile or trade. And of course nut-job survivalist communities who'd decided that This Was It, the end of civilization that they'd been waiting for. They all told the state governments to pound sand.

Shelly said that when the states cried to Washington for help, President Touches Clouds refused to let them use the distributed US military units to put down the "insurrections." Governors tried to use National Guard and militia units to do it themselves, but in a lot of places the guard and militia units weren't willing to fire on fellow Americans who weren't looting or shooting at *them*. Where they *were* willing...

Before the Pulse, the ATF (the Bureau of Alcohol, Tobacco, Firearms and Explosives) had estimated that there were around *three hundred million personal firearms in the US*. The DSA had estimated that for every three *known* breakthroughs there was at least one unknown breakthrough. They'd both been conservative; there were a *lot* more guns than that and independent-minded Americans could shoot back. Adding the startling number of unaccounted-for civilian breakthroughs to the mix...there were pitched battles in a few places, and a lot of people died. With the legitimacy and continued authority of the national and state governments on the line, Washington had to do *something*.

And it did, just, according to Shelly, not what the states wanted. She was almost grinning ear to ear as she told me the story; President Touches Clouds addressed an emergency session of Congress, and they worked out the Freehold Protocols, which strong-armed the states into backing off of the insurrectionists by withholding ammunition (most of the armories were in *federal* hands). The states had to stand down military operations and settle for holding onto what they controlled.

Then she sent in the US Marshals—augmented by CAI heroes recruited into the Marshals Service for the purpose—and they made sure that the freeholds were being run according to God Bless the USA principles. The freeholds that were nothing more than gang lord fiefdoms, self-declared white supremacist "states" (or black supremacist—there were a few of those), or otherwise not honoring democracy and freedom, were Taken Care Of as soon as the marshals and the US Military could get to them.

"The one exception to that rule is Haven," she finished up. "It's a *breakthrough*-supremacist enclave on the California coast. They dodged the wrath of Uncle Sam by setting up their operation where there were no normals already and then only letting breakthroughs and their families in. They're democratic, just exclusive."

"So that was it?" I really found it hard to imagine. "The government just let them form their own states?"

She shrugged. "The good ones, anyway. Washington is still negotiating the freeholds' actual legal status with the state governments. Touches Clouds wants the states to voluntarily cede freehold land to the federal government as self-administering territories, and everyone's leaving us alone while they work it all out."

"So what about this place?" My wave took in all the box towers we could see. "This is just... I don't know *what* it is."

"This is Vulcan's place."

I put down my chopsticks. "Vulcan. The mad scientist in the basement?"

"Nnnnot following you."

"He's a Sentinel here, right?" Wait, he hadn't been on the plaque.

"Huh? No! When did *that* happen?"

"Blackstone recruited him after—" My stomach sank and I tasted bile. *Please* no. I hadn't been around for the Villains Inc. fight, here. "What happened to Blackstone and Chakra? Rush?"

"Rush was killed last year. Blackstone works for the DSA now, and Chakra went back to Heroes Without Borders. Why?"

I felt both guilty and grateful. I'd light a candle for Rush the next time I was in church, but hearing that Blackstone and Chakra were still alive filled me with relief. "And you?"

"I joined up with Vulcan before the Pulse for the prosthetic bodies. He liked me for the Galatea and Prometheus Projects."

And that made it *three* realities where Shell and Vulcan got involved by different routes. When I got home I was going have to give more serious thought to questions of fate. "Prometheus?"

"That's what started all this." Her wave to the world outside matched mine, and now she was actually smiling fondly.

"Eric's—Vulcan's—polymorphic molecules let him make a lot of different things, but most of that's just harder or more durable versions of modern alloys. The two things he really dedicated himself to were transformative technologies; molecular switches and networks capable of the sort of organizational processes needed for a neural network supporting a true artificial intelligence, and a way of producing a durable, safe, high-energy fusion chain power source."

She frowned, considering. "I have no idea how the Sentinels recruited him in your history. *Here* he built his workshop just outside the Fermi National Accelerator in West Chicago for access and buried himself in it. He's...focused."

I sighed. "If I understood all those words, he accomplished most of that back home. Maybe the team offered him more resources?"

"Maybe. Anyway, just before the Pulse he had one of his eureka moments and came up with the Monsatt Power Cell. He fabricated a bunch of them—compact little suckers the size of beer kegs. Just one can replace a trailer-sized power generator, and their self-sustaining cycle lasts *forever*. Well a few hundred years, maybe. And yep, now you're getting it."

I wanted to laugh. "He built a self-fueled power source just before everything collapsed?" Wow, that was practically *fate. Again*.

"Yeah. It's all Verne-tech shortcuts, but give us a century and we'll be able to do it for reals. When the Pulse happened and the power grids fried like bacon and collapsed everywhere, he handed five power cells to West Chicago in return for the deeds to the land around his property. Then we used the rest for ourselves and for barter—plugging into local distribution centers whose refrigeration centers were warming up, into hospitals so they could keep their drugs fresh and do their jobs, all that stuff. We got food, material, and labor for it and by the time West Chicago and the municipalities around it fell apart anyway, this had become Westcamp. It's amazing how much professional and superhuman labor you can get when safe and warm places with enough food are suddenly scarce."

"Okay…" That all made sense, sort of, but— "Freehold?"

"Yeah, well, things were going great and then the Great State of Illinois got pushy. And greedy."

The way Shell explained it, it sounded like a total bureaucratic train wreck. Illinois had "assumed emergency oversight" of the failed county and city governments—not that they could do much from Springfield—and in the name of West Chicago it tried to come in and regulate Westcamp zoning and construction according to city licensing and codes. Which would have ground everything to a halt since by then nobody had cash to pay for permits, inspections, and licensing (they were already paying with Westcamp Bucks inside the camp) and they were using non-standard materials anyway. The government also tried to tax Westcamp's power production, *which it was mostly giving away.* Hey, the state needed revenue, right? Then they found out that the power cells were "nuclear," and moved to seize them "for safety reasons."

Dumbasses.

Westcamp declared itself a Freehold, and had enough superhuman and armed refugees to make it stick unless bigger guns like the Sentinels backed by US Army troops came in to enforce the state's authority. Which as she'd said, Washington refused to do.

And that was how *Vulcan* came to own his own mostly independent micro-state. Or all the land and buildings, at least.

"So…he's a benevolent tyrant, right?"

"If you don't catch him in the morning."

We stacked our bowls on Charlie's washing station and Shell took me two floors down to a tiny Public Safety station on the fifth floor—because why wait for them to come find us? Like Charlie's Wok, its front door opened onto a wide balcony walkway. The single officer there checked my pass—yep I was Susan Evans—checked with Shell, and issued my guest card with a new pic because of the wig. (And no she didn't ask. What?) She also formally welcomed me to Westcamp, entered me in the tower's book, gave me the *Westcamp Guest and Visitor's Guide*, and let me know I'd need to check in here once a week until I left or made the stay permanent.

Finally she asked me if I kept or carried a gun. When I said no she handed me another brochure, *If You Keep a Gun*, just in case I changed my mind. Really?

Shell's explanation freaked me out all over again; places like Chicago had actually *stiffened* their gun laws post-Pulse—and been ignored by their own police departments after the first few horrible weeks. Chief Redmond ignored the General Confiscation Order after the first *day*. Why? Because in the food riots, the neighborhood breakdowns, the whole bloody anarchy after the Pulse, they couldn't even begin to disarm everybody—in a lot of places they'd had to deputize armed citizens just to keep from getting overwhelmed.

Did they try gun confiscation elsewhere? Some places, and it hadn't worked out at all well. Even if they'd been able to get all the *guns*, they couldn't disarm *breakthroughs*.

So armed self-defense had come back in a big way and the laws were slowly catching up to that, but in the meantime local law enforcement was openly practicing *selective* enforcement; when stopping someone carrying, an officer might do a criminal background check. If they didn't have one, no warrants or convictions, then they were cool.

And Westcamp Freehold pretty much *started* with armed civilian militia.

I couldn't imagine how my oldest brother Aaron—who Shell told me had worked at Johns Hopkins here, too—had managed to get his family safely out of Baltimore in all that. Shell wouldn't say, except that it had involved a contract and they were safe in Chicago now.

This really was Grimworld.

We walked around Westcamp, and went back to Shell's apartment. She offered the bed, since she could lie on the floor while recharging just as easily, and the evening became a session of "Did this happen?" I could have looked up a lot of stuff online much easier, but Shell could tell me what happened *instead*. Most of it was purely depressing; after hearing about Blackstone's fight with the new Mayor of Chicago—who was Mal *Shankman*—I covered my face and may have screamed a little. It beat putting my fist through something.

Shell laughed. "You okay?"

"*No.*" I lowered my hands with a sigh. "You know the old story about someone who gets three wishes? And he wastes the first wish because he's not taking it seriously, then he makes a second, *big* wish, and screws things up so bad that he has to use the third wish to undo it?"

"Um, okay?"

"The moral being that, most of the time if we got our wish we'd regret it? Well this place feels like that big stupid second wish, so now I'm feeling dumb and awful."

"Okay, now you've com*pletely* lost me."

I laughed too. It wasn't a happy laugh.

"Do you know how many times I wished that this had never happened to me? That I hadn't been under that underpass? That I'd never had my breakthrough—that I'd—that things had been *normal*? Getting you back was *great*. The rest—I always imagined that without this I'd be living in Polasky Commons with the Bees, hanging out between classes, doing just, *stuff*. Stuff that mostly didn't matter to anybody but me. And now I know that, if I hadn't—that there'd have been *this*."

"Plus a dead President."

"Don't remind me. The first day was bad enough, *that* day was the worst day of my life." And they'd made a *memorial* out of it here. That was just...

Shell stayed uncharacteristically silent until I looked up. "What?"

"It was for me, too."

"Oh." And just like that I was done. My BFF had seen me die; I couldn't top that, not ever. I nudged her with my shoulder. We'd sort of fallen together on her couch. "At least I did get *you* out of it all, back there. Here it looks like you didn't get jack."

"Till now."

And I couldn't stay. "Shell—"

"If the Teatime Anarchist had asked to copy you, would you have said yes?"

"Wait, what?" Where had *that* come from?

She turned to me, drawing her legs up, and her eyes were big and dark in her face, luminous. "He asked *me*, you know. He went back to before I jumped, told me I was going to die and said he couldn't change that but you were going to need my help later."

"He—what? That's— You were *fifteen*!"

"And not going to get any older. He needed consent, and when I gave it he wiped my memory of the whole ask. Then I went ahead and jumped."

"That's just— How do you know he did that?"

"Duh." She shrugged easily. "Recorded it. All nice and legal by late twenty-second century standards. So, would you?"

"I—" I *really* had to think about that one. "I suppose so? Yeah, I would have. There was still stuff to do and I'd want to leave *something*. But he didn't ask. Did he?"

"He had no time to go back, after. He and his twin finished their fight before he could."

The bitterness in her voice made me shiver. Mutual annihilation, leaving Shelly all alone without the job she'd been made for. Without me. *Wow*. The two of us could hold the world's biggest pity party. Despite everything I realized I was smiling, even—yes, the giggles started and I didn't stop them.

Now it was her turn. "What?"

"Do you remember—when we both had that crush on Jeremy in seventh grade? So of course when he picked *Alison* we binged on double-fudge ice cream together and puked our guts out?"

"Hey! You puked first—mine was sympathy vomiting."

"Yeah, right. Sympathy? You said *ew, gross!* and turned green as grass before hurling your load of dairy. Your mom was so maaaad..."

"My room smelled like sick for days. We had to steam-clean the carpet."

I put my head on her shoulder. "Ah, the good old days."

She shook with laughter and everything was better. Not good, but better.

"So, tell me some good came out of all this? Blackstone's alive, so the Sentinels stomped Villains Inc. just fine without me—tell me they got the Wreckers? The Ascendancy?"

She shrugged. "The *Wreckers* are active in LA, not here. And the...Ascendancy? Who are they?"

My head came up. "That *can't* be right. Dr. Pellegrini? The Foundation of Awakened Theosophy? The Ascendant, the L.O. Stadium Killer?"

"They never caught the nut-job who called himself The Ascendant." Her eyes unfocused. "Dr. Pellegrini, founder and leader of the Foundation of Awakened Theosophy. He's right here in Chicago. Are you saying..."

Oh my God. I actually felt faint.

"He's the L.O. Stadium Killer, and the Wreckers work for him! He's also the breakthrough that enabled the Dark Anarchist to trigger the California Quake and kill *fifty thousand people*. Back home he's the most wanted man in the US, and we can't *find* him! He covered his tracks too well when he—"

I froze, paralyzed. I didn't even close my mouth.

"Hope?" She nudged me.

"He's here Shell, he's *here*, and he hasn't launched the Ascendancy yet. He's in the open and he's *vulnerable*."

"Well, yeah and that's great, but you're just passing through so why are you—"

"Because if we can stop him *here*, take him down *here*, then I can get hold of all the leads he buried! All the tracks he covered up when he was closing shop on his legitimate businesses and getting ready to go full supervillain! When I get back home—"

Shelly was nodding. "You can use it all to come at him from directions he doesn't know you know about."

"Heck, I might be able to find the location of his super-secret villain's lair!" I laughed, almost giddy at the thought. If there was any rhyme or reason to my jumps, this was *it*.

After that bombshell, Shelly decided to go hunting and carefully let me know that she was going to "step out" of her prosthetic body for a bit. I didn't understand quite why she wanted to prepare me until she closed her eyes and opened them again to study me.

"Hello, I'm Galatea."

I blinked. "Yes...yes you are. How are you?"

"I am operating within acceptable parameters. Shelly told me to take care of you."

"'I'm fine' is a better way to—you know what, never mind. Is there anything you need to do?"

"I can recharge if there isn't anything you need me to do for you."

I patted her hand, filled with a crushing sense of déjà vu. "You do that. I'll just take a look around."

She went into the bedroom and lay down. A *click* told me something had connected, and I got up off the couch to wander the apartment.

Shelly and I had practically lived in each other's rooms as kids, and they'd been total expressions of our childhood and teen personalities. This place...made me wonder if Shell expressed herself elsewhere. It was neat, clean, artistically decorated, not the home of a teen or even a college student. Checking her fridge turned up guest-food—she didn't eat here by herself.

There weren't any pictures, of us or Mrs. B, but I didn't expect there to be. Shelly wasn't Shelly here; she was Elizabeth Parks, El to her friends. It wasn't like her rooms in the Dome.

Making sure my wig was in place, I finally went out to lean on the balcony. The breeze blew warm, and I watched joggers threading the walkways below me. The white of the buildings, broken only by business signs and the flowering plants everywhere, reminded me of whitewashed and sun warmed Mediterranean villages. I spotted the occasional orange-helmeted Public Safety officer, but children ran about freely. I heard laughter.

Vulcan had made a *city*. A small city, but *still*.

The sun flooded the horizon with oranges and pinks before Shelly came out to join me.

"Any luck?"

"Yes. No." She scowled. "The Foundation of Awakened Theosophy has the latest and best security. I think a Verne might be involved—it shouldn't be that good. The *government's* isn't that good. But that's something, isn't it?"

"Why would a legitimate private business be that protected? You think?" I turned away from the view. *So much for easy.* "Should we—do you think the Sentinels can help?" I'd take that hit if I had to—even if Blackstone wasn't there anymore, even if I had to see my dad, let him see me. For this I'd do it. Was that selfish?

Shelly looked...trapped? "Not a good idea. Hope, there's—something. I'm sort of a..."

"Sort of a...what?"

"Sort of a supervillain."

The world went weird for a moment, kind of like a punch to the head in training. It had to be purely psychosomatic, but my ears rang. "*No. Not* possible."

She started babbling. "Everything's broken! I know it looks—things are getting better in a lot of places, but none of it's *right*."

"Is this about the, the Public Safety and..."

"The Public Safety and Security Act, and that's just starters! After the Pulse—legal restrictions on breakthroughs are tightening everywhere. President Touches Clouds is fighting it, but with the last election Congress is mostly against her and a bunch of the states are—it's getting bad. Everybody's scared, lots blame breakthroughs for the Pulse and for making things worse afterward. There's a *resistance* forming and I'm a part of it. As Cypher I'm on the DSA's wanted list."

"But— What do you *do*?"

"Mostly low-level cybercrime, information theft, intelligence. Some pranks—the kind of embarrassing and non-lethal stuff the real Teatime Anarchist used to be known for. I help the new Underground move breakthroughs from places where the law is, you know, to places where they're welcome or at least won't be labeled and lojacked."

My perspective of the entire day shifted. "Mrs. Lori and Henry?" I almost squeaked.

"Hey, Grey House is a station on the Underground—at least it was. I don't know how soon we'll be able to use it again."

"And the Sentinels?"

"They're the *law*. They're not happy to chase down unevaluated breakthroughs, but they'll do it if it's public. They're on thin ice with the state for not helping against Westcamp before the situation got regularized."

"And today?" This couldn't be happening.

"They had no evidence Henry was escorting anybody, so they accepted his Good Samaritan story. The CPD's Superhuman Security Division might not, but we've got a guy inside who'll tell us if they decide to pull Henry in for questioning."

"Detective Fisher?"

"How did you— You know his secret, don't you?"

I nodded. "His literary roots? He told me, back home. This is just— messed *up*. What really happened this morning? How did you 'take care of it?'"

Shelly managed to look proud and guilty at the same time. "Hey, I know a guy. C-Class Mentalist, only talent is making people not notice things, but he's really *good* at it. You've met him, you just didn't notice him. He's a supervillain who calls himself Blindspot."

"Wait, when did I not notice him?

She laughed. "He was sitting in the back seat of Mrs. Lori's town car until you got most of the way out of town—why do you think Henry made that stop in the middle of nowhere? So until they served the warrant and searched Mrs. Lori's, they thought you were still there."

"He was invisible? But I didn't hear him—and I sure didn't see the door open."

"He's not invisible. People just don't pay any attention to him unless he interacts directly with them. And that goes for things he does around them, too—the cops on watch didn't see your car because he was in it and didn't want them to."

"Wow." Now *that* was a scary power, and not a little creepy. "I'm surprised you didn't mess with the traffic cameras, too."

"I did, sort of. I looped minutes here and there to edit out the town car—worked it with Henry so he only passed under a street-cam when there were no other cars in the frame with him. I could have just shut down the whole system, had him drive straight here, but then the CPD would know someone could do that."

"Right, and that would be bad."

She nodded seriously, looked at me funny. "What?"

"Nothing." I shook my head. "You just seem—older? Older than my Shellys." She wasn't justifying herself, or asking for my approval. She'd had to go up against the CPD to keep me free, and she'd done it. She'd done it, it was done, and that was it. Kind of cool, and a little disconcerting.

"Well, duh. You *died*. And then the world went to shit."

"It wasn't *on purpose*—" I shut up. Shelly looked just...*bereft*.

We went back inside.

I got a bottle of water from her fridge and tried to think. So Shelly couldn't just hack into Dr. Pellegrini's files and peel his secrets like an onion. "Can you find enough dirt on him to turn over to the government and get them started?" If the DSA even *thought* that he just might be the L.O. Stadium Killer, they'd go after him with every tool they had.

"There *might* be enough iffy stuff to make them open a case file and assign an investigation team to it if, oh, I don't know, the whole country wasn't in the toilet."

"Maybe we could talk to Blackstone? If I—"

"You sure you want to go down the DSA rabbit hole? And all Blackstone knows about me is I'm..."

"A supervillain?"

"Yeah, that."

I put the bottle against my forehead for the chill, resisted the urge to scream in frustration. *Come on, Hope. Think it through.* "So you can't hack the foundation's cybersecurity. How about if we got you inside?"

"Find their server and gain physical access? Hells yeah, nothing could stop me, then—I could copy and ghost-drive his entire system. Easier if it's a public system."

"It's not, and I know where it is. I've *been* there. Sort of."

Shelly was nodding hard. "And that could be enough for you, *and* for us to get the DSA onto him here. It won't matter if the source of the information is 'tainted' since it will come from private parties—an anonymous drop and what's one more crime to Cypher?"

"Okay." I was smiling, and pretty sure I looked a lot more like Jacky than myself doing it. "Because I really do know where The Ascendancy kept their secret server before they went public back home." I took a deep breath; I couldn't believe I was saying this. "But it's not something that you and I can do alone. We're going to need to put together a supervillain crew."

Shelly's eyes went wide, and a matching grin spread across her face while I tried not to think about all the ways this could go so very, very wrong.

And now I was a supervillain mastermind. *It's official, this reality completely and truly sucks.*

That night I used Shelly's bed, and with everything that *should* have haunted me, I dreamed of Kitsune.

It started in my bedroom at home, where I sat in my sleepshirt watching the latest Sentinels movie with Greymalkin in my lap. Except it wasn't Greymalkin, it was a silver haired and seven tailed fox I was scratching behind the ears. No, it was Yoshi, lying with his head in my lap while I ran my fingers through his silvered hair.

He stretched and sighed. "Miss me?"

"Hmm?" I could hear footsteps on the stairs.

"Did you miss me?"

Mom knocked on the door. "Honey? Don't you think it's about time you introduced us to your fiancé? You're marrying him in the morning."

I stood in front of my bedroom mirror, admiring myself in my wedding dress. "You really shouldn't be here. It's bad luck."

"Don't worry," Yoshi said behind me. "I'm not. I'll bring the rings."

I woke up with a yell. I wasn't in my bedroom, I wasn't wearing a wedding dress, and I was sitting up and floating a few inches off the bed.

"What?" Shelly asked from the floor beside the bed, where she'd gone into sleep mode. "Bad dream?" I just breathed until my racing heart settled down to not-paNikking rate.

"Not...exactly?" flopping back on the bed, I pulled the pillow over my face and screamed into it.

I hadn't had a regular Kitsune-dream since before Japan, but this hadn't been one of those; no goddess hiding in a cherry tree was pulling us together so he could pass messages. No, this had just been my luridly dreaming brain, like the fevered stuff I'd dreamed about Atlas and later Seven. It was one of my crush-symptoms.

I remembered that Shell knew perfectly well what pillow-screaming meant from me when I felt her tug on the pillow. I didn't let go.

"Okay, who is he?" She stretched out on the bed beside me.

"Nobody."

"Liar. Pillow-screams are always about boys."

"No they're not."

"Give it up." And she *tickled* me. I shrieked and brought my arms down—then panicked but she moved fast enough that my hit only pushed her hands away instead of snapping them off.

"Don't do that!" I gasped. "I could have—"

"Damaged some molyfiber muscles or joints, maybe. Doubt you could break my carbon-weave bones that easily and Vulcan would fix it. So, give. We don't have to go save the world until later and— *There's your smile.*" Bright green and not at all artificial looking eyes twinkled down at me. I groaned again but didn't replace the pillow. Sighing, I sat up and told her all about Kitsune. She listened with surprisingly few Shelly-type interruptions.

"Geez, Hope," she said when I was done. "You never do anything by half, do you?"

"It's not my fault! Everything was fine until the fairy woods!" Elbows on my knees, I wrapped my arms around my head. "It was just an *arrangement*!"

She laughed, nudging me hard enough I nearly fell over. "An arrangement where he was stalking your dates? And rescued you from the king of the fairies? You suck at arranging things and you've got feeeelings for him. Or her. Whatever."

She was right. I shuddered just remembering what it had been like. I'd opened my eyes in the woods, seen Yoshi wearing Puck's face, and *had to have him.* Then. There. Under any conditions. Love, lust, just the memory of that hot, desperate need rushing in my veins made me warm again, but at least the intoxication was gone. The love-juice hadn't just screwed with my affections, it had been a drug stealing my reason. When Titania had countered it, I'd practically felt it evaporate from my brain to leave every thought and action after opening my eyes feeling like a dream. Someone else's dream. *It hadn't been me.*

Head against Shelly's shoulder, I groaned and pulled into a tighter ball.

Because it *had* been me. A little. I *had* thought about Kitsune before—especially after we'd wound up kinda-sorta *engaged*. But it had never been in that pulse pounding and laser-focused way that signaled a serious crush. Now... *This can't be happening.*

"Hey," Shell poked my knee. "Did I break you?"

"No." Uncurling, I flopped on my back and sniffed, wiping my eyes. "But this is so *wrong*." On top of literally *everything*, I was crushing on a foreign superspy. Or a supervillain. Which was worse?

"Hey, don't— Do I need to stock up on double-fudge?"

"*No.* I need to shower."

"Okay..." She stood up. "And put your wig on, we're going to go recruiting. I'll get breakfast."

I smelled the bacon when I came out of the shower—Applewood-smoked bacon, she was getting the good stuff from somewhere. She'd gotten fancy cheese from somewhere, too, and she knew me—launching into an explanation that while a lot of things were still messed up, food production and distribution was back to more or less normal and nobody was starving. The way she rolled her eyes when she said it got a smile out of me, and the omelet really was amazing.

She had an omelet, too; Vulcan had given her great taste-buds, and she said she never wasted them.

We hashed out our initial plan over breakfast. I'd been on the other side of these things often enough working with Fisher and the CPD that I knew generally what we were going to need. The most important thing was a *driver*—if the caper got noisy then we needed a speedster, teleporter, or other breakthrough who could either extract us quickly or hide us from detection while we left the scene of the crime on our own steam.

The scene of the crime. *Am I really doing this?*

Shelly didn't see, or ignored, my stuttering attention as I tried to buck myself up. Because I *was* doing this; to get *the Ascendant* I'd do a lot more and pay whatever penance I had to after. Father Nolan would tell me how wrong that was. *I* knew how wrong it was. This time I didn't care enough to stop.

I tapped the table with my fork. "We need at least one more muscle. And someone who can drop normals without hurting them is really, really important." The best of all possible outcomes was a job where we got in, did our thing, and got out completely undetected and unopposed. Yeah, like that was going to happen.

She nodded seriously. "I can handle the unpowered opposition with my anti-riot stuff—I've got a suit for times I don't want to look like Galatea, completely expendable and untraceable. For the rest, I know where to find them. Speaking of..."

A chime at the door turned up a package that Shelly presented to me with a "Ta-dah!" Opening it I found boots, tight black leather motorcycle pants, a black cotton shirt, a green and black motorcycle jacket with an anarchy symbol stitched into the back, several pairs of panties and sports bras, and the coolest pair of dark shades I'd ever seen, black with green details.

"I know, right?" Shelly was grinning ear to ear. She'd found me a villain-rap outfit; with it and the wig I'd be ready to go on stage. "Get dressed!"

Of course she had a suit too (black with red details, same symbol), and helmets for both of us. And a black and silver street bike with room for two in parking storage. Shelly's supervillain-recruitment hunt wasn't in Westcamp, but I hadn't expected it to be; Shelly wasn't going to do anything that might jam Vulcan up, and I respected that even if this reality's Vulcan was sounding a little monomaniacal. Or more monomaniacal.

Did this Vulcan at least get out more? Maybe Shelly chauffeured him on her bike? Was this *just* a bike? Maybe it transformed into a backup for Shell? We passed through another Army checkpoint on our way to Southcamp.

"We're going to a den of vice and supervillainy," Shelly spoke in my head after the checkpoint. "It's called Dante's, used to be a sports bar. Still is, just a different clientele."

"Super!" I yelled over the wind. Her low-slung bike had me leaning far forward to get my arms around her waist, putting my helmet by her shoulder. "So they're going to think we're a couple of style-villain wannabes?"

"Maybe, but Dante keeps the place peaceful—the state would love any reason to shut it down. And I'm pretty sure the DSA actually pushes local law enforcement to keep it open so they've got all the poison apples in one tub where the damage can be contained, you know what I mean?"

"So we're going to a public supervillain hangout the DSA is probably watching, to find people to contract a crime with?"

She laughed happily. "Dante does a good job of making sure the law doesn't bug the place or get any ears inside—I'm pretty sure he pays a psychic and a witch or two to boost his security. This will be fun! Awesome Girl and Power Chick, rocking it old school!"

Yeah, if old school is the dark mirror-world where the good guys are the bad guys. This was feeling more and more like a bad idea. Our Japan adventure had started out a lot the same—and ended with me in government custody and doomed to be exposed if the Japanese government hadn't been desperate to catch bigger fish than a trio of ronin. The problem was, I couldn't think of a better idea—at least not one that involved my leaving here without getting what I needed.

Shelly drove us through the kinds of half-abandoned neighborhoods I'd seen on my way to Westcamp, but these streets got worse the further south we went. At last she turned us off the street and into a fenced-in parking lot. The building it was attached to looked like the only open business on the block, and a man in a muscle-shirt accepted a twenty and gave Shelly a numbered red ticket before letting us past his little booth.

As she coasted us into a space I removed my helmet, careful of the wig. "Nice security for a villain hangout."

"Shapeshifters."

"What?"

"Auto theft ring out of Southcamp. Uses at least one shapeshifter, so we get tickets we need to show to leave with our bike. I'm fine with that—my bike can take care of itself, but we don't want them to know that."

The secure lot was half full, with lots of pieces of junk but also some *very* high-end cars and bikes. Shelly tucked the ticket away in her jacket. "Come *on.*"

"Great. Two girls who look like they can't legally drink yet and blew out Daddy's credit card. This can't possibly go wrong." But I was smiling.

The smile dropped off my face when we stepped inside; my tactical mind took one look at the threat environment and replaced it with my warface. I'd learned it from Jacky, a straight-lipped *Don't mess with me and I won't mess you up.* I wasn't Jacky and on me it was less than intimidating unless I was in uniform, but it was the best I had.

The bar was divided into three parts; the bar itself, a table area with a big-screen TV, and a playing area with pool tables and dartboards. The interesting bit was someone had removed one wall of the playing area to widen it into a new room that was built along the lines of the inside of a bunker. I saw a weight machine built for pressing tons, and a firing range with steel targets at the end.

Because if you're a Projector-Type, why play with darts?

Except for that, it pretty much looked like a working-class sports bar—or at least what they looked like in TV shows, since silver spoon girl that I was, I'd never actually seen the inside of one. It also smelled like I'd imagined one would, like stale beer and men who weren't that concerned about hygiene, but a lot of that was just my super-duper sense of smell. It was the occupants, some of them fragrant, that had me ready for action; maybe one in four was an obviously transformed breakthrough of some kind, and half of them dressed in the street-villain version of biker gang wear.

And from the looks thrown our way, I was pretty sure that half the bar patrons were wolves checking out the two stupid lambs who had just wandered bleating into their dark little cave. Shelly started to head for the bar, but I grabbed her arm and took us to a tall club table by the wall. We drew attention away from the soccer game on the big-screen, but most of them kept it covert.

"What can I get you girls?" Our muscled server's arm tat said *Mother*. Seriously?

"A bottle of Jack and two glasses!" Shell replied before I could open my mouth to order a beer. "What?" she asked at my look. I just nodded and our server carded us and left.

I watched her go. "Do you think *Mother* is her, or her mother?"

"Does it matter? I'm sure she loves her mom."

Maybe, but I was willing to bet it was her "villain" name. Two closer patrons were transformed breakthroughs; one had little licks of flame crawling along his shoulders and through his hair, the other had sharp bone spurs sticking out of rhino-tough skin and a huge knit hat that covered his misshapen head. Both of them were obviously more than a little "happy" as they watched the game, but *Mother* didn't act scared or even cautious of either of them. Was she just really used to the clientele? Or was she an Ajax-Type?

Maybe, and a criminal record or lack of interest in military service or moving really heavy stuff around all day would explain why she worked in a supervillain bar.

She came back with the bottle and glasses, set them on our table. "Now," she said to us, "Before I open this bottle, you girls are going to have to show me that you can take care of yourselves. If you can't, you're gone."

I kicked Shelly lightly before she could protest. "That's fine. It's nice to meet you. Shake?" I held out my hand and when she took it I squeezed carefully, feeling for the strength in her muscles and bones. Her eyes widened but she squeezed back. Feeling what I'd half-expected to find, I squeezed harder before letting go. Ajax-Type. At least C Class, maybe B.

I hadn't gone for the crush, but she flexed her fingers anyway. "And her?"

"El could drink the whole bar dry, it wouldn't do a thing."

"Okay, then. Enjoy." She opened the bottle and walked away, gathering empties as she headed back to the bar.

Smart—we had Rich Victim written all over us, and she wouldn't want it to happen here. *Or maybe she just doesn't want anything bad to happen to us at all.* I caught a few eyes turned our way and stopped watching Mother. A wiry guy with a scarred and pinched face looked away when I stared back at him, and I almost laughed when I realized I was getting protective of *Shelly*. It was too easy to forget she was remote-operating a prosthetic body.

Watching her out of the corner of my eye, I hid a smile with my fingers; her eyes were darting around the bar, stopping on each patron. She was having an adventure, but it was business too. "Can you give me a virtual report?" I whispered.

"Oh! Yeah, easy." Virtual tags began popping up in my vision as I sipped my drink. I'd been far too optimistic; close to half of the bar had criminal records, and most of the rest had Public Safety and Security files. Shell supplemented those with notes from the Future Files on the ones whose breakthroughs predated three years ago. She obviously also had some kind of underworld connections; a few listed "known jobs and reps."

Honor among thieves, my tiny white butt. I wanted to arrest half of them. I had no problem with thieves except in general principle, but most of what I saw here went way beyond that into all sorts of anti-social behavior. How were we going to find someone competent, trustworthy, and not vile in this place?

"Supervillain" was a tag the press applied to any superhuman who used their powers in a public, colorful, and criminal or anti-social manner. *Villain* meant the same thing in the cape community, but we drew distinctions. There were "professional villains," who used their gifts to get money or power. Professional villains ranged from street-villains who controlled their own gangs to underworld mercenaries, thieves, and other sorts. We'd find a bunch of them here, and they'd do just about anything for money. But could we trust them and control them? It wouldn't be their normal heist-job, there'd be restrictive rules of engagement.

Then there were "cause villains," like superhuman green activists. They came with every flavor of cause—political, national, racial, ethnic, or religious—and they ranged from principled vigilantes to bloody-handed terrorists. I'd be amazed if we found any here, and they'd be unlikely to be recruitable if they were—though some might do it for money to advance their cause and they might be more trustworthy than a lot of professionals.

And finally there were "thrill villains," breakthroughs who just reveled in their powers. They loved to show them off and stroke their egos by pulling off supervillain capers as flamboyantly as possible. Since they tended to be egomaniacs as self-centered as spinning gyroscopes, if not a little crazy, I'd rather just give up than trust one of them.

A second read of the tags confirmed my sinking hopes; Dante's was full of mostly professionals or wannabe professionals, maybe three or four I'd fit into the other categories, but none of the ones I might take a chance on had the right power-sets. Where—

"There!" Shell exclaimed gleefully in my head. A patron she hadn't tagged since all we could see was the back of his head turned to laugh at another guy at his table, and we saw him in profile. "There's our driver!"

I almost spit my drink. The boy she tagged was *Jamal*.

I never read a virtual tag so fast in my life. *Juvenile record sealed (multiple assaults), adult conviction for marijuana possession, one charge of trafficking in stolen property (dropped).*

All that because I hadn't been there to steer him to Sifu? Something *cracked*, and looking down I realized I'd crushed my shot-glass. Whiskey and tiny shards dripped from my fingers and made a mess on the table.

Heads had turned for my oops, and Mother came back with a bar towel and new glass. "You alright, honey?"

"Yeah, sorry."

"You sure? New to your strength?" I could just see her wondering just how young I really was—forget about what my ID said.

"No, ma'am. And I'm fine, really."

She laughed softly. "I'm nobody's ma'am. Call me Mother, everyone does."

Hah! I grinned. "Okay, Mother. Um, that boy over there? Black, cornrowed hair?"

"The one who shouldn't be drinking either?"

"Um, yeah. Could you give him a strawberry lemonade? Strawberries in it? Virgin?"

She narrowed her eyes at me. "That's pretty specific, hun."

"Yeah. Could you give it to him?"

"Sure." She finished wiping the table and went away. I watched her make the order and wait for it. Shelly nudged me. "What's going on?"

"I know him, back— You know." I wasn't going to say *He's a Young Sentinel in my own reality!* Not where someone could easily be listening in with their X-power. Shelly's eyes widened.

"You trust him?"

"I trust him *there*. Here, we'll see." We watched Mother deliver his drink. He looked at it, asked her something I didn't hear over the noise of the soccer game, and looked at us as he tasted it. Dropping a bill on his table and laughing at the guys he sat with, he was sitting at our table with barely a detectable blur of super-speed motion.

When I didn't flinch, he grinned. My Shellys thought he was the bees' knees, and this Jamal had it too. He set his drink down.

"Which one of you girls thinks you're my mother?"

I raised a finger. "I'm pretty sure Mother thinks she's your mother, but I bought the drink. I want to talk shop and alcohol shouldn't be involved."

He looked pointedly at our bottle of Jack. "Yeah, right."

"I burn it off fast. Are you open for business?"

"Do I look stupid?" He sipped his drink and I smiled. He did love his iced strawberry lemonade. "Look at you two, all clean and shiny. Are you slumming, or cops?" When Shelly actually stuck her tongue out at him I nearly put my face in my hands. Had I thought she was more mature here?

"Shows what you know," she snarked. "Call Calvin, ask about El."

Jamal looked as stunned as I about the whole tongue thing, but he found his grin, pulled out his cell, and started texting. He looked at the reply, back at Shelly.

"Black hair, smart ass, yeah I guess that's you. Say cheese." He took her picture and sent it, read the next text. "You really pay that well?"

"Well enough to get you to Disneyland, so, yeah."

He turned back to me. "Smarty here is your moneybag?"

"She knows him."

"So what do you have in mind?"

I shrugged like it was no big deal. "Some B&E with not much B. The package is digital, not physical. We just need a designated driver to make sure we're home in time for dinner."

"How many?"

"Four."

"And no cut of the package? Then it's ten grand a head." He held up his hands before Shelly could get her word in. "Hey, driving safe is worth it." His eyes stayed on me. *So who's the crew boss here?*

I smiled to let him know that was me. "Ten grand a head. You can ride all the rides in the Magic Kingdom. In all of them."

"Deal. What's your number?" It was evil, but I gave him Shelly's. He put it in his phone and then a hand came down on my shoulder. It was a big hand, but I managed not to jump. I turned my head to follow the hand up back to its owner. Its big owner.

I named him Harry, because he was; he had a mullet and a dark beard that hadn't been washed in too many days. His muscles had muscles, pumped like he'd just come from the gym after curling a few hundred pounds while snacking on raw steaks and steroids. Another Ajax? Lots of Ajax and Atlas-Types didn't look any different after their breakthrough (I was a regretful example of that), but lots more got transformed outwardly as well as inwardly—if you're going to *be* strong you should *look* strong.

He checked me over with the kind of eye that saw a potential toy instead of a potential threat. Not very experienced? Well, I could be his first real experience if I had to. "Do you want to lose that?" I nodded at his hand.

He actually leered. "Be nice little girl, and you'll enjoy it."

"I'm not charmed. Go away."

"You're not *listening*." His leer turned nasty and he squeezed, which confirmed what the virtual tag Shelly popped up said about him. And that was good, since beside me Shelly was getting to her feet; my BF was going to *do something*, and I couldn't let her do that. Our little drama had caught the attention of the tables around us, and whatever she pulled out to smack him with would be a lot less generic than what I could do.

I sighed theatrically. "Fine, I'll enjoy it. Gimme a second." I grabbed the bottle of Jack with my free arm and guzzled it down, dropped it back on the table. "Alcohol does it for me." I wiped my lips, and hit him.

He really was stupid; when his squeeze hadn't made me shriek in agony and start begging he should have realized I was one of *those*, but he didn't even try and move as I rose and pivoted around his grip to punch him into the wall behind us.

Not *through* the wall; it had obviously been reinforced. He stuck in it comically, like a cartoon-character trying to exit and leave a human-shaped hole, head buried deeper than the rest of him. His bellow and the smash grabbed the attention of the rest of the bar.

Harry didn't seem that popular; only two guys stood up looking indignant at my refusal of his advances. Unfortunately, one was Rhino Skin, and he didn't seem all that impressed by the way I'd turned Harry down. He cracked knuckles and more bone spurs popped out. *Aha.* I kept the shock off my face, but even though that changed things up I still needed to play it out. I reached for Harry; he'd make a great first missile.

Whangggg.

The sharp sound startled me, and Rhino Skin sank to the sticky floor. Mother stood beside him holding a baseball bat that I had to guess was made out of a piece of steel girder.

She pointed it at the rest of the bar. "Sit down, you posers! She's paying for the wall, Billy and Bony are paying the bar fine for starting shit, and who else wants to pay?"

Nobody else wanted to pay. "El?" I said softly. "Bony?"

"A Class Ovid-Type."

"Riiiiight." I sat back down, scooting my chair out of the way as Mother stepped around me to yank Billy out of the wall and drag him through the tables as he protested feebly. I might have hit him a bit hard. "Pay up, El, we're leaving."

"Really? But—okay."

Jamal had sat there through the whole thing. "Call tonight," I told him on my way past. Shelly threw some bills on the table and scooted after me, but didn't say anything until we made it to the parking lot.

"That was *sick*," she exulted as soon as we were clear. "Again! Alcohol does it for you? When did *that* happen?"

"It didn't. It doesn't." Actually, chugging almost the entire bottle of whisky hard was hitting me a bit and I did feel a little light, but it would go away in maybe five minutes. "It was a show."

"It was badass is what it was. Why did you do it?"

"What were you going to do?"

"I've got a capacitor in my left arm with enough juice to drop an elephant."

"Oh." That would have actually been subtler than what I'd done. Was Grimworld getting under my skin?

"But we didn't find another muscle for the crew!"

"Yes we did. I'll just have to make our pitch privately."

We road back to Westcamp, and as we wound our way through the different neighborhoods I realized that I was beginning to get a feel for the gradations of control. The ones closest to the Southcamp I still hadn't seen were half-abandoned, and a lot of the people we passed on the street seemed to be "loitering with intent." Their business was street business, and the police I could see patrolled in armored cars.

Getting closer to Westcamp we passed fewer abandoned businesses and empty streets. People were using the streets, on foot or by car, to get somewhere. I actually saw fewer armored patrol cars, but I also spotted marked private security vehicles and even security kiosks.

More private solutions to government breakdown?

Westcamp itself had a two-block ring around it where I saw police, conspicuously armed citizens, and even a pair of orange-vested Westcamp Public Safety Officers. Only one or two businesses were abandoned, and the streets bustled. So maybe West Chicago was recovering.

We put the bike back in parking, showing our passes at the Public Safety booth—the officers didn't even blink at our "villain-rap" outfits—and got beef kebobs for lunch at a Greek food kiosk.

And I felt a tug on my leg.

"Hello." Big brown almond eyes under a dark mop looked up at me. He had a firm grip on my leather bike pants.

"Hello back. What's your name?"

"Jun. What's your name?"

"It's—" What was my name? Jun watched me expectantly, and I had no idea how to answer him. I'd lost track.

Peeking around my shoulder to see who I was talking to, Shelly leaned down. "It's Susan, but you can call her Awesome Girl. Or you can call her Awesome."

I almost squeaked, glared at her before making myself smile. "That's right, I'm Awesome Girl. Are you alone, Ju—" Obviously not; a harried looking Asian woman bearing down on us with an eye lock on the little guy said otherwise.

"Jun yah!" She grabbed his hand and turned to me. "I'm sorry—"

"It's alright, ma'am," I cut in hurriedly. "It's nice to meet your son. Really."

"She's Awesome Girl!"

My blush matched Jun's mom's.

"I am sorry," she repeated. "Jun collects capes, their pictures for his wall and webpage."

"He already has mine," Shelly laughed. "Piggy-back." She gave me a look I read easily.

"Would you like one with me, Jun? Is that alright, Mrs…"

"Bae. And yes, thank you."

"Okeydokey!" I handed Shelly my kebob and when Mrs. Bae let go of Jun I snatched him, screaming laughter, into the air to lightly turn and drop him onto my shoulders. Obviously a veteran of such maneuvers, he didn't even grab my hair. Mrs. Bae took the first picture with her phone, after which I held the little guy upside down by one leg for more pictures just for good measure. I'd have tickled him, but he was already laughing so hard I was pretty sure he'd pee himself.

With a last lift and flip, I set him down and held onto his shoulders until he looked like he wasn't going to fall over.

"Thank you!"

A beaming Mrs. Bae echoed Jun's sentiments with more restraint, then captured his hand again to lead him away while lecturing him on touching without permission. I watched them disappear into the crowd as the knot of people who'd stopped to watch us broke up.

We started walking again, me watching Shell out of the corner of my eye. "Jun's webpage? Awesome Girl? You did that on purpose."

She shook her head, grinning. "Nope. But it's a good thing. The pics will be up before dinner."

"But *Awesome Girl*?" That had been my teen cape-name with Shelly before. I didn't think anyone would recognize it—it had been a private joke—but still not a good idea. Even so, dark shades, wig, generic if colorful villain-fashion, I was safely unrecognizable. (And if Jun thought I looked *cape*, the lines around here might be blurring a bit.)

On our way back to Shelly's place, I told her which muscle I'd spotted at Dante's. She got the abstracted look that said she was doing her cyber-thing.

"Dante said he'd pass along your message, but don't come back to the bar. He'll get us a contact number if there's interest."

"That hardly seems fair." I'd been banned from a supervillain hangout. Cool, but *still*.

"Billy's out, too. Dante doesn't give a lot of second chances, and Billy was on his second. As for you, he apologized but said if you came around again there'd be a line of idiots wanting to test themselves against you."

"What, to fight?"

"No, to drink. That whole bottle of Jack thing was cool, but not smart."

I threw back my head and laughed. I felt good. Winding my arm through Shelly's, I tugged her along. "C'mon, let's get off the street and out of these clothes before someone else wants to fight or take pics."

Back at her place Shelly "stepped out" again to devote more of herself to Vulcan stuff, leaving Galatea to act as hostess. When I asked, she set me up on Shelly's completely-for-show personal computer (I assumed she kept the thing as both a red herring and Trojan horse for anyone who actually penetrated "El's" physical or cyber security). I spent the next few hours web-searching the post-Pulse legal situation (it was cool to see that Legal Eagle was leading the plaintiff's legal team in *Turner v. Illinois*) and the status of people like Jamal who I'd met post-Whittier Base. Then I made the mistake of looking to see what was going on with friends.

Annabeth was *dead*.

The New York Red Bulls had been playing in Kansas City, and Annabeth had flown down to cheer for Dane. He'd survived the night of the Pulse, but her plane had gone down over Kansas.

It wasn't possible. I felt like I was floating outside my body.

Cold, barely breathing—breathing meant I was *here* and not dreaming—I did multiple searches, even found a federal post-Pulse database of the dead and missing. Everything confirmed it, and I stared at the heartbreaking memorial on her social page.

Had she been scared? Had it been quick?

And what had they gone through, Julie, Megan, and Dane? Oh God, *Dane*. Just the thought turned my heart to a lump of ice in my chest. He'd been my second young crush and never, ever, known because wonderful, beautiful Annabeth had picked him out for herself. It wasn't that I couldn't have worked up the courage to let him know, but I'd have never done that to Annabeth. He'd always been her Lancelot, her faithful and devoted knight. They'd been a fairy tale.

I read *everything*, carefully and over again. Not because I disbelieved it anymore but because I hadn't been there, with Dane and the rest of the Bees, to live it with them.

"Do you need anything?"

I blinked, tore my blind gaze from the screen. Galatea watched me with an expression as close to concern as she could manage.

"No. No, I'm fi— I'll be alright." I couldn't lie now, not even to a gynoid robot who was sometimes possessed by my friend.

"Your heartrate is elevated. Your breathing is irregular. You're crying. How may I help you?"

"You can't. But thank you." Standing without thinking, I threw open Shelly's closet and found my bag. I'd carefully repacked everything, and now I dumped it all out on her bed, tore open the protective box I'd picked up for the snow globe two realities ago.

Flakes of snow floated loose around Chicago's skyline. Sometime between yesterday morning and today it had recharged. I could go. Now. Before I saw any more. I couldn't *take* any more. I couldn't.

"Hope, I'm sorry."

I looked up and Galatea's face had changed, filled with pain and regret. Shelly was back.

"You *lied*. You said everyone was alright."

"Yes, I did." She dropped to the bed beside me, wrapping her arms around me as I clutched the globe in both hands. "Tell me everything I need to know about the Ascendant and I'll finish the job. You shouldn't be here."

"This place *sucks*." I choked on a sobbing laugh, sniffled wetly and messily.

"It hasn't been much fun for me, either." That brought more choking laughter as I cried into her hair.

"I *hate* this thing." I shifted my shaky grip on the globe, held it close in my lap. "I want to go *home*."

"Go."

"Can't." I straightened with another sniff. "You know that."

"Yeah." She sighed and let me go. "I know. Not until the job's done. You always were stubborn."

"*Me*? Right."

"Well, when you really knew what you wanted. Which wasn't that often—usually you left that to me. Come on." She took the globe and set it on my pile of stuff before pulling me up. "It's time for the double-fudge."

We toasted Annabeth with clinking spoons over ice cream while I told her all about the best of the Bees.

Then we got in our first fight. Dante reached out to Cypher and let her know that the muscle we were interested in was interested back, and gave us a time and a place. I insisted on going alone to minimize exposure, and Shelly didn't think being my virtual wingman would be enough.

I finally argued her around to my plan, and she countered by bringing out extra insurance. While I'd been traumatizing myself surfing the internet, she'd been busy; now she presented me with my new costume. Apparently the villain-style biker outfit had just been for barhopping.

"Ta-dah!"

It was a black skintight bodysuit that covered me from ankles to wrists to a high closed collar. It wasn't all black; my crest and thick white seam lines broke the suit's darkness. The center seam bisected the suit down the middle of the front from collar to crotch and up my back, and matching seams ran from my collar down my sides, arms, and legs. Despite the seams and texturing it felt sprayed on, and the white crest...

"Real subtle, Shell." The crest lay across the center seam and it was my white eight-pointed star, only with a thick black diagonal bar through the center to cut it in two broken pieces.

She snickered. "Really, it is. You'd be amazed how many female capes have adopted some variation of your star since you saved the president of the freaking country and killed Seif-al-Din with his own sword."

"And died. I did that too." I swallowed, looked away from the mirror and grabbed the matching white gloves and boots. "The cleaning bill is going to be huge."

"It's Vulcan's stuff—dirt and blood will come right off and it's almost as tough as you are. It's chameleon cloth, too—it's got a stealth mode."

"And the helmet?" The white shiny-visored half helmet matched the suit.

"That too. It's rigged with full heads-up-display and com links, not that you'll need them with me."

It also came with another black wig, visible below the helmet once I'd put it on. I hadn't worn a wig with my mask since being outed as a cape and wasn't really used to it anymore, but it was a smart precaution. Still...

"And check this out. Bibbity, bobbity, *boo!*" Shell wiggled her fingers and the suit shifted to brilliant white with blue seams and crest. Even the helmet changed.

I laughed. "So you're my fairy godmother now? Well the back seam is riding up my— Anyway, I don't think I'll be using this setting. It's way too on the nose."

She sighed and the whole outfit went chameleon-mode. "But you look good. I'll arrange to get Jamal into Westcamp as soon as he calls, you go close the deal with muscle-guy."

I was beginning to think that any actual supervillain organization that had Vulcan and Shelly as their suppliers would be unstoppable. Giving her a mock-salute, I stepped out on the balcony and went straight up into the deepening blue of the evening sky.

The suit and helmet covered everything but the top of my neck and lower half of my face, making me virtually invisible from more than ten or a dozen yards away in its chameleon mode. "*Helmet telemetry and coms check,*" Shelly—Cypher—said in my ear. "*If we're going to do it old school, this'll work.*"

"Paint me the rendezvous?"

She brought up a targeting icon on the visor heads-up display, thoughtfully added a countdown to the meeting time, and I grinned. "More detail than I needed, but thanks."

"*Any time, I'll leave you to it.*"

I dropped into a swoop, gliding along about a hundred feet above the rooftops. The chosen spot sat north of Southcamp, about equidistant from Chicago and West Chicago, in an abandoned vehicle park. Storage buildings hid the park from the street, giving us open space and privacy; it was just us and some feral cats. Landing lightly, I dropped my camouflage and my potential recruit stepped out of the shadow of an unhitched semi-trailer.

"You're early," Bony said. His voice sounded like grinding rocks, and the bone spurs that pierced his tough hide gleamed white in the moonlight. He glowed like a furnace in my infrared sight.

I laughed. "I thought I'd get here first and see how you arrived. At least that was the plan. Is Nix with you? Or Nox?"

I take my priceless moments where I find them, and this was so absolutely one of those moments. Grendel *flinched,* his whole body one big twitch. And that answered my question; whatever the reason for his really different look, this Grendel worked for Ozma. Or had.

"And you can take off that ugly hat. I know how you are about *the hair*."

He actually *growled*. It had sub-harmonics in it, and I couldn't keep the wide grin off my face. "But thanks for almost coming to my rescue, back at Dante's. That is what you were doing when Mother clocked you, right?"

"What do you want?" Not *How do you know me?* Not *Who are you?* And that told me something else. He took something out of his pocket and looked at it before scanning the night sky. I didn't ask; I had bigger questions.

"It was the Question Box, wasn't it? It told Ozma to send you on up here to meet me, and you don't even know why. I wonder how she decoded that poem."

"Some shit about finding the maids with Virgil's disciple." He still sounded like he was contemplating ripping my head off, but that was just disgruntled Grendel and he did take his awful hat off to release his beautiful dreadlocks. However he might change himself for disguise, he'd *never* get rid of the hair.

Speaking of change... "So what's with the thorny look? Isn't that a bit uncomfortable?"

"Not for long." The bone spurs started receding as I watched, his skin smoothing out. A few breaths later he was the Rastafarian troll I knew and loved.

I just wanted to hug him; he wasn't my Grendel, but ever since he'd carried me out of the Ascendant's base—how we first met—I'd always had a warm spot for him. He might be terrifying to others, but to me he was like a Bengal Tiger, beautiful and wild (and his deep growly voice seriously did it for me). Also *my* Grendel was a complete softy under his trollish exterior, and I really couldn't see this Grendel being any different. Not if he was still working for her royal majesty the Empress of Oz.

"So are you going to tell me who you are and why you know all my shit?" He still stood balanced and loose, ready to rumble—probably why he'd gotten rid of the decorative spikes that could only get in his way. I forced a serious look.

"I'm part of the Royal Army of Oz, at least I am where I come from. I can't stay, but if you'll help me I'm pretty sure I can add to Ozma's army here. And I'm going after the Ascendant." This was *twice* the enigmatic Question Box had directed Ozma and Grendel into a situation where he could learn who'd killed his parents; I had no idea why it was so important in Ozma's campaign to regain the Emerald Throne, but it obviously was.

And I'd pushed the right button; just hearing *the Ascendant* had Grendel bulking up, hunching his shoulders and adding muscle mass until he forced himself straight

So I gave my pitch, bare facts and no spin. I wasn't going directly at the Ascendant, just his organization. There'd be no room for personal vengeance, just justice if we succeeded. He didn't like that, and I was pretty sure that if he ever did actually encounter Dr. Pellegrini then he'd try and rip the man's head off—which made it good that the odds of a meet were pretty low.

Even with the stakes involved I couldn't quite keep the cheer out of my voice; it was great to see him. He picked up on it, which just deepened his scowl. "You'd better not be jerking me," he said when I finished.

"No jerking. Promise. I wouldn't dare." I tried to look serious. He didn't buy it, but obviously decided that my only half-successful attempt not to grin wasn't a sign of untrustworthiness. "So here's the plan," I went on. "We need—"

"*Hope, you've got incoming!*" Shell shouted in my ear.

"Brian, get out! Now!" I launched into the night sky, doing a three-sixty spin as I rose. Hearing a roar of wind below me, I didn't look down. Travel Dust—Grendel was gone and I only had to worry about me.

There—coming in from Chicago, a glow I instantly recognized, Variforce's softly shining golden force-fields closing on me fast. *Oh, crap on a—*

The hit sent me tumbling, and I pushed into the vector of my spin as the sparks cleared from my eyes. It had been Watchman who hit me, and looking back and up I could see that Variforce had decoupled his towing field to float on his own. And he'd brought Lei Zi and *Dad* with him, netted in his Watchman-pulled fields for speed. Turning I found they'd bracketed me between them: Lei-Zi, Dad, and Variforce to my north, Watchman to my south. So why was Watchman just hanging there instead of being all over—

The second hit blacked me out with a star bursting in my brain. This time I cleared to find the ground rushing up at me, barely had time to twist so that whatever weight was clinging to me hit *first*.

Which didn't soften the bouncing, rolling impact at all. My diaphragm froze on the first smash, locking my lungs into gasping spasms as the world spun around me. Completely disoriented, I didn't even know which way was up and barely noticed the concrete wall that gave its life to stop my sliding crash. When the world stopped hitting me and I finally got a lungful of air I struck out blindly at—*Iron Jack*.

My swinging fist caught him beside his ear, but I didn't have the right angle for it and he barely moved his head. Lei Zi had fired my *dad* at me; he still sizzled and sparked from the after-effects of being shot at me like an iron bullet from a virtual railgun of her electromagnetic fields—I'd seen them practice the move back home.

"Stand down!" he yelled. "Stand down! We don't want to hurt—" My bear hug wasn't any kind of fighting move at all.

I let go instantly, but not before Variforce's fields settled over us both like a tide of mercury, fluid and heavy, to forcibly separate us. I didn't resist; a wrong move now would bring a bolt of current down on me that I'd survive but not enjoy one bit. I could take Lei Zi. I could take Variforce. I could escape Dad, maybe even Watchman. I couldn't handle them all. Variforce' field loosened its hold and, and I put my hands on top of my helmet (which Vulcan had designed *really* well). Shelly wasn't talking, electronically or virtually, and I could only guess that she'd gone silent to avoid discovery or she was being blocked. Either way, I was on my own for now—the good news was that having all of their attention on me meant that Brian had likely gotten completely away. No roaring or sounds of things smashing gave me hope of that.

Dad—Iron Jack—stood and pulled me up. I let him, rising slowly and making no move to take my feet off the ground, as the others touched down around us. The whole heavy team. Somebody really wanted me bad.

"You're under arrest for violations of the Public Safety and Security Act," Dad said. "An arresting officer will be here shortly to read you your rights. Don't be stupid."

I'd never thought faster. I was not going to let myself get taken into custody by the CPD in a city run by Mal Shankman; the police might be staging a covert Blue Rebellion, but I couldn't count on that meaning anything for me and Shankman's people. Can't run. Can't fight. Can't be taken—

"I demand to be taken into federal custody," I blurted, dropping my hands.

That set them all back. Lei Zi's eyes narrowed. "This is a city and state matter."

"No, it's not. I'm an incursion, and that puts me directly under the jurisdiction of the Department of Superhuman Affairs."

Incursion. Someone or something entering the world from an extrareality. By definition from somewhere else, therefore foreign, therefore the DSA's concern, not to mention the State Department's. Lei Zi's eyes widened, and then her face set. Sparks crackled along her skintight bodysuit.

"Take off your helmet."

I shook my head. "Not until you order a coms blackout for Dispatch and stand the police down. National security." It was a bluff, but a small one. Clenching my fists to hide shaking hands, I didn't look at Dad.

Lei Zi didn't like that, either, but she half turned away and started talking into her Dispatch link. I could have listened, but the approaching sirens were more than a little distracting.

They stopped approaching, and I stopped breathing.

She turned back. "Dispatch has routed us directly to the Chicago DSA office, and is not listening or recording at the Dome. That's the best you'll get."

I nodded, took a steadying breath, and slowly reached up. Unbuckling my chin strap, I lifted my helmet and wig off and dropped my hands to let it swing at my side.

"Hi, Dad."

I ended the night in a nice hard cell.

Before the wagon arrived—a DSA bus, not a CPD one—they had me put my helmet back on and then cuffed me. The Blacklocks were wide and thick, joined by only a thin wire, and Watchman promised me that if I broke the wire the cuffs would put enough volts into me to knock out Atlas. And of course a GPS trigger would do the same if I tried to just fly away.

The DSA agents—all of them Platoons—didn't lock me down in the bus. My team stood and watched, Dad taking an aborted step towards me as they closed the doors and got us moving. On the other end of my ride, the doors opened on a familiar bay and I relaxed. A little. They'd played it straight and brought me to the DSA's Chicago center, and they had their own hard cells and guards. *Good so far...*

It was a risk; if I'd gone into the CPD system, I could have yelled for a lawyer immediately and been pretty sure of getting one quick— possibly Legal Eagle—before the federal government learned of my existence and moved to take custody. But the *DSA* could drop me in a hole for days with only their own cleared federal judge knowing of my existence while they determined my status. Technically an illegal alien and potential security threat, I could find myself in the cells of our Guantanamo naval base without ever speaking to anyone else. So if things were too dicey since the Pulse...

Platoon treated me nice. Maximum-security procedure called for a strip-search, but they just took my boots, gloves, and helmet, letting me keep my costume on after passing a wand over it—not that I could have hidden even a credit card under it. One of them had me recite my Miranda Rights and I ended with "I understand these rights as I have just stated them."

He smiled. "Good to see you again."

"Tell Bob, Tom, and Willis I said hi. Oh wait, you don't have to."

Nothing looks funnier than synchronized smiling, but that was the only unprofessional word out of the five Platoons escorting me as they logged me in at the processing station, took me to my cell, and detached the wire on my Blacklocks, leaving the wide cuffs on but my wrists freed.

The only non-Platoon agent present, a young woman probably just a couple of years older than me, logged my lockdown on her epad with one of their thumbprints and her own. Agent Alexis Grace had me state my own name for the record as well, let me know that she was my custodial agent and I could call if I needed anything, and closed the cell door. It closed on hydraulics and with a decidedly solid sound, telling me it was as thick as the walls.

Not that I needed to be told, having escorted a few villains into them myself.

Still no Shelly. Did the DSA know enough about quantum-signaling transmission to detect or block her? Or was she mum since I was most certainly being monitored at every level—probably right down to a brain-activity scan.

I shrugged. It *was* a nice cell, much nicer than the ultra-secure one Defensenet had put me in a few months ago. It had a connected bathroom that offered the illusion of privacy, a bed, and a wall-mounted table with two chairs; it even smelled fresh, in an institutional way. It was the kind of cell given to a breakthrough whose powers made her tougher and more dangerous than anything in the cell she could possibly use as a weapon.

And I was glad to finally be "alone." Dropping to the bed, I stared at the ceiling.

"I need to talk to Veritas," I informed my listeners, and closed my eyes to think.

Or try not to think.

Dad. He'd just *stood* there, not saying a word. Which had been exactly what I'd wanted him to do, at least until I wasn't under arrest anymore, or not until they understood anyway. I really couldn't begin to imagine what he had to be feeling. I was *dead.* Heroically and horribly dead. So what was I now? Who was this person, who looked and sounded like his daughter? I could be a trick—a shapeshifter (even if one strong enough to mimic an A Class Atlas-Type was pretty unlikely). I could be a delusional Astra fan who became the object of her obsession. Really, I could. Or I could be a lost Hope Corrigan, from a world where she hadn't broken her promise to her parents and died.

I sat up, rubbed my eyes with fisted hands. Would he tell Mom? *No.* Not until he was sure, one way or the other. Maybe not even then— how could it be good for Mom, for anybody? It was my worst-case scenario come to awful life.

And this wasn't doing any good. Folding my legs into lotus position, I began Chakra-taught breathing exercises. Getting half blind-sided by Watchman and shot with my dad had left me a bundle of aches, but I eventually relaxed enough to sleep.

They provided a toothbrush and a laundry service with a nice robe until I got my costume and underwear back, making this officially the nicest cell I'd ever been in. Just the thought of how wrong it was to be able to make that kind of comparison made me smile, but if it wasn't for the vault door and the titanium cuffs with voltage I was still wearing I wouldn't know I was detained. Breakfast was butter and syrup-drenched Belgian waffles.

I hadn't been dressed and finished eating for more than a few minutes when the door opened again and a guard—not a Platoon— appeared with Agent Grace; nobody ever came through the door without her attendance. The guard took my breakfast tray under the agent's watchful eye, and left. Which left me with my custodial agent. She gave me a friendly smile. "Are you ready for visitors?"

The waffles settled uncomfortably. "Who?"

"You asked for Agent Veritas last night. He's here."

Yes! No. Wait. I felt hot and cold at once. I'd said it almost as a test—to see if the Cutter of Gordian Knots was still alive in this reality and if I had enough juice to get him here. I couldn't lie to him, but did I want to? Did I have anything, now, to lie about? And my encounters with the man had left me with the sneaking suspicion that he couldn't lie to me, either; he might not tell me everything, but maybe, just maybe, he had clearance high enough to tell me what I now desperately wanted to know. *How bad is it? Really?*

I swallowed and nodded, staying in my chair. "Yes, please."

Once I'd thought him the evil minion of the Director, head of the DSA. Now I knew he was just the Director's main fixer, the man sent to Get Things Done, good or bad. He looked at me with hands on hips, head cocked and eyes hidden behind shades, and when he nodded to Agent Grace she closed the door to leave us alone.

We'd be recorded, of course.

"We meet again, Miss Corrigan. How many times is it, now?"

"This makes it three times, in person."

He nodded. "Interesting. Our first was in the Dome? After the Freakshow Riot?"

"Yes."

"And the second?"

I swallowed hard and played my first card. "You took me to Littleton to meet an interesting snake."

He looked up at the ceiling. "Stop all recording. Clear and seal the observation room, and flip the lights when you're done." He took off his shades and waited. Maybe a couple of minutes went by, and then the lights flickered. He pulled out the second chair, and sat.

"Miss Corrigan, given the nature of this cell, we are now as private as two people can possibly be. Tell me about the snake."

"The Ouroboros Group. Do you know who they worked for?"

"Do you?"

"The real Teatime Anarchist."

"And now they work for us. Likewise, in your reality?"

Letting out my breath, I nodded; I hadn't been sure of anything that might have happened here, after I'd died. I remembered that John—Atlas—had left a message and video files for Blackstone, but...

"Miss Corrigan. We could waste a great deal of time playing *do you know*. You have proven that you are not a delusional breakthrough—there is no way that a mere Astra copy could know about something that highly classified that you never experienced here."

I blinked. I hadn't even thought of that.

"So let's move to the next big question. You believe that you are Astra, from another reality?"

"Yes. And I think that this reality was the same, until I died at Whittier Base here. It might have diverged earlier than that, but not enough that the Whittier Base Attack didn't happen."

"What kinds of divergences have you noticed since arriving?"

I bit back a laugh. "The Pulse, and everything after."

He looked at me for a long silent moment. "You stopped the Pulse, in your reality?"

"I was part of the Omega op. And I had help."

"I see." Sitting back, he rubbed his brow. He looked tired. "For want of a nail, indeed. What do you want?" *Why did you come here? Why are you recruiting supervillains?*

Sitting on my shivering excitement, I played my second card. "I want complete freedom of movement until I leave. I can give you The Ascendant, next best thing to gift-wrapped, if you'll let me—"

"No."

Just that: *No.* No bargaining.

"Why?"

"Because we are on the edge of the abyss and skating very carefully past it. Because since the Pulse we have managed, with the Ouroboros Group, one psychohistorian Verne, and a quintet of variously-gifted precogs, to push ourselves back towards hope for the Good Future that you undoubtedly know about. A couple of days ago, something happened that put two of the quintet into comas. The other three are still uselessly incoherent. And now here you are—an incursion from outside of history, a piece of a road not taken. We don't know for certain, but the smart peoples' consensus is until you're gone and no longer an outside agent of change we're flying blind."

I slumped back, stunned.

"So, can you return home on your own?"

"I— I know how to leave."

"Can you do it from here?"

"No." There was no way I was calling Shelly to have my stuff delivered.

"Then I will see about putting together a detail that will escort you to wherever you need to go to accomplish that and only that. Until then, you will remain here. Do we understand each other?"

I nodded weakly.

"Good. Will you promise not to say anything of what we have spoken of? If you can promise me that, there are a few people who wish to speak with you. The detail will be ready tomorrow, and until then you can decide how much you want to tell us about the Ascendant and what other intelligence you can leave with us."

"Yes. I promise."

"Good." Veritas stood, donning his shades with a thin smile. "And Miss Corrigan? It is...heartening, to see that somewhere you are well." He touched the panel by the door and the lights flickered again. "Open up." The bolts in the door thunked, unsealing it to swing open. Agent Grace signed him out, and they were gone.

Which left me regretting my breakfast and wondering if I should have refused to speak to anyone. Because I knew who wanted to see me. *I don't know if I can do this.*

The next one through the door, just before lunch, wasn't who I'd expected. I should have. Agent Grace gave me a sympathetic smile before stepping out to leave me alone with Lie Zi. The tall, athletically fit electrokinetic field leader of the Sentinels (and team leader now that Blackstone was gone?) looked me over before pointing to the table. We sat.

This Lei Zi wore a bodysuit with more armor elements to it than my Lei Zi's did, and her hair was cut so short it barely touched her neck, but she was still Lei Zi and she studied me coolly. "You are a Sentinel?"

I nodded.

"Then report."

And I did: my survival at Whittier Base and every team action taken after the attack, the post-attack lineup, the formation of the Young Sentinels, everything not classified (like Shelly and Littleton and the whole Japan thing) right up to the bad result of my mission to trap Red Jack. I didn't tell her anything about The Ascendancy, but even with that omission it took a while. Another guard brought us lunch.

She raised an eyebrow when she heard that in my reality both Crash and Grendel were Sentinels, and silently considered it all when I finished.

"So two nights ago, when you arrived, why didn't you come to the Dome?"

I winced, partly from her look—*Why didn't you report?*—but mostly from the memory. "I saw the memorial."

"I see." And Lei Zi did; she might act like an almost emotionless commander sometimes, but she was good at seeing what was in front of her and acknowledging it. "And after? I assume that, given the current situation, you dropped underground? I won't ask if that was you with the carjack gang yesterday, but it was a good job."

"And I don't know what you're talking about, but thanks." A lie she understood and let pass. I straightened up, tried to look only politely curious. "Why did you come after me, last night?"

"We didn't. We came after an unknown A Class Atlas-Type. And we wouldn't have, except that after disappearing with only a parting gift for the police, twice, you popped up again. Apparently to recruit a villain crew."

"You have eyes at Dante's? How did you know it was— Oh."

It was obvious how they knew. I'd screwed up. I'd shown too much in Dante's when I put Billy into the wall; only an Atlas-Type could have done what I did.

Sure Ajaxes were *strong* enough to do what I'd done, but Billy had to have massed maybe three hundred pounds—while I, as Mom liked to say, weighed as much as a goose. Physics meant that no matter *how* strong I was, a slip of a girl like me couldn't move a pile of bricks like him unless I had either leverage or a lot of force behind my swing—and force meant momentum, which required mass and velocity. Less mass required more velocity, and even leaning into it my small fist would have needed to be traveling fast as a bullet for my little weight to have pushed him more than a step or two, forget about into the wall.

No, for me to do what I'd done required the extra *push* that Atlases came with—the invisible push that allowed us to fly by will alone. What I'd really done by *leaning in* was fly behind my fist without going anywhere or taking my feet off the floor, and *that* was what had given me the force put Billy into the wall.

I almost put my head on the table; so much for staying *covert*. Atlas-Types were lots rarer that Ajaxes, and since Billy was a B Class Ajax, what I'd done to him told anyone with an experienced eye all they'd needed to know about me. For anybody looking at both incidents, the probability that I was also the mystery-girl who'd raced a missile over Chicago was pretty close to certainty.

The corner of Lei Zi's mouth twitched when I didn't speak. "Yes, *oh*. And you were very impressive both times. Drawing out that Paladin team is a gift we owed you for."

"So you put me low on your priority list until I made you take notice by recruiting."

"Yes. Will you tell me what you hoped to do?" *That couldn't be done by us?* Biting my lip, I shook my head.

"I see. Veritas informs me that you are a federal matter now, and will be departing shortly. Is there anything I can do for you?"

Don't let Dad see me. Biting my lower lip I almost drew blood with my teeth, I but shook my head again.

Lei Zi stood. "Very well. It was interesting to meet you, and I wish you well with your departure." *Don't stay in my town.*

I wouldn't. Not for long, anyway. We shook hands with military precision, and once the door closed behind her I collapsed into my chair.

Well, that wasn't too bad. Who was I kidding? It was going to get a lot worse.

The day passed, dinner came, and I'd almost decided that Dad wasn't going to come visit, when he did. Agent Grace actually had the decency to ask if I was okay with seeing him, and I didn't say no.

Which didn't help me prepare at all for when Iron Jack stepped into my cell.

It was a good thing that Dad was ironed up; I managed one shaky smile and calm breath before I launched myself at him hard enough to bounce us both off the closed door. I almost took us down, and he would have had an easier time keeping his feet if he hadn't wrapped both arms tight around me as I clung to his neck and did my absolute best not to fly apart into a zillion pieces.

He held me, a warm iron statue, while I shivered and gulped air, only setting my feet back on the floor when I finally made myself let go.

Inhaling with a long sloppy sniff, I wiped my eyes. "I'm sorry. I just— I'm sorry."

He pulled me into another hug, kissed the top of my head, and held me at arm's length.

"You look good."

I choked on a laugh; I had to be a red-nosed mess now. "I broke my promise."

Dad frowned. "Promise?"

"Not to die. I did, I mean, here."

That stunningly obvious confession bought me another hug, and Dad sat us down on the bed to tuck me against his shoulder. "Well I'm glad you didn't, there. How long have you been gone?"

I blinked. "Gone?"

"From home. From where you're supposed to be."

I had to totally shift gears. Velveteen's world, seeing Faith, the fairy world, my adventures under the Blue Moon, San Francisco, the others, here... "Um, a couple of weeks?"

"Can you get back?"

"Yes," I nodded against his shoulder. "I think so. Sant— I have a—a thing that lets me jump. I thought it might take me straight home, but now I'm beginning to wonder if it's going to take me all twelve. This is number seven."

"Seven, huh?" He chuckled. "I'm glad we were on your travel itinerary. Mind telling me where you've been?"

I could *not* tell my dad that I'd meet Santa Claus and was jumping realities with the help of a magic snow globe. But I could tell him about pirate adventures under the Blue Moon. I told him about Velveteen, the detective and her writer, and Oberon and Titania (editing that story a little). And I told him all about Faith.

We just held each other after that, my head tucked in, Dad rubbing my arm and shoulder the way he used to when I'd had a bad day or a bad dream.

Finally he sighed. "Thank you."

"For what?"

"For letting me know that both my girls are alright, somewhere." He straightened. "I watched your debriefing with Lei Zi this morning, spoke to Veritas. I know you need to go, tomorrow."

I brought my head up, pushed away. "But—"

"You need to go home. I'm sure your mother and I are going crazy, there. Whatever you're trying to do, here, it's not worth the risk. Here is *our* responsibility, not yours."

"But—" Good grief, I was ten again. I closed my mouth. "I won't risk not leaving. I promise."

"Good." He kissed my hair again. "Now, do you think you can see your mother? She's waiting back at processing."

Dad promised to come back tomorrow and be part of my escort detail, and I wondered what he'd think of Shelly if they met; I intended to use an available cell to call her number, arrange a drop for my bag so that she wouldn't have to expose herself at all. Mom announced that she was coming, too. She'd handled our reunion with fragile aplomb, and I'd wanted to tell her *so* much—like about Shelly, who'd be alone again once I left—but couldn't because *Cypher* was a supervillain and every word would be parsed by DSA analysts somewhere.

Long after they were gone, I stared at the ceiling of my fancy cell and mentally listed all the things I absolutely needed to pass along before I turned the globe. At minimum, if I couldn't go after him myself then I was passing everything I knew about the Ascendant to Shelly; she could at least see that he was captured *here*—and might be able to leverage the information for things like legal immunity for her past crimes.

Hours after lights out, they came back on again. Blinking in the sudden light, I sat up; the digital clock told me it was one in the morning. *What?*

They'd made me comfortable here, but even for sleep I'd kept my Shelly-designed costume on and now I was glad; the thing was a second skin I still wasn't comfortable with, but psychologically it beat an institutional jumpsuit or the bathrobe. When the door unbolted, I stood. Agent Grace stepped into my cell, and I pushed my bed-fluffed hair out of my face.

"Agent Grace?"

"Good morning, Hope." Dropping her epad on the table beside us, she reached up to frame my face in her hands and *kissed* me.

What. The. Hell? I jerked my head back, grabbing her wrists, and that's when I smelled her. A musky scent, like a fox. "Kitsu—"

Her brown eyes danced as she broke my slack grip to put a hand over my mouth. "Yes, sorry but Agent Grace is romantically impulsive." The touch of an electronic key sprang my shackles loose to roll on the floor and, retrieving her pad, she took my hand. "Checkout time." The door closed behind us as she led me out of the cell and down the hall. Just short of the corner, between one blink of an eye and the next, I realized we weren't alone; Kitsune passed my hand to someone I hadn't noticed and I found myself looking at—*Mal?* Megaton? In jeans and a button-down, he was still the chunky but athletic geek-jock I knew.

"I'm Blindspot, ma'am," he said politely, hand tightening on mine. "Cypher said you'd know. Don't let go until we're outside." I nodded automatically, completely at a loss as the two of them took me around the corner. Kitsune—Agent Grace—walked right up to the processing station, handed her epad to the station officer to sign.

"That was quick," he grumbled good-naturedly. "What needed to happen with our mystery-guest at one o'clock in the morning?" His eyes never went to Mal and me for a second, not even a flicker.

"Classified," Kitsune returned cheekily.

"Yeah, yeah." He touched a button and the door behind him unlatched. "Be safe—caught a Driver Alert earlier, the Sentinels are cleaning up on a street action a couple of blocks north."

"I saw on the way in. Tell Amanda I said hi."

Mal kept us in front of Kitsune as we left processing, slid us behind her as we passed a second monitored gate and then through the outside doors as she swiped her card and said goodnight to each checkpoint guard along the way. The street was empty except for a lonely cab just turning our corner, and then Crash appeared out of hypertime on his street bike. Mal dropped my hand to climb on and they disappeared before I got out a "Hey!" Kitsune took my elbow.

"This way, darling girl," she laughed and pulled us to the street as the approaching cab slowed and its trunk opened. Kitsune gracefully hopped in and waved an invitation. "Go go go!" Shell yelled in my head when I hesitated. I ran and flew, landing in the trunk and closing it on us as the cab sped up again. Agent Grace—Kitsune—chuckled in my ear as I scooted around trying to get comfortable, throwing and arm over me so we were spooning in the tight space.

The cab turned a corner, and Kitsune shifted behind me. "Comfy? We'll be in here a little while—we could play." I nearly squeaked as she rested her hand on my stomach and puffed a breath over the sensitive skin behind my ear.

"You said Agent Grace is—"

"The young lady is romantically adventurous, yes." I could hear the laughter in her voice. "When I become someone completely enough to inhabit their memories and manners, I become them a little, too. You would call it extreme character-acting."

"Then why are you still her? Is she alright?"

"She's fine, asleep at home. And I'm still Agent Grace because I want to keep her knowledge of local DSA assets and their likely response until we're reasonably safe. She is also fun to be. Her neighbor was much less so."

"Oh." Okay, so my fox-spirit had become at least two people in the process of breaking me out. But— "Why are you *here*? Did you talk to the team?"

She chuckled, stirring the air and making me shiver. With her scent in my nose it didn't matter what she sounded or felt like—in my mind's eye, I was sharing a very intimate space with Yoshi, Kitsune's *courting* form, the one he'd worn formally presented himself to me in Chicago after our Japan adventure.

"Yes, I did. And I'm chasing you, of course. I find myself reduced to the roll of messenger these days, and you should know that your friends are on your trail. They can't follow you, the way you are jumping now, but they found the first world, the one you fell into with the mirror-killer."

"They could have found me there?" My stomach rolled, and not because of the taxi's bumpy ride—we'd obviously left the better streets of downtown Chicago.

"If you'd stayed, which you didn't." Kitsune sounded dryly matter-of-fact about it. "But they know that you're well, or at least you were when we met in the wood." Her voice dropped almost to a purr and suddenly I was hyper-aware, having the opposite of an out-of-body experience. An in-body experience? My heart moved in my chest, beating against its cage of ribs. my blood pulsed in my ears, and I felt the heat of my skin—could have counted each small hair standing at the nape of my neck where her breath floated over it. My eyes had to be dilated a hundred times, and when her hand moved over my stomach I dropped my own to cover it.

"Dream of me?" She whispered.

"Wh-what?"

"Have you dreamed of me?

I gulped a breath. "How did you—that was *you*?"

"I didn't send you one, but it's flattering to know you dream of me on your own."

This time I did squeak in indignation. "You tricked me!"

She laughed playfully and I shivered. "Trickster, don't forget. I didn't lie. I never do, that would be cheating. I would love to play with your Agent Veritas, sometime."

Just the thought of *that* meeting shut down my brain for a moment. It took me a few distracted breaths—she wasn't touching any place on me that stepped over a line, exactly, but between her intentionally aimed breathing and her hand I was finding it hard to think of anything relevant—but I realized she hadn't really answered my question.

"Why are you here? Twice?" *Why did you find me in the wood?* She'd—he'd practically declared war on King Oberon for me then, and I'd been trying very hard not to wonder why since.

I felt her sigh.

"I'm a kami. A kitsune. A fox spirit."

"I know that." Why was I whispering, too? We were in the *trunk* of a *moving cab*.

"Mortals are who they are, not what they do. Kami are what they do."

"Um, what?"

"When you put on the cape, you didn't become Astra *inside*. Astra remained a title until you committed to it, and you could give it up if you decided it wasn't necessary anymore."

"Okay?"

"Kami are different. We *are* what we do. I trick, therefore I am. And one thing we always do is keep our promises. Once we make a promise, we want to do it. We *change*."

Her hand was totally distracting me, but I tried to make sense out of that. "But we didn't make promises—we, we promised to promise? Someday?" A bill with no due-date. Right?

"And a promise creates anticipation, a shadow of fulfilment." Really, her *voice* was as distracting as her hand. Just how adventurous *was* Agent Grace? "I am a wild fox, but I promised to serve your family one day and so I want to. I don't want out of my promise. I don't want to kill every Corrigan so there is no family left to serve."

"Y-yes, but you're not the one who promised *marriage*."

"No, but our promises are linked. They cast the same shadow, and to desire one is to desire the other. A consummation, your great playwright once said, devoutly to be wished." Her voice deepened at the end, his hand changing under mine, growing rougher and more masculine, and he kissed the back of my neck. *Oh my God.*

"Yoshi?" I gasped when I could breathe.

"You like Yoshi. I live to serve."

The cab hit a curb, bouncing us both. Agent Grace had been tall but Yoshi took up more space—or the trunk was shrinking on us. I fought for air, light-headed.

"Yoshi—"

"Your dates were amusing, but I tire of chasing after you."

"But we haven't even really—"

"Easily remedied." And I found myself expertly turned so we weren't spooning. *How did he do that in a trunk?* Then we were kissing. *We* were kissing—I could have stiff-armed him into the backseat of the cab, but instead my shaking hands grabbed the narrow lapels of the suit he now wore and steadied us.

Oh, my.

His lips were smooth and slick as satin, and weirdly I fixated on that. "Do you gloss?" I gasped, leaning back for air. Almond eyes that had started visibly sparkling in the gloom of the closed space crinkled with laughter.

"Do I—" The laughter reached his voice. "Of course I do. You will not meet a more metrosexual creature, darling girl." And then he used those lips on other parts of my face.

"Oh. That's, nice. Really." The Bees would love him.

He worked his way around a cheekbone. "Any more questions?"

"Not now." I stretched up to catch the corner of those beautiful smooth lips.

"Good." He kissed my nose. "Because we're here."

"We're—what?"

The taxi stopped, and a door slammed. Frozen somewhere between *Damnit!* and *Oh God, what was I just doing?* I barely had time to get space between us and turn to face up before the hood of the trunk opened. I blinked in the light.

"Nice thing about skintight suits," Shelly observed, reaching in to help me out. "They don't get wrinkled." She wore a cabbie uniform.

"I— You—" We were in a closed-up service garage, surround by taxies.

"And it's a very clean trunk." Kitsune gracefully unfolded and dismounted behind me. His silver-gray suit, tailored so closely it looked sewn on, hadn't wrinkled either. He could have smirked. Or smiled knowingly, or winked, or done something else to make me want to slap his face off. He didn't; we might as well have been discussing post-Pulse politics.

Shelly pulled me into a quick hug, hooked my arm and led me away from the cab with Kitsune following. "You do seem to get captured a lot."

"The last two don't count. They were the good guys."

"Point!" She laughed, glanced back at Kitsune. "Thanks, hot-stuff. The crew is meeting in an hour in the break room over there. If you go outside, wear someone else's face."

He looked at me and his perfect lips twitched, widening into a smile as my face heated up. "I do wish to stretch my legs, and will see you ladies in an hour." He turned on his heels and headed for the door under the green-lit exit sign.

"Wow!" Shelly fanned herself. "So *that's* Kitsune. I can see why you want to get home so bad."

I groaned, ran fingers through my hair. "You couldn't have, I don't know, *stopped and let us out* after we got some distance?"

"Couldn't." She led me into the breakroom. It smelled like stale takeout and mildew. "I picked up my fare, dropped off my fare, called in a mechanical problem and drove right to the garage. Keeping it clean means fewer street-cams I have to mess with as Cypher."

I plopped down on the ratty couch. Did we stop during the ride? I vaguely remembered a car door slamming but I'd been... *Admit it, you were hot to trot and eating his face*. It was like the teenage party game Seven Minutes of Heaven except we hadn't been sharing a closet with clothes. *And now you're going to dream of teenage party games with Kitsune*. I didn't think it was possible for me to flush any hotter.

"So, you really drive a taxi?" My voice broke on *taxi* and Shelly snickered.

"Hey, they're everywhere. 'Course I usually look a bit different—I wore my Shelly-shell tonight because of the meeting."

"The meeting?"

"Sure. I pulled Brian and Jamal in after you got picked up last night, figured that the protectors of truth and justice would sweep them up too, since we'd reached out to them. Brian got away from your ambushed meeting with something called Travel Dust? Then when Kitsune showed up and we realized we could pull a rescue, I decided to keep us to The Plan. What does Kitsune *do*, back there? She has mad resources."

"Rescue—" The whole trunk thing had completely derailed my moment of befuddlement at seeing—"Mal! Blindspot is *Mal*! How is that possible?"

Shelly sat in one the steel chairs. "Mal had his breakthrough after the Pulse, hiding his family from looters. You know him?"

"Yeah, as a Young Sentinel named Megaton! He is *not* inconspicuous! He blows stuff up!"

She whistled. "Wow, that's an interesting data-point." In the Future Files that we both knew about, new potential futures always meant a whole new crop of breakthroughs; people experiencing breakthroughs in more than one future event were *rare*. "So he was a natural just waiting to happen, I guess?"

I rubbed my eyes. "At least tell me his family is okay and all together?"

"Well, yeah. Sydney is just the cutest little thing."

"That's nice." At least *something* had turned out better, here. Even if Mal was a supervillain, he'd choose his family in a heartbeat over being a cape. "So with Blindspot and Kitsune, and I assume Cypher to hack their video records, you guys pulled a complete Blackstone on them. Thanks."

"Don't mention it—the best kind of jailbreak is one where they didn't see it happen and will always wonder how the hell it happened. And your bag is right over there in the third locker. I packed everything and added some stuff, we can get you on your way any time." She sucked at sounding casual about that.

"Shelly..."

"I know, you've got to go. But we've got the crew together. We can complete the mission!"

I dropped my head back to stare at the ceiling. Since Veritas had shut me down I'd avoided thinking about The Mission at all. And now it was back on the table. A digustingly sticky breakroom table, sure, but what had Veritas said? My just *being* here was putting DSA precognitives out of commission? He, or his boss, was scared enough that they were willing to basically get me out of town on the next bus instead of take a chance I could make things better.

But bringing the Ascendant down had to be a *good thing*, right?

I scrubbed my face. The *responsible* thing would just be to follow my half-formed idea of earlier tonight, dump everything I knew about Dr. Pellegrini, The Ascendancy, and the Wreckers on Shelly, and *go*. She and Vulcan could figure out what to do with it—even with a shady source, the DSA *had* to move on something like that.

But could they do it by themselves? Back home, after the Ascendancy announced itself by hitting the Detroit Supermax, internal investigations had shown that Dr. Pellegrini's government connections had been *deep*. Could the federal agencies launch the kind of quiet investigation they'd need to, confirm what I could tell them, without Pellegrini learning about it in time to disappear and erase his trail again? Or would history just repeat itself?

And what about *home*? Here or there, the Ascendant was *dangerous*. Nobody knew, *nobody*, when he might make another Temblor or Green Man, trigger another city shattering quake or a bigger disaster with some ultra-boosted breakthrough. Even without that, the Ascendancy was all about superhuman supremacy; the post-Pulse chaos had to suit them just fine. They'd probably helped it along.

Hadn't Shelly said something about a superhuman freehold? I'd almost bet that was them, and she'd said that the Wreckers were active.

Maybe that's why they haven't come out in the open as the Ascendancy here—they don't have to. They're getting it done.

And back home, Dr. Pellegrini could decide they'd benefit from just this kind of Grimworld mess, and *make it happen*. If I didn't take this chance, here, where I could get to him in a way that he just wasn't vulnerable to anymore back home...

Shelly let me sit and think, not trying to press her argument; another way she was just a bit different from my Shellys. Finally, I straightened up with a sigh. "Is there bottled water in that fridge? And how much time is left before the meeting? I need you to research, and can I go outside?"

It turned out that the service garage sat in a basement below a mixed business-residence building, and the rooftop featured an urban vegetable garden (apparently a new trend accelerated by peoples' experience of post-Pulse food insecurity). The screening trellises for the climbing plants blocked easy line-of-sight observation from anything not directly overhead, and Shelly was watching for that. I took the elevator to the top floor and the stairs to the roof.

Clouds hung low over the lit city, with the smell of rain. The low clouds forced the jetliners descending on O'Hare into a closer approach, and their distant engines glowed like a string of giant fireflies in my sight. I couldn't see any human flyers out, and wondered if any capes flew regular night patrols anymore. Too dangerous?

Finding an old lawn chair I sat, rested my chin in my hands, and tried to empty my mind. I pushed away thoughts of my family here, of Kitsune's apparent new plan to seduce me into marriage, of Shelly and Jamal, Mal and Brian.

As a cape, a CAI hero, I was duty-bound to uphold the rule of law. That duty hadn't disappeared because I was in another reality. I'd severely bent that duty last year in my trip to Japan, violating the territorial sovereignty of another nation, but I'd never tried to physically resist the legal authority of its representatives.

Now I'd passively participated in a jailbreak, after fleeing the proper authorities here and recruiting a crew for a very criminal caper. And I was still planning on breaking and entering. Property theft. Very possibly assault and battery, depending on if we met any real resistance.

I laughed unhappily. When had I become a vigilante? I'd always tried to keep *Jacky* from that dark side of "superheroing" once we had dragged her into the Sentinels. Jacky... I straightened, breathing a little easier. I'd never condemned Jacky's whole Dark Avenger vigilante project, back when we first met; she'd been fighting very bad people, in ways the police and courts couldn't. She'd made whole street gangs stop victimizing their neighbors and fear the night. I'd only ever worried about what she'd been doing because sooner or later superhuman vigilantes ended with jail.

That, and I didn't think the role of night-stalking Dark Vigilante could be healthy for anybody, especially not for a friend who was already something dark.

But at least I wasn't being hypocritical—or I didn't think so. Veritas wanted me gone, I'd get gone. Tomorrow, succeed or fail, I'd turn the globe and jump to my next adventure. Whatever *that* would be. And I'd try and manage it so that my teammates here—and they *were* my teammates even if they'd never met me—could get what Jacky got; a chance to come in out of the cold.

I felt the first drop on my head, and then the night filled with the light patter of an easy spring shower. Tilting my face up, I let the rain bless my decision.

I spent my last few minutes on the roof going over Shelly's discoveries and finding out if she could deliver what I thought we'd need to pull it off tonight, and when I came back downstairs I found everybody waiting in the garage, where Shell had dragged the breakroom table to give us more room. With no visored helmet or wig and shades, the broken star of my costume crest was enough that Jamal made the connection first and his eyes widened.

"Holy shit—you're *dead.*"

Mal didn't look surprised—but he'd walked out of the DSA station with me so he'd gotten a nice long look. Brian looked like he'd seen weirder things and didn't much care. I folded my arms. "I get that a lot. To clear the deck, yes I'm Hope Corrigan, Astra. No, I'm not back from the grave. *I'm—*" I tapped my chest "—not from around here. You guys have seen enough 'alternate world' shows where the hero is the villain or we're all anthropomorphized mammals or something. Back home, I didn't die at Whittier Base. And here's the thing, where I came from I know *all* of you. Back *there*, Mal, Brian, Jamal, you're *Sentinels*. The Young Sentinels. You're *capes*. The good guys. You called us the freaking white hats, Jamal." I looked at each of the boys in turn, ignoring Kitsune for now.

"I didn't get a chance to tell any of you what this was about, before, but tonight I need you to be my team again. Because tonight I'm going after the Ascendant."

I smiled tightly at the growl I heard coming from Grendel. "Brian here has a score to settle with the Ascendant. It might not be personal for the rest of you, but even here and with everything that's happened since I've been...gone, the Ascendant's at the top of the DSA's most-wanted list. Before I leave I intend to make sure that they get him. But here's the thing."

Channeling Lei Zi from every action briefing I could remember, I leaned forward and I locked eyes with each of them again, even—this time especially—Kitsune. "This is going to be a clean job. We take it as far as we can, with cutouts when we can abandon it if we have to, to make sure that no civilians get hurt—not even bad guys. We're not the *law*, we're not serving a warrant, we don't have the legal right to use force. That means I'm not getting you guys into anything that would look worse on a rap sheet than a B&E unless it goes completely south.

"And how's that going to work?" Brian had control of his vocal cords, but I heard no deep subharmonic undertones like he got when he was ready to seriously tear into somebody. "How do we get The Ascendant without fighting anybody?"

"I didn't say no *fighting*, I said no *hurting civilians*. But we're not going at him directly—we're getting the evidence the DSA needs to do it for us and they'll do it good and hard. I'm sorry, Brian." I tried a smile on him. "I know how bad you want him, but it has to be this way. Ozma wouldn't want you in jail, and neither do I."

Jamal folded his arms. "This doesn't sound like my usual delivery job. What's in it for me?"

"Triple the fee for your last delivery job—I've got a good paymaster. Or if you want, I can get you what you have back home, a second chance and an apprenticeship with Sifu." I shrugged like his choice didn't matter to me. "Mal? I don't know what you need, but—"

"Forget it, I'm in." He coughed, looking almost embarrassed. "I owe crazy-girl here too many markers not to." He tipped his head at Shelly. "Besides, if it all blows up you'll need someone to get you out without every Chicago Sentinel and Guardian chasing you."

I nodded, blinking repeatedly to keep the rush of gratitude from getting obvious. I was *so* far from home, but tonight I had my team. "Kitsune? If you're in, those are the terms."

"I live to serve." There was nothing reserved about his smile, and now I had to fight down a flush.

"Shelly?"

She unrolled a screen on the breakroom table, projecting a 3D image of our target on it as we gathered around.

I put both hands on the table. "Here, all the DSA knows about the Ascendant is that a few years ago he claimed responsibility for several mass-casualty attacks. The biggest was the LO Stadium attack, where he gassed a whole interstate band and cheerleading competition and audience with a synthesized psychotropic." I didn't look at Brian. He'd lost his family and had his transformative breakthrough there, and had signed on with Ozma because she'd promised him justice. "All of the attacks were designed to generate trauma more than fatalities, and DSA profilers concluded the Ascendant was interested in creating more breakthroughs—all the deaths were a byproduct. He went silent before the California Quake."

Now I looked at Brian. "The LO Stadium attack wasn't the Ascendant's worst. He was responsible for boosting Temblor, the psychotic terrakinetic responsible for triggering the California Quake. Back home we know that because he *told* me."

"Well, shit." Jamal spoke for all of them and I nodded.

"The Ascendant is a secret breakthrough named Dr. Simon Pellegrini. He has the power to inhibit or boost the powers of other breakthroughs, and he's fanatically delusional. He believes that breakthroughs are transcendent humans, sleepers who have been awakened. His goal is racial apotheosis."

"So he's a superhuman supremacist," Mal said.

"Yes. Back home the DSA now believes that his two goals are to increase the number of breakthroughs and to unite us against control by sleepers. We awakened are inherently superior to sleepers, so of course we should rule."

"That is *so* messed up."

"You think?" Shelly quipped.

I shot her a quelling look. "I think we all agree on that one. Until a bit over a year ago, Pellegrini was the known cult-leader of the Foundation of Awakened Theosophy. They preached superhuman supremacy, just not that explicitly. They were also an organization dedicated to using meditative imaging techniques to trigger "soft breakthroughs" and strengthen weak ones. Their success rate wasn't much better than for normal traumatic breakthroughs, but the foundation had thousands of followers. We know now that reports of foundation-enhanced powers were because of Pellegrini's gift, and his inner circle knew what he was really about. You know some of them—the Wreckers."

Mal raised his hand. "Sounds like he had a sweet thing going. Behind the scenes supervillain mastermind, all that. What happened?"

"The Sentinels happened. We tried to capture the Wreckers when they were killing anti-breakthrough criminals in Chicago. We failed, but we exposed one of them and the police investigation revealed his link to the foundation. Pellegrini knew he couldn't hide anymore, so he covered his trail and took the Ascendancy completely underground."

"But he's still in the open, here."

"Yes. Shelly?"

She touched the screen menu bar, pulling up a map of the US. It had a *lot* of bright dots on it. "His foundation here is even bigger than before the Pulse. Rising anti-breakthrough sentiment since has increased his following among low-level breakthroughs. He has more Awakening Centers than ever, and a lot of low to mid-level Crisis Aid and Intervention capes are registered members. Not so much for A and higher B classes."

I tapped the screen to bring back the blueprints. "That's really the good news—the foundation is still in business, and that means we have an opportunity. This is the foundation's biggest Awakening Center, and it's just north of Chicago. They only use it a few months out of the year and the rest of the time it's rented out for big group events, but they've always kept their own site maintenance staff and there was a reason for that." I used my hands to "lift" the 3D image to expose the building's sub-level. "I never saw this myself, but back home Blackstone briefed everyone on the DSA's investigation of the site after the team raided it." Everyone leaned in to see what I'd brought up.

"The foundation's secret Ascendancy operations are large enough that communications security is a huge issue; even before discovery they coordinated through the dark net, and they kept their own central secret server for it. They kept it here." Another gesture centered the blueprint on one basement room and I expanded it. "It's physically secured, and it's one big burnbox, a room-sized version of the kind of box embassies and criminals use to completely destroy documents, computer drives, and physical evidence. It's basically a concrete bunker rigged with thermite to cook everything in it into a useless pile of slag."

I looked up. "The room isn't secret. It's a maintenance room and the hub of the building's landline network. The foundation's server is there, with what my DSA guessed was their 'dark server.' Cypher confirmed that at least their legit server exists here, too, and based on power usage she's close to one hundred percent certain that the other is there too."

Brian smiled toothily. "They haven't burned and run, yet."

"No. If we can get in, physical access will allow Cypher to bypass their cybersecurity and make a ghost copy of the dark server drives. So we do it completely quiet, copy the drives, and Cypher can crack it all for everything the DSA needs to get warrants and take down the whole Ascendancy. Even if we don't manage to stay completely quiet, if we copy the drives then the DSA will have what it needs to dig them out of their holes when they go underground. That's the mission."

"And that's what you want, too," Mal concluded. "The stuff they burned where you're from."

"That's right. It may be enough to roll them up completely, back there. And they'll never see it coming."

From there it became a matter of details, mostly Shelly explaining what Cypher and Galatea could do to defeat the foundation's security (she was keeping the two firmly separate—I was pretty sure that even Blindspot didn't know they were one and the same). She confirmed that, as of now, the Awakening Center was empty except for its four-man resident "maintenance staff." Of course we didn't have time to do real recon and investigation to confirm that they were who employee records said they were.

I was assuming they were all boosted low-level breakthroughs.

And all of this felt *so* strange. This was my team—most of it—and they were together for the first time and didn't know me at all. We should be in the Assembly Room at the Dome. I should have Lei Zi on one side of me and Blackstone on the other. Instead I was in the middle of a dimly lit garage, surrounded by half a dozen taxi cabs in various states of work, taking command point on a mission that really needed days more planning and every possible backup.

After the second round of questions over best approaches, I made myself step back in. "Alright, everyone. We've got three stages to this job. Penetration of the center's security layers, duplication of the drives, and extraction. We'll equip in two hours and review each of our roles, then go. If we can achieve the first stage without undue risk of discovery, then the second stage is a go. If the first stage proves too risky, we cut out; we can't let the Ascendancy know that they're vulnerable from this direction until the ghost-drives are in our hands. After that it's best if they *still* don't know, but either way the DSA will be able to use the information in those drives to hunt them down. Any questions?"

There weren't any, and as everyone broke up I was able to pull Shelly aside.

"What?"

"Two questions," I said quietly. "First, are you *sure*, if we get you into the room, you can shut down its hellfire function? Second, I'm not that computer literate but I know that the things can do a lot to mess themselves up. Can you keep the system from wiping its drives or whatever, if we don't manage to stay completely quiet?"

"Maybe, and yes."

"That's not reassuring."

"Hey, all computers call me God but some are too simple and secure for me to mess with without lots of work. Don't worry, I've got this."

"Okay." I sighed. "And equipping the team?"

"Got that, too—in about forty-five minutes we're getting a trunk load of gear, a bunch of it fresh off of Vulcan's forges. We'll be ready."

"But?" I studied her. There was something she wasn't telling me.

"You're gone when the job is done, right?"

I hitched a breath, swallowed around the sudden knot made of wishes and guilt and impossible choices I'd managed to push off by thinking about everything else. "Yeah. I wish— I *can't* stay, you know that."

"Well yeah, but you are, sort of." She'd been steering us to the breakroom and now she stopped at the door, *pushed* me the last couple of feet, and shut the door on me. *What?*

"Hi," the tiny blonde who appeared by the fridge said with a worried smile. "Don't freak out, okay?"

She—I—wore our original skirted Astra costume, minus the completely unnecessary mask and I *instantly* knew what had happened. It didn't help at all. There are moments for which words just don't cut it, like describing a nuclear explosion as "hot and loud" but I finally understood how Shelly must have felt when, shoved back into a live body by me and Ozma's Wishing Pill, she found herself saying hello to...herself.

"...hi," I managed. "When did you wake up?"

"Yesterday? But I've been in an accelerated environment for two weeks. Shelly's had me staying with Mistress Jenia. The Western Warden?"

"In her virtual cloudhome?"

I—she—nodded. "Yeah. I'm 'experiencing' myself and reality through an interface that lets me perceive everything as physical analogues so it's all not too much of a shock. Still trying to wrap my mind around it, you know?"

I finally found one of the steel chairs still in the room, dropped into it. "So you're me, until I died? Whittier Base was two weeks ago, for you?" I'd been nearly a walking zombie then, and it hadn't been because of my physical injuries. My heart ached in sympathy when she nodded again. "Are you—are you okay? And why did Shelly wait till now?"

She actually laughed. "Hey, the bioseed that the Teatime Anarchist had us swallow didn't just grow a beacon and cyber-quantum link. But you know that now, right? It grew a neural net capable of supporting a—just like Shelly, I had a quantum mirror copy of my brain up and running when I died. But she says that Twenty-Second Century biocybernetic ethics are backed by unbreakable protocols."

I choked on the thought that the Teatime Anarchist had had *any* ethics—the guy had never told the entire truth any time I'd met him.

"I know, right?" She rolled her eyes. "*Shelly* gave the Teatime Anarchist permission, but he didn't have time to go back and get *mine* after I died so I stayed dormant, asleep without my own authorized wakeup call. Shelly's been looking for another time-traveler ever since to—"

"—go back and get permission." And again I just *knew* what had happened. "She asked *me* if I'd have let TA copy me—"

"—and you said yes!" She struck a dramatic pose. "Ta-daaa!"

From there it got interesting; talking with myself was...weird. This me, younger Hope, was still dealing with Whittier Base, but at least she didn't have the added mess of killing Volt with one gory punch to try and bleach from her brain. She also didn't know what had happened to the Teatime Anarchist, here. (Shelly had sealed it, but I was willing to bet that it had involved direct action.) So we *looked* the same—a no-brainer since I wasn't aging anymore and the only injury that had stuck in three years was my chi-torn shoulder and that was invisible—but younger me acted *tentative*, hesitant. Had that been me, two years ago? Or had actually dying changed me—her—already?

"*This is weird, right?*" We both spoke in stereo and then broke into laughter. "*Jinx!*"

She wiped her eyes. "And you said your Shellys are like this? Siamese twins, joined at the brain?"

"Worse. They merge through their link when they get really focused. What are we going to do about Mom and Dad? About everybody?"

"Take care of them."

Okay, *that* was totally me. I couldn't help the grin and when she saw it she fell into giggles. I waited it out, stood when she finished.

"I've got to get back out there. Leadership stuff to do."

She rolled her bright blue eyes. "I know. And, we're awesome. *You're* awesome—really Awesome Girl. I just, I couldn't let you leave without knowing that I've got your back. That everything will be alright, here. And tonight I'll be watching. With popcorn." She vanished with a spirit-hands wave.

Wow. I opened the breakroom door to find Shelly "guarding" the other side.

"All done?" She gave me a quick once-over. "Need anything?"

What I needed was two weeks of my own to get over having my world changed *again*. I settled for a mock glare. "All done. You know you could have *said*. Something like 'Well, you know TA quantum-thingied *your* brain, too.'"

She snickered cheekily. "Where's the fun in that?"

"Not as fun, but you might live longer."

"A longer life not as fun. Our presents have arrived." She drew my attention to five big hardshell suitcases with a sweep of her hand. Everyone except Kitsune was already gathered around them.

"Good grief, they're like children."

Mal had obviously worked with my BF before; he was laying them out and opening them for everyone's inspection as they stood over him.

"They're boys with toys," Shelly agreed happily. "Your fox *wants* to—he's just too adult to admit it." I looked and smothered a smile. Kitsune was watching the proceedings intently, only distance preserving the illusion of disinterest.

"You know this could go really bad, right?"

She gave me a look. "Second thoughts? Doubts?"

"No." I smiled fondly, but it faded. "No. I know what the boys can do. I know what *you* can do. It's just—unless we have a perfect run, and what are the odds of that happening, there could be blowback. And I won't be here for it." I would be the *only* one not here for it. "I think—"

Shelly's eyes narrowed when I stopped. "What?"

I had to fight hard not to start laughing. It was turning into that kind of night. "I—I just realized something, not *funny*, but—"

"Spill, or I start tickling."

"You know how, in all the movies, the heroes always manage to find the villains for one big boss-fight scene in their secret lair? We—well, I'll bet right now the entire Chicago DSA station and probably the entire team is trying to find me and whoever busted me out—the classic supervillain jailbreak. And—and we're all right *here!*" I waved helplessly at the dim and dirty garage with its fleet of busted cars.

Shelly looked around, snickering. "Some supervillain's lair. There's not even a big red button. There's a grease pit over there we could fill with really small sharks. Or alligators. Come on, lets gear up."

It all looked like a delivery from Villains R Us; my only gear was a new helmet, gloves, and boots to replace the ones I'd left behind with the DSA. No new wig—at this point that piece of disguise was completely superfluous. Shelly ran through the telemetry and communication links with me to make sure I was tied into everyone else's.

Everyone else got *team costumes*. Black and white bodysuits (*not* skintight) and helmets, they all more or less matched my own pattern but with individualized cuts and crests. We looked like a professional motorbike-racing team; the only thing we needed was team patches.

Nope, there it was. Shell handed me a black and silver utility belt to add to my outfit; it came with sandman packs, zip cuffs, and other handy items, and its buckle sported a stylized "S".

"Shell, you going to tell me about this?"

She looked up from the elaser she was checking. "Well I couldn't make it a 'V' for Vulcan's Villains, could I? We're going after the group that fields the Wreckers and calls itself the Ascendancy—so I figure we're the Spoilers."

"We sound like weirdos who sneak into supermarkets and turn off their refrigeration."

"All the cool names were taken. Help me with this." She handed off the stunner to Blindspot and opened the fifth and biggest case, packed with a suit of her armor. It was styled very different than her Galatea gear and in the team's black and white. We stepped behind one of the cabs, and five minutes later she was dressed in her own skintight black bodysuit with white webbing-sheath overlayer supporting her armor and weapon racks with full riot-control loadouts Power Chick.

She tested her own helmet links. "You're going to be carrying me if we need to fly—these jet-boots are only good for about ten minutes in the air. Mostly I'll be on the ground anyway, and I'm not extracting myself—hey!"

I set her back down and released her shoulder grips. "Good enough. I'm used to carrying Grendel into fights. Dropping him into them, really."

"A Grendel bomb? Sounds insane."

"It's a show stopper." Even for most breakthroughs, a dropped Grendel usually inspired a great desire to leave the area or give up before he hit you. "Okay people, equipment-check! Shell, read it off. Everyone, if you don't know why you've got something, ask. If you don't know how to use something, ask."

I had to show Jamal how to administer a sandman pack and Shelly demonstrated the stunner for Kitsune, but other than that everyone was good. We even did the power-walk leaving the garage. I almost hallucinated music and a slow-mo effect.

No, the music was Shelly.

My new and lively sense of the ridiculous only got livelier as we moved out. It was four in the morning, less than three hours until sunrise, and the gear-drop had included a service van left parked outside, backed up so that we could board without seeing the driver or the driver seeing us. Blindspot joined the driver, Crash would meet us there, and the rest of us loaded into the back of the empty van.

The van wasn't rigged for anything but passengers; benches and safety belts secured us comfortably against the sides, with room beneath our benches for gear we couldn't hold. Resting my head against the van wall, I watched everyone and tried to look cool, calm, and serious. Which was hard since I was again trying not to giggle.

We looked like an elite supersoldier strike force from some action movie. Especially with Grendel (his outfit made him look like someone had wrapped him in heavy-duty spandex bands from neck to feet, covered with a layer of armor-supporting web harness like Shelly's. When he put his helmet on nobody would be able to see any skin at all—he'd look just like any other Mister Universe built Ajax-Type. Across from me, Kitsune had changed his face again; now square jawed and practically Nordic, with a decorative scar running down the left side of his face, he could be a hardcore Paragon-Type mercenary. Beside me, Shelly had her head back and eyes closed. In her powered armor and weapons rig, she looked like our artillery expert.

The Spoilers. God help us.

Shelly opened her eyes. "Stage One is go. I've got a drone out at the Awakening Center, triggering their grounds alarm and staying out of sight. They've had three 'false alarms' and an automatic call from their security company, and they're expecting a van. That'll be us, since the company van has been redirected to the rendezvous. I've tapped their landline and local cell tower, and am monitoring their calls. So far nothing to anyone else."

I nodded. "Tell Blindspot and Crash we're good for the rendezvous. Their service person is taken care of?"

"Yup. He'll be waiting for us."

I nodded again and closed my eyes. Since The Plan was rolling on rails now, half my job was to look confident and not do anything worrying until it went off the rails. I could tell when we hit the freeway, and fifteen minutes later we got back off of it and then pulled into a parking lot. Crash opened the van before I could unbuckle.

"Security van secure, ma'am!" He mock-saluted me as I climbed out. The Apex Security van was waiting for us, and our driver had turned and backed us so that he couldn't see it or us as we got out. Crash had used the sandman pack on the Apex serviceman; she sat slumped behind the wheel of her van. I motioned to Kitsune.

"How long will it take you to get ready?"

He straightened the sleeper up, winked at me. "Five minutes, ten if you wouldn't want her husband to be suspicious."

"Five. Shelly?"

"On it, boss." Finishing her walk around the Apex Security van, she turned back to ours and waved her hand. Our ride turned white and the AS logo unfurled itself on the side. "Can I paint, or can I paint?"

"Chameleon-layer finish?"

"Oh yeah."

I found myself watching the sky in the direction of Chicago. Variforce's glowing fields weren't at all subtle at night, and nowhere to be seen.

"I'm listening in on Dispatch," Shelly said softly beside me. "Figured it was a good risk, for this."

"What are they doing?"

"*They* aren't doing anything but staying ready to move. The CPD and DSA still have no clue how you got out, but they think it was a security system hack to take down the hard cell's barriers and a teleporter to get you out."

"They haven't spotted Kitsune's work?"

"They know about the substitution—they just don't think you walked out with 'Agent Grace'."

So they weren't looking for a suspicious taxi, probably weren't looking at traffic at all. I relaxed a little. We might get away with two impossible jobs in one night.

"All done." Kitsune came up to stand beside us. She was a stocky brunette with a weathered and freckle-covered face. Her costume had morphed into company coveralls, and she'd acquired our sleeper's tool belt and equipment box. She shook my hand. "Charlene Waters, nice to meet you and let's go—I've got kids to get up and get to school."

I blinked. "Shelly..."

"Got it covered, boss." A van door opened, and Shelly moved us all to the other side as our driver got out and came around. A few minutes of movement, and the company van door slammed. We watched it back up and pull out of the parking lot. "He'll take Sleeping Beauty home, park in her driveway and administer the wake-up when we call. She'll be bright-eyed and bushy tailed five minutes after he's gone. She might be too busy with her company and police report to get her kids to school, though."

"So let's go. Sooner begun, sooner done." Charlene handed me her belt and box, pulled her company cap low on her head, and headed around to the front of the van.

I stared after her. "I'm never going to get used to that." Blindspot joined us in back this time.

Another five minutes on the freeway headed north, another five minutes of surface streets, and we came to a full stop. "Charlene" opened the tiny window separating the cab from the back of the van so we could hear as she talked into a gate speaker, and Blindspot had the other three of us leave our benches to stack up behind him. Shell showed us how to fold down the bench-backs with their safety straps so it looked like a van with empty drawers and racks. Clever.

We braced ourselves awkwardly as the van lurched back into motion, and watched the gates close behind us through the rear windows. A turn up a long drive and Charlene stopped us again, getting out this time. The rear door opened and she collected her tool-belt and box as a guy in a blue security uniform looked at the inside of the van.

And of course didn't see us.

"So what's the problem, tonight?" She hitched up her belt and closed the doors.

"Twitchy system," I heard him answer as they walked away. "Went off again just before you got here, and we've got to go out and check every time." Another door opened and closed.

"Stage One complete," Shelly announced needlessly as we all sat down again. "Now we just wait until she jacks me in." She passed out water bottles. "Hydrate. There may be a lot of yelling soon."

I hated waiting, and chugged water to cover it.

Which didn't fool Shelly. "Worried?"

"I don't like not being where it could go bad. Kitsune isn't bulletproof." *And we're flying blind and don't know what kind of detection powers they might be using.*

"Do we sneak, much? Back home?"

Now Grendel and Blindspot were listening. "Not really. We're more the 'kick in the wall and serve the warrant on the supervillain' kind of team, when we're not doing public appearances and emergency response stuff. Which is most of what we do. That and train, a *lot*."

Blindspot looked dubious. "I'm not exactly a wall-kicker kind of breakthrough."

"You have your moments."

That led to a brief discussion of *home*. I didn't tell Blindspot that back there his codename was Megaton and he blew stuff up. I did tell him his parents were divorced and his mom and sister lived on the west coast. I didn't tell Grendel that he'd already missed a shot at the Ascendant; he didn't need any more motivation. I tried not to ask Shelly how long it had been, and then I didn't have to.

"We're up," she reported. "Kitsune has jacked me in, and I've sweet-talked their security system into playing for our team. Let's go, people."

"Helmets on," I called out, only just keeping the relief out of my words. Blindspot opened the van doors and we piled out behind him. Shelly took the lead at the service door, and I could hear the electronic locks disengaging as she pulled the latch.

I went over the blueprints in my mind as we marched down the service hallway, stopped us at the stairwell doors. "Brian—Grendel—"

"I know. Nobody gets past."

"Right. Blindspot?" He nervously hitched his belt with its holstered elaser.

"Join Kitsune in security. Don't let anyone mousetrap us in there. If you can't immediately take whoever comes through the door, give Kitsune a big hug and walk her out of there."

"What about the guard with her now?"

"Handled," Shell said. "We're down to three on-sight risks." She unlocked and opened the stairwell door and we headed down the concrete well.

Just feet from our goal I was winding tight again; all senses alert, above the echo of our descending steps I could hear the hum of a light getting ready to die, the skitter of a few roaches below reacting to the vibration of our feet on the concrete stairs. The place needed an exterminator. At the bottom of the stairwell and through another security door the way branched, a service tunnel made close by the power and water lines running along the opposite wall. We went left and there was the steel door with its expected lockpad.

I watched the approaches, listened for anything on our team link, tried not to pay any attention to what Shelly did behind me.

"We're in." She pulled the door open and took us through a second, inside door. And we were, in fact, in; in the white room with its power and phone lines, blocky boxes on the walls, and beautiful, beautiful, computer station and caged server stack.

Really, if I wasn't so relieved I'd be disappointed; somehow I'd thought that it would be more physically secure.

Shelly looked over the stack, then took a finger-sized jack from her belt, plugged it into a USB port, and completely froze for the space of four heartbeats.

"Okay, good news and bad news."

"Good news."

"I can do it. Give me eight minutes and I can copy the entire drive. The bad news is you might have to work for those minutes. Any use of the system triggers a query with an outside key; if the use is not cleared first by the key, then it triggers the thermite. I can disable the thermite trigger first, but it's in constant handshake-mode through the server with an outside link and I have no idea what will happen when I disable it. Best guess, an alarm somewhere else is going to go off. So, plan?"

"Why can't we just disable the trigger, rip the server out, and go?"

"It's got its own internal capacitor; we disconnect and it will discharge. I have no idea how much data we'll lose."

"Okay." We had three threats left in the building, and no idea if they'd get a Kill On Sight order from elsewhere the moment we pushed the button—they should be taken care of first, but again no idea if they could see us coming and sound their own alarms. *Damn it.* "Kill the trigger, kill the landlines, kill the local cell tower if you can, and copy that drive."

"Just did one and two, can't do three, working on four. Countdown!"

I put my hand to my helmet by reflex. "All Spoilers, this is it. We have begun copy and have triggered an external alarm. Be prepared for on-site action and possible visitors. We will extract in eight minutes."

Eight minutes. What's eight minutes. Just four hundred and eighty seconds. How much could the Ascendancy bring down on us in eight minutes?

They had a teleporter somewhere.

"*The on-site staff is moving!*" Kitsune sang in my ear from security. Yoshi's voice—the body he was most comfortable with in a fight?

"Someone just tripped a security program," Shelly informed me. "All exterior and interior doors are unlocked now."

"Well..."

"You so want to swear right now, don't you?"

I swallowed a hysterical giggle. "Grendel, retreat to the top of the stairs, hold the door *closed*." The thing was steel, fireproof and probably bulletproof. Anything that got through it would be able to survive rough handling by Brian. "Blindspot, get friendly with Kitsune. Anyone enters security, it's your call to engage or leave. It's also your call to yell for extraction." Bright side, all the doors being unlocked left an open road for Crash. "Shelly, time?"

"Faster than I thought, just under six minutes."

The floor rocked, and a horrible thought almost choked me.

"Shelly, can they cut power to the server from outside?"

"No— Crap on a cracker! There's a junction box out in the tunnel. If they blow that then we're dead in here and the capacitor goes!"

"Are you *kidding* me?" I almost ripped the useless doors off their frames getting out. And then I went blind.

"Shell, build me a view!" Helmet-cam feed, blueprints, echo location and GPS, whatever sources Shelly was using, she threw up a virtual overlay that gave me a real-time neon map through our neural link. One man, racing up the tunnel from whatever access stairs he'd come from. By his silhouette, he carried an assault rifle.

"*Just so you know,*" she observed, "*your optic nerves just stopped working.*"

"You think! Talk about a blind spot!" He opened fire and I got between him and the junction box, arms up to shield my helmet. It took him five squeezed shots to realize that I a.) wasn't falling down and b.) could obviously see him. I took a step, and he ran. "Kitsune! Anyone else down here with us?"

"No!"

I launched myself down the tunnel, flattened the guy against the wall where it turned a corner and crushed his gun.

"You're a neuralkinetic? Unblind me, please. Now."

"I can't! Optical paralysis! It'll wear off!"

"Fine." I pulled a sandman pack, slapped it on him, and counted to three. He sagged and I checked his pulse and respiration before lowering him to the concrete floor.

I should have taken him back with me but a room full of thermite, even rendered 'safe', probably wasn't the best place for him to sleep it off.

The floor shook again.

"All Spoilers, who's *knocking*?"

"*Mine*," Grendel came back, a roar in his voice.

"Need a hand?"

His *No* was a primal scream and this time when the floor shook concrete dust drifted from the tunnel ceiling. "*Great camera angle,*" Shelly quipped. "*I am so keeping a copy of that.*"

I walked back to the junction box. "Stay on task, Shell."

"*At this point I could make you a cake and do your taxes, the drag is on the server end. Damn slow 21st Century tech—Hope! Teleports!*"

I flew back into the room.

Three somebody's had joined Shelly—one close to Grendel-size and two more reasonably male adult proportioned—and I couldn't see anything but their outlines but Shelly's virtual-tags froze my blood: Dozer, Drop, Doctor Pellegrini. What the hell was *Pellegrini* doing here? And then it didn't matter; Drop and the Ascendant looked unsteady on their feet—I remembered that DSA briefs suggested Drop's jumps took it out of people—but Dozer turned and took two steps before I cleared the inner door. Sweeping Shelly aside to bounce hard off the wall, he crushed the server stack and the steel cage that housed it.

No.

I didn't slow down; I'd already unbuckled my pouch full of sandman packs, and now I leaped forward to slap one on Drop, catching him right in the neck with it. He vanished in a space-twisting blur before it could finish the job but I was already turning—

Dozer caught me in the side.

Managing to let myself go with his hit, I bounced off the other wall but stayed on my feet. My head rang and my virtual-vision got weird before coming back more clear; he'd damaged my helmet feeds but Shelly was in the same room to live-stream it for me.

I put Dozer between me and Pellegrini, took off my helmet. "Eric, please don't. You don't want to do this."

Eric Ludlow, Gantry, Dozer—war veteran, supervillain, the first superhuman I'd ever fought (briefly, he'd been drunk), looked just like I remembered except the hay-colored hair he'd cut military-short again. He wasn't wearing anything but an extra-large pair of jeans—obviously they'd mobilized fast. And now he stood there, literally stunned.

"Eric, it's okay." I lowered my hands. "You can stop now." *Really? Why? Because back home he seemed to not like fighting you?* I desperately tried to remember what Blackstone had said about him; that my sympathetic arrest of the guy had maybe helped him sober up, get straight, at least before he'd meet and been recruited by another Ascendancy member during the cleanup of the Big One. Blackstone had suggested I might have leverage. How much leverage did I have here, where I'd died?

Hearing Shelly rise, I took another two steps to put her behind me. "Really, Eric. I know it's been tough. You've done things you—you didn't want to do. But you don't want to fight me, do you?"

"You're dead."

"Yes, but not where I come from. I fought you there, too. You *made* me fight you." *And you gave me a beating I still remember.* "I asked you to stop, before more people got hurt. Aren't you tired of it, Eric?"

"Don't listen to her, Eric!" Pellegrini finally decided to open his mouth. What the *hell* did he think he was doing, coming here himself?

"You attacked a town there, Eric." I kept my voice low. "A whole town full of people who'd done nothing to anyone. And you're going to do that here." *As soon as the Ascendant decides that he wants his own pocket-reality.* "I asked you to stop, and then I made you stop. I'll stop you here, but I don't want to have to. Don't hurt anyone else, Eric. Please."

"Hope—" Shelly whispered behind me but I didn't take my eyes off him. I didn't look at the shattered server. If I did I might be sick. Chest heaving, fists flexing, Eric stared back. I didn't move. Eric didn't move.

But the room wasn't that big, and my steps to put myself between Eric and Shelly had moved me off-side; with my focus on Eric I didn't move fast enough when Pellegrini lunged. "Hah!" He brushed my instinctively up-thrust arm and I staggered back as my senses shattered.

This time I hadn't been half-concussed. *This* time I managed to keep reality from going away even as I fell to a knee, feeling like a puppet whose strings had been cut. I'd been de-powered. Again.

"Get the other one, Eric!" Pellegrini shouted. "Get the—" Coming up off my knee, I clocked him with my helmet and he went down like a stunned ox.

Breathing hard I stared at Eric, ignoring Shelly still behind me. You'd think that a Verne's sound-dampening field had gone off in the room. Finally, he straightened up, relaxing his fists.

"Miss Corrigan, you can't fight me now. I could take the doc and go."

I dropped my helmet to the floor. "You might."

"But I won't."

"Thank you. Hold me up?" My head spun, and he lunged forward to catch me before I face-planted into the smashed server or concussed myself on the concrete floor. "Thank you. Shelly? Did you tell the boys upstairs who showed up? Do they need your help?"

I couldn't see her face behind her dark helmet, but she shook her head. "They were busy. And no, they've handled it. Grendel pushed the A Class upstairs through every load bearing wall in the place, and if you'd believe it, Blindspot stunned the other one. Some kind of telekinetic, never saw him coming."

"Eric? Anybody else coming? I dosed Drop before he left, so I don't think he's coming back."

He shifted his hold on me. "If you did, then we're all there is."

"Good to know. Shell, tell everyone to stand by. What?" My brain wasn't quite working, but Eric wouldn't stop looking at me funny.

"Are you scared of anything? At all?"

"Trees. Doctors. Clowns. Telling a guy I like that I'm into him. Lots of things. Shell, check Pellegrini, then sandman him and glue-tape him till he's a mummy." I swallowed a hysterical laugh; he'd never even got a chance to monologue. "*Don't* tell Grendel he's down here. Just, don't." I decided my legs were working, pulled away from Eric to drop into the steel chair by the computer station. His hands empty, he just stood there with no idea what to do with them.

Checking and dosing and taping took Shelly a moment, which at least gave me time to *think*. Not that it really helped.

The job had gone completely pear-shaped. Off the rails. I had no idea how much useful information Shelly would be able to reconstruct from what she'd managed to copy, no idea if *anything* could be recovered from the pile of bits Eric had turned the server into. And we might have *Doctor Freaking Pellegrini* taped up on the floor, but *I wasn't the law*. With this mess, I couldn't believe that his attorneys wouldn't be able to turn any investigation and prosecution into a circus. He'd *walk*, powers or no—

I blinked. "Shell, the Public Safety and Security Act—the detainment requirement."

"What about it?"

"You said any licensed CAI cape was *required* to detain any unregistered breakthrough for evaluation? Are there any circumstances that supersede that requirement?"

"No, but—"

"I didn't finish certification here, before I died, but I'm a fully licensed and certified CAI cape back home. Is there any legal recognition of that, for visitors like me?"

"Well..." She got that distant look, then a grin spread across her face. "The Supreme Court has been finessing it. In one case they ruled that an extrareality double of someone real and deceased couldn't claim that person's property—they're just not that person. But in another decision they recognized the professional qualifications and legal certification of an extrareality visitor from a parallel history, even though certification had been granted in an alternate Mississippi..."

"And I'm CAI certified and licensed to wear the cape in the Great State of Illinois!" I was *legit* in a weird sort of way, at least until they stripped my credentials here. It made me dizzy; if I hadn't insisted on hiding when I'd arrived, I'd have probably been completely fine.

Then I'd run of course, and hadn't stopped breaking laws since, but while they could try and prosecute me for all that if I stayed, I wasn't a state agent for *this* Illinois. It wouldn't affect their prosecution of Pellegrini. And they didn't even need to arrest him *now*—they just had to "detain and evaluate him" when I reported his power. So whatever they did to me, this would give them plenty of time to analyze whatever

Shelly had retrieved and nail him with it. But that meant I had to stay to report Pellegrini. And first...

"Eric?" I had to clear my throat. "Eric. I think you should go. I really think you should turn yourself in, but you should make that decision yourself, and not here. There's always Canada, and I'm sure Shell can arrange a new identity for you. If you could phone in Drop's location as a tip, that would be great."

"Hope—" Shelly started, but I shook my head. "Go on, Eric. Maybe we'll share a cell in a day or two."

Eric never had been a man of many words; he nodded and left.

"Hope, what are you doing?"

"Isn't it obvious? I'm detaining Pellegrini. Make sure that everyone upstairs is alright, secure the foundation guys, then have Crash take Kitsune out of here. Put yourself and Grendel in the van with Blindspot, and drive out of here as soon as you see the team landing. Oh, and call the team. They're looking for me, after all."

Of course my Best Friend Anywhere argued. But she'd had two years of making hard choices herself, and she could see she wasn't going to move me on it. I explained to everyone that I had to stay as a witness, without going into detail, promised Kitsune that he could break me out again if he had to. I felt bad about not telling Brian who we'd captured, but de-powered as I was nobody here could even try and stop him if he decided to come down and rip the mass-murderer's head off. I hoped he'd forgive me.

Kitsune left with Crash. I stood outside with the pile of foundation staff and Pellegrini—after some thought I'd had Shelly tape up his face and then bring him upstairs with the sleeping neuralkinetic—and less than ten minutes after Shelly's call I spotted Variforce's familiar Watchman-propelled fields. They brought the whole team, and of course didn't see the unnoticeable van that drove away as they landed.

"Hi guys. I'd like to make an official detainment? And is there any chance I can get Legal Eagle? I might need representation."

A week later I stood outside on the garden veranda of our Oak Park home with my bag slung over my shoulder, carefully holding the globe. Mom and Dad still couldn't quite bring themselves to believe that it had been a gift from Santa.

It had been a busy week. This time the Sentinels had gone by the book, and I'd been okay with that. Veritas had listened to my voluntary statement, promptly made a call, and suddenly Springfield was declining to prosecute. I still didn't know if anyone had spoken to Mayor Shankman directly, but the City of Chicago also declined and I was free to go home.

Less than a day after our caper, Shelly had sent a huge packet of electronic files to the DSA—backup for what they were managing to extract from the dead server (it turned out that Eric's big smash had disconnected the capacitor from the drives so they'd been able to recover almost everything). They hardly needed the server drives anyway—which might not have been accepted in trial—since Eric had called in Drop's location and then turned himself in before the day had ended. He'd given testimony and named names. Lots of them.

There was no reason they had to, but the state also declined to prosecute our vigorous breaking-and-entering and granted amnesty for the Young Sentinels—which was what Brian, Jamal, and Mal were calling themselves in their press interviews because of course the media was all over it. We'd outed and taken down the *Ascendant*, and the Wreckers with the help of teams in California who served the warrants Eric's testimony generated. The whole web of what had become the Ascendancy back home was being exposed and rolled up and Congress gave us medals (all except Kitsune, who'd never been there). I had mine in my bag.

Kitsune disappeared with a flash drive full of everything we'd recovered. I had a copy, too, but whatever happened to me the secrets of the Ascendancy would make it home with him. I never got to introduce my "boyfriend" to the parents, but of course I did get to introduce both Shelly and Younger Me to everyone. Mom and Dad grasped the fundamental twinned nature of their Hope and Shelly right away, allowing me to feel a lot better about leaving them all to take care of each other. Mom convinced Shelly to get in touch with *her* mom before our show-and-tell evening was over.

So I couldn't fix the world but at least I was leaving it a lot better off than I'd expected to be able to—and it mostly hadn't been me. (Okay, so I'd made some calls, too. Doctor Cornelius and Jacky knew what his Words of Power could do now, and Chakra knew she and Blackstone had become an item.)

Mom touched my arm gently. "Are you going to be alright?" We'd known that it would be time to go as soon as my powers came back and I'd woken up all better this morning, called Doctor Beth at the Dome so he could log it, and packed after breakfast. Dad and Mom stood with me, his arm around my shoulders and hers around my waist, watching the birds in the garden. Shelly and Hope hovered, virtually present but quiet (we'd all talked a *lot* the past few days).

I tried on a smile. It didn't feel completely fake, at least. "'But all will be well, and all will be well, and all manner of things will be well.'"

Mom's eyes crinkled. "Look at you, quoting Julian of Norwich."

"Hey, Father Nolan's favorite text." Sunday mass had been interesting, though he hadn't used that one. Dad cleared his throat and I turned my head.

"You'll be careful?"

I hugged him back with one arm before pulling away and turning to look at everyone. It was almost too much. "I'll be careful, Dad. Really. I—"

What could I possibly *say*? Nothing, apparently, and I didn't have to; Mom and Dad leaned in for synchronized kisses to my cheeks, giving my shoulders a last squeeze before stepping back as I blinked away sudden tears.

"I love you. Goodbye." I took a deep breath, and turned the globe.

DSA Field Report: Agent Smith.

"The time is out of joint. O cursèd spite, that ever I was born to set it right!" Hamlet, boss, and my Harvard degree wasn't wasted. Ozma promised daily updates, but Crash is dropping back in a lot more frequently than every twenty-four hours—there's some kind of time-slippage between the termini. I have no idea what that even means, but if it flips the other way then what do we do? If a day passes there while a week or more passes here, we could lose control of our end of the rift. I don't like it. Japan has all sorts of trouble with incursions, boss, and their practice is to ring sites like this with mecha or at least a lot more firepower than we've got on call. I know we've got a budget, boss, but it's better to explain overruns to the Congressional Oversight Committee than try and explain why we lost Portland. I've attached the Need More Firepower form.

Odysseus Case File 1-F429 B.

Wargames

by Marion G. Harmon

"Jump #9. What can I say about Jump #9? I was tired, I was more than just a bit detached, and after the stress of #7 and the weirdness of #8 I was treating the whole thing like a waking dream. Still pretty sure I did the right thing, for all the good it might have done there."

Astra Cross-Reality Debrief Session, 14.2

She was a *twist*. She had to be. Yeah she wore an inner-city outfit, all bright and clean and what had to be the newest fashion since I didn't recognize it from any vids—was the star a campaign symbol? And yeah she looked peachy-fresh and gene scrubbed, practically Aryan which wasn't something you saw much these days; most parents wealthy enough to afford selection preferred the dark-light contrast of ebony and gold or cream skin and jet-black hair for their kids. But she grabbed the cybered war-twist who'd pinned me screaming to the wall, hammered him into the ground with one hand, so she had to be a twist, right? But who made pretty twists? When she pulled out the spike pinning me to the shattered wall with a whispered apology, I screamed higher and passed out.

"I can't fly," she said when I woke up in the dark.

"What, you get motion sickness?" My side felt tight and hot, but she'd found my med-kit and if she'd never seen one before she'd known to read directions; my probing fingers told me I had a brace patch on, and not being in agony said I had at least one dose of pain-block inside me.

"I can't fly," she explained patiently. "So I don't know where we are." Her soft words had a precision to them that sounded...

"Are you from Greater Chicago?"

"Oh, it's greater, now?" Her teeth shone in the glow of the hooded camp light—light! I panicked for two heartbeats until I realized she'd found us a shielded refuge, spread a camo-sheet over our heads. A quick eyeball-recon painted a steep ditch blocked by some old burned out wreck. On our open side the ditch went maybe twenty feet before turning sharply; nobody would see us unless they were right on top of us or coming up the ditch at us.

"So where are we, soldier?" Her question brought me back to her. Like she could be *lost*?

"A long way from Greater Chicago." I moved a little, experimenting. "The foot of the Rocks."

"The rocks?"

"The mountains? Western North-Am?"

She nodded, smile fading. "And what are we doing at the foot of the Rocks?"

Ratshit. It was the smoothest interrogation opening I'd ever seen, and I clamped my jaw on more stupid words. She sighed.

"So I'm supposed to Sherlock you? You're a soldier, got it. From your dirt and smell you've been in the field for a while. You're carrying full pockets and pack, lots of ammo, so either you haven't had a serious fight yet—other than back there—or you had a resupply. I can't think of any elites that go out alone except maybe snipers and you're not armed for that, so I'm guessing you lost the rest of your team since your last resupply. I'm sorry."

And she sounded it, too, which was starting to freak me out. Who *was* she? The only stuff in the ditch with us that wasn't mine was a fancy handbag, stuffed full but looking as bright and clean as she was. And with those blue, worried eyes watching me I had to keep reminding myself she was a twist.

A twist who hadn't killed me.

A twist who'd killed or maimed another twist to save my dead ass.

A twist who'd patched me up and hadn't even tied me.

She kept going. "And from the condition of, well, everything around here I'd say this ground has been fought over for years. Right?"

"Who *are* you?"

That brought back the smile. "And you don't recognize the star. So, just Hope. You can call me Hope. Should I just call you Soldier?"

"Flynn." I gave her that much. She nodded and sat back, giving me space.

"Nice to meet you, Flynn. I don't know how long I'm here for, and this ditch seems quiet. But is there somewhere I can take you? Anywhere you need to be?"

What. The. Hell?

She left me alone, except to check that I was comfortable a couple of times. She even stacked my gear—guns and all—by me in easy reach before disappearing down the ditch, walking confidently into the dark and coming back with a full canteen.

I tried to figure out what the actual flaming pile was going on. She'd killed the other war-twist so she'd wanted me alive. But for *what*? Had she called in, told her makers where we were while I was out of it? Were we waiting for pickup?

But I'd tested the hole in me while she was gone; I wasn't hurt bad enough to immobilize me—not with her care and the patch and the blocker and the stims and regen in my blood. I'd counted the empty injectors to see what she'd given me. I'd also had my loaded service pistol in my hand when she walked back up the ditch, and she hadn't even looked at it, just put the sloshing canteen down beside me before sitting back down.

And she was still *freaking me out*. She didn't look like any twist I'd ever seen, didn't talk like a vat-grown, brain jacked twist. She looked young and fresh and would be totally invisible in any in-city crowd, a monster among sheep, blood and horror waiting to rage.

If the Biolords had made her, we were all dead—the war was over except for counting the bodies. But if they'd made her, why was she *here*?

"Where did you come from?" It took me a moment to realize I'd said the words.

She brightened. "Depends. What year is this?"

"Twenty seventy-three."

"Then I'm from sixty years in the past."

I laughed, a chopped bark before I could stop it. "Yeah, right. Nobody made twists back then—" She shook her head.

"Not *your* past. I'd have guessed this was one of the Bad Futures, but since I can't fly the rules are different here, and nothing I'm saying is making sense to you, I'm guessing a Stage Two Reality from a theme or fiction. So, future war? Maybe a hugely popular computer game."

Ratshit. She was a *crazy* twist. But the Biolords terminated those mistakes fast, so why was she *alive*? An escapee? But that didn't explain every other thing about her.

Blue eyes blinked slowly. How much could she read in my face?

"So, tell me about this war? Whatever's not classified, I mean, I get that. There's probably a reason I'm—hold on."

She scrambled to the top of the ditch, put her head just below the edge under the camo-sheet, and listened. I couldn't hear anything but light rain on the sheet. A minute later she slid back down.

"Some kind of heavy engines out there, moving pretty slow. If you have mechanized units in the area I can take you to them? Or just yell real loud?"

"No!" I clamped my jaw on anything else.

"Okay, okay." She made calming motions, returned to the top of the ditch. This time she stayed up there longer, I almost drifted off before she slid back down. "They're moving away, I can't spot anything like drones, so unless they're using something like keyhole satellites to watch us, I think we're okay. So, what are they? I mean, what are you fighting? I can't automatically assume you're one of the Good Guys, but you're human and the thing that tried to kill you—well I'm not sure what it was. So call it blind solidarity but until I learn different, I'll side with the human. What's going on?"

What's going on? I coughed on a laugh, a mistake. A twinge got around the pain blockers. If she wanted non-classified intel, I'd give her a history lesson.

"The Biolords are what's going on. Genetic supremacists. They control North-Am from the Rocks to the Pacific. We've been trying to keep them contained for ten years." I waxed lyrical for most of an hour on the history of the war that any schoolkid would know. Either she really didn't know or she was the best actress in the whole crapsack world; as I went on she looked progressively less confused and more horrified.

"Perspective is a bitch," she said when I wound down.

"What?"

"Don't worry about it. And you're out here because..."

The fading stims made it hard to think. Why did she want to know? It wasn't like the mission wasn't blown; I'd lost my team, and the beacon, in the ambush. Game Over; the cache I'd found had been pointless—I'd just been wandering with no way of completing the mission when the lone war-twist caught me.

She killed a war-twist!

It had to be the drugs; there was no way she could have done that. I blinked, a long one, and she looked concerned. What had she wanted to know? Oh yeah.

"Recon. Biolord forces made a push three weeks ago, overran five counties before we pushed them back. They emptied a bunch of small towns, and we have intel that says most of the residents are interned somewhere in this zone. The sons-of-bitches use prisoners for biomaterial. Men, women, children, it doesn't matter."

The pain block was failing, but with the stims losing their grip the jabbing spikes only made me more confused. I tried to find a better position, tried not to think of the children. What had we— Right, the mission. "My team was one of three sent into the zone to try and find the internment camp. We were supposed to locate the camp and plant an LZ beacon."

"So it was a search and rescue mission."

"Was. It's completely burned, now. Team's gone, beacon's gone. My team had the best shot—the other two were covering the outside bets." I pointed vaguely in the direction of the Rocks. "The whole division is waiting for a signal, telling them where to push. That was the mission. Game Over." Why were my eyes watering?

The girl—Hope—patted me on the shoulder that didn't scream hurt. "Stand down, soldier. Everything's going to be alright."

"Really? Because it's one bottomless crapsack, now."

"I promise. Go to sleep." She had a real nice voice. Soft. I hadn't heard soft voices in a while. Yelled commands, barked orders, stealth whispers, screams. Nothing soft. I made myself nod.

"Yeah. Good idea. I'll be okay tomorrow."

"Yes you will. Goodnight." I felt a brush on my sticky forehead, permission to close my eyes.

My eyes slammed open and I looked up at sunlight through camo-cloth. *What?*

The war-twist. The impossible girl. The ditch. We'd...talked?

I tried to stand up, couldn't manage more than elbows and ass as I looked around. No impossible girl, but someone had laid all my gear out neatly. Someone not me, I could see that. My med-kit was spread beside my right elbow, empty injectors lined up where I could see them. And a full canteen with a note.

Corporal Flynn. You're running a fever so I decided not to give you any more stims, but I administered another pain-block after you went to sleep. You've got four left. I'm sorry but I've taken your compass-map. It was very nice to meet you, and it's never Game Over.
Sincerely, Hope Corrigan.

What? I rubbed my face, probed my side, and looked at the note again. If it wasn't for the wrinkled and pressed piece of paper—she'd used the wrapping of a field-ration—I'd think that part of last night a mind-warp hallucination from blood loss, shock, and stims. *What—*

The soft roar of the lifter passing high overhead told me what had woken me up. A second. A third. I scrambled, nearly passing out again, to the top of the ditch to look out from the edge of the camo. The laughter should have hurt; *seven* trails in the sky, the whole airlift capacity of the division. Turning my head to look east I could see dust clouds that signaled landlift on the move.

I ripped the camo-away and pushed myself to my knees, waving. The drones would find me.

"I don't even know how to begin writing this up." Captain Beaur scratched the back of his head, looked out the window of the command bunker.

I smoothed out the note without looking at it, my hands shaking on the cold table. "She really did it?"

"I don't know about *she*, corporal. High-altitude drones picked up the explosion at around oh-six hundred hours this morning, analysis said it was big enough it had to be a whole Biolord munitions camp. We lost a flight of drones getting a closer look, and the heat-signatures headed east from zero said civilians. We didn't have your beacon signal, but the general ordered go, and it was the internment camp. Also what was left of an armor camp. The explosion took out its camo."

"The civilians?"

"We're still counting, but it looks like most of them—maybe all— are still here. They're in a bad way, but we're evacuating them to the rear and pushing forward now that we don't need to worry about them anymore. We may push the Biolords all the way back into the Rocks in this sector. Do you want to add anything? A squad couldn't have done it. A brigade might have done it, maybe. They were still shooting at *something* when we came in. Whatever it was ripped into a whole platoon of war-twists like they were toy soldiers. Is this some kind of rogue monster war-twist we should be worried about?"

Not a war-twist. A war-angel. Wherever she was now. I shook my head. "Nothing to add, sir. Maybe after more sleep. When can I report—"

"You can't. We're sending you home. Debrief, physical rehab, probably move you into instructing after this. This breakthrough is good, we'll probably win the sector. Hell, the way their offensives have slowed, we may finally be winning the war." He pushed back his chair and stood up. "But it's Game Over for you—you're going to help train the next wave. Whatever happened out here, good work, corporal." He snapped a salute as I pushed myself up, held it until I returned it.

"Thank you, sir." I left with the note. Outside, I could see the pillar of smoke still rising from the armor camp.

She'd been wrong; it was always Game Over for somebody. *Right, Flynn, but twelve thousand live civilians is a pretty good Mission Accomplished. Be a little less cynical.* Carefully folding the note, I tucked it in my breast pocket and limped back to the medical bunker.

DSA Field Report: Agent Smith.

Really, boss? A team of Platoons? Much as I like him—them—whatever, I'm not sure five synchronized agents is going to do it if something big and nasty comes knocking. At least if something eats all of us then the Platoon keeping your calendar will be able to tell you what it was. Sorry, boss. This site is giving me the heebie-jeebies; I don't like standing beside an open door when I can't see what's on the other side. *Sides*.

Odysseus Case File 1-J238 D.

Astra Gets Grrl Power

by Marion G. Harmon and Dave Barrack

"You'd think, after everything I'd seen, I'd have expected something like that. Right? But Jump #12? I did not see that one coming."

Astra Cross-Reality Debrief Session, 21.8

Nobody felt the cold but brief gust of arctic wind that blew papers and city dirt into sudden motion in the narrow service alley, and the light flurry of snow that came with it melted quickly in Chicago's first spring heat. Nobody saw Hope blink into existence, either, like a 1960s stop-motion cinema photography trick.

She straightened her cape, slipped the now useless snow globe into her canvas tote-bag, and studied the alley. She hadn't changed location this time, which she decided was a good sign. But the alley hadn't changed, either, and her shoulders slumped a little.

Bright side, there *was* an alley. She hadn't jumped into a primeval forest again, or a landscape of flattened and scorched rubble. But the building beside her shouldn't be there; the old residential tower was one of the pieces of Chicago landscape destroyed in The Event and replaced with something newer and shinier.

Which meant she'd just made her last jump with Santa's gift, and still wasn't home.

Pull it together, Hope. Straightening, she tugged off her half-mask and tucked it away with the globe. No Event probably meant no superheroes, and for some reason masks made people nervous where there was no tradition for it. *Go figure.*

The sarcastic thought made her smile; she should probably be worried at how much her inner voice had started to sound like Shell. Compensating for the awful silence in her head where her virtual BF should be, obviously.

Yeah, well, as long as you know it's just you talking then you're not crazy. Yet. Now get out there.

Stepping carefully over the trash and oily patches that littered the alley, she emerged into what looked like the same Wabash parking lot she'd just walked through. The lot was emptier and the cars had changed, but they were still Toyotas, Fords, and other familiar brands. There were no flex-fueled *Terras*, and that was encouraging. No fliers in the sky, either, other than planes and a traffic helicopter; confirmation she'd jumped to another "mundane" extrareality.

"Hey! Nice Astra costume!"

Almost jumping out of her skin, Hope barely kept her feet on the ground. The young business-suited man heading for his car gave her a friendly laugh. "Are you headed for the convention? I've got tickets for tomorrow, and good thing—you can't get them now that it's official the Arc-SWAT team is here! Maxima! Yeah!"

"What— Yes. Can't wait." Hope clutched her bag.

He threw his briefcase in the back of his car, loosened his tie. "Well, you'll knock them dead in the cosplay contest—I've never seen a better Astra. I'll cheer for you."

"Thanks." She started walking to cut off any more comments or questions, but he was slipping behind the wheel and closing his door; perfect city-etiquette, don't ignore but don't meaningfully engage unless obviously invited to and Hope hadn't. He backed out and exited onto Wabash before she made it to the sidewalk. She watched him disappear into traffic. Something made her look up.

It was a single flier, a blonde girl wearing big glasses and some kind of paramilitary uniform crossing the sky west over the city. Hope counted five glowing spheres orbiting her head, and she held two more in her hands.

Time to find a library. *Really? You think?*

The Harold Washington Library on State Street had a nice computer center, and fifteen minutes of waiting and three more compliments on her costume got Hope an open screen. One search-term told her how wrong she was.

This wasn't another mundane world.

The confusing word her businessman had used was *Arc-SWAT* — SWAT being the unimaginative swapping of *Special* for *Super*. Super Weapons and Tactics, which made her wonder how many police department SWAT teams had objected. Arc-SWAT was the action arm of Archon, this America's version of the Department of Superhuman Affairs.

ARC. Atypical Resource Commission. Someone had really wanted to spell "Archon."

Since the word meant ruler—it came from the same root word as mon*arch* and no less than three supervillains back home had grabbed it as their nom-de-guerre—she could only hope someone here wasn't being *that* clever.

And Archon was new. Finding a video-file of Arc-SWAT's debut, Hope watched them beat up a tank. It gave her chills; their leader, Maxima, could easily have waxed *Atlas*. Or Seif-al-Dinn. A quick search of news and fansites turned up a power-scale that made her heart sink. Little Hope Corrigan might rate a 6, Ultra level here. The scale rated Maxima as a 9, *Penumbra* level.

The articles Hope scanned only referenced superhumans—supers—this world's version of breakthroughs. A bunch of bloggers speculated about the source of the superscience stuff used by a super named Dabbler (she sounded like a Verne-Type to Hope, but apparently they weren't common here), and nobody knew what to make of Halo's spheres. Halo, the girl she had seen flying over Chicago.

Hope sat back and tried to absorb it all.

So, almost no *superheroes* in this world, but they could be terrifyingly powerful. And superhumans had been around forever—it looked like most of the ones with truly useful abilities earned big money in the private sector. Weirdly, the one unifying feature of all superhumans was that, whatever their powers, every last one of them met the classical Greek conception of physical perfection; if they never used their powers they could all get jobs as fashion runway models. Victoria's Secret would take every last female one of them.

It would be nice if breakthroughs worked like that... She shook the image of a six foot tall C-cup Hope Corrigan out of her head and did a search for superhuman history. There was no trace of an Event in Archon World's history, and she frowned.

Without an originating Event, it didn't make a lot of sense that no supers had been especially high-profile until recently (although lots of online sources speculated that earlier superhumans were the basis for most myths). Archon was the first *publicly* known association of supers—and now the first superteam was a government-run military team that could roll right over the Sentinels without breaking much of a sweat. *Not* good. Another search let her relax a bit; although some people were calling for it, this America had no compulsory registration of supers—her "unregistered" presence here wasn't illegal. Archon wasn't *hunting* superhumans; just acting as super-cops and coming down on the ones breaking the law. So she was safe. Although technically she was an illegal immigrant...

Hope set that aside and entered one last search word: *Astra.* Despite the fact that she'd arrived physically instead of slipping into an Archon World analogue of herself, being "recognized" by half a dozen people who thought her Astra costume was great had left her expecting to find herself a member of Arc-SWAT. So, why no mention of her? The generated links told her why, and she didn't know whether to scream or giggle hysterically. Neither was appropriate for a library.

She was *fictional*. Even worse—Stacia Ellis, the young actress playing her in the new *Sentinels* TV show, looked just like her. *Just* like her; looking at the publicity stills was like looking at any news image back home. She was amazed that nobody had asked for her autograph yet.

At least she wouldn't need to worry about running into any Corrigans in this Chicago. Twice had been enough, and she didn't want to risk it again.

And I'm wasting time.

Surrendering her station, she exited the library. Back outside, she found herself standing on the street with no idea which way to go.

The snow globe was a paperweight now—she'd used up all "twelve days" of jumps it had in it and according to Saint Nick it wouldn't recharge until Christmas. She'd started jumping confident she'd make it home in time for Annabeth and Dane's wedding; now she was trying not to admit that she might not make it home this *year*.

Which left her two options.

She could try and fit in here until she could jump again.

And that was laughable; she didn't exist, legally, and if she tried to get a private-sector job with her powers the *first* thing prospective employers would do was ask for her social security number and run a background check. And whether or not superhumans had to register, this Archon entity absolutely had to *investigate* the backgrounds of new superhumans who popped up.

So they would look into her background and realize she had no document trail. And that she looked like Stacia Ellis' clone... For one hysterical moment, Hope wondered if the production studio needed a stunt-double. *No.*

But regardless, Archon would still be coming to ask her pointed questions.

Or she could introduce herself to Archon and ask for help, or even for employment until next Christmas...

Yeah, like that couldn't possibly go bad.

She shushed her Shell-voice. She'd found no hint that there might be other extradimensional travelers wandering around, and had no idea if Archon would even buy her story since the articles she'd scanned had only referenced superhumans of local origin. Did they have anyone like Veritas? Then they'd have to believe that *she* believed it, and if they still certified her sane then she might have a job. She might have a job if they thought she was crazy but functional—it wasn't like her skill-set was that common around here (although their insurance company might have something to say about hiring a crazy person).

Or—wild hope—they might actually have a way to get her on her way again; just because the *public* didn't know about other realities didn't mean Archon was ignorant. If they already knew about other realities then maybe Dabbler could whip her up a jump-belt or something.

Hope started walking before she realized she'd made up her mind; the Chicago Comic Con was being held at the McCormick Place Event Center, and she'd figure out how to get in once she got there.

⊕

Sydney was still getting used to using landmarks for navigation, but the GPS function of her wrist-com had gotten her to Chicago. From above, the City by the Lake looked just like it did on Google Earth, and she only had to check her map once before she found the convention center. "Gotcha!" she laughed when she saw it. "You're mine, now. All mine..."

Hovering over the roof of the parking garage across from the convention center, she let go of her violet shield-orb and it rose to join the five others orbiting her head. Her airtight force field dissipated, Chicago's relatively bracing (and polluted) air rushing in to replace the more verdant air she'd picked up over a forest a few hundred miles back. Airtight force fields had their advantages, but it meant she'd had to stop and refresh her air supply during her otherwise supersonic trip.

Letting go of her blue flight orb, she realized that she was slightly off-axis when local gravity reasserted itself; stumbling and flailing wildly to catch her balance, she reached up and grabbed an orb without thinking—willing it to *be still* while she steadied herself with it.

"Yes! Scoville saves!"

Congratulating herself on not eating roof and giving her face a gravel rash, she looked up and yanked her hand back—she'd grabbed *Pew Pew*! Released, the red sphere dimmed, feeling almost *disappointed* to Sydney, and she wiped imaginary sweat off her brow.

She still wasn't sure of Pew Pew's safety feature yet, and Arc-SWAT had labeled her red orb "Bad for A *Tank*." Not needed to cut anything in half (or into discrete flaming particles), Pew Pew drifted upwards to rejoin the other six spheres orbiting just above her head in the configuration that had earned her the "Halo" moniker. (Or as Sydney insisted everyone call her, "The Mighty Halo"; it was never too early to stake out the name of your comic book.)

"Scoville saves..." she muttered, shaking off the near-disaster as she rubbed her cold hands. Spring in Chicago definitely wasn't spring back home; her urban camo Arc-SWAT Field Dress uniform was warm enough, but not for the first time she lamented the fact that needing skin contact to use her orbs kept her from wearing gloves. Checking the time on her wrist-com, she unpacked the thermal-wrapped spicy breakfast burrito she'd gotten from Fusion on her way out; in her hurry to leave Archon headquarters before Arianna or Maxima figured out a reason why she couldn't fly up early to give herself a little time at the comic con before "supervision" arrived, she'd skipped breakfast.

It wasn't bad—the habanero salsa wasn't what she'd call *hot*, but it had enough bite that her lips felt it. Finishing it, she checked the time again and reached into her jacket to pull out a dog-eared blue notebook to look at her schedule.

The List, as she named all her notebooks, had started as her mother's earnest attempt to help her scatterbrained daughter organize better. Sydney was on her twelfth pad, and while she'd mostly filled the first one with daily to-do lists, number twelve was chock-full of lists, doodles, movie screenplay ideas (mostly involving lots of shirtless men), and notably, grievances; the newest entry simply read "That guy in the grocery store who only bought whipped marshmallow in a jar, Nutella, and a box of Golden Grahams."

Sydney shook a mental fist. *Damn you, evil genius!* It wasn't fair—certainly not Sydney's fault that she ate herself sick on the same, fiendishly brilliant, concoction. And not "ooh, my tummy hurts" sick, either; more like "Why does the shower curtain smell like s'mores?" sick. She flipped past it to her schedule. Her wrist-com contained an electronic version, but physically writing things down helped solidify information in her attention deficit-addled brain.

"Yesssss!" She had about an hour to kill before the rest of the team arrived to debut at the con—time enough to wander the floor for a bit. Snapping the notebook shut, she zipped it up in her jacket.

Time to implement her fiendish plan.

Being one of the few superheroes working in the states came with the double-edged sword of immense celebrity status. One of the perks was getting invitations to all manner of superhero themed events (just thinking about the open invitation she'd received to the premier of *Avengers III* made her drool a bit). The obvious downside was being nearly as recognizable as any A-list actor—*especially* in uniform. Fortunately, the place below was one of the few places on Earth where she could pass unnoticed with minimal effort. *Hee hee hee.*

Sydney *loved* cosplay, and normally she'd cosplay as someone else entirely, but she hadn't wanted to haul a whole separate outfit up to Chicago with her. The solution was to simply dress up as The Mighty Halo!

Sliding off her knapsack, she set it on the ground away from the puddle she'd almost face-planted into. Transferring her very real pistol, tazer and pepper spray to shoulder holsters inside her jacket, she knelt down and opened the pack to produce obviously-fake plastic replicas and holster them on her belt. Pulling out and unfolding a spoked metal ring about the size of a medium pizza and a pole about two feet long, she slid the pole into a narrow pocket on the back of her pack so that it would stick up over her head when she put it back on. The pole slotted into the center of the spokes on the ring, and seven wire frame bowls attached to the outside of the ring, facing up. Perfect!

She slung the pack on again and looked up, mentally adjusting the orbits of her orbs until it looked like they were resting in the bowls, almost cackling as they settled into place and the whole thing began spinning slowly.

This was going to work! She *had* considered adding a wig to cover her very distinctively floppy "rabbit ear" bangs with much less convincing distinctive bangs, but thought she'd chance it for now. If anything was going to give her away, it was probably the fact everything she wore was professionally made, even her "orb-rack." To be really cosplay-authentic, she should have made the contraption now attached to her backpack out of bent up coat hangers; instead it looked like it had been made by someone who had access to a machine shop. Or who had access to someone who knew how to make stuff in a machine shop without injuring themselves or others.

Sydney wasn't allowed in the Archon headquarters machine shop.

Ready to mingle in anonymity, she summoned the flight orb to her hand and drifted down into the service alley between the parking garage and its neighboring business building. *And...we're safe!* Exiting the alley and walking to the intersection with a gaggle of con goers, she was invisible; nobody pointed and said "Look! It's the real Halo disguised as fake Halo!"

Standing at the crosswalk, waiting for the light and watching people streaming purposefully towards the center with their reserves of pre-con energy, she did a little happy-dance. No stranger to comic book and sci-fi cons, having traveled the circuit for years with her father, Sydney Scoville Senior, she expertly "weighed" the crowd.

An experienced eye like hers could always tell what day of the con it was by the energy level of the attendees. First day, everyone was chipper and excited to be there. First night, the enthusiasm was still there, but the energy would have waned considerably and most people were looking to turn in or find a party. The second day was equal parts energetic new arrivals, the caffeine kick-started, and the bravely beating back a hangover crowd. The third day had fewer new arrivals and a lot more caffeine fueled zombies. Today was obviously First Day.

Sydney named each cosplay as she spotted them. A Master Chief shared the corner with her, carefully not crowding her halo rig. Across the street she spotted two Doctor Who's, one of whom held the hand of a little girl wearing a TARDIS dress. A tall woman of better-than-average attractiveness wore designer paramilitary gear, probably from a video game but maybe SHIELD. (She was too far away for Sydney to get a good look, but based on the quality of the outfit she guessed the woman was a professional cosplayer.)

She also spotted Naruto, a better Naruto, several Star Wars characters, and an Astra from the new *Sentinels* TV show. *Probably another pro*, she judged from the authenticity and well-cut fit of the blue skater-dress-and-cape costume. Even the blue calf-high boots perfectly matched the rest of it, and footwear was where most cosplay costumes fell down.

"Is it actually legal to dress up as one of those Arc-SWAT dudes?" The question snapped Sydney out of her appraisal and the guy waiting behind her leaned in, eyeing Sydney's uniform critically. "I mean they're cops, right? Like, federal super cops? Aren't you impersonating an officer of the law if you dress up like them?"

Hah! She knew the answer to this. "You can dress up as one as long as you don't actually represent yourself as law enforcement. Also your outfit can't be exactly correct, it has to be obviously different in some way."

"Yeah, well yours looks pretty accurate except for that blue plastic gun. Where'd you find the patches?"

Crap! She'd meant to replace the Arc-SWAT seals with dummy patches. *Oh well, it's not like I can get in trouble for pretending to be me.* She opened her mouth, paused. *Can I?*

The guy watched her think for about twenty seconds before waving his hand in front of her face. "Hello?"

"Oh, uh, thanks! Ordered it made special—hopefully I won't find out if it's too accurate, right? Quality stitching! That's the key to proper cosplay! Feel that!" She tilted her shoulder towards the guy, and he ducked to avoid her halo rig, taking her up on her offer and tentatively pinching the fabric.

"What kind of material is this? It feels like a cross between silk and canvas."

Oops. "Well it's not a proprietary fiber coated in a non-Newtonian liquid making it even more bullet resistant than Kevlar if that's what you're asking! Hah hah... Hah!" Sydney gestured excitedly as if to cast a spell of forgetfulness on him. *These are not the droids you are looking for!*

It worked, or at least he leaned away from her. "Uh..."

"Welp! Time to make like a chicken and cross the road!" Sydney turned and bolted through the crosswalk—*finally* the light had changed.

Behind her she heard Master Chief say, "You know what? I think that might have been the real Halo disguised as a fake Halo."

The rig kept her from ducking through the shuffling crowd like she wanted, but nobody came after her whatever Master Chief thought.

"Should have brought the wig..." she muttered as she carefully wove her way towards the convention hall. Someone in Archon's PR office had had the foresight to get every attending member of the team a plus-one guest pass in addition to their VIP passes, and she used hers to enter the con without drawing any more attention to herself. *Safe again!*

Wandering the convention floor, she studied the map and checked the schedule, collecting comments and compliments on her costume and even stopping a couple of times to take and pose for pictures. Arriving at the dealer's room, she found the doors still closed. *C'mon!* She'd half-frozen her ears and hands off—whatever the season, high-altitude air was *cold* and her shield sphere was thermally conductive—to get here early and make her grab without anyone being the wiser, dammit! *Nooo!* Couldn't the convention *cooperate?* Turning, she heaved a sigh that turned into a hiccup when she almost ran into Maxima.

Well, not *Maxima*—a tall and busty girl wearing a purple wig, gold body paint, and a pretty good approximation of the Arc-SWAT team leader's uniform. Sydney's brain switched from near-panic to professional evaluation. *Not bad—the purple wig's a bit too red – wait, not a wig, she actually dyed her hair. The body paint doesn't shine like buffed gold chrome, but—*

"Hey, cool Halo costume!" Maxima's obvious boyfriend said. "Can we get a picture?"

Sydney nodded, swallowing her all-too-familiar body envy; while six or seven inches shorter than the genuine article, something the woman had gotten almost exactly right was Maxima's chest measurements. Trying not to stare, she estimated that the woman's bra was taking up some of the slack and suppressed a snicker. She wasn't sure Maxima would have appreciated the attention to that particular detail; bashful was never a word that could be used to describe The Golden Glamazon, but she always wore heavy leather jackets in public to downplay certain dimensions.

She could testify from experience that, almost without exception, superhumans looked very much like the supers of comics: taller than average, muscular, zero excess body fat whatever their diets. Yet female supers were still... How did that one article put it? Blessed with womanly abundance? *Yuck*. Most of the women on the team didn't seem to mind—why would they?—but Maxima hated it, grumbling that it distracted from her authority and ability to intimidate. Definitely a soldier first and a woman second.

All Sydney's powers came from the orbs she'd discovered scuba diving off the Florida Keys (which showed the universe was fundamentally undramatic—she should have found them in a mysterious antique store). *Not* a superhuman, she would have been happy if her body were even of average build but she was more on the leeward side of that particular bell curve. Before joining Arc-SWAT she'd been no more prone to A-Cup Angst than any other woman not better endowed, but given that most of her teammates were supers, sometimes it wore on her.

Wait, Boyfriend's mouth had been moving. What was he saying?

"Yeah Maxima's definitely my favorite... We're going to make a mess on the sheets tonight, right honey?"

Eww.

"Paul!" Maxima exclaimed, then turned to Sydney. "Sorry about that. I'm Casey by the way."

Sydney cheeks heated but she managed a shrug. "What are boyfriends for if not embarrassing us? Also, opening jars."

"Right! And protecting us from spiders." Casey smiled.

"Absolutely. I'm Sssssssssss..." *A name! Think of a name!* Committed to a name beginning with an "S", she'd totally blanked on all other women's "S" names. *C'mon, brain!* "ssssss...." Wait! Sydney was the name of the main character in the movie *Scream*, but in the spoof version, *Not Another Scary Movie*, her name was super similar and also began with an "S" sound...

"ssssCindy! Yeah, Cindy. Sorry, I have a tic."

"Oh. Well, nice to meet you." Casey allowed only a slight wrinkle to crease her brow as she moved closer to pose with Sydney.

Blame a disability to cover errant behavior! Score! Tourette's syndrome, good for a thousand public missteps.

"Anyway Paul!" Casey smacked her randy boyfriend in the chest. "I only painted my arms and face down to my... you know... V-neck."

"That's why I brought all that extra paint!" Paul leered smugly as he backed up to as he snap pictures. "Why mess up the sheets at home when we can leave the mess to the hotel?"

Casey looked struck. "...that's actually pretty solid," she muttered as the heat in Sydney's cheeks turned into a burn.

"I don't... really need to know about that."

"It actually shouldn't be too messy. This paint is... Paul, did you bring the alcohol wipes also? Cause this stuff is really hard to get off without them."

He paused in the act of taking another pic. "Define 'bring'."

"Paul..." Casey sighed.

"Well, thanks for the snaps, The Mighty Halo," he said, pushing his phone back into his pocket, obviously immune to his girlfriend's exasperation. "We're off to find us a Dabbler. An Anvil if we're lucky!"

"I guess *you* have a type, huh?" Sydney smirked.

Paul just laughed. "And I guess you have to play your body type, huh?" He slapped her on the shoulder.

"Paul!" Casey slugged him in the arm, rolling her eyes. "I swear to God! See you, Halo!" She grabbed his hand and pulled him away, mouthing *Sorry about that!* behind his back. Sydney watched them go with narrowed eyes before reaching into her jacket, ready to make a new entry to The List when a voice like a melodramatic stage actor called from behind her.

"Your attention, Orb Maiden!"

She spun around to see a man dressed in elaborate armor under vaguely druidic robes. He carried a helmet under one arm that looked like Daedric plate if it had been made for a spider. The metal looked real and the stitching on the robes was excellent work, too. She couldn't place the costume, though—which was weird, given her encyclopedic knowledge of the genres represented at conventions. The man wearing it didn't match the quality of the outfit; he might clean up nicely, but he currently looked like he'd gone several weeks without any serious attempt at grooming.

He gestured wildly at the doors to the dealer's room floor. "Have you the knowledge of whence this Room of Dealers avails itself to the cretinous masses?!"

At least he was staying in character, whoever it was. *Maybe he's a bad guy from some obscure TV show. Ooh! Maybe he's a new villain from The Sentinels!* The series' production studio was supposed to have a big presence at the convention. "Wow, uh, who are you dressed as?" she blurted, already forgetting his question.

"Your ignorance of His glory does you disservice, for I am a servant of the mighty Oryxarch! Destroyer of all he surveys! Consumer of hope! Engine of despair! Architect of Doom! Tipper of..."

"Oryx... like the deer thing?" Sydney interrupted, suspecting Oryxarch's resume was *really* comprehensive.

"Test not mine patience Orb Maiden, and render unto me the knowledge I require!"

"Uh, I think it opens at eleven? Never made sense to me why they wait so late. If I was a dealer who dragged my kit across the country, I'd want as much time..."

"YES! The eleventh hour!" he cried, curling his fingers into claws. "An auspicious tolling that will HERALD THE DOOM OF MAN!"

Sydney blinked. Usually she was the one providing melodrama. "...okay. Well. Good luck with that." She backed away slowly then turned to wander the floor until eleven.

Twenty minutes and many, many cosplay pictures later (and nobody suspecting a thing, ha ha!), she followed the tide into the opened dealers room. Resolutely ignoring the Marvel Studios booth (even in the face of drool-worthy pecs on the costumed Thor model) and the *Sentinels* booth (it wasn't like the *actors* were going to be there), she still found herself sucked into Artist's Row before she could find the booth she'd come for.

Ooooh.

She tried to decide if she could also sneak some The Mighty Halo art back to Archon Headquarters without getting caught. Maybe she could... "You're Halo." The soft words, spoken right by her ear, shot panic through her wiry frame and she jumped back, coming down in her patented anti-ninja Dancing Crane pose.

"Ayahhh!"

The girl standing beside her—the Astra cosplayer Sydney had seen outside the convention center—blinked, looking worriedly at the orbs wobbling in their swaying baskets above Sydney's head. "Okaaay..."

"I'm not—" Sydney came down from Crane stance, looked around wildly. "They look great, don't they? Ha ha." Right, left, front, back, a few con goers had looked their way when she'd screamed and hopped on one foot, but the room was full of weird and they kept walking.

"What was that?" the girl asked, smiling when Sydney turned back to her.

"What?"

"That." She gave a small hop, lifting her arms a little. As solemn as she'd sounded accusing Sydney of being herself, now she looked ready to laugh.

"My anti-ninja stance."

"Do ninjas attack you often?"

"Always. Expect. Ninjas."

The girl's laugh broke free. "Smart thinking! I'm Astra." She held out her hand.

Sydney took it, shook hard. "Not Halo. Because, obviously." And couldn't let go.

Really, she couldn't, which was just nuts—the girl in front of Sydney was almost exactly her height, maybe a smidge taller but hardly any curvier; if they'd been roomies she and Sydney could have raided each other's closets, but her grip had less give than a marble statue's.

"Don't panic," the fiendishly harmless-looking girl said, sighing when Sydney automatically reached down to try and pry herself free. Wrong move—the Astra's other hand joined hers and now they were holding hands like a couple of lesbians. *Stupid, stupid!* She should have gone for Pew Pew.

But what the hell? Seriously, what the hell? Super strength—but not *built* like a super. Android? A Sydney-sized Illusion cast over a stone golem? Or over a giant, talking spider with grippy spider hands? The possible talking spider-thing was talking *to her*, breaking in on Sydney's building eruption of *fight, flight*, or *crippling-case-of-the-willies*.

"The video files I saw showed you holding your orbs to use them? So if I let go, that means I'm handing you your guns back, right?" She let go. Hands-free, Sydney raised them high and then yanked them back down before she completely blew her cover, tried not to hyperventilate. What. The. *Hell*?

"Hey! Cool!" A con guest already loaded with two stuffed cloth bags of swag and overpriced action-figures stopped beside them. "Halo and Astra! Can I get a picture?"

"I— Um— Sure!" Sydney nodded spastically. The Astra shrugged and straightened into a one foot forward, hand-on-hip pose like she'd done it a million times. After flapping her hands indecisively, Sydney chose Maxima's fists-on-hips pose and the guy enthused enthusiastically as he took a bunch of shots, bags swinging from his arms as he held up his phone. A half dozen other booth browsers took advantage of the girls' team pose to get their own pics.

"Awesome!" Their fan tucked his phone away. "Thanks, I'll cheer for you guys at the contest!"

"Yay!" Sydney cheered weakly, giving him two thumbs up as the crowd broke up and everyone resumed the usual convention-walking Brownian motion. "Whew! That was close!"

"Right?" Astra *was* laughing. "Like they'd believe that Halo was masquerading as...Halo?"

"Right— Hey!" Sydney jumped back *again*, but kept her hands and foot down this time. "You're not going to trick me again!"

The Astra looked around. "I hope not. Listen, there's an empty booth the next aisle over. I'll keep my hands to myself, promise, but let's get out of traffic? Please?"

The empty booth sported two tables, a trash can, and four folding chairs, but whoever had rented the space obviously hadn't arrived yet. Squeezing around behind the tables, they put their bags down. The Astra took off her mask as well, shaking out her bobbed platinum-blond locks.

Sydney stared. "You're the *actress*?" She'd DVR'd the *Sentinels*' first eight episodes so far, watched them all at least three times to list all the superhero tropes and clichés the series used, and the girl in front of her looked *just* like the actress playing Hope Corrigan, new Sentinel and teen sidekick. "And a *super*?"

Smiling wryly, the girl shook her head. "No, it's so much worse than that. I'm Astra."

"...right." *Smile. Smile and nod...* Sydney looked the crazy girl—crazy *super*—over. Everyone had at least one body-double somewhere, and obviously—what was her name? Stacia-something, yeah Stacia had hers right here. In an Astra costume that looked like she'd stolen it right off the studio set. And a *super*. That was *too* crazy. Wait—

"Ahhh! I get it! It's like *Last Action Hero*! You've come out of TV-land to catch a supervillain who's escaped from the story! This. Is. So. Cool!"

Astra opened her mouth, shut it. "That's— Huh. Surprisingly close."

"Are they all here? I *so* want autographs! I should introduce Chakra to Dabbler— No, no reason to do that, ha ha. Is that Atlas guy as much of a tool as he is on the show? How about—wait—shake my hand again!"

"Okay. Why?"

"Seeing if you vibrate differently than me."

"You vibrate?"

"No, *I* don't. *Dimensions* vibrate. At least in all the sci-fi stories. I just thought maybe we'd be able to feel the difference if we touched."

Hope laughed again. "Right. Well, good thing I'm not from an anti-matter universe or we would have both exploded."

Sydney snatched her hand away and froze, casting unblinking eyes around. It was only after several explosion free moments lapsed that she uncoiled, nodding her head smugly. "That was a close one. High five! WAIT!" She yanked her hand back again, narrowly avoiding another non-disaster. "You won't get me that easily!" she yelled at no one in particular, shaking her fist at the sky. And now Astra was looking at her funny.

"What? Have I got something in my teeth?"

"Um, are you sure you're a federal agent?"

"In training! They need me for my vast genre-savvy!"

"Okay. Are more of them coming?"

"Yeah, we're—crap on a cracker! I've got to go!" Sydney almost vaulted the tables before realizing that a.) despite all of Peggy's drill-sergeant work with her she was still a spaz and likely to face-plant comically, and b.) wire baskets or not, the move would probably send her orbs everywhere. Instead she edged undramatically around the booth tables.

Astra followed. "Are you meeting them?"

"Not yet! Special mission! Incognito! Mask!"

"Oh! Right." The girl pulled her half-mask back on. "Where are we going?"

Sydney froze. "Wait. Swear you won't tell *anyone*. Swear it by Grabthar's hammer! Say it!"

"I...swear by Grabthar's hammer I won't tell anyone where we're going?"

"Excellent!" Sydney looked left and right. "Screw it. Memory blows." Pulling out *The List*, she turned to the page where she'd written the booth number. "D-12. No more distractions—let's go!"

Astra followed gamely as Sydney did the best she could to imitate a meth-hopped ferret without assaulting strolling convention-goers with her orb rack. Three requests for pictures got shut down with a "Can't!" Two aisles over, she found it.

"Yes! Come to me, my pretties!"

Hope watched as Halo rushed the table of a...My Little Pony booth? Stopping just before collision, the other girl leaned over the table, pointing and waving like a kid calling for *that one* and completely ignoring the other customers at the table. She wasn't being intentionally rude—at least Hope didn't think she was—she just didn't seem to see them. She waited until the booth's owner finished with the purchases they were making before grabbing his collar and *pointing* again.

Hope almost apologized for her, but the guy was obviously used to interesting patrons; he verified the pony Halo was pointing at and got it down. It was...

Okay, it was kind of clever. The booth was dedicated to everything MLP, but pride of place had been given to a couple of shelves of obviously handmade special items, *not*-canon ponies of fictional characters (Hope spotted a Captain Kirk pony and a Sherlock Holmes pony). And apparently ponies of very real people; she'd only watched a few minutes of news footage, but with its purple mane, gold-chromed hide, and—was that a mushroom cloud cutie mark on its rump?—the one Halo pointed to was obviously a *Maxima* pony.

"Eeeeee!" the superhero and federal agent bounced on her toes while the man carefully wrapped and boxed it. Thrusting a black credit card at his face, she looked hilariously stumped at how to cram the box into her backpack—which was still on her back while it supported her halo-rack.

"I've got it," Hope said, taking the box and gently deposited it in her own bag. "You wouldn't want it bouncing against your rack, anyway."

"Thanks! Remember! Grabthar's hammer!"

"Grabthar's hammer," Hope replied gravely.

"Right!" The other girl relaxed as they walked away from the booth. Or got less wound up, anyway—Hope wasn't sure she could *do* relaxed. "We go this way! The team—the part of it coming with Maxima and Arianna—will be here any minute and Arianna threatened to dock me more than I used to make in a month if I'm not at the event stage to meet them."

"Great—I mean, that's fine. So, this whole...not-Halo thing was so that you could get your...pony MacGuffin? Without anyone on the team knowing about it?"

"Obviously! I've been tracking this guy's stuff online for ages—he makes hilarious one-offs for sale at conventions. One of *Max*?" She cackled gleefully. "Hey! How did you penetrate my fiendishly clever disguise, anyway?"

Hope fought bubbling laughter as Halo scowled at her suspiciously. The other girl *might* be a little older than she was, but Halo was worse than Shelly had ever been—hyperactive and seriously ADHD. "Master Chief? And then when I looked at your spheres they weren't there."

"Huh?" Sydney tipped her head up, squinting at her orbiting friends. "They don't do that!"

"Not to you, maybe, but super-duper senses? When I look at them they're there, but they're not *there*, there. My visual resolution scale isn't quite microscopic but it's way better than 20-20, and I see more of the electromagnetic spectrum than other people—near-ultraviolet and into the infrared bands. Let's just say that they're not really emitting light? It's like they're *faking* it. And—"

Hope sneaked another look at the spheres, trying to find better words than *they freak me out*. "The more I focus on them the harder it is for me to say where their edges are? Or even that they're right over your head and not, I don't know, a few miles closer to my visual horizon. And they've got more *depth* than their radius should allow. Looking at them is like looking through holes in a wall—there's a lot more on the other side? They give me a headache."

"That's—so cool!"

She shrugged. "Non-Euclidian, anyway. Hyper-dimensional? They're not the weirdest thing I've ever seen, but they're close. So no, your wire hanger setup didn't quite fool me. Where did they even *come* from?"

"Maybe they're really from another dimension." Sydney's eyes widened. "Maybe they're from *your* dimension! Ooh! Maybe your dimension is in one of these orbs!" Hope didn't think the girl's eyes could get any wider, but they did as she whispered, full of awe, "Maybe *my* dimension is... or..."

"We're all on Orion's belt?" Hope laughed. "I don't think we really need to go all *Men in Black*. Anyway, I suggest covers next time? Some cheap plastic balls would work, just open them up and slip the orbs in? Even lit up they'd be a lot less noticeable."

"Thanks! I'll remember that." Halo pulled a notebook out of her uniform jacket and wrote something in it, snapped it shut. "So—hey wait! You've just started! Eight episodes in! When did you see weirder stuff?"

"Um, I'm actually two seasons ahead of you?" Hope couldn't believe she was saying this. "What happened in the last episode?"

"You yelled at Atlas and stormed out after he let a supervillain fight go down so you could arrest everybody. And met a vampire at the hero-club."

"Oh," she said weakly. For one, absolutely insane moment, she wanted to watch that show. "Well, a lot's happened since then."

"No spoilers!" Sydney frantically flapped her hands and Hope blinked.

"Uh, sure."

"Unless..." Her eyes narrowed deviously. "Does Vegas take bets on what happens in TV shows?"

Hope stared at the girl. "Um, I'm not really sure it works that way. In fact I spotted two changes in the pilot episode recap."

"Hmm, yeah. Stupid rewrites! Still they're bound to get the big things right. Okay, *one* spoiler, like can you tell me what the season-ender cliffhanger's going to be?"

"Um, no. So when are—"

"There!" Halo waved and Hope spotted the group headed their way. Only in a place like this could they not stand out like hippos dancing the Nutcracker Suite. A swirl of convention goers and assorted press followed, taking pictures, asking questions, but none quite coming within an arm's length of the group, almost as if Maxima was projecting a fear aura with her glower. All but two of the group wore tailored fatigues like Halo's, dark urban camo with black collars, Arc-SWAT patches on their shoulders. They looked more like US Army supersoldiers than superheroes to Hope, but then they had sounded more military than government-agency from what she'd read. They even kept military ranks and discipline; Halo snapped to exaggerated attention with a salute in front of Maxima.

"Sir!"

Maxima's eyes narrowed. "What did I tell you about that Scoville!?" she barked.

"Sorry!" Sydney grimaced dramatically, repeating the salute. "That's how they do it on Star Trek! Ma'am!"

Maxima returned a far less formal salute, dropped into a more normal voice. "Who's your friend, Sydney? And what is that?" She pointed to Sydney's orb carousel.

"My disguise! Cool, right? And this is Astra. Shake her hand!"

Cameras swung towards the two of them, making Hope glad she had her mask on; her similarity to Stacia would not have gone unnoticed. She also decided that Maxima had had a lot more exposure to Halo than she had; the gold-skinned and intimidatingly tall Amazon looked at the girl's improbably innocent grin and a crease appeared in her forehead.

"Alriiight... And take that thing off."

"Got it, boss! It's served its excellent purpose, anyway. I went totally incognito!" She pulled her pack off her shoulders, twitching her head at Hope and mouthing *Go on!*

Hope sighed. This was not how she'd wanted an introduction to go. On the other hand, what would a *good* introduction look like? She held out her hand.

Maxima took it, enveloping Hope's small hand with the obvious care but ease of practice of someone who knew just what she could do to a non-super. They shook. And Hope held on.

"What the *hell*—" Purple eyes drilled into Hope's, the crease in Maxima's brow crinkling into deep scowl lines.

"Maxima? What's going on?" The crisp office-dressed blonde beside Maxima—one of the two party-members not in a uniform—looked between the two of them.

"She's strong." More cameras focused on Hope along with the blonde's full attention. She knew what the lady was seeing; now old enough to drink, she *still* looked like a teenaged pixie in her skirted outfit. Add to that the apparent Adonis or Amazon figures that went with superhuman powers in this world and...

"Is this a joke? She can't be a—"

"Shut up, Arianna. Squeeze, kid."

Hope squeezed helpfully and Maxima grunted, shifting her hold. "Grip strength says she could match Stalwart or Super Hiro."

An explosion of questions came from every direction but Maxima cut them all off.

"Why are you asking...?! We literally know as much as you do right now!"

Sydney grabbed the now carousel-free blue orb and floated up to cover the height differential between herself and Maxima to whisper in her ear, easily heard by Hope. "Told you! She's the *real* Astra!"

Maxima released her and she flexed her fingers; the golden super hadn't tried to win the knuckle-crushing contest, just to see what she was capable of, but her hand still felt hot and tight. The Arc-SWAT leader's eyes drifted to one of the many publicity banners advertising the *Sentinels* booth—and apparently an actor panel tomorrow. Hope winced.

"Okay, *now* we know more than you do." Maxima grinned slyly as the cavalcade of shouted questions resumed. Then she ignored them, to the office-blonde's obvious consternation. "Right." She started walking and everyone fell in around her moving center of social gravity. "Let's take this back to the green room, we've got a few minutes before today's dog and pony show."

"Max," Office-Blonde protested. "We were going to mingle."

"Sorry, Ari. Safety first."

The designated "green room" behind the stage was a tight space for the group—obviously doubling as a storage space although now it held a fridge, a single table, and half a dozen folding chairs. Hope, Halo, the office-blonde Maxima introduced as Arianna, and five other Arc-SWAT members made it almost claustrophobic, more so because they were all looking at Hope while Halo loudly expounded her *TV Land* theory.

"Astra?" Maxima cut Halo short. "The TV show?"

Hope had *no* idea what to say to that, but Sydney took a deep breath as if ready to regurgitate an entire wiki on the subject. "It was an indie comic first. Actually before that it was—"

"What else can you do?" Her scowl had faded a bit, but the set of her mouth told Hope that she was still assessing her as a possible threat she needed to get the measure of.

"I can fly." Hope helpfully raised herself a foot, keeping her feet flat so it was obvious, and set down again. "And I have expanded and sharpened senses. Pretty vanilla, really."

One of the uniformed ones, a goth-girl with purple streaks in her raven hair who reminded Hope of Kindrake, laughed hard. "Only you, Syd! Whoosh out here on a super-secret mission and meet a fictional superhero? Really?"

"Doubter! We're *super*heroes! We've got an al— We've got a mad scientist on the team! How could we not run into heroes from the comic-books! It's practically destiny!"

Maxima ignored her. "Dabbler?"

The other out-of-uniform member of the party shrugged. A statuesque blonde with a deep copper tan and swirling tattoos covering her face, she wore a gold bustier to show off her generous figure. Tight pants and high boots completed an outfit made only marginally less stare-worthy by an open coat. It was a costume that would fit right in with the fashion-hero clubbing scene back home, but Hope stepped back when she raised her hands.

"Relax." The woman gave her an easy smile. "I could eat you up, but this is just diagnostics." A glowing holographic net of connected circles and lines laced with lettering Hope couldn't read filled the air between them. Dabbler's fingers danced over the changing pattern.

Maxima watched, arms folded, as Dabbler switched from simple circles to more complex and densely lettered forms. "Well?"

"Patience, hot-stuff," Dabbler smirked, cocking an eyebrow at her leader. "It's always best to take your time, don't you think?" She smiled wider at Maxima's glower, turning back to her work. Despite the uncertainty of her situation, Hope was fascinated. A civilian contractor? She could give Chakra lessons in workplace inappropriateness—was that what Halo had meant about introducing them?

The woman chuckled at whatever she saw. "Hmmm. You *are* a fascinating thing. Halo, you may be onto something."

"See? See? Tell them, Dabbler!"

"So?" Maxima cocked an eyebrow, watching Hope over the rim of her dark shades.

"It's a little complicated. First," she waved at Hope. "She's not a super."

"I beg to disagree," Maxima said.

"Yeah!" Sydney protested. "She's wicked strong!"

"And that's so cute. She's not a *super*, Max. She's got *powers*, but...whatever it is that flips your switch and makes all you guys so yummy and strong, she hasn't got it. Even better, she reads like any normal human being—I'm getting nothing off her, not physical, mental, magical, *nothing* explaining her powers. Just based on what I see, I'd say she didn't have any. And you don't seem surprised."

Hope started—that last had been directed at her. "I'm not, really. Back home that's pretty normal for breakthroughs. We've got no power-gene or detectable common source. The only way anyone can detect our powers is when we use them."

"Well it's *fascinating*. Now I don't know about TV Land, but you're as real as anybody is. And your tick is off."

"My what?"

"I've got no hu— English word for it." Dabbler spread her hands and the light-board went away. "Your quantum-signature? That's not what it is, but it's as close as I can get. The universe we see is just a hyper-dimensional substrate of a much bigger thing. It's not as simple as the parallel worlds Sydney is talking about, but you can spot a visitation from another substrate because its *tick* won't match the local tick. So you're definitely not from around here. Immigrating?"

Not in a million years. "I'm just trying to get home. I ran out of juice here."

"So you're wandering. Well, maybe I can help with that. But I'd need to tinker."

"Hmm." Maxima considered the situation for a moment, her eyes traveling between Hope and Dabbler.

Hope tried to maintain a pleasant but hopeful expression. "I appreciate whatever you can do for me—and while I'm here, if there's any way I can help out..." The Arc-SWAT leader shrugged, looking more thoughtful and less scowly. Obviously Dabbler's "Not from around here" was good enough for her—which didn't mean Hope wasn't a *problem*.

"There are going to be liability issues with that," she said finally. "At least until we can read you in on our specifics of super-powered law enforcement."

Hope nodded hard. "Of course ma'am—I'm *good* at rules. If nothing else, I could pay my way flying payloads for NASA."

Sydney perked up like someone had lit a light-bulb over her head, but before she could jump in one of the others, a tall and seriously buff woman standing behind her gave her shoulder a playful dig.

"Wicked strong?" This woman's thick Bostonian accent did *not* match her dark skin, copper-red hair, and sharp facial features. Her family roots were clearly Latin American—an impression strengthened by a trio of feathers woven into her long, side cut hair. Just shy of Maxima's towering height, she was muscled like a decathlete-in-training. "You're finally stahting to tahk like a civilized person!"

"Well I learned from the best you peaky blinder—" Sydney comically tried to match her accent, laughed. "Nope, that was cockney." She shook her head, blinked and brightened even more. "Oh, Astra, this is Varia! She's *Aztec*, and a fan of the Red Sox, but don't hold that against her..." She paused. "The... sports thing, not the Aztec thing, because... I mean, don't hold the Aztec thing against her at all, obviously..." Sydney wound down. *"Sports burn!* Am I right?"

"Yeah Sydney, wicked burn." Varia shook her head, laughing.

"But! Astra, you've *got* to shake Varia's hand! I mean—" She tried hard to look innocent. "Don't give her the clamps, just hold her hand. Oh, and take off your glove."

"Okaaay, and that will do what?" Hope started working the fingers on her right glove.

"That's what we're going to find out. I've got a five on... armor!" Sydney dug into one of her pockets, pulled out a bill.

"No!" Maxima said flatly. "We're not doing that in here. Not after the telekinesis vs force beam argument."

"C'mon, pleeeeease?" Sydney made puppy-eyes at her boss. "It's hardly ever that dramatic."

Hope lowered her hand, wondering if she was being punked. "Should I be worried?"

Varia shook her copper-maned head. "Nah, if anything, you'll be the safest of us." But she stepped back. "We'll have to try it later, definitely if you're hanging around awhile."

All-business and apparently satisfied that Hope wasn't any kind of immediate threat, Maxima let Arianna herd them all back out of the Green Room and to the stage. Hope got the impression that this wasn't their first rodeo; with the team less than a year old, she wondered how many comic cons and sci-fi conventions they'd barnstormed to get this unique demographic of American society behind them.

And now they were back on-mission. Which didn't mean that the Arc-SWAT heroes ignored her; when the rest of the team took the stage behind Maxima and Arianna, one of them—the uniformed goth-girl—attached herself to Hope. "So, do you guys do these things?"

"Hmm?" Hope listened to Arianna's pitch with half an ear. She was good, and everything she said confirmed what she'd read online—minus the conspiracy-theorists and worriers who declined to join the Arc-SWAT mania.

"PR events? I've caught your show; I like the superhero-procedural stuff—it's like *Law and Order: The Tights-Division*—but I don't see you doing a lot of media work."

Hope pulled her attention from the stage. "We do a bit. Enough that I've learned about studio makeup and the special smile-and-wave." A sudden, crushing weight of homesickness stopped her breath. She shook it off. She was going to get home, darn it. She *was*.

"Hey, you okay?" The goth-girl gave her a look, obviously wondering if she was about to become a problem. Hope fished for a new subject.

"And what do you do?"

"Me? I'm a duplicative-combinatory teleporter. I've got five of me sharing one mind and occasionally one body with the strength of five."

"Oh. Okay."

"Okay?" The girl blinked. "No questions?"

"Nope. I've got stranger friends. Five yous, one mind, and you combine for extra umph. Got it. So then you're with me since the other yous will be able to tell the rest if I do something off? Are you up on stage now, too?"

The girl barked a laugh, held out her hand. "Harem. And yeah, I'm the white-haired one in the glasses."

They shook hands solemnly, Hope repressing a triumphant smile. Score one for Laconic Acceptance of Weird Shit, to use Jacky's name for the important social skill. It was almost as important as Not Commenting on Crimes Against Fashion, needed for meeting a lot of capes; at least Arc-SWAT didn't require her to use *that* skill.

Hope opened her mouth to ask another question when Harem stopped her and pointed at the stage.

"Let's just enjoy the view for a moment," she said, watching the presentation with sparkling eyes.

Hope turned and looked up at the only male member of the team who had made it to the convention today. A muscular and ruggedly handsome Asian American, he stepped up beside the podium to a crescendo of mostly female squeals from the audience. It didn't hurt that he had ditched his jacket and was wearing just a tight fitted black t-shirt. Hope had shaken his hand earlier, but spent the rest of the time trying not to stare at him. He wasn't supernaturally attractive (Hope had met her share of those), but he was definitely easy on the eyes.

And his pants seemed awfully snug for combat fatigues.

"That's Super Hiro. Great angle to watch from, isn't it?" Harem sighed as Hope flushed, tearing her eyes away.

"Super *Hiro*?"

"I know, right?" The two girls giggled, and Hope could see the Harem up on stage trying to suppress her laughter as well. Sitting next to her, Sydney wanted in on the joke; Hope couldn't quite hear the explanation over the noise of the crowd, but the hand gestures Harem made brought her flush back.

"What are you telling her?" she asked, not at all sure if she wanted to know.

"I promise it's nothing about you wanting to spank him." Harem said, contradicting her pantomime on stage.

"Hey—no!" Could she get any redder?

Maxima snapped her fingers at the pair on stage, an unmistakable "I will turn this car around" expression on her face. That stopped the laughter as Arianna retook the podium to wrap up the presentation.

The smartly-dressed woman neatly stacked her notes, smiling at the avid crowd. "As always, if you do happen to have super powers, we will be conducting preliminary interviews to see if you're Arc-SWAT material."

Maxima pushed in to commandeer the lectern. "And if your power is to manipulate butter, then get a job at Parkay!" A ripple of laughter ran through the audience as she openly scowled at the room. "And I want to remind everyone that having a neat *idea* for a power set and superhero name is *not* a power! Neither is a cool design for a costume! We don't even wear costumes!" The laughter only climbed and Hope hid her smile behind her hand, imaging an apparently humorless Maxima fuming at a line of imaginative applicants. "I mean it! We don't do pitches! Save that crap for publishers!" She stepped back and Arianna resumed her place at the mic as the laughter crested and died.

"And!" The publicist shot a glare at the Arc-SWAT leader, who ignored it, before smiling widely at the settling crowd. "We will be doing handshakes with Varia as well. I would like to remind you all that it is Varia who gets the power and not you, and while you will be immune to whatever she manifests, the floor might not be. So we have moved that session out from under the *sprinkler systems* to the picnic field on the west side of the convention center." More laughter and applause told Hope everyone knew the story there.

She should have done more research at the library.

"That said," Arianna finished smoothly, timed perfectly to fading claps. "It is pretty cool to be able to stand next to someone made out of fire without getting burnt!"

Hope had to admit that Archon's PR girl knew how to rock her podium—she imagined Arianna and The Harlequin having "a productive power lunch"—but something was going on behind her as she put a cap on her speech. Hope watched Sydney nudge Varia, and when the bronzed Bostonian waved her off the girl called her fuscia orb to her hand. Hope blinked as the ball sprouted a tentacle that looked like a flexible blue glowing tube, what you'd get if you animated a neon bar sign.

The thing was as thick as Hope's forearm but longer, and Sydney used it to prod Varia up next to Arianna, who'd segued into attempting to dismiss websites devoted to "what Varia's power gestalt says about your personality." Seeing Varia being herded toward her, she gave the crowd an "Ok I guess I will" eye roll, sparking more applause, and held out her hand. Varia took it and—

Holy crap on a cracker.

Hope blinked as the big Bostonian burst into pure white light, an aura of yellow flames enveloping her silhouette. She shielded her eyes—darned super-duper vision—but still saw Arianna waving her hand through the flames licking around Varia without harm.

Sydney flew up above the stage as the audience cheered, calling another orb to her hand. This one popped a blueish shield into existence around her. "Don't miss!" She called down playfully.

Varia aimed her free hand at Sydney but Arianna desperately intercepted, hopping on her toes and waving her free hand in between the two of them. "Not in here! Sprinklers! You'll melt my tablet!" She tried to twist her hand from Varia's grip while keeping the free one interposed between the two heroines, the cheers turning to laughter as the two women danced about.

Maxima finally barked at her rambunctious private (in what organization was a woman that powerful a *private*?) to fall in and Varia released Arianna's hand, returning to her caramel colored self. It looked like the show was over.

Hope had started to relax, when a crack like the first peal of thunder shook the hall and a brilliant flash of red struck Sydney's shield with an air-splitting boom. Hope found herself in the air without thinking, ready to help the girl before her clearing vision showed no help was needed; unharmed by the blast, Sydney looked as confused as everyone else.

Hope turned to track the source of the beam. It wasn't difficult to find, but she couldn't believe what she saw. In the crowded hall a clear space had sprouted around a man dressed in a blue full bodysuit. Short brown hair stuck out of the top of his attached costume mask. His boots, gloves, belt, and crossed bandoliers were vibrant yellow and only the black "X" over a circular red badge where the two straps of the yellow bandolier connected broke the blue-yellow color scheme—that and the golden mono-goggles attached to the mask, shaped as a single red lens across his eyes. A *glowing* red lens.

You've got to be kidding me.

"Whoa, nice cosplay!" Sydney declared.

Maxima looked at the much too familiar fictional character, then back at Astra with an arched eyebrow before returning her attention to the new player.

"Attacking a federal agent is a serious offence!" She barked. "Stand down and explain yourself immediately!" Maxima didn't use his name, as if that would validate the weirdness of a second fictional superhero appearing at the convention. She stared down Halo's impossible attacker, giving cover as behind her her team slipped earpieces into place and unsnapped holsters. Even Arianna was going to work as she backed off the stage, phone in hand.

Hope couldn't fail to notice that none of them were moving like they were in the exposed sights of a shooter, which told her everything she needed to know about their confidence in their leader's ability to intercept and take the hit.

Impossible guy wasn't as impressed.

"You imposters can't be allowed to fool these people any longer!" the man who *couldn't* be who he was yelled out. "I'm here to put an end to this sham!" He pressed a button on the side of his visor and another red beam struck Maxima. The golden woman simply held her hand out as if trying to keep a bright light out of her eyes, the beam hitting it with another flash and crack of released energy and as much actual effect as a flashlight beam. *Not* what her attacker had been expecting; the goggles hid his eyes, but his body language told Hope that he'd been looking for a much more dramatic result.

"If you're who I think you are," Maxima said in a measured tone, lowering her hand, "then you don't want to do this with civilians present. I don't know what you think is going on, but let's not have some misunderstanding-based superhero crossover fight that we can easily avoid."

His response was to twist a dial on his visor and fire a much more powerful beam. This time the effect was more dramatic; it would have punched Hope through the *wall*, and the shockwave from the blast forced the crowd back further back. Some of the audience headed for toward the exits, but others just applauded, obviously thinking it was part of the show, and a good number of the ones who didn't already have phones out for the presentation produced them and started recording. Hope felt herself coiling. This could go bad in *so* many ways.

All it did to Maxima was toss her hair around—an irresistible force meeting a determinedly immovable object—though she did have to lean into the blast to hold her position on the stage. And Hope could see her decide this wasn't going to be resolved peacefully. "Harem!" she barked.

Hope expected the Harem who'd been standing next to her to respond, but instead a third Harem appeared in a burst of purple energy just behind the assailant. *This* Harem, an athletic strawberry blonde, swung a pneumatic syringe straight at his neck and would have got him if his hand hadn't already been up working the visor. Catching the new Harem's wrist before she could plunge the needle home, he tossed her with a textbook Judo shoulder throw. Hope instinctively dropped hard to cover her as he turned to track his would-be assailant, but she vanished before connecting with the ground.

Where—

Twisting back around with impressive speed he fired a blast behind him—he'd obviously dealt with teleporters before. The beam cut empty air to strike explosively halfway up the wall, showering convention goers with drywall as Harem appeared several feet *above* him. She turned the momentum of his throw into a vicious axe kick that connected with top of his head and staggered him into the arms of a *fourth* appearing Harem. This one got her needle in where it belonged, and he slumped to the ground as the crowd began to cheer.

Hope moved to put herself next to the fallen superhuman, but again it wasn't necessary; the team went into what had to be a well-rehearsed processing mode. The newly arrived blonde Harem pulled off his mask while the other did the same with his gloves. One teleported away, then back again with a small kit and they began fingerprinting and photographing him. Halo floated down from her perch to land beside Hope.

She released the orb that generated her force field. "Well that was... I'd say weird, but that's a pretty relative term in our profession."

Hope nodded agreement. "Are you guys usually a nexus for fictional superheroes?" She considered what she'd just said. "Um. I want to emphasize that I'm only fictional in your hyper-dimensional substrate."

"Evidently... he really *was* fictional," the Harem beside her said. Hope and Sydney traded a *Huh?* look.

"Meet me over by him." Harem gestured where her bespectacled self knelt by their fallen attacker.

The pair stepped closer to find Harem kneeling over a man who looked *superficially* like the one who attacked them. He was taller but much skinnier, and didn't come close to filling out his uniform, which was, there was no other word for it, cheap looking. His bandoliers were made out of yellow duct tape, and his blue bodysuit wasn't made of unstable molecules or even spandex. He wore dark blue cargo pants and a matching turtleneck with custom stitching on it.

"It's a cosplayer." Halo said, as obviously bewildered as Hope. "Did he have an illusion over him earlier?"

"His beams were real enough." Maxima loomed over them. "The wall is still damaged."

Dabbler was already scanning him with another spell. "Mmm, there's a trace of energy leading out of the room, but it's fading fast. Whatever fueled his transformation may be in the merchant bazaar or beyond."

"You mean the dealer's room?" Halo poked the sorceress.

Maxima nodded and started issuing orders. "Right, Dabbler, come with me, we're going to find..." She didn't get any further as screams swelled from the audience. The main door to the dealer's room burst from its frame as a giant creature stumbled through, and Hope blinked again; it looked like a robotic gorilla. She wasn't the only one stunned by its appearance, and nobody moved until it hauled back to take a swing at a terrified convention goer.

Stunned as everyone else, Hope moved far too late but Maxima covered the distance to the Mecha-Gorilla in the blink of an eye to smack the descending arm away from its target with enough force to send parts of the armor flying into the wall and spin the entire beast on its feet. Turned around, the thing presented a very obvious "this is my power source" pack on its back, and Maxima tore it off like it was cardboard.

And then it was; the cosplayer who hit the ground with a yelp where Mecha-Gorilla should have landed seemed as confused as anyone else.

"Hey what the hell are you doing to my costume!?" He started to push himself up, fell down again. "Ow! Ow! My arm! I think it's broken! Why did you *attack* me, it's just cosplay!" He rolled on to his side, cradling his arm and crumpling more of his cardboard Mecha-Gorilla outfit.

If he was dressed up as something from a movie or comic, Hope, trying to slow her racing heart, couldn't identify it. But she didn't recognize the next two who came bursting into the room, either—not so much through the broken door where Maxima stood as through impromptu entryways where parts of the wall used to be. One of them could only be described as a big pile of tentacles with an eye on top, either an alien-of-the-week from an old Doctor Who episode or something inappropriately Japanese, and the other one looked like an evil magician complete with top hat and twirlable moustache. He also had a purple cape and golden gauntlets, one of which he aimed at the podium where Arianna stood trying to direct the crowd.

"N'ya hah! Who wants to see a lady disappear?!" he cackled in a cartoonishly evil nasal voice, firing blue rings of energy. Hope launched herself, but Hiro intercepted them first and Hope shielded her eyes from the blue flare. When she uncovered them she saw that the only thing to disappear had been his shirt, blown off like ash, his torso obviously immune to the effect. His sharply chiseled, depilated and buffed torso.

"Oh my." She realized she'd said it aloud when Halo smirked.

"It happens. Every. Battle."

Harem laughed. "That's another five bucks for the Wardrobe Malfunction Jar." Then she yelped—pulled away from the group by a tentacle that snaked around her ankle while everyone was distracted. Another one whipped around Hope's waist and tried to pull her with no success. It did drag several con goers toward it—male *and* female, and Hope noted with relief that it wasn't pausing to rip anyone's clothes off, so its origins remained blessedly inconclusive.

But if it was another transformed cosplayer, how could she attack it safely?

As she hesitated Halo yelped and popped her shield back into existence around herself when one of the flailing tentacles made a grab for her. Shocked into action, Hope grabbed her own and squeezed to crush it in half—they *had* to be just faked-up extensions from the costume body. The rubbery limb started to give, but then sprang back into shape and jerked free of her loosening grip. Attempting to grab it again, she realized she could barely close her hands around it.

Oh, crap. On a cracker.

A tingling numbness begin to spread from her waist where the tentacle held her, and her knees threatened to give. Seeing her wavering, Halo tried to bat the tentacle away from her with her own blue neon one but the rubbery appendage just twisted with the strikes. Hope gathered herself to leap into the air, but Dabbler came out of nowhere to put a hand on her shoulder as she chopped through the tentacle with an improbably demonic and glamorous sword.

Dabbler continued to brace her, which was weird because she had both hands around her sword. "Don't worry, cute-stuff, it only had you for seconds—the paralyzing effect should wear off quickly." The "civilian consultant" let her go and spun around as a vortex of light swirled up her body. In its wake, she changed from a copper-tanned beauty to a purple something. Something still humanoid and beautiful, covered in iridescent green stripes, sporting two different kinds of horns, digitigrade legs with cloven hooves and another pair of arms.

Hope's Laconic Acceptance of Weird Shit was being seriously challenged.

Transformed Dabbler gripped her sword with all four hands and leapt over a row of chairs to slice through the tentacle dragging Harem away, leaving Hope to slide to the ground, the tingling in her limbs half numbness, half returning sensation.

Halo landed to help her up. "I'm sorry! I just stood there smacking it like an idiot! I thought you had it, I didn't realize..."

"Itslokay, I dibn't..." Hope stopped and tried to rub feeling back into her jaw. *Oh, my hand works again.* "I thought I did, too."

"I could have used my particle beam to cut it," Sydney babbled, pointing to an orb with fire and lightning dancing around inside it, "but it's so powerful I can't use it near civilians."

"I think they've got it covered." Hope watched an exotically inhuman Dabbler chop away at the tentacles, dancing through them with an expertise that suggested this wasn't her first time fighting this sort of creature. "What *is* she?"

"It's her...*cough*...battle form." Sydney explained, an expression on her face that said *I'm absolutely lying right now but that's what we tell the public. If you'd like to know more, please speak to someone well above my pay grade.*

Hope knew all about those sorts of explanations. "Okay."

Severing the last of the tentacles from this monster changed it back into a guy wearing a cloak covered in popped animal balloons. He looked as bewildered as Mecha-Gorilla guy had. So did the evil magician, once Hiro tore off his gauntlets and, after fending off an ineffectual but comical deluge of rabbits, squashed his top hat.

Taking it all in, Hope winced. *Yeah, it's going to be so much fun trying to convince everyone I'm real now.*

But not her problem right now—her super-duper hearing picked up Maxima's orders coming from Sydney's earpiece. Arc-SWAT's leader had advanced through the shattered doors into the next room and found more business.

"*Move it, people! Transformation threats are proliferating in the dealers' room—engage with non-lethal force and ensure the safety of untransformed civilians! Whatever's going on, knocking them out or destroying key parts of their costumes seems to revert them back to normal! Dabbler, we need to identify the source of this shit ASAP!"*

An unruffled Arianna returned to the lectern, calmly urging the con goers still in the auditorium to remove their costumes before they were affected by whatever was happening, and asking if anyone knew a way to get a message to the entire convention center. A *good* thought and one that made Hope wince again; this was turning into a full-scale bystander-threatening event and she wasn't trained to work with this team. She turned to Halo.

"You guys have your hands full, let me help!"

Goth-Harem hopped up to them, one leg obviously still numb, and held out her hands. "Here, take my choker and earpiece! Only one of me really needs to be wearing one anyway, have you used a tactical mic before?"

"Yes!" Hope took the offered choker, snapping it around her neck and wiggling the earpiece into place. Halo pressed the button on her own choker.

"Maxima, Astra is going to help! She's using one of Harem's sets, so if you see a Harem flying around on your HUD, that's why."

Harem fiddled with the earpiece as Maxima replied. *"Astra, do not engage unless you feel you have an easy takedown. Stick to defending civvies and helping keep exits clear."*

Hope felt around on the choker and quickly found the switch. "Yes Ma'am."

Still fiddling, Harem adjusted what Hope had thought was the tip of an earpiece mic (of course it wasn't—if it was, they wouldn't need the collar's throat-mic) until it sat just inside her peripheral vision. A light on the tip projected a heads up display into her eye, overlaying her vision with icons of the team members matching their chokers. Harem and Halo's icons floated over their heads, and Hope panned her head around to see other Arc-SWAT icons from members already on the other side of the ruined wall. A compass, GPS coordinates, and a wealth of other information ran in neatly organized rows along the top and bottom of her vision. It was almost like having Shell back.

"Is that in focus?" Harem asked.

Hope nodded distractedly. "Yes, thank you. Wow, this is really handy."

"We used to have goggles that did the same thing but they kept getting punched off and smashed. These are..." Harem tilted her head. "...*slightly* more durable."

"Oh, crap!" Beside them, Halo started. "Uh, Max, I get why you don't want her on offence, but people don't know she's with us! They'll think she's one of those—"

Crap. Halo was right. Panicked con goers wouldn't know her from all the other fictional heroes popping up—the fact that she wasn't attacking the Arc-SWAT team would only confuse them.

"*Damn it!*" Maxima shot back. There was a pause, then a thud that made the convention center shudder, knocking several ceiling panels loose. "*Hell with it! Astra—engage as you see fit but DO. NOT. KILL. ANYONE. Minimum force takedowns, am I clear?*"

Hope nearly saluted. "Yes Ma'am, absolutely!"

"*Then get your butts in here!*"

"Thanks, Harem. On it, ma'am!"

As fast as Hope moved, Halo moved faster. The girl grabbed two of her orbs—the flight and forcefield ones, obviously—and went through the hole in the wall at a trajectory aimed to take her high into the next room. Hope followed; clearly Halo intended to make herself a target—smart move with an indestructible forcefield to keep her safe, and it gave Hope a perfect opportunity.

"Yikes!" Halo flinched with a yell as a short hafted war hammer rang her shield like a bell. Hope followed the hammer back down to the mighty-thewed Norse god who'd thrown it.

"Well met, shield-maiden! At last, a worthy foe—hey!"

Letting her drop carry on past his shoulder, she snatched his billowing red cape from its silver clasps as she passed. The transformation was almost instantaneous, but she snatched the professional model's returning but suddenly much lighter hammer and crushed it against the floor for good measure before grabbing his molded plastic armor and shaking him.

"Listen! Everyone in costume's in danger! Make them take masks or gear off before they change, too! If they change, leave them to us! Move people out!"

And Arianna must have found someone who knew the PA system; Hope could hear similar instructions blaring over the crash and din of the fight. Just feet from them, Halo's lighthook snaked out and yanked a lightsaber from a red-skinned Jedi's hands and the sight shocked Hope's man out of his paralysis. She let go.

"R-right!" He easily hoisted the dazed Jedi and retreated down the aisle between the smashed kiosks.

Over her new earpiece, Hope listened to Halo dispense genre-savvy tips. "Harem, pop down to a restaurant and see if you can find a banana—the guy Hiro's fighting is afraid of them! Don't give me that look, I didn't write the character! Also see if you can find dish soap, we need to de-oil the guy Dabbler's facing off against. Who would even dress up like him? Ug, you'd get oil all over your pants and..."

Then someone jumped Hope from behind and tried to drive a knife into her temple. The knife bounced, but when she reached back for her attacker whoever it was flipped away, leaving a beeping grenade tucked under the top of her cape. Grabbing the live grenade she doubled over to curl around it, tucking it tight against her stomach and clenching in anticipation.

This is going to sting.

The whump of the explosion felt like a boot to her stomach, but her next breath was relief—mostly showy fire and boom, the grenade had little in the way of actual impact. A realized version of the Hollywood prop? Whatever it was, it had barely scuffed Hope's costume and she spun around looking for her assailant.

The woman in a catsuit adorned with paramilitary gear might have been stunned at Hope's lack of gooey red explosiveness, but she ducked aside fast enough when Hope lunged. A series of impressive looking but impractical backflips later, Hope caught her in mid flip and tore the catsuit in half, leaving a dazed woman in a sports bra and panties to tumble into a pile of shipping boxes. Hope helped her to her feet and gave her the same briefing she'd dropped on "Thor."

Turning about, she took in the room. Halo had landed to use her lighthook, whipping it around to knock back transformed cosplayers while flicking her forcefield off and on, each flicker expanding the field to encompass more uncostumed con goers as she moved back towards the hole they'd come through. Smart. Maxima and Hiro took turns playing clay pigeon, popping up to draw fire as Halo had, while purple flashes told Hope that Harem was keeping busy at ground level with her syringes. But Varia fought—

Hope almost groaned. Not the Big Guy.

The Bronze Bostonian hung onto the hulking green giant as he roared and spun around, trying to peel her off his back. Whatever power Varia was getting from contact with him wasn't obvious—she was glowing and Hope didn't think even contortionists could bend like she was bending—but she was keeping the lumbering engine of mass destruction from taking out his rage on anyone else while she tried to get at his—

You've got to be kidding me. The transformed cosplayer only wore one obvious piece of costume to remove.

When Hope pantsed him he turned back into a wiry kid with Styrofoam muscles. His ragged purple trousers smelled like ass and body paint.

"Thanks!" Varia laughed, holding out her hand. "Let's see what—"

"*Guys!*" Halo yelled over the com link. "*One of these things is not like the other! In the middle!*"

Looking back, Hope saw that Halo had managed to herd her charges out of danger and pop back up for a new look. She followed the bespectacled girl back into the air, scanning the convention floor, and saw that Halo was right; the guy she wildly pointed at *was* different.

First, like Hope he was the only powered-up "fictional character" in the room not attacking the Arc-SWAT team or other con goers. Hope could tell he was powered up because he was glowing and sparking and the staff he waved around pulsed with light. It also twisted, the dragon carvings on it slithering around the staff and sniffing the air as if searching for something. Every time the staff pulsed another nearby cosplayer blinked into his played character.

"Who's he supposed to be?" Hope yelled, forgetting about her throat-mic. The guy looked like a scruffy Phantom of the Opera, minus the mask and plus a hooded cloak.

"*Don't know!*" Halo returned.

"*And don't care!*" The pinpoint-honed blast Maxima shot at his staff sizzled the air past Hope's ear. And disappeared into the staff's own glow with as much effect as the optic blasts had had on her earlier. The disreputable villain, whoever he was, started at the burst, looking wildly around for its source, and broke into mad laughter.

⌌H⌏

"Wait a second!" Sydney *knew* the guy. "He's the tool from out in the hall, talking all fancy about the Doom of Man! Sexist little vole shart! What about the Doom of Women?"

"*Sydney! Focus!*" Maxima yelled over the earpiece while firing more ineffective blasts at the staff, all negated by the glow surrounding it.

"Right, uh, he didn't have that staff then... I think he... He must have bought it in the dealer's room! What kind of idiot would sell a magical doomsday staff..." Wait a minute...

"What is it?" Astra asked. She'd gotten off to a rocky start, but was handling herself pretty well now.

"I recognize the staff! It's a prop... I mean, it was used as a prop on that show that only lasted one season. Legend of the... Uh, Legends of the Under Moors or something. It was the wise man's staff—but it didn't do anything on the show! It was just a walking stick!"

"If it doesn't match anything, could it be the source?" Astra suggested distractedly. "So maybe the studio prop department found it at an estate sale and thought it looked cool? They didn't know what it was, but this guy saw it on the show and did?"

"My money's on Chinese antiquity shop," Sydney nodded sagely as Astra dove to chase what looked like a ninja with a pair of panties over his face. "They have the best MacGuffins."

Maxima ignored the debate to fly at the staff wielder, only to run into an invisible force that sent her careening through a row of abandoned booths. She bobbed up from the wreckage, forehead-vein pulsing. "Is there any lore from that show that could apply in this situation? Did the wise man have any weaknesses?"

Sydney shook her head. "He didn't have any real powers! And that staff is the only bit from his costume!" She used her lighthook to wrestle a huge gun with a chainsaw bayonet away from an equally huge guy in equally huge armor. Finally disarming him, it took her a moment to realize he'd reverted back. "Props on the authenticity!"

She gave the confused guy the three-second version, then floated back to her vantage point to observe and mull over options. Below her Astra's ninja ducked and wove with what bordered on super-speed, utterly frustrating the girl's every effort to grab him. Fortunately, he didn't seem intent on harm—just on collecting underwear from the fleeing con-goers—which he was somehow able to do right through pants and from around waists without hurting anyone or even tearing their clothes.

Halo decided the ninja-trick was pretty impressive, but since he wasn't hurting anybody Astra gave up on him to tackle a... well, it looked like a velociraptor from Jurassic Park, but those were grossly misnamed. Real velociraptors were the size of turkeys and had feathers, but this was the size of a horse. So, probably a utahraptor? Astra knocked it on its side, braced one foot on its hips and popped its tail off.

That did the trick and it reverted back to a rapidly deflating inflatable raptor outfit.

Geeze, navigating a convention floor in that must have been... no, not important now!

Then the battlefield changed as an array of force walls sprang up throughout the convention hall. Sydney glared accusingly at Crazy Druid before spotting Varia holding hands with a Hispanic gentleman they'd met at another convention handshake lineup a couple of months ago. She sighed with exaggerated relief; *he'd* gone on the emergency contact list, but had to have already been here at the con.

The walls helped a lot, but didn't shut the battle down; they protected fleeing attendees from ongoing fights, but the transformation beams emanating from the staff went right through them and Varia had to continually reposition the walls as victims were transformed within the evacuation groups she herded along. Still it mitigated a lot of the immediate bystander threat, and that allowed Sydney to focus on the problem at hand.

So, back to Maxima—who was still having no luck. Trying to smash Crazy Druid Guy with tables or blowing up the floor near him to pelt him with shrapnel was as ineffective as charging or shooting at him. The staff just sucked in energy attacks, deflecting physical attacks like its wielder was standing in the eye of an invisible tornado.

Hmm. Time to experiment a little.

Since Sydney could only hold two of her orbs at a time and she wasn't about to drop her shield so close to the bad guy, she landed outside the radius Maxima had bounced off of. Releasing her flight orb, she swapped it with the lighthook to try and bat at the laughing fool. *Yep.* The energy tentacle twisted aside without hitting him, even when coming from above.

Ok, so it's like a spherical tornado.

She looked around at the trashed convention hall. The dealer's room was emptying, and at least no one had been killed—that she could see anyway, but keeping that from happening was tying up most of the team and she was a nerd, gamer, and comic store owner; all the flattened booths and broken and burned merchandise made her blood boil.

"*Focus*, Sydney," she muttered, shifting her brain into tabletop gamer mode. She might not be military-trained like a lot of the rest of the team, but she had freakin' *skills*. A decade-plus of twisty tactical thinking honed in tabletop roleplaying games against some of the worst rules-lawyers, munchkins, and min-maxers anybody could dream of, and on Arc-SWAT she'd found that walking herself through a problem like she was looking for the winning move in a pen and paper dice game often brought her surprising solutions.

She let her lighthook orb go and struck an arms-folded, chin-stroking thinking pose. "Okay, he's transforming people at a rate that's making it difficult to manage, but he should run out of those once we finish evacuating the convention center. Wait him out?" She mulled that over for a moment. Her recent experiences with the team had taught her that battles like this tended to be chaotic enough to make the fluid dynamics of crowds unpredictable. People would run in the wrong directions and get trapped, or might try and hide in bathrooms and under tables, giving him a long tail on his supply of targets. And the longer it went on the greater the odds that *someone* was going to get hurt. So, no.

"We can't trick him into transforming someone dressed as a good guy since everyone who changes seems to either have it in for us or wants to run amuck like the Utahraptor and the Panty Ninja. Hmm."

She wondered if they could get the Panty Ninja to help them de-costume people. Maybe, but that would probably only work if their costume primarily consisted of lingerie in the first place. Given how so many anime characters and superheroines dressed, that might actually work. *I guess he's probably already doing that anyway though.* "The best bet seems to be to stop it at the source, but we can't get at him, at least at the moment."

Sydney checked again and, nope, Maxima was still having no luck. She'd shifted her tactic to just trying to push into his spinning deflection field, "flying" down into the ground to steady herself and cratering the floor with each dug-in step, but the staff seemed to have some sort of reverse event horizon around it; the closer Maxima got, the harder it turned her away until she was ripped from the ground and spun halfway across the hall. It took a frightening amount of power to be able to do that to *Maxima*, and that made Sydney wonder what the ultimate purpose of the staff *was*. This random transformation-slash-possession shtick couldn't be it.

I guess I could just ask. She shrugged and walked up to where Crazy Druid's field just barely began battering the edge of hers. He'd stopped laughing and had started shouting, the words drowned out by the crackle of his defensive field. Sydney had assumed that it was either mystic incantations or general megalomaniac ranting—now close enough to make him out over all the noise, she realized he was arguing with his staff.

Nope, not crazy. At all.

"Mighty staff of the mightier Oryxarch! You have made enough guardians to defend you! Waste not your energies! Summon the great ArchoDemoMagus, I am prepared!"

The staff paid him no heed and zapped a woman dressed as Slave Leia, who jumped on Varia's back and tried to strangle her with the chain dangling from her collar. Fortunately Slave Leia was only as strong as an actual human woman and other con goers pulled her off before Varia got distracted enough to bring the force walls down. *Whew!*

The situation had gotten static. Crazy Druid, who Sydney decided to name The Servant Of, ignored it all to continue arguing with The Staff Of while Maxima tried closing the distance again. Again no luck. Finally servant and staff seemed to agree on the same thing.

"Perhaps once we have answered your damnable persistence, we will finally be able to complete our sacred task!" he shouted, pointing the staff at a group of con-goers who had been cut off from the exits by an altercation between Hiro and a mechanical beetle from... um, probably one of those short lived lines of toys that weren't Transformers but were cashing in on their success.

Who would dress up as one of those? They'd be pretty easy to deal with, anyway. Then Sydney spotted Casey in the crowd. Still dressed as Maxima.

She'd ditched her jacket, but her hair was dyed and the paint... She couldn't take off her costume without a serious shower. *Oh, no frickin'—*

Frantic, Sydney jammed the priority com button on her wrist comp. "Corner of..." She paused and checked the compass on her wrist. "Yeah, northwest corner of the dealer's room! There's a cosplayer dressed as Maxima! Someone get her out of here before..."

Maxima tried to disengage and the deflection field threw her again as she lost her "footing." *Astra* shot across the room, landing hard enough to crater the concrete floor but in time to set and brace herself as a beam of energy shot from the staff.

Ooh, I hope that isn't bad. Sydney winced in anticipation—and the beam passed straight through the plucky heroine with no effect at all. Whatever it was, it couldn't turn her into *herself.*

Which meant nothing prevented it from striking Casey, except for her skeevy boyfriend who shoved her out of the way to take the hit himself. Sydney had to give him props, but the beam simply turned in mid-air and stuck her before she hit the ground.

Oh, shit.

Sydney always understood intellectually that Maxima was frighteningly powerful, but it wasn't until this moment that she really felt it. The new Maxima (*Fauxima?*) rose into the air with an indifference and confidence Sydney had seen so often that she didn't think about it anymore. Normally Maxima's *whatever's-happening-had-better-not-annoy-me* body language inspired confidence in her allies, but at that moment Sydney wasn't sure the doppleganger-Maxima floating above them wasn't projecting a fear aura like an elder dragon.

Nope—Sydney's shield was up, and even psychic stuff like that couldn't get through it. She was just good old fashioned *afraid*.

Max rose to meet her and, ignoring Astra and the other heroes between them, the two Maximas hovered in the air glowering at each other.

Maybe if that's all they do, Sydney thought hopefully. *Like two samurai staring each other down.* Then the real one shot up through the roof, scattering ceiling tiles and dust below. Sydney didn't realized she had holding her breath until the other one followed a second later. Already half way to the ceiling, Astra started after them and then decided not to follow. *Smart girl.*

"You idiot!" Sydney turned back to yell at The Servant Of. "One stray shot from either of them could level this entire—"

"The powers false guardians cling to is *nothing* compared to the *might* of Oryxarch! Razer of civilizations! Gardener of conflict! Harbinger of darkness! Sautéer of—"

A white flash from outside shattered every remaining window in the convention hall with the accompanying boom. Tiles fell from the ceiling and most everyone without powers was knocked on their ass, stunned. In the echoing silence, a thousand car alarms sounded in the distance.

"...Souls." The Servant Of finished, his confidence somewhat attenuated.

"Yeah, ya big dummy, what are you going to do about that?" The teams' throat mics sucked at picking up ambient sound, so Sydney turned on the one in her wristcom. Hopefully she could get this guy to slip up and spill something useful. *Keep talking, crazy-guy.*

Getting him to shut up would have been easier. "Concern yourself not of the future, Orb Maiden! Once Oryxarch the Interminable chooses to reveal himself, all your worries will be at an end!"

"Yeah yeah, 'cause he'll poach our spleens, I get it, so what's the hold up?"

"Oryxarch the Turmulent is not beholden to mortal timetables!" The Servant Of waved his arms in the air.

"But?" Sydney prodded.

The Servant Of set his jaw and visibly seethed, too angrily sullen for someone who seemed to be *winning*.

"I am prepared to serve as his vessel..." He grabbed the hem of his robes and flipped them up exasperatedly.

Finally Sydney understood. He was cosplaying as Oryxarch!

"This outfit is a perfect recreation of The Consumer's accoutrements." The Servant Of shook his head, his bombastic oration slipping into a frustrated whine. "I... I mean I didn't hand stitch it *all*. I used a sewing machine on some of it, but I had to rush when I discovered the staff would be here."

"Guys," Astra whispered over her com. *"Do we want to help him transform into Oryxarch?"* Yup, the girl had figured it out. The idiot's costume wasn't *complete* enough.

Dabbler came on. *"He might be vulnerable during the transition. And even if he isn't, we might only have one enemy to deal with once the change is complete—someone we don't have to pull our punches with."*

"Or it could make the existing transformations permanent." Harem suggested.

Sydney couldn't contribute to the discussion without letting The Servant Of know others were listening in, so she took a breath and made a command decision, which is to say, she rolled the dice.

"Well, where's your helmet?"

The Servant Of froze for a moment, then slumped. "Geeze! Lewis, you bonehead!"

He trotted off across the convention center floor, his deflection field pushing Sydney and her shield out of the way. She grabbed her flight orb and followed along just above him, Astra joining her in the air as they watched him search.

He finally found what he was looking for in the mess of the wrecked hall. The booth had been largely destroyed, but one banner still stood: "Stan's Movie and TV Props." A helmet Sydney recognized from their earlier encounter sat on the floor next to a knocked-over table.

Sydney and Astra gathered themselves as he slowly placed the helmet on his head with the reverence of a crown.

"And thus, I unleash the darkness," Lewis, The Servant of The Mighty Oryxarch intoned.

Several things happened at once. The staff began seriously glowing. Lewis began glowing. All of the transformed cosplayers began glowing.

Oops. This might not have been one of my best ideas. Beside her, Astra just waited to see what came next.

The transformed cosplayers jerked, erupting into glowing auras that pulsed and flew back into the staff as—*Yes! Thank Kirby!*—they all reverted. Visibly gathering its power back into itself, the staff fired an eye-watering beam directly into Lewis. More hugely impressive than the others, this blast of power was practically anti-light, a snaking coil of thorns and tentacles made of purple-black smoke and shadow that obscured Lewis in an inky tornado.

Sydney wasn't at all sure if she'd executed a brilliant plan or royally screwed the pooch, but Astra dove at the writhing mass without hesitation. Sydney shot her lighthook at Lewis, who was either screaming or roaring—it was impossible to tell over the noise of the dark tornado's wind. The seething field battered Astra and Sydney's lighthook away, but not with the same force as before. *Not so tough? Big bad transformation draining you a bit?*

Not enough. Astra dropped to the ground and pushed into the savage coiling wind, battered as she tried to remain upright against the sheering force. Her cape stood straight out over her shoulder like a full windsock—it had to be like walking into an ongoing explosion, and Sydney could see the girl still couldn't get close enough to Lewis to pull his costume apart.

Sydney threw her lighthook out far past the twisting winds to go with the flow and wrap around what she hoped was still Lewis standing in the epicenter, but it vibrated so hard in the turbulence she had to drop her shield and grab the orb with both hands, exposing herself to peppering with the smaller debris caught in the fringe of the winds. Whatever was happening in there, she couldn't see a thing through the whirling vortex. Then her lighthook jerked.

Eyes on her feet as she leaned in, Hope nearly lost her footing when Halo's lighthook flailed out of nowhere to hit her in the waist. Grabbing it with both hands, she realized that the spin of their opponent's protecting field had wrapped the energy pseudopod around its rim before flipping it at her, anchoring it around the...whatever at the center of the storm and her against the whirling vortex. *Yes!* She leaned more deeply, using it like a lifeline to pull herself closer to the source of the whole mess. They could *do* this.

Except *Oryxarch* had started making some interesting noises, not the typical deep-throated gravelly laughter that seemed to emanate from all cartoon arch-villains. *Not* a good sign.

Hope dragged herself closer to the crazy idiot—*Why do half the guys who get serious power just go nuts?* The wind finally tore her cape from her shoulders, and in the thick of the roaring storm she felt the sudden presence of something else in the vortex besides the wind. The savage gale obscured even her super-duper vision, but she felt too-real thorned vines wrapping around her, trying to pull her arms away from the lighthook. She fought against it, but it already took all her strength just to inch her way forward.

Her grip was starting to slip on the smooth surface of the energy tentacle when Oryxarch began *growing*. Ominous thorn-like spikes sprang from his armor. *Seriously? Peachy. Just, peachy.* This reality had seemed nice enough, but now it was *really* starting to suck.

She held on as tight as she could, teeth clenched, while half-seen thorned vines tore at her arms, and then something smacked her from behind. She yelped, pushed forward, and spun—to see Hiro being thrown back out of the storm, his flying push *just* enough to shove her past its repelling sheer and into the calm eye. She was in!

And not out of the woods yet; *Lewis* was already twice as large now, purple light streaming out from beneath his armor. His head turned slowly towards Hope and more than just two glowing eyes shone from within the helmet. More eyes opened to focus on her as his features reshaped and he looked less and less human.

No, not at all freaky.

But Hope had faced Seif-al-Dinn and an enraged Grendel; Oryxarch was only scary. Leaping onto his swelling shoulders, she grabbed hold of the helmet and tried to snatch it off his head. A wave of nausea hit her as lightning danced through her arms and legs, but she refused to let go. Another *pull*, and she felt it start to give, but the transformation was fighting her. A new spike sprouted from Lewis' shoulder, shooting right through her boot and—miraculously—between her toes. A second sprang from the side of his helmet, piercing her hand and she shrieked through clenched teeth, but the pain gave her a final shot of adrenaline and she yanked the helmet free.

She *hoped* it was just the helmet.

Resistance gone, Hope tumbled up through the air. Below her Oryxarch , thankfully with his own—albeit mutated—head intact, screamed as the dark tornado blew itself apart. Finally seeing her target, Sydney slid her lighthook down the back of his outfit and up the front before contracting it to tear the whole thing to shreds. In falling pieces, the costume turned into smelly black sludge and splattered everywhere as her teammates tackled the exposed Lewis from three different directions while his mutations melted and slid off him like he'd just stared into the Ark of the Covenant.

Ewww...

Ignoring the evaporating mess, Dabbler kicked the staff away from him. It lay inert, dark and smoldering, but she pulled her sword out of a fiery pocket in mid-air and chopped it in half anyway.

Hope landed by the pile of Arc-SWAT agents, crushing the costume helmet dramatically as she touched down. It felt good, but *she* didn't; the thorns in the wind must have been illusory—her arms and sleeves were intact—but there was still a hole in her boot and her hand throbbed hotly.

"Well," Sydney chirped, covered in papercuts and small bruises from the debris but still grinning like an idiot. "That's the first time I ever saved the world by pantsing the villain."

Hope thought through her own internal scorecard. "Yeah, me, too."

"Freeze frame high five!" Halo yelled and jumped into the air, keeping herself airborne with the flight orb in her other hand. She hung there motionless for a second, looked down at Hope. "Come on, freeze frame!" Hope looked around the room. Most of the team was already doing after-action stuff; securing the unconscious prisoner, coordinating with authorities, etc. (only convention security so far, but she heard sirens). Goth-Harem took out her camera phone to give the moment its proper due. "Might as well."

Hope laughed. She couldn't help it. But she still bobbed up for the high-five while Harem snapped the shot.

⌣H⌣

Sydney needn't have worried about Maxima and Casey; their fearless leader had taken the transformed girl far out over Lake Michigan to fight it out away from any breakables (like the rest of the city). The need to fly Casey back more slowly once she changed back explained why Maxima hadn't dropped in on the Final Boss Fight.

Both had taken a beating—which translated into serious bruising and wrenching for Casey, who didn't have Maxima's superhuman recovery powers anymore. When the EMTs checked her out, her skeevy boyfriend made a comment about having to miss out on Maxima-action in their hotel room before realizing that Maxima was standing behind him. His wet fear-response was priceless. (And given his priorities in the face of his girlfriend's traumatic experience, Sydney figured Casey would be kicking him to the curb before they left the convention.)

Astra gave Maxima an informal after-action report like a pro— which Sydney guessed she was—while handling the first aid Harem applied to her hand with a *been there, done that, no big deal* attitude about her injuries. (How many *Sentinels* seasons ahead was the girl? Maybe Sydney would have to rethink her opposition to spoilers.)

The cleanup took most of the rest of the day, but it was all good to Arianna—she practically salivated at the PR opportunity for the team to be seen helping out with their powers instead of just blowing stuff up. Plus, doing cleanup kept Hiro from going and getting another uniform shirt (why he didn't just slip on something from one of the seller's booths was beyond Sydney—she was starting to think he liked flashing the beefcake).

And Sydney finally got her wish. "Varia! You've got to check your Astra-power! It could be something useful for all this!"

The bronze giantess looked over where Astra was stacking fallen security doors out of the way. "Come on, Syd—you think she'd be happy holding onto me while we work?"

"But it could help us finish *fast*. Don't know until you try!" Sydney turned to appeal to Maxima, who shook her head with a chuckle.

"Go ahead, Varia. Even if it's nothing useful, Halo will get back to cleanup."

"Okay. Sure, why not? Astra?"

The girl put down her doors, dusted her hands and smiled sunnily. She'd confessed to Sydney that her jumps had been consistently dropping her into "interesting times," and being done with this one had turned her practically bouncy.

"Sure, why not? New experiences can be fun!" Astra's deliberately cheeky children's-show voice made even Maxima smile. Sydney moved to make it happen before their fearless leader thought better of it.

"Okay! Just to be safe, I'll provide security." She quickstepped to meet Varia and Hope halfway, and grabbed her shield orb to enclose all three of them in a sphere that covered the center of the hall. The rest of the team gathered outside the shield to watch.

"Um," Astra hesitated. "Doesn't that mean *you're* vulnerable to whatever?"

"Relax! Varia's never manifested anything omni-directional and explody yet, and I'll give you guys room." Just in case, she stood behind Astra and called her lighthook orb, stretching the energy-tentacle into a woven shield between her and the other two. Astra eyed it dubiously.

"Well, okay. Varia?"

"Like she said, relax. And put 'er there, partner." She held out her hand and Astra took it gingerly.

Varia didn't explode. She also didn't transform, start glowing, or otherwise do anything remarkable except blink. Several times in rapid succession.

"Holy shit! You really met *Santa Claus?*"

"Varia?" Maxima watched with arms folded. "What's happening?"

"Ya' got me, boss. I'm kinda seeing an array of Astras, like a trail of her. I think I'm looking back at the places she's been. And I think I can give her a push."

"You can affect her with your power?" Sydney gaped. "Doesn't that violate your rules?"

"Nah—what I should have said is, I think I can sorta...fold? Fold the space where we're standing. Then if I just let go..."

"She'll drop through before it *un*folds! Got it!"

"Can—can you see my home?" Astra's voice was tight, all her easy humor gone.

"I don't *think* so, unless your home is a blown up glass factory."

The girl slumped. "No, that's the first place I jumped to."

Varia let go. "Don't know why I can't see further. Maybe because of the way you got there?"

"Maybe." She laughed unhappily. "I certainly got there a different way."

"Dabbler?" Maxima looked at their resident alien mad scientist.

She shrugged. "That's as good a guess as any—different modes of travel carve different paths. And you know what? This might be the best solution we've got. Interdimensional magic's outside my area of expertise so I can't help her recharge her own jump device. I've been querying my catalogue of goodies for something to adapt, but any jump I can give her will be pretty random."

"You can't match her tick to the tick of her dimension?"

"It doesn't work like that. I can break her loose of her alignment from *our* reality, and there's a chance that if I just toss her out there, she'll be attracted to her home reality, but I can't promise anything. Sorry, kiddo."

"No," Astra protested. "You've all been great." The girl gathered herself, straightening with a look of determination. "And Varia, I'll take your solution."

"But it won't get ya home!"

"No, but now I have friends looking for me and I know they've gotten that far. If I go back prepared, then I can just wait there for them or maybe even send a message. Besides, I'm getting sick of magic snow globe travel—it's got some kind of karma element that keeps popping me into places where I think I'm supposed to 'learn something'. It's like being caught in Dickens' *Christmas Carol*, and I'm a little tired of it."

"It brought you here!" Sydney interjected, realizing. "To meet Varia, obviously!"

She considered that. "Probably. Amazing coincidence that the reality I run out of juice in just happens to have someone I meet who can send me back to the start. Right?"

"Drat! You're right. So she's obviously your ticket to wherever you need to go next."

"I think so. But if I'm going back to the Super Patriots' reality to wait for rescue, then I need to stock up on a few things. I've got some cash, but I don't know if it's valid here?"

Sydney cackled. "Are you kidding? The dealer's room wasn't totally trashed—The Sentinels booth is fine. And everyone saw you fighting right beside us—I'll bet a couple dozen attendees recorded you on their cell phones!"

"Okay. So?"

"So the TV studio will pay huge just to get the real Astra's signature on a bunch of their merchandizing! I'll bet they pay even more for a few posed pics. A couple of hours for their convention rep to get approval, and you'll be able to buy anything you need and still have big bucks left if you ever drop back here again. We could keep an Archon account for her, right Max?"

"Don't forget, we need our own pics for you with Arc-SWAT!" Arianna broke in. "Please?"

The studio proved more eager than even Sydney would have guessed. With Maxima glowering at their tele-conferenced legal representative and marketing exec, not only did they drop a six-figure ton of cash into an Arc-SWAT account in Astra's name, they dragooned their convention staff into becoming Astra's personal shoppers so she didn't have to go civilian and hit Macey's herself.

By the time the team had finished the cleanup Astra had done her turn with a hired photographer, who also got shots supervised by Arianna (Hiro found a replacement shirt), and her shopping list had been filled: complete vacationer's luggage set, several sets of clothes, prescriptionless glasses and a fitted wig, more rolls of cash, everything she needed to pass herself off as a tourist for a while.

"I'm not going to hang around in the states," she explained. "Even Oregon is too hot for me now, with the Super Patriots looking for me. I'm headed to Toronto, and I can call friends from there to keep their eyes open in case my guys come back through looking for me in Portland."

Of course then she had to explain about the Super Patriots; by the time she was through Sydney wanted to invade their reality to Set Things Right. Superheroes shouldn't act villainously, dammit!

The wheeled luggage set, with the bag Astra had brought with her, nearly outweighed the girl. Dressed in high-class civvies (pink shorts, white and glittering t-shirt), she looked like a teenager who shouldn't be on the road or checking into hotels herself—half the reason for the new and expensive luggage; Sydney had argued that the best way to not look like a runaway or fugitive was to look like someone who obviously paid her way wherever she went without even thinking about it.

To contribute to that, Dabbler, who had restored her sexy tan and blond glamour that hid her true four armed officially-not-a-demon form, produced a card holder in a flash of blue light from one of her now invisible hands.

"Here, kid. I *don't* use it around here, but I've preset it for you. You're Sydney Ellis now—check your new Connecticut driver's license—and any card reader will recognize your shiny new credit card because it will take over the system and *make* you an open Visa account wherever you go."

"Really?" Hope handled the card like it was unexploded ordnance. "What's its credit limit?"

Dabbler shrugged. "It's better to ask how big a purchase you can get away with without looking conspicuous. Buy a plane ticket, not a plane. Right?"

Max choked, scowled. "Dabbler..."

"Relax, hot-stuff. I said I'd never use it around here—it's not like I'd need to, with my own fabricator arrays and my Arc-SWAT paycheck. Speaking of fabbers..."

She nudged Goth-Harem, who handed Astra an Arc-SWAT com choker. This one was blue and white with a silver eight-pointed star in front; Astra's crest.

She turned it over in her hands. "Thanks?"

"If you do pop back here for any reason, this will link you right up to the Archon communications net," Harem explained. "Yell and we'll come get you. If you don't come back, it's a souvenir."

The girl actually sort of misted up. "Guys... Thank you. All of you."

"Anytime, Astra," Maxima said. "You did good work today."

"So, ya ready?" Varia held out her hand. Astra took a breath and looked around, nodded.

"Yeah. Sydney? One spoiler. Artemis becomes a BF."

"Really? Coooool!"

Astra took Varia's hand and the Bostonian's eyes unfocused. "All the way back to the beginning, right?"

"Right." Astra, making sure of her grip on her luggage stack. "No, wait! The North Pole, I think. Do it."

What happened next made Sydney's eyes water—one second Astra was there, smiling bravely and ready to go, and the next second she wasn't. And between those seconds, Sydney's brain told her that the girl had taken forever to recede to a horizon a lot further away than the wall of the dealer's room.

"Wow. *That* was—"

"Totally weird?" Harem shrugged. "Welcome to Archon. If it's weird, it's Wednesday."

"I know, I just keep forget— Shit! Shit shit double donkey paté fart cannon Rorschach splatter!"

"Halo?" Maxima scowled, concerned.

"I forgot to get my Maxima Pony back! Oops." Sydney slapped a hand over her evil, traitorous mouth. Too late.

"Your *what*?"

DSA Field Report: Agent Smith.

See attached incident report. Boss, I don't know what to make of it either—the thing that showed up on our end is freaky as shit and that's my professional opinion. Yeah boss, those pics of the thing are the real deal. It has no face. Agents Todd and Royce and one of the Platoons are in stable condition, and we've flooded the site with proximity-sensors and suppression systems. Anything coming through now that doesn't look familiar is going to go down hard; we're shooting first and asking questions later.
We got lucky. I recommend again we call the Young Sentinels back and seal the site. Now.

Odysseus Case File 1-G168 C.

Everybody vs. The Team-Up

by Marion G. Harmon
(with permission of Seanan McGuire).

"It is a law of the universe that if a new superhero comes to town, no matter how big the town, he will run into its current protector and there is going to be a misunderstanding ending in a fight. Then they're going to team up to deal with a situation that neither could have handled alone. It's one of those karmic laws of superheroing."

Yelena "Polychrome" Batzdorf.

Jacqueline was halfway between the workshop and the reindeer stables when the girl came out of nowhere to face-plant into a snowdrift. It was the least elegant North Pole arrival she'd ever seen—it was like the girl had been shot from a cannon. She dropped the trim she'd been carrying and hurried over.

"Christmas! Are you alright?"

"The snow tastes like peppermint, so yeah, I think so." The girl rolled over, blinked up at Jacqueline. "Do you have a sister?" A young, fresh-faced blonde, she wore a skirted sparkly blue ice-skater's costume over white tights and had a sprig of holly in her hair. Who knew what she'd been wearing before being outfitted on arrival?

The girl panicked for a moment before finding the stacked wheeled luggage set that had arrived with her, heaving a huge sigh upon finding it buried beside her.

Jacqueline gave her a hand up and watched her brush snow out of her skirt. "A sister?"

"Well you're not blue and glowing and you don't look like you're in training for the Winter Olympics, but other than that you could pretty much be her twin."

Her mouth dropped open and she stared, eyes wide. "You *remember?*"

"Remember Jackie Frost? Hard not to, the girl makes an impression. I'm sorry." She held out her hand. "I'm Astra—Hope—it's hard to know, should I use my codename here when I'm not in uniform?"

They shook, Jacqueline holding on longer than was probably polite. "Are you a personification?"

"Of what?"

"Of hope." The girl wasn't quite a child, so if she was mortal how had she gotten here?

She blinked. "I don't *think* so, although it's kind of hard for me to tell these days. I've been on the road for a bit and not always myself. But I'm back here, anyway. Is Jackie around?"

Jacqueline closed her lips on what could have been a hysterical scream. "Jackie— Come with me!" She grabbed the girl's hand and pulled her, luggage and all, away from the workshop and around to the family door. Mama wasn't in the kitchen, thank Winter, and she got the girl—Hope—to her room unseen. Closing the door, she started to lock it when a hand settled on hers. It was a small hand, but it might as well have been made of bronze for all the give it had. "I didn't get this part of the tour last time," Hope said softly. "And I went in the front door. Also, why am I dressed for the Ice Capades? That didn't happen last time."

Oh. The strength in the girl's hand sparked a memory. "It happens sometimes when you cross the boundary, especially if Christmas doesn't consider you appropriately dressed. Your outfit fit pretty well, before."

Hope let go. "You know about that?"

She nodded. "I remember now. Sort of." A wave lit the logs in her fireplace and she pulled out the chair for her guest. Hope looked at the master-crafted wood chair and shrugged, taking it as Jacqueline sat on her bed, sinking into the eiderdown cover. "I'm Jacqueline Claus, the adopted daughter of Santa and Mrs. Claus. But I *was* Jackie Frost, the daughter of the Ice Queen and Jack Frost. And nobody remembers her at all except you."

She spilled it all out, or as much as she could. She couldn't tell the bewildered girl everything—too much was Winter business and not for someone from the Calendar Lands—but it felt overwhelmingly good to be able to talk to someone who remembered what she'd been.

And isn't that pathetic—I only met her once.

The tiny blonde didn't say anything when she finished, and Jacqueline could see her trying to organize it all in her mind.

"Okay, to make sure I understand this you were Jackie Frost, but you did something against your nature as a spirit of Winter. So now you're not the sexy selfish smurfette, you're Jacqueline Claus, wholesome selfless spirit of giving. And now that you're *you* you've always *been* you, but you remember being her *and* you. And even though you are all anyone else remembers, you're not supposed to be you, here. I guess I remember because I wasn't here when things got ret-conned? Do you still go by Jackie?"

Jacqueline shuddered. *"Jack*, please."

"Well that makes sense, I guess. Even your *parents* don't know?"

"No. I don't know. I don't dare ask." She was astonished when the girl's eyes darkened in sympathy.

"That's terrible. I was—well, another me on my first jump away from here. I had only my own memories and was just there for a day, but as wonderful as it was to meet my sister Faith I still felt like a horrible intruder. Like I'd pushed myself aside or stolen something. And at least Faith knew—this just sucks. Is there anything I can do to help?"

Jack blinked rapidly, eyes burning. "Thanks, but I don't think so. But—why are you back?" She straightened. "It's been months, you couldn't get home?"

The girl laughed, startling her again. "No... I think the snow globe has been sending me where it thought I needed to be, not where I wanted to go. Big coincidence, the last place I jumped to giving me a way to get back here, right? Wait, months? I've only been gone a few *weeks.*"

That was another long conversation about temporal non-linearity between realities, especially between the Calendar Lands and the Seasonal Lands. After a moment's thought, Jack also gave her a quick sketch of everything that had happened since she'd left. The last bit left Hope grinning. "So Velveteen took out the Super Patriots, huh? That's awesome! On a purely selfish note, that means I can go back to Portland to wait, right?"

"I suppose it does." Jack tried to set aside her current fears and consider all of the angles. "Vel's gone, though. She left a couple of days ago, Calendar Land Time, to take care of a promise. We don't know when she'll be back." Or what she'd remember when she returned. What if she didn't remember Jackie Frost either? Or forgive her for what had happened? Jack pushed the nearly nausea-inducing thought aside and focused on her guest. "I can take you to see Papa."

"Um, could you not?"

Jack looked at her as if she'd just started speaking Latin, and Hope flushed. She couldn't explain why, not to his daughter. His *daughter*—and Hope was *not* letting herself think about how the Powers That Be here were powerful enough to rewrite the script and impose retroactive continuity on the whole *world*. It was pure nightmare fuel.

Pushing *that* aside, it felt weird and a bit awful to be pissed at Father Christmas.

Santa Claus hadn't promised the snow globe would get her home, but she'd had a lot of time to think while she'd been jumping, and now she wondered why he'd offered such an iffy solution in the first place. Couldn't she have simply hung around the North Pole—which would have been *amazing*—until Jackie heard from Velveteen that the Sentinels had shown up in Portland looking for her? Or couldn't Jackie have used mirrors to take her to Canada to wait, out of the Super Patriots' reach?

She was pretty sure that the personified Spirit of Christmas had sent her on some kind of inscrutable mission without asking her if she'd wanted to go. And while some of it had been pretty amazing (and some of it would never, ever, *ever* be believed), a lot of it had been horrible and he Should. Have. Asked. "Can you still use mirrors? I mean—did it take ice powers?"

Jack shook her head. "I use snow globes or dedicated mirrors now, but I can still get you to Portland."

"Good." Hope smiled, relieved. "Then can you take this?" She rifled through her bags, found the box with her nested snow globe and held it out. "I don't need it now—I can't imagine using it again. And I'd rather not tell your dad why I don't want his gift anymore."

Despite what she said, she had a hard time letting go of the box when Jacqueline reluctantly accepted it. Returning a magical gift of

Christmas like it was an unwanted present to be dropped at the returns department at Macy's had to break some kind of cosmic rule.

Jack read her hesitation and smiled. "Here." She took another globe off her mantle, this one with a scene of the North Pole. "As long as you're on the Nice List this one will bring you here, from wherever you are. Just—you know, make sure you have a way to get *back*."

"Thanks." Hope cradled the globe, trying not to look stunned. Like the one she'd just given up, it felt cooler than the room, like the snow inside wanted out. Santa's daughter smiled at her encouragingly.

"And we can go any time, but before we do I can at least introduce you to Mama." She opened the bedroom door. "There are cookies."

Trust Mama to know just how much to fuss. Mrs. Claus (*Mama*, and Jack didn't know if she'd ever be able to think that naturally) treated Hope like a favorite granddaughter who she hadn't seen in much too long. That was how Santa's wife treated any boy or girl with a shred of childhood left in them who made their way to the North Pole, but for Hope she kept her expressions of concern to a minimum. Even that much warmly maternal affection was enough to briefly bring tears to the young girl's eyes and Jack wondered just how much had really happened to her in twelve turns of that globe.

Her Jackie memories were unreliable—no matter how hard she fought to remember the *true* history, Jacqueline Claus memories kept trying to layer themselves on top. But still, the Hope she remembered had seemed less assured but also less...worn and tightly wound. Jack's guess was hard lessons and travel fatigue, and so they lingered in the kitchen until cocoa, cookies, and Mama's magic could do its work.

Finally she gave her mom the expected kiss and told her she was taking Hope to see Carrabelle.

"That's nice, dear. Stay as long as you like, you should see more of your friends than you do the penguins."

"I—okay, Mama." She got a smile in return and—again—wondered if Mama *knew*. It was all screwed up; she had to imagine it was like some boy or girl finding out that, somehow, they'd been switched at birth. Did *they* know? She wished she was as fearless as Jackie had been. Jackie wouldn't have been terrified of hurting them; she might have felt bad, after, but she'd have *asked*. It was driving Jack crazy.

They returned to her room, where Hope made sure her luggage was secure before they stepped up to her vanity mirror. Maybe she thought the trip was going to be as kinetic as the one that dumped her in the snowbank.

"So, Carrabelle?"

"She's Vel's friend. It's easier for me to get to the Calendar Lands through the Crystal Glitter Unicorn Cloud Castle than directly from the North Pole."

"The *what*?"

Jack sighed. "Carrabelle's The Princess, the current personification of the beliefs and dreams of all the world's little girls about fairy tale princesses, alright? I know that's hard for someone from a less anthropomorphically determined universe to grasp, but just go with it."

"Okay, but the...Crystal Glitter Unicorn what? Will there be talking animals?"

"After decades of Disney? What do you think? And musical numbers on demand, complete with drafted extras." Jack touched and instructed her mirror, which began frosting up. "Ready?"

"Sure—wait." Hope touched her shoulder. When Jack gave the girl her attention, she took a breath.

"Before we go— About what you said?" She flushed, fumbling for words. "I don't know anything about how that worked for you, but I have a—a friend who made a decision that may have fundamentally changed him. Maybe he wanted to be changed, I don't know, but he did it for me and I didn't find out what it did to him until he told me a few jumps back and it's pretty big and absolutely binding and he knew that when he did it. I still don't know how I feel about that.

"You said you did something selfless and that changed your nature, right? I don't understand that, but maybe you wanted to *be* selfless because that's what friends are. Jackie couldn't be, and stay Jackie, and she knew that. Just, you know, saying. Maybe you'll find out you're supposed to be you."

Jack just stared at her. *Christmas! Maybe she is the personification of hope. Or might be if she hung around here long enough.*

The girl turned to the mirror. "So, um, we can go?"

"Yeah." Jack blinked. "Just touch the mirror." She raised her own hand, giving her time to follow her lead. Their fingers touched the glass, and—

Hope flinched. She needn't have; her one mirror-trip to the North Pole previously hadn't exactly gotten her over the whole trauma of mirror-abduction-by-insane-clown, but just like last time the transition was practically seamless. It was certainly nothing like the wild ride Varia had sent her on, falling back through eleven realities in vertigo-inducing succession to crash land back where she'd begun. Touching the mirror, she'd felt a tug and stepped into it, and now they were stepping out of a full-length mirror in a huge arched hall. She still had a grasp on her luggage, wheeling it behind her. But—

She looked down at the unexpected *swish*, and nearly stumbled as she swallowed giggles. Her skater's costume had been replaced by a sparkling blue and white off-the-shoulder ball gown, the full kind with layers and hoop skirts that made her feet disappear. She had to grab the front in her free hand and lift to keep from stepping on her floor-brushing hem, and letting go of the luggage handle to reach up told her that her bobbed hair was now in an elaborate updo with extensions. Spinning, she looked at herself in the mirror they'd just come through.

"You have *got* to be kidding me!"

She hadn't worn anything like this as a *debutant*, but now she was dressed for the ball. Not just any ball, either, but the one where she'd meet her prince sometime before midnight. For a heart-stopping moment she wondered if the Crystal Glitter Unicorn Cloud Castle would instantly provide the prince just to accessorize her properly; if he was Kitsune she'd be calling totally unfair *deus ex machina*. The continued mundane existence of her (admittedly top of the line) luggage set reassured her a bit.

"Sweet, isn't it?" Jack spun gracefully, gave Hope a deep curtsy—an impressive feat in her own red and green gown. Hearing gentle silver chimes, Hope looked up and realized that the hall was gradually decking itself for Christmas as tinsel, wreaths, and silver snowflakes shimmered into existence. Jack followed her gaze, looked embarrassed.

"I'm kind of a personification of Christmas myself," she admitted. "It bleeds over since like the North Pole the Castle is more conceptually than physically real." Hope wondered why the admission made Jack blush, but before she could ask a bluebird flew down out of nowhere and landed on the junior Claus's shoulder. She reached up and let it carefully transfer itself to her finger.

"Hello," Jack said to it. "Could you tell Carrabelle that we're here? If she's busy we only need to use the garden gate." It chirped once and flew off through the hall's open doors. She watched it go and then caught Hope's expression. "What?"

Hope blinked. "I thought you said they talked."

"They do. They speak Animal and understand Human. Carrabelle understands *them*—it's one of her powers."

"Oh, well that makes sense." For a given value of *sense*. She shook her head. She really should be used to this by now.

The bluebird was back in a moment, flitting about in place until Jack touched Hope's arm and followed it. Hope followed, wheeling her luggage behind her as the bird led them through the castle. They passed suits of armor and framed pastoral landscapes, tapestries, and open galleries. Jack's Christmas theme followed them as they went, decorating around them and, Hope saw, fading behind them as the castle reasserted its own décor. It was all as rich as any European palace, and she had to hide her smile; *Jack* was sweeping along grandly, but towing her own luggage just completely broke the picture for her.

A couple minutes' walk brought them to another tall pair of open doors, this one leading into a library. Huge of course, with high windows letting in warm sunlight to dance in beams along the floor-to-ceiling shelves.

And there was The Princess, in comfortable jeans and a sweatshirt, which Hope thought totally unfair.

It had to be The Princess; she sat at an oak table spread with papers, going over some sort of accounts with a raccoon in a waistcoat wearing bifocals. She looked up with a smile when they swept in, Jack grandly, Hope semi-grandly.

"Hi Jack! Nice of you to visit, even if it's only for the door. You know that just because Vel's gone doesn't mean that you shouldn't come around. But who's your friend, sugar?" Her smile extended to Hope, her voice as warm as her smile and dripping with southern charm, and something in Hope wanted to curtsy. Another supernaturally flawless blonde, even casual with her hair down and held back in an easy Alice band, Carrabelle struck her with the same presence as Ozma but without the hard edge—though something told Hope that she could bring plenty of edge if she needed to.

"Hope, Carrabelle, Carrabelle, Hope," Jack provided the introduction. "You remember Vel telling you about her, Carra? The fight with The Projectionist in Salem?"

"Oh, yes! It's wonderful to meet you!" She stood up from the table, nodding to her helper who seemed to sigh. Coming around the table she stood before Hope and offered her hands, squeezing when Hope took them, releasing her to give Jack a quick cheek-kiss before directing both her guests over to a pair of couches. "But that was months ago," she went on once they were seated. "And you're back?"

Hope had argued with Ozma, played games with a god-fish, diced with Davey Jones, had cookies and hot cocoa with Santa and Mrs. Claus, and now something in Carrabelle's open smile and friendly concern wanted to emotionally reduce Hope to eight years old, the tail end of her princess-phase. She wanted to drink tea and tell The Princess all her problems. She shook her head. Jack seemed unaffected. It probably wore off with exposure?

"For now, your highness," she replied. "Jack tells me the situation with the Super Patriots has changed, so we've decided it would be best for me to return to Portland to wait for my friends instead of wandering."

Carrabelle looked to her friend for confirmation and Jack nodded, rolling her eyes. "*Long* story, Carra."

"Good stories always are." She studied Hope for an intense moment, smiled again. "But why rush back to Portland? Vel's not there right now—" her eyes darkened briefly "—but Polychrome and Victory Anna are guarding Portland for her, and they'll certainly be able to keep an eye out. And I can have some animal friends watch over your point of arrival and let us know when someone shows up. Vel liked you, honey, and no offense but you look like too many miles of hard road. Thousand-yard stare, if you know what I mean?" She turned her smile up several brilliant watts. "The otters give amazing mani-pedis and the rose-petal baths are to die for."

Oh my God. If Hope had been dropped into Middle Earth and had to contend with the seductive power of the One Ring, she didn't think she'd have so hard a time. The Ring of Power would have been dumped in that volcano as fast as she could fly, but the thought of a long soak and pampering—by otters!—almost melted her into a puddle. But— *No, darn it.*

She summoned up her own smile. "I really, *really* appreciate the offer. But..."

The Princess sighed, wattage only slightly dimming. "Stubborn. All you heroes are. Okay, but if you find yourself sitting around for an extended period of time, the offer of a castle spa weekend stays open. Jack, promise you'll bring her back and you'll come, too." She rose, moving more elegantly in her jeans and sweats than Jack and Hope did in their gowns.

Carrabelle bibbity-bobbity-booed a ball gown for herself—a trick that didn't surprise Hope at all at this point—and led them to a smaller door, opening it to reveal a small castle garden. As technicolor as the rest of the castle, all flowers and fantastical topiary, at its center, the garden sported an arched gateway framed by climbing roses. Every rose was a solid color, but collectively they spanned the full spectrum of the rainbow and glistened, dew-fresh, in the afternoon sun. Carrabelle swept up to the arch, reaching out to stroke a petal.

"Portland, if you please, and—sweet Disney's stepchild!"

A little while earlier.

Polychrome stood on the edge of the roof and listened to the quiet night.

A couple more streets, and we're done. The summer night had cooled down a bit, but was still making her costume stick in uncomfortable places. A skintight bodysuit might scream *superhero* and look awesome, at least on her exhaustingly toned and trained body, but it was skin*tight* and since it couldn't be thin enough for sweat to go right through and evaporate (it would show way too much then), it was almost as miserable as latex would have been.

And Portland's criminal element was learning; after-dark violent street crime had dropped almost to zero. It probably had something to do with just how much *fun* Victory Anna had stopping it; word like that got around. And they'd also not seen hide nor hair of the black vans that the Portland PD had reported street-talk about.

Which were probably nothing, but when something didn't fit the normal mold the police kicked it to the city superheroes just in case.

"*Epona*, this is boring!"

She fondly looked at her partner from the corner of her eye; it got worrying when Tory started swearing upon the patron horse-goddess of the England of her vanished home reality, but she had to admire her enthusiasm for smiting evil-doers. When she smote, they stayed smitten.

That can't be right. Stayed smote? Smited? Hmm.

Tory couldn't be much more comfortable than she was; where her own outfit was at least just a single layer, black from head to toe with only a rainbow sash around the waist for accent, Tory's was a Victorian (of course) steampunk ensemble complete with leather boned corset and heavy skirts. She also carried a gun that looked like the orgiastic mating of a blunderbuss and a laser. She was always tinkering with it and, amazingly, for all its menace she mostly used it as a simple Taser-gun (which, admittedly, incapacitated targets with excruciating pain and left them aching and noodle-limp for hours). She seldom got the chance to raise its setting (the scorched holes it made then were too inconvenient), which didn't keep her from always improving it.

"Did you say something, Victory Anna?"

"The criminal lot has gotten cowardly. It's hardly worth our while to patrol anymore. We could be snuggling, Pol."

"We could." She looked down at the empty street. "But all it takes is one night when we're not out here for something bad to happen and the media to start asking 'Why weren't you there?' Besides, we get seen by a few people, they know we're here, and the rats stay underground. Portland stays quiet." *And Vel comes back to find her city in one piece.*

"That is fair," Tory allowed grumpily. Polychrome hid her smile again.

"But really, two more streets and we can—" The scream rang out with inevitably perfect timing and before it died she'd grabbed Tory (who said she was working on a jet-pack but hadn't perfected it yet) to fly from the roof on a stream of black light. The scream echoed between the buildings again and long training let her zero in on it, down a block and into an alley between two older business buildings where she evaluated the scene: body on the ground, screaming woman (her clothes said hooker, although in Tory's opinion all women in her new reality dressed like whores), and *big hulking grey humanoid.*

"Monster!" Tory shouted, firing as Polychrome dropped her to the street. The lightning discharge lit the thing up; when it didn't drop, Tory just laughed and changed the setting.

"Wait—" Polychrome squeezed her eyes shut and covered her ears as the thing went off with a sound like unbottled thunder and lit the alley. Opening her eyes, she thought Tory'd vaporized their target until she saw it sticking out of the brick wall.

"Dammit, stop *shooting* me!"

"Surrender, monster!" Tory shot back, changing the setting again.

"I'm trying to!"

Polychrome stopped gathering photons and laid a hand on Tory's arm as, with a tumble of loose bricks, the thing pulled itself out of the hole. *He*, definitely a he, and the scorched and burning button-down and casual slacks didn't match the gray skin, tusks, and massively muscled body. Or the meticulously kept tight dreadlocks now lightened by mortar dust.

"And now I'm on fire. Shit." He patted himself out. "Aren't you supposed to say something like 'Hands up or I'll shoot?'"

"You threatened this—" Tory looked around, gun still up. The woman, whatever her moral status, was gone. The body was still there, but now it was groaning.

"I didn't *threaten* her, I knocked out her pimp. Or boyfriend, whatever. *I* was coming back from a snack run," he pointed to a couple of filled plastic bags against the alley wall, "and he decided to slap her around. So I good-Samaritaned her."

"A likely story."

"No, Victory Anna, I think he's got it right." Polychrome walked over and toed the bags. They were stuffed with enough candy and chips to fuel a guy's football night. It was practically a law of nature that when one superhero wandered onto another superhero's turf there was going to be a misunderstanding and someone would get punched in the face (metaphorically and often literally speaking).

Tory didn't lower her gun. "How can we be sure he's not a supervillain in disguise?" Polychrome snickered. Some disguise; the guy filled the classic Beauty and the Beast mold—monstrous appearance, beastly voice with educated diction, random do-gooder...

"He could monologue and then we'd know. You just want to test your highest setting."

"Are you ladies done? Or is this the obligatory witty banter? I'm Grendel, FYI." The big guy stretched, popping his back rapid-fire. "Nice boom stick, point it somewhere else." Stomping over, he retrieved his bags. Reaching into one of them, he retrieved a pair of glasses and put them on before looking at the groaning man on the ground. "You might want to check his eyes, I hit him kind of hard. Dudes that slap women around just piss me *right* off." He turned to go.

Polychrome blinked. "Hold on!" Privately she agreed with him, but rules were rules. "You're an unlicensed superhero—at least I sure as hell don't recognize you so I know you're not licensed in Oregon."

"Do I *look* like a superhero? Mask? Spandex? I'm a private citizen, going about my private business."

"You gave a superhero name. Your mother didn't give it to you, unless you really *are* Grendel and if you are you're a little far from home."

"Damn. Well I'm on vacation, then. And you have no idea how far. Give me a break, ladies? You've already destroyed my shirt, do you really want to ruin my night?"

He had a point. And the paperwork for an unregistered superhuman was a bitch. Also, their damsel-in-distress was gone, and their concussion victim probably wouldn't remember what had happened (and couldn't be counted on to tell the truth in an incident that involved him taking the first swing). Even if Grendel was telling the truth, his Good Deed was going to land him in jail overnight.

Polychrome, Yelena Batzdorf, had been a stick-up-her-butt, by-the-book girl for *years* with the Super Patriots; she could close the book at least for tonight.

"You said you're on vacation? Why don't you just show us where you're staying." She called it in while he thought that over, ordering an ambulance for their sleepy perp with notice that they wouldn't be there when it arrived due to *pursuit of potential incident*. "Let's go."

He gave them a long look before turning to walk out of the alley, and she realized that there was something else going on. Now that adrenalin wasn't turbo-charging her focus, every time she looked at him she had to remind herself that yes, he was huge, gray, and tusked. She barely noticed his singed clothes.

She shook her head. Her Super Patriot training let her recognize the subtle mental manipulation and ignore it, but she'd bet a box of donuts she didn't dare eat that the average person wouldn't look twice at the guy. Magic? Psychic Power? Well, now she knew how he'd managed to stock up on snacks without tripping a hysterical call to the Portland PD and from them to her. What else would they learn about Grendel tonight?

It felt wrong to be proceeding down the street in costume and on foot, but Grendel obviously wasn't a flier and she wasn't about to give him a lift—she doubted she *could* lift him even if that would have left Tory out. A few blocks brought them into much nicer streets and she was silently surprised when he held the door to usher them into the Kimpton Hotel. His psychic unnoticeability didn't extend to cover her or Tory, and the night clerk behind the long desk went bug-eyed when they came through the door. She showed her card and assured the clerk that they weren't here on business, which probably didn't reassure the man.

In the elevator, he swiped his keycard and hit the button for the top floor suites. Between him and Tory's gun, there was barely enough room in the elevator for Polychrome. She could see his reflection looking down at the top of her head. "See something interesting?"

"Not really." His eyes slid to Tory's gun and he rubbed his chest. "If you want more banter, wait a minute."

The elevator dinged and opened into a warmly decorated hall and he used his keycard on the doors to the nearest suite. They followed him in, and it was about what she'd expected from the lobby and hallway: the kind of VIP suite that sported its own bar, floor-to-ceiling TV, and fireplace. What she *hadn't* expected was the other occupants and the symbol-covered whiteboards, the mirrors, and the sand table occupying the suite's main room. Vicky almost leveled her gun.

"Thank you, Brian," the blonde in the green lab coat said without looking away from the furthest whiteboard. "Jamal, would you please offer drinks to our guests? I'll be just a moment." A black kid wearing a red hoody over his cornrows dropped the handheld game he'd been playing to blur over to the bar and line it with a selection of alcoholic and non-alcoholic drinks before Polychrome had a chance to breath.

A speedster. Hell's bells.

Beside her Tory grimaced and very carefully lowered her gun. The best defense against a speedster was to be off the ground and where he couldn't get at you, or shoot him when he wasn't looking. They were standing on the carpet, and he was looking.

He just grinned. "What'll it be, ladies? If you're not driving anywhere tonight, this place has some *fine* stuff."

"The year's not bad for the wine." That came from the woman who looked like an undead Snow White; no cheeks like roses or lips red as blood, just hair black as night and skin white as snow. "It's kind of fruity." She slouched on one of the couches, innocently teasing an annoyed coffee-and-cream cat with a piece of string, but every instinct Polychrome had shouted that the woman wouldn't have looked out of place at any bloodbath of a crime scene coolly confessing "I did it, they deserved it, and can we move this along?"

A speedster, a beast, and—crap, probably a vampire. We're so screwed. At least sunlight might take out the vampire. She started gathering photons, keeping it subtle and hoping that none of them would notice the minute dimming of the room's lights. Then the blonde turned around and she realized who she really had to worry about.

The girl—and she looked like a schoolgirl, sixteen or seventeen at best—was also pale complexioned but a healthy complexion that could only be described using words like *milky skin* and *completely unfair*. Her eyes sparkled and her lips were like perfect red jewels, set off by high patrician cheekbones and a smooth brow under golden hair that tumbled perfectly around her shoulders, and she made the green lab coat look like the only possible accessory for her flawlessness. Her perfection was the opposite of cold, but the look she gave Polychrome and Victory Anna was a lot older than her biological age.

Then she smiled, and it was like being smiled at by Carrabelle; the Sun had decided to be your friend.

"Please, sit down. We have a great deal to discuss but first let me assure you that we mean no harm, to you or your city. The Question Box said that we needed to introduce ourselves to whomever Brian would meet, and now here you are."

"And we're thrilled," the cat said with a yawn.

Grendel had to admit, neither girl blinked at the talking cat and that said something. Or not; *Shell-Cat* (she said she and Ozma had learned the trick wherever they hadn't been a couple of months back) had been surfing the net since they'd arrived two days ago, and had been telling them all some pretty weird shit about the place.

The lady with the big-assed gun gave him a seriously disgruntled look before leaning her boom stick against the couch and sitting down to arrange her skirts. The hot blonde in the black bodysuit did the same without the look; that one was a leader, he could tell, even if right now her team was only her and the trigger-happy one. She kept her eyes on Ozma because, well, *Ozma*.

So why had they corralled two of this strange Portland's protectors? Jamal shrugged and tossed him a coke. He joined him at the bar to watch.

Of course her witchy majesty had to do things properly; she introduced everyone by codename and inquired as to their guest's names even though they already knew who they were from Shell. They also knew they were two of the winners in this place's recent spectacular superhero civil war, and he'd half expected to meet the *other* local cape, Velveteen, who was normally the ringleader of this little team.

He'd *wanted* to meet Velveteen. She'd disappeared from all media sightings a few days before they'd arrived, but they'd been hoping she was just laying low; she was the one they'd wanted to talk to since finding out about Hope's little adventure in Salem *a few months ago*. What the hell? Hope had been gone less than a *week*, so really, what the hell?

The suite door opened and Kitsune stepped in, carrying an unconscious club-dressed brunette over his shoulder. All conversation stopped as he looked at everyone

"Seriously, dude," Jamal laughed. "What happened to catch and release?"

"The young lady passed out in the cab. I have had enough exposure, but the situation I removed her from was not the best and it seemed ungallant to leave her considering the condition of the street. One moment."

He disappeared into the smaller bedroom, emerged straightening his jacket, and bowed to our guests. The guy could out-polite Ozma. "*Konbanwa*. I see my evening's adventures may have been unnecessary."

Ozma considered him. "Perhaps. What precisely do you mean by the condition of the street? Brian and our guests arrived only shortly before you."

He shrugged. "Only the black vans with the speakers and the crowd."

"Black—*what*?" Polychrome was off her couch and at the patio doors in an instant, outside to look over the rail as they followed in a rush.

"What is that?" Jamal asked for all of them. It had to be the most bizarre thing Grendel had ever seen.

At least twenty black vans had parked directly in the street outside the Kimpton, a crowd of at least two hundred pedestrians filling up the street around them and more arriving by cabs that joined the gridlock. Some of the vans sported big speakers on their roofs, the kind someone might use to rally an outdoor audience. Others were open as workers unpacked loads. Some of them started inflating. Others turned out to be full of tiny black drones that launched in swarms to dart about the street.

Artemis looked at their guests. "This isn't normal, right?"

Victory Anna shook her head. "I have not been here long enough to be certain of that. Pol?"

"Uh, no? It looks like—"

The fire alarms went off. All of them. They could hear them up and down the street, and there were three tall hotels on their block. The alarms almost drowned out the sudden base beat from the speakers and the thrum of motors beneath the inflating balloons—which were rising.

Shell climbed Grendel's back to perch on his shoulder and look down at the street. "Jamal, could you do recon? Use the stairwell."

"On it!" He blurred away. *"Bunchofuglyfacelessguys injumpsuitswith—morelookslikehomeless gettingoutofvans. Noweapons butwatchthetinydrones latchingontobystanders!"*

"Swell," Shell said. "FYI, just checked and city shelters have reported a slight downtick in beds filled and requested. Someone's been sweeping the streets."

Grendel turned to Polychrome. "It's your town." The weird beat and tone from those speakers was driving an icepick into his brain, and the balloons lit up with a strobing light that jabbed in through his eyeballs. He grew filters. Below them, the hotels started emptying out.

"I can shoot the hellish balloons!" Victory Anna announced.

That broke Polychrome's paralysis. "No! You might hit the crowd! Everyone, remain here until we know it's not some kind of mind control!" She launched herself off the patio, streaked towards the balloons, and instantly caught flack. She dodged like a pro.

"They'reshootingbeams fromtheirheads!" Jamal announced. *"Thefacelessguys!"*

Grendel watched Victory Anna's gun twitch as she struggled hard to not just lean over the rail and start firing at the whatever-they-were things trying to shoot her friend. Ozma looked up at Shell on his shoulder. "And the behavior of the drones?"

"They're like little Frisbee-copters—they're attaching themselves to the backs of bystander's necks at the base of the skull and, yeah, controlling them. There are thousands of them."

"I see. Brian?"

"Gotcha, boss." Detaching Shell and handing her to Ozma, he flexed his neck, popped his spine, and grew a bridge of armor up from between his shoulder blades to a Mohawk crest. It left him barely able to turn his head, but nothing was getting to him there. While he was at it he grew thick membranes over his ear canals, around his earbuds. The "sound" from the speakers was unfocusing his world. Then he jumped.

He aimed for one of the trucks, trusting Crash to get the heads-up from Shell and track his descent to remove any bystanders in the impact zone. Smashing down on a truck close to the center of the two-lane convoy got the no-faces' attention. They were freaking ugly suckers; not just no face, but no ears and no hair, just eggshell-white skin with the fronts of their skulls squashed inward in a deep ridged horizontal crease.

The nearest turned and shot him with flattened pulsed beams that erupted out of those creases with a sizzling *whooom*, the pulses burning without burning. He staggered, growing another thick layer to get his nerve endings as deep below his skin as possible as he charged the next speaker van.

"Jamal." Ozma had elected to talk over the open channel. *"Shell is doing signals analysis to try and understand the clinging drones. What are they doing to the people?"*

Grendel smashed into the side of the second van, flipping it as the bystanders around it vanished into Jamal's blur.

"They'rejuststandingthere! Lookingat thecenterof thestreet!"

Overhead one of the balloons blew up. Checking first to see Polychrome weaving above them as she continued to engage, he oriented and looked to see what Jamal was talking about. *Okay, that's not good.* It had to be some kind of trick; in the center of everything the lines were all curving, bending in towards a point like an optical distortion at the center of a photograph. "Ozma, they're doing something freaky to the world!"

Another balloon blew, another, and the jabbing pain of the flashing lights became a little less intense.

"*I understand, Brian, thank you. Jamal, I need you to start removing the controlling drones from their victims as quickly as you can.*"

"*Toomanydronesare makingmorezombies!*" The kid was right, the air was thick with the little suckers, zooming all over the place like guilded starling swarms and plenty of fresh victims were still coming out of the hotels.

"*We are working on a solution, but we need you to stop as many as you can.*"

He smashed a third van, heard the *snap-snap-snap* of Artemis' elasers, and spotted her dancing through the crowd; she'd wrapped a towel around her head and was ignoring the no-faces and the drones to drop zombie bystanders as fast as she could shoot. *That'll work, too.* To his left a swerving flight of drones blew up sequentially as Jamal blurred through swinging something Grendel couldn't quite see.

The brain-hurting thud of the speakers cut out. "*I've jacked their feed!*" Shell crowed. But the distortion was still growing, like a stretched membrane. *We're not going to stop—*

"What in the name of the Brothers Grimm is going on here?"

Three women in ball gowns dashed out of a suddenly-there arch of climbing roses. The one leading the charge, a regal blonde in pink and a tiara, had the interesting curse words. The one right behind her was—

"Astra! Don't get caught!"

They pushed through the rose arch and into a street full of smoke, pulsing light, and the ugliest critters Hope had ever seen that walked on two legs. Brian—*Brian!*—shouted a warning and she twisted to look as *Jamal* came out of nowhere to smash a tiny something flying for her head. A flying blonde hero in a black bodysuit dropped down beside them, landing hard enough to stagger her.

"Carrabelle, we need to stop the crowd!"

The Princess looked around, wide-eyed and determined. "With what?"

Grendel smashed ugly whatevers out of the way as they turned towards Hope and the girls, shouting about *no-faces!* She got the message, flying into them to knock them flying like bowling pins as a blonde woman in black spandex laid into them with precision shots of weirdly physical light-blasts from above.

Jamal blurred to a stop beside The Princess. "Shell says she can give you a soundtrack! Like your origin story!"

"Really, sugar?" Her eyes lit up. "Orchestra! Sleeping Beauty's waltz!"

The van-mounted speakers around them erupted into a full symphony orchestra performance of a tune Hope instantly recognized—one known to millions of children and adults who had been children sometime in the last fifty years—and The Princess broke into song, Shell getting her voice into the broadcast (probably through one of the team's mics). Beside The Princess, Jack tossed what looked like fist-sized Christmas-poppers into the air and they exploded into multiplying and cascading fireworks as Hope dropped to the street and her feet started moving to the piped music.

What the heck? Oh no, the drones— But she saw Jamal blur again before the song could grab him too, going back to swatting drones away from The Princess as *everyone* else on the street—the no-faces (who could hear somehow, obviously, even if Hope couldn't see any ears on them), *Artemis*, Polychrome, and a whole crowd of zombie bystanders—formed up in the biggest flash-crowd dance routine she'd ever seen.

A dance that ripped everyone's attention away from the growing distortion that Hope only now spotted in the street, which popped like a soap bubble as the Princess sang and everyone danced. Grendel grabbed and spun Hope into the waltz as she turned to him, and she could have danced all night, twirling partners in the glorious swirling synchronicity. The bit of her brain not lost in The Princess's song wondered how long everyone else could.

Then they didn't need to; the street lit up with a blinding pulse and everyone else fell down. She and Grendel stood in the middle of a street full of sleepers as shorted-out drones fell like rain.

So how did one end a night that featured an attempted extra-dimensional invasion that turned into a self-choreographed street ball? Even for this place Hope could tell it obviously wasn't just another night in Portland. By some unspoken agreement, Jacqueline, Carrabelle, and two more women introduced to her as the Polychrome and Victory Anna she'd been told were watching over Velveteen's city, got her and her team (she was so happy to see them she almost cried) off the street and up into the hotel suite they'd set up in.

Something about avoiding explanations and paperwork.

Collapsing onto a couch, she sighed and adjusted the skirts of her ball gown. It was a little the worse for wear, but since a magic mirror in an enchanted castle had made it she didn't feel too bad (and it was disturbingly okay that that thought made sense). Shell, after clinging and babbling for ten minutes while Hope and the rest watched Polychrome and The Princess handle the live report on the big screen TV (both of them *very* good at handling the media), curled up in Hope's lap and let her scratch her ears.

Artemis—*her* Jacky—stepped in from the patio to drop to the couch beside her. "So, that's a new look."

"This old thing? I just threw it on. Been waiting long?"

"A few days. You?"

Hope hugged her favorite fiend of the night. The gown and protesting cat barely got in the way. "Glad you're here. Hey, so what was that flashy-thing at the end?"

"This place's Verne-type rigged her big gun for max dispersal and Ozma hot-shotted it with the Magic Belt. Turned out the drones didn't like being tased any more than people do. I wish she'd waited; Shell's got great video of Grendel twirling you. I think she's saving it for blackmail."

"And what did we stop, exactly?" *Talk. Just talking is good.* She kept looking over at her guys, even Kitsune, making sure they were here too.

Jack sat down opposite them, easily arranging her own gown. "Nothing less than an attempted incursion from a Dada anti-realm. They're related to the Seasonal Lands, but...not."

"Nasty little things," Victory Anna sniffed, coming into the room. "Not even respectable universes." She stalked over to the bar and started rifling through it. "I traveled through my own share to get here and most of them were *balls*, without even proper—ha!" She pulled out a wooden tea box.

"There is an electric pot and filter here," Ozma informed her, leaving the whiteboards she'd been playing with to join her at the bar. "A bit of tea would be most welcome."

"Thank you, ma'am. I can prepare—"

Ozma didn't let Victory Anna finish her protest, simply locating the pot and water as she stammered. From what Hope understood, the woman was a survivor from a vanished Victorian steam-punk world; Ozma's old world royal demeanor probably pushed every one of her class-buttons.

"Tea sounds great," Carrabelle agreed, entering the suite ahead of Polychrome—the flying photon-manipulator who'd helped Hope and Brian keep the uglies off of Carrabella while The Princess had gone to work. All done dealing with the police and press, Hope supposed, stifling a giggle. The Princess of Oz and The Princess were certain to start a more-royal-than-thou contest any moment now; she hoped poor Victory Anna didn't have a meltdown.

And she was *way* too...jet lagged? The littlest things felt insanely funny. She found Jacky's hand, ignoring Kitsune's considering look from across the room (or trying to—her rebellious eyes kept wandering). She also ignored the part of her wishing it had been Kitsune on the street and caught in the dance with her instead of Grendel; Kitsune *anything* would have to wait. *Right. Absolutely*.

In any case she needn't have worried about Victory Anna; as soon as Polychrome joined her at the bar all of the woman's attention focused on her. "Are the policemen satisfied, Pol?"

"For now. Since we identified it as an attempted incursion, federal agents with all their science stuff are going to be here tomorrow." She looked at the suite's grandfather clock, sighed. "Today, actually. Till then the street's sealed off."

"They will find that the point of distortion is safe," Ozma informed everyone from the bar. "I know nothing of them, but my tests have determined that they came through the same weak place that we used to get here. I believe that they were attempting to use their technology and captive minds to create a wider beachhead at the closest point congruent to a more stable point in their world."

"Great." Polychrome's face said it really wasn't. "So Portland is going to become a weirdness magnet, now?"

Hope laughed, slapped a hand over her mouth.

"I think not." Ozma finished measuring tea and let Victory Anna take control of the pot. "We kept our own presence quiet, but now that you know about the rift you will be able to monitor its terminus here with minimal difficulty. It does not support large incursions, the reason for tonight's attempt."

Polychrome sighed. "We'll need to think about getting more city heroes, anyway. Or getting our science guys to rig something up."

"Actually, guys," Jack put in. "Do what you want, but the Seasons are going to be learning about these Dadas as soon as I get home. Protecting the Calendar Lands from disruption by anti-realms is part of our job. The whole cosmic Order vs. Chaos thing."

Hope took a breath and straightened up. "And that gives us our deadline, doesn't it? We should be on our way home before your people start sealing off our arrival point." *And I can go home.* The *best* news she'd had was that, back home, it had apparently been not even a week since she'd left for her adventures. Which didn't mean she wasn't going to hug the stuffing out of a lot of people.

Ozma nodded agreement. "It is best that we not dawdle. However, there is always time for tea, and I would like some time to speak to both Victory Anna and Jacqueline Claus. Perhaps you could nap in Kitsune's room, once he removes his young lady."

"His *what*?"

"And perhaps while he does, you may discuss your courting arrangements? He's already met your parents, and they would like to know as well."

She covered her eyes and groaned. Maybe home could wait a few more days? One? Two?

In her lap, she could feel Shell laughing.

DSA Field Report: Agent Smith.

Okay Boss, everybody's home and accounted for. Apparently Astra brought souvenirs, one in a very large garment bag. We've mapped the current edges of the rift, and they haven't expanded beyond the warehouse walls; my recommendation, *again*, is if the science boys can't figure a way to make the rift go away completely then we seal the entire site inside a cement cube and forget about it. SP1 is weird and dangerous enough—it sounds like a lot of their capes are Ultra Class and they know a lot of Omega Class entities—but Ozma has informed me that our faceless dudes launched an invasion on the SP1 side of the rift. Boss, if we leave it open then one of these days Cthulhu is going to come knocking on our end.

Odysseus Case File 1-K612 B.

Operation Odysseus: Director Kayle.

Madame President, Per Agent Smith's recommendation assets are being mobilized to seal Gate SP1. Initial reports are confident that total seal is possible; if not, steps can be taken to make the open rift less accessible and more hostile to intrusions. I understand the potential of the site, but further mapping of accessible destinations on the other end of Gate SP1 does not appear worth the risk of leaving the door open. See summary of Operation Hellmouth for a review of the downsides of such a venture. Also, see full Astra debrief; I found her observations succinct, and our analysts are going to be rethinking many of our suppositions regarding extrarealities in light of the data she brought back.
Finally, given what we have learned regarding the Ascendancy, I request approval of Operation Icarus.

Director Summary, Odysseus Case File.

Historical Accuracy

by K.F. Lim

Chapter One
"To be honest, one of the most useless bits of advice I've ever heard was "prepare for the worst, hope for the best." The thing is, when you're dealing with six active military bases, one NASA facility, one highly active government-funded physics lab, and one of the biggest shipyards on the east coast, all in one area code with a propensity towards hurricanes and flash floods, it's really impossible to even predict what the worst could be, let alone prepare for it."

Nikki Aguilar, aka Typhoon

2 PM, March 31st: Virginia Beach
　　I sat in my mother's obnoxiously pink catering van, stuck on the Hampton Roads Bridge Tunnel, with 300 loaves of Filipino breakfast rolls in my trunk. Grimly leaning against the horn, I contemplated the futility of my own existence, wondering just how furious my mother would be if the *pan de sal* at my cousin's wedding was served slightly stale and smelling of sweaty diving gear. My earbud chirped, thankfully interrupting my gridlock nihilism.
　　"Dispatch to Typhoon, do you copy?"
　　Groaning, I put the catering van in park. Given the fact that I hadn't moved in 20 minutes, I probably should have done that ten minutes ago. "Typhoon, here, General. What's the what?"

I could *hear* his disapproving grimace at my non-regulation response over the headset. Whatever; I was technically off duty, and The General could use some informality in his life.

"*We got a Level 5 Pinocchio. Some idiot decided to animate the King Neptune Statue over by the Boardwalk.*"

I groaned again. Spring Break had just broken on the Ocean Front; the beach was probably overflowing with tourists and locals alike. "Well, shit, General, that sounds like a real Charlie Foxtrot just waiting to happen, but I don't know how I'm gonna get down there when my van's not moving and I haven't even crossed the tunnel yet."

"*I have a Navy chopper waiting for you at the coordinates I just sent to your headset. Cold Front will meet you at a rendezvous point closer to the Ocean Front. Nightingale is already there on crowd control duty. Just jump in the drink and zoom over there, Typhoon.*"

Muttering something a lot harsher than "shit" under my breath, I dug through my purse for my waterproof, Verne-type-engineered set of goggles. "General, this is supposed to be my *day off*. Do you even know what "day off" means? I have 300 bread rolls in my van and—"

Of course, he overrode me. "*Somebody will be by to pick up your van and deliver the baked goods to their final destination. Good luck, Typhoon.*"

I sighed and started stripping, eyeing the waves with a suspicious glare. I hated diving off the HRBT; you just never know what weird litter lurked underneath the foamy, smelly water. Finally free of my jeans and dressed only in an ergonomic tankini, I climbed out of the van, locked my door, stashed my keys in a waterproof wrist pouch, slid on the goggles, and positioned myself to jump off the bridge. For a second, I contemplated how ridiculous I looked—a short, muscular, dark-skinned Filipina girl, dressed only in a silver mesh two-piece, struggling to get her half shaved, half shoulder-length black wavy hair under a swim cap, all while preparing to jump into some seriously sketchy water.

"DON'T DO IT! TRAFFIC ISN'T THAT BAD!" somebody yelled over the cacophony of car horns.

"I PROMISE YOU, THIS ISN'T WHAT IT LOOKS LIKE!" I yelled back.

And then I jumped.

Maybe I should take a moment to explain why jumping off a bridge doesn't mean certain death for me.

Hi, My name is Nikki Aguilar, and I am an actual mermaid.

OK, maybe not a mermaid *all* the time. But five years ago, me and a bunch of my swim team buddies accidentally got caught in a hurricane. In our defense, it was only a *little* hurricane...well, as little as a hurricane can get while still officially being labeled a "hurricane."

We decided that taking a boat out to sea without checking the weather report was a great idea. The experience was life-threatening and adrenaline-pumping enough to induce my breakthrough. My best friend was drowning, and I was (and still am) an enormous fantasy nerd. Result: I grew gills...and yes, a fish tail where my legs had been. What I didn't grow was a pair of conveniently placed seashells, which 15 year-old-me was more upset about than the fact that I had turned into a frickin' mermaid and wasn't quite sure how to turn back. You'd think that a big honkin' fish tail would make me more self-conscious than a little nip slip, but that's high school for you.

After the Coast Guard responded to our SOS call, rescued us, and ensured my modesty was protected by a big towel, my parents and I hitched a ride with a couple of scientists to Camp Peary, since I was still awkwardly flopping instead of walking. A group of super creepy CAI, CIA and DSA scientists put me through my aquatic paces (or rather, swim strokes). We discovered that I wasn't *just* a mermaid. The scientists determined that I was an aquamorph: able to change my anatomy to any sort of aquatic creature (or creatures) that I knew about. Sure, I had to study up on what each animal was capable of and their specific musculature, but by the end of the first week, I could mimic the tail of a marlin *and* the bioluminescence of an anglerfish. We also discovered that shifting back was just as hard—I had to have intimate knowledge of my own skeletal and muscular systems.

In the General's words, I was "tactically useful" to the US Government.

Flash forward to now. I'm a certified and fully trained member of the Hampton Roads CAI team. We're officially known as "The Nauticals," but the locals know us as "The Pirates." We're a relatively small team; just three, sometimes four, of us. The 757 isn't really that big of a supervillain town; it's simply not Metropolis-y enough for the average attention-seeking-bad-guy. Local authorities mostly call us in when some government/military experiment goes haywire. The pay is good, the benefits are ace, and I'm not stuck at an office job like the rest of my friends are.

But the hours are crap, and sadly, jumping off a bridge into sketchy, sludgy Chesapeake Bay water wasn't nearly as disgusting as my average workday could get.

I hit the water feet first (there was no way I was going to risk a head injury by jumping into murky water) and propelled myself forward, melding my legs into a sailfish's tail (bursting the seams of my tankini bottom in the process) and cutting through the water with gills and arm-fins. The coordinates The General had sent me flashed red against the plexiglass of my goggles, superimposed over a GPS display. Ten seconds later (it was a familiar morph), I was fully finned and zipping through the Bay at a brisk 68 miles an hour and gritting my teeth against the icky feeling of polluted bay water flowing through my hair.

I really hope Mom doesn't mind her catering getting delivered by military copter.

Ten minutes later, I was grabbing a harness attached to a Knighthawk helicopter. The crew carefully winched me up into the cabin, where two (blessedly well-briefed) sailor boys grabbed a large towel and formed a discrete changing screen for me. Another tossed me a ready-made "modesty bag" that the General must have sent. I chirped a grateful "thanks!" to the embarrassed young men (it wasn't the first time I had made sailors blush). Quickly (and discretely) de-morphing, I toweled myself off, and slipped into the swimsuit bottom provided by the pack. I rifled through the bag for an energy drink, popped it open, and covertly tried to check for a wedgie (pulling on a swimsuit over damp skin is *hard*). The pilot banked the chopper towards the Ocean Front as one of the sailors tuned the chopper's comms to my earbud frequency and began to brief me on the situation.

"Ma'am. At approximately 1330 hours today, tourists reported hearing a loud cracking sound coming from the King Neptune Statue on the Boardwalk. Witnesses saw the statue break free from its foundation, point its trident towards the crowds of beachgoers, and said, quote, "MOTHER NATURE WEEPS AT HER DEATH BY CAPITALISM," end quote. The statue then proceeded to crush several taffy stands, hot dog carts, and cabana rental stations under its feet as it marched towards ocean. Current status reports from Virginia Beach Police say that it is ripping up beach umbrellas and generally destroying anything in its path."

I grimaced. "What about Cold Front? What is his location?"

"Cold Front is currently flying recon above the Ocean Front. He will rendezvous with us shortly to plan your attack strategy."

"Understood!" I yelled back, wiping my arms and legs while chugging the rest of my energy drink. Cold Front could harness hurricane-level winds to speed him wherever he wanted to go, and while I was used to riding in the eye of his storm, I still got cold when I was wet and that high up.

A loud *thunk* sounded behind me.

"Hey Nikki, how's it going?" a deep voice yelled over the noise of the chopper's blades, "...*Swimmingly?*"

I grinned and turned. "Charles! That depends on *weather* you're ready to go or not."

"*CODENAMES!*" barked The General in both our earbuds.

We rolled our eyes at each other. The General was a stickler for security protocol—a left over from his covert ops days in the Middle East.

"*Report, Cold Front.*"

Charles nodded politely to the four Navy boys. "Looks like a typical automaton to me, sir. Doesn't seem to have any sort of extra firepower or anything; it's just really damn big. Also, the trident's kinda pointy, and covered in bird droppings."

Muting his earbud for a second, he turned to me and grinned. "So *look sharp*, Nikki."

I could practically hear the General gritting his teeth over our coms. "*Any civilian casualties?*"

"No, sir. King Neptune seems to be more fixated on structural damage, not human beings. And he doesn't really move that fast; people have been able to get out of the way. It's just the potential for mass panic and further property damage."

"*Nightingale is in charge of crowd control, Cold Front. You and Typhoon are responsible for minimizing property damage.*"

"You got your lightning under control yet, *Cold Front?*" I asked.

He shook his head ruefully. "Not good enough with this many civilians around, *Typhoon.*"

I nodded grimly and strapped my goggles back on. "Guess it's up to me to provide the *shock value*, then."

"*Now approaching the Ocean Front.*" The pilot's status update buzzed through both our earbuds.

"Roger that," Cold Front said. He stepped out of the helicopter and floated in place on a whirling platform of wind and reached his hand out to me. "Ready for action, *Typhoon?*"

I cracked my neck from side to side, "Let's *storm this beach!*" I yelled, and slapped my hand into his. Gripping my arm like a taut spring, he launched me into a steep fall towards the ocean.

I took a deep breath as I punched through the surface of the water like a missile. Fifteen feet ahead of me, the tacky, bronzed King Neptune smashed up and down the surf yelling "SMASH THE CAPITALIST PATRIARCHY!"

Breathing deeply through my gills, I sped towards the marauding statue. Along with the HUD, my goggles improved my underwater vision (I could do it by morphing, but I preferred to save my energy). Spotting the muscular bronze legs of the statue stomping about 15 feet in front of me, I flared my webbed hands out in hard stop. Gritting my teeth at the thought of getting *that* close to King Neptune's crotch, I zoomed under my target and popped up between his legs, gasping as my gills sank back into my chest.

"Hey, you dirty hippy!" I yelled, as I popped up through the surface. "Why don't you just get a job?"

King Neptune didn't pay any attention to me—which told me that he was definitely not an AI, but probably being controlled by an actual person through some sort of remote. I grimaced—an actual AI would have been easier to clean up (overcompensating dorks are easier to scare than bronze automatons). I quickly morphed my arms into something resembling electric eel skin and slammed my fists into King Neptune's bronze, muscled legs.

"FEEL THE BURN, BIG BOY!"

The automaton creaked, crackled and froze. Just as I was about to congratulate myself on a job well done, Charles yelled, "TYPHOON, GET YOUR ASS OUT OF THERE!"

Aww, *fuck.* In my rush to stop the statue from stomping on civilians, I had forgotten about one very important thing: gravity. Frozen in mid-stomp, the 20-foot tall obnoxious merman monstrosity toppled forward like a felled tree. Desperately wishing that seagulls counted as "aquatic," I frantically morphed my legs into a sailfish tail, then went for fullbody manta ray as I dove because *dammit dammit dammit not enough time too slow piece of shit vertebrate skeleton—*

CLANG.

Diving as deep as I could into the water, I winced as my half-morphed human pancake shape scraped against the rough sandy bottom as I flapped away from an impact...that never arrived?

I cautiously bobbed to the surface, breaking through the waves with a disgusting *schlorp-pop* sound. Spitting out a mouthful of foul-tasting, briny gunk, I was greeted by the sight of a tiny blonde girl in a seriously cute bright blue bikini supporting the entire weight of King Neptune with her bare hands.

Her very small, perfectly manicured, bare hands.

"Hey!" she yelled down at me. "Need a *lift*?"

Nodding weakly, I watched her casually float downwards, gripping King Neptune by his waist. "So, what should I do with him?" she asked, eyeing the statue critically. "And, um, are you okay?"

An embarrassingly flatulent sound came bubbling out of my flattened mouth-slit, and I realized my flattened manta-shaped face was high-octane nightmare fuel. Shaking my head furiously, I quickly re-inflated my features.

"I....I....ummm...." Imminent death made words *hard*. "Are...what?"

"'Scuze me, Astra, ma'am." Charles had swooped down to check on me and make sure I hadn't been turned into a sea pancake.

"...ASTRA?" I hissed to him. "*Are you fucking serious?*"

He frantically shushed me and pointed towards the Navy chopper. "There's a Navy crew right here who have a real strong harness, ma'am. If you could be so kind as to strap King Neptune in, we can move him somewhere safe."

Astra (*Seriously?! Astra*?!) nodded and slowly flew upwards, keeping her grip on the statue as the helicopter buzzed over to us, slowly lowering a large harness down. Astra nonchalantly gripped the straps and started buckling them into place, like she disabled enormous socialist automatons every day.

"You OK?" Charles asked quietly, checking my arms for any damage.

"Yeah...I'm fine, I think," I mumbled, still in shock. "Did I get hit on the head, or is Hope Corrigan flying around King Neptune in a designer bikini?" I paused, squinting my eyes. "...A *Marc Jacobs* designer bikini?"

"Well, I'm not sure if you're brain damaged or not, seeing as you *immobilized a giant statue while you were underneath it,*" Charles quipped. "But yep, that's definitely Astra, in the bikini-clad flesh." He double-checked my pupils. "You good? I'm gonna help her buckle up King Neptune and guide him in."

I nodded, dazed. Charles left me treading water with my tail as he and Hope guided King Neptune in midair to prevent a big, dangerous splash.

The loud, angry buzz of a jetski interrupted my big-dumb-brush-with-death reverie.

"HEY GIRL HEY!!!" a familiar, cheerfully demented voice called out.

I looked to my right. A muscular girl with a bright pink buzzcut and several piercings splashed to a stop next to me, a big red megaphone in one hand, throttle in the other.

"Hey, CeeCee," I said, tiredly. "Where were you?"

"*I* was making sure that y'alls butts didn't get trampled by a rampaging stampede of panicky tourists," she replied, gesturing to the megaphone. "While you were busy getting pancaked and staring at Astra's bikini, I was hypnotizing beachgoers into "please form a single file line towards the nearest exit where emergency personnel will assist you shortly."

I blinked, impressed. "Wait, I thought your voice only works on like, one or two people at a time?"

Cee Cee—Cecelia Tyler, code name "Nightingale"—had super siren powers. Her voice could seriously damage a person's body, *and* hypnotize them to do what she wanted. She was only 21, but several private military companies were already courting her. Which was ironic, because she was basically your typical hippy, vegan, feminist, anti-war college kid.

CeeCee giggled. "Turns out that when my voice is amplified, so's my powers. Some local DSA Verne-type totally hooked me up." She slid her megaphone in a customized bag hanging from the jetski's handle and then slipped it over her shoulders. "Want a ride back to shore? I think the General may want us to escort Super Girl over to HQ for a debrief."

"Great, more chances for the General to yell at me on my day off."

She shrugged. "Either you get barked at over comms, or you get barked at in person, first thing tomorrow, with an extra lecture on promptness, timeliness, and responsibility. You really want to put up with that for, like..." she checked her watch, "8 more hours of freedom?"

I gave a long-suffering sigh. "You're right. Totally not worth it."

She tossed me a waterproof bag. "Here, make yourself decent and I'll give you a ride to shore."

I gratefully caught the bag, fished out a pair of bikini bottoms (seriously, my life would be so much simpler if public nudity was acceptable), and quickly demorphed my tail into legs. Shielded by CeeCee's jetski, I covertly slipped on the hikini bottoms, grabbed her hand, and swung myself onto the jetski behind her.

"So...you talked to Astra yet?" I yelled over the buzz of the jetski, "How did she even get involved? Where the hell did she come from?"

CeeCee gunned the jetski towards shore, yelling over the roar of the engine. "I dunno, dude! I think she was, like, sunbathing on the beach or something? King Neptune started yelling about, like, the Hegemony of Consumerism and she just sort of tapped the nearest cop on the shoulder like, "may I assist you in this situation," or whatever? By the time I got there, she was already flying overhead, to like, coordinate evacuation routes, or some shit."

"Show off," I muttered. "Who shows up on vacation and says 'you know what I should do? Coordinate an evacuation plan for the locals when a giant marauding statue takes over the beach. Following instructions and taking a back seat to things, nope, not at all something that makes sense."

"Sorry if I stepped in your sandbox," came a chipper voice overhead. "As my friend Jacky always says, I have a compulsive need to *save anybody, ever.*"

Oh Shit. I looked up. Yep. Of course. There she was—Astra, in the flesh, just in time for my petty rant. "Um...errr..." *How do you apologize in this situation? "Sorry I was a raging bitch and talking about you behind your back right after you saved my life because I was embarrassed about trying to turn into a sea pancake and thus incredibly defensive?*

CeeCee shot me an amused, shadenfreude-laden grin over her shoulder as she docked the jetski into the pier.

Astra shrugged apologetically. "I get it, I do. I'm an interloper. You guys are the local crew, and since I was first on scene, I ended up running the show. I didn't mean to step on anybody's toes. Or fins."

I turned bright red. CeeCee just casually jumped off the jetski and tossed me a rope to tie it in place. "Don't mind Typhoon over here," she told Astra in a conspiratorial whisper. "She's just pissed off because the General called her in on her day off."

"You guys get days *off*?" Astra asked. "And people actually *respect* them?"

CeeCee laughed. "Yeah, for the most part. It's not that busy of a beat." She grinned lasciviously, giving Astra and her bikini a long, appreciative stare. "You coming back with us for the de-brief, hot stuff?"

"Um...yes? And...Thanks?" Astra's blush was even redder than mine.

I winced and heaved myself off the jetski. After that many rapid morphs, my body felt like jelly. "Don't mind CeeCee. Her sexual preference is 'all of the above.'"

CeeCee smacked me on the forearm. "Don't scare her! All the blogs say she's a *good* girl."

I rolled my eyes. "I'm not scaring her. I'm *warning* her."

Astra gave us a quizzical look. "...Are you guys always this casual over group comms?" She silently tapped a finger on her ear.

"What?" CeeCee and I yelped in unison.

I grabbed my earbud, desperately wishing I could morph a foot into my mouth.

On cue, the General's voice barked in my ear. *"Typhoon! Nightingale! Your jobs are done. Escort Astra to wherever she requires and report to HQ at approximately 0800 hours."*

I glared at CeeCee.

She rolled her eyes. What's the big deal?" she scoffed, "The General packs you go-bags filled with underwear. My sexuality is so not the most embarrassing thing he's had to overhear."

Astra looked at us, confused. "Who?"

"The General," I said. "You talked with him before stepping in to run the show, right?"

Astra still looked puzzled. "Um...I talked to an abrupt, older gentleman on the police channel? He told me to proceed with caution and rendezvous with the local DSA team?"

"Yeah, sounds like The General. He got trained out of extraneous emotions and social niceties during his long and mysterious military career."

"But he's actually super serious about everything, including letting us blow off steam after what he calls "a successful campaign," CeeCee added. "Speaking of which, wanna get drunk and sing really loudly into a microphone in front of strangers?"

I face-palmed "CeeCee, could you please at least *try* to seem semi-normal to the very famous visiting Super Girl?"

"....I honestly cannot tell if you're joking or not," Hope replied. "Like genuinely, one hundred percent, I feel like this could go either way."

"Does that actually make you fifty percent?" CeeCee asked cheerfully.

I glared at her, got an unrepentant goofy face in reply, then turned to Hope. "Does it matter to *you* if it goes either way?"

Hope cocked her head to the side, as if listening to somebody. "Well, the little voice inside my head says to trust you and not be such a wimp. Not that she's always *right*."

I grinned. "Well then, Super Girl, we'll show you a good time."

Chapter Two

"I believe in three things: the necessity for absolute social equality between human beings, the power of music and poetry to foment social change, and jello shots. Lots and lots of jello shots."

Cecelia "CeeCee" Tyler, aka Nightingale

7 PM, March 31

After dropping off some spare equipment at the local DSA offices, I took Astra and CeeCee back to my place to clean up (and wasn't that a fun thing to explain to my parents: "Hi Mom—Astra, the most famous young superhero in America, needs to use our spare bathroom; do we have any extra towels?"). After some seriously necessary showers, we dragged our (super) girl Friday over to Frankie's Place for three out of the four B's: beer, bourbon, and barbecue (obviously, we supplied the bitches).

"So what exactly makes good pulled pork anyway?" Hope asked as I navigated the car around clumps of roaming, bathing-suit-clad tourists to get into a cramped parking spot.

CeeCee shrugged. "I tend to just suspend my veganism to support local businesses, so I'm really the wrong person to ask."

"...What?"

I rolled my eyes. "CeeCee here is vegan except when being not-vegan will simultaneously benefit the local proletariat and also get her schwasted." I explained. "But to answer your woefully Yankee-ass question, it's the tenderness of the meat and whatever secret is in the sauce. Good pulled pork is juicy, falls apart on the fork, and melts in your mouth like a meaty rich snowflake."

"Ah...that sounds...really, REALLY delicious." Hope replied. Her stomach growled audibly, totally agreeing with her.

I grinned. "You got a weird, hyperfast metabolism too?"

"Not exactly. My super-duper strength isn't based on anything biological. But when I'm hurt, I heal real fast and then—" She giggled as her stomach made another loud, grumbly noise. "One time I ate ten bags of beef jerky without realizing it. Super-stomach."

"You're in the right place then. Frankie's is the best barbecue joint in the city...AND their portions are the biggest."

"Also, tonight's karaoke night at the Salty Mermaid next door," CeeCee piped up.

Hope snorted. "I can't possibly drink enough alcohol for you guys to get me to do *that.*"

I smiled wolfishly. "Challenge accepted."

As we all got out of the car, my cellphone started buzzing in my back pocket. I pulled it out—*aaaaand crap.* It was my mother. "Y'all go on ahead and get us a booth. I've got to take this."

CeeCee beamed and grabbed Hope's hand. "Sure thing! We'll order an onion loaf for the table."

"What's an onion loaf?"

I rolled my eyes at their retreating backs. "Hi, Mom. What's up? Did I forget something at home?"

"*Nikki,* ai nako, anak! *Why are you not answering* Tita *Maria's texts, huh?*"

I quickly glanced down at my phone screen. Ten messages total, seven from *Tita* Maria, and three from mom. Oops. "I was driving, Mom. You know I don't have a hands-free for my phone."

"*Whatever, Nikki. No excuse! There is a crisis! What type of* ate *are you, that you can't even pick up your phone when there's an emergency?*"

I grimaced. If mom was invoking my status as "*ate*" (a Tagalog term that strictly speaking means "older sister" but *really* means "older female relative of any kind") things were about to get real. "Which cousin is it this time? Is it Isabella? Did she get *another* piercing? Where is it this time?

"*Aiyah, Nikki, don't joke! It's Ollie! He's all over the news,* bah! *Something about that silly Neptune statue earlier today. It's on the Facebook and the Twitter,* Tita *Maria says!*"

"What do you mean, it's all over Facebook?"

"*I don't know, Nikki, I can't get to my, my, my, thing. You set it up, daddy messed up our tablet again. Check your text messages, OK,* Tita *Maria sent you all this.*"

I barely stifled a frustrated scream. "Yes, Mom, OK, OK! I'll check them."

"And what time you gonna be home, huh? It's not good for three girls to be out so late alone, with no boyfriends. Some man might follow you home, hurt you or something."

"Mom, I can literally electrify any man who touches me, CeeCee can melt their brains with a single note, and Hope Corrigan *is a frickin' indestructible, flying human tank.* I think we'll be fine."

"Don't take that tone with me! I'm your mother! I'm just worried about you!"

I grit my teeth. "Yes. Yes. Sorry, Mom. I'll get right on this Ollie situation. Bye."

Pressing the end button on my phone before my mother could launch into a lecture about healthy eating, (so not a possibility at Frankie's) I slid my finger over to my texts and groaned.

Tita Maria, who was decidedly more tech-savvy than either of my parents (she was less an auntie, and more like a distant, slightly elder cousin), had sent me five different news article links that all embedded the same video. I hit play to be greeted by the sight of my kid cousin Ollie in cheesy, movie-villain half-lighting, voice enhanced by many, *many* echo-y filters. And a fedora. He was wearing an actual fedora. I could only pray it was ironic.

"I AM THE FUTURE." Another Ollie appeared on screen, facing the first Ollie.

"I AM HERE TO FREE YOU FROM THE TREACHEROUS SLAVERY OF THE PAST." Both Ollies turned to face forward and spoke in unison.

"I CLAIM CREATOR STATUS FOR THE AVANTE-GARDE PERFORMANCE ART PIECE, 'NEPTUNE AWAKENZ (GAIA WEEPZ)'"

(Yes, he pronounced the parentheses. I almost smacked my smartphone screen).

"BE TREPIDATIOUS, MY DOPED UP DENIZENS OF DEGRADATION! MY THOUGHT CAMPAIGN TO ENLIGHTEN YOU MINDLESS DRONES OF WESTERN SOCIETY HAS JUST BEGUN! JOIN ME FOR MY INTERACTIVE AUTOMATON LASER RECREATION OF THE BATTLE OF THE MONITOR AND THE MERRIMACK! IT...IS...A METAPHOR!"

Seriously? How many SAT words can he fit into a single Vine?

"Information for the event is listed in the box below, and don't forget to like, favorite, and subscribe!" he continued on the video. "And ladies," he said smirking slyly at the camera, actually tipping his fedora at audience. "*My* information's down there too. HMU, kk?"

I growled, dropped my phone into my purse and proceeded to bang my head against my car door. "I am going to *kill* him!" I growled.

"No, I'm going to disable his Facebook and crush his laptop between my shark jaws."

"Now that I'd *pay* to see," CeeCee called out cheerfully from the restaurant doorway. "Bee Tee Dubs, our table's ready."

"Be right there," I sighed, "Just let me make one more call." I waited until CeeCee went back inside before I pulled out my phone and dialed Ollie. It went straight to voicemail.

"*Yo, this is Ollie's phone. I'm probably awakening the proletariat to my artistic vision's cause for social justice. Leave a message at the beep, or text it, cos I'm lightning fast with the emojis, ladies.*"

"Ollie, you little shit," I hissed into my phone, glancing up to make sure nobody was eavesdropping. "You are *so, so* very dead. I am so *not* going to be able to cover your ass this time. Call me, you little twerp. Before I have to convince the General that vaporizing your *pretentious little ass* is overkill."

Three pulled pork platters, three orders of coleslaw, and five St. George's Hard Brewed Lemonade's later, Hope was giving CeeCee and me a knowing grin. Well, I was getting the knowing grin. At that point, Ceecee was lost in her own barbecue-and-beer fueled world, dancing to the jukebox in the corner.

"You're kidding me," I growled over the rim of my (sixth) hard lemonade. "What are you, a cyborg?"

Hope shrugged. "Alcohol's a poison—my body fights it off. I thought you had a super-metabolism?"

I glared at her. "I'm also Asian. Alcohol will fade on me much faster than the normal person, but it hits me twice as fast."

"HEY GUYS! WE SHOULD TOTALLY GO NEXT DOOR AND GET JELLO SHOTS!"

I leaned back against the booth and sighed. "CeeCee, I'm DD for tonight. You know even my mighty morphin' body has limits. Not to mention, I need to—well, I've got a family thing." I snuck a look at my phone again. Ollie hadn't called, or even texted back.

"Awwww man, not a family thing!" CeeCee replied in a totally obnoxious, totally drunk sort of way. "Come on, Nikki! I called Missy. She's at some protest or something but she'll be done in time to pick us up!"

"I have my car, CeeCee. And yes, a *family thing*. You know my mom; she's not gonna let me off the hook for this. And besides, Missy—"

"Who's Missy? And what family thing?" Hope, completely unfairly, was not even a little drunk.

"Missy is CeeCee's on-again-off-again girlfriend. She's a wonderfully non-judgmental straight-edge," I explained, side-stepping the family question. I wasn't sure I was ready for Hope to know about my crazy family issues yet. CeeCee knew Ollie already, but CeeCee was part of my team. I had no idea how Hope would react to my cousin Ollie's megalomaniacal, evil-Verne-genius, teenage horndog status.

"She's not my GIRLFRIEND," CeeCee slurred happily, sloppily draping herself over the table. "She's my enlightened polyamorous partner."

"Right, sorry. What CeeCee said. And by the way," I glared at her, "I am NOT dealing with my car getting towed."

CeeCee grinned. "No big; call HQ. They'll totally take care of it for you."

"Oh hell no," I replied, "You know the General would go ballistic. "

Besides, I wanted to avoid HQ for a little bit. The General was probably going to find out about Ollie sooner rather than later; I just didn't want to be there when he did. Between losing my job and pissing off an army of rabidly over-protective aunties, I would take the aunties...but only if I was forced to make that choice.

I still had a slim hope that Ollie would turn himself in, in a weird attempt to look more badass by getting arrested. A very slim hope, fueled by the knowledge that Ollie was obsessed with looking like a badass for the ladies.

"You know," Hope interjected helpfully, "I could always airlift it back to your house and be right back."

"WHAT?" I yelped. "Are you serious? I thought you didn't want to even GO to karaoke. And isn't there some kind of rule against that?"

"Against what? Utilizing my own powers to ensure the safety and wellbeing of my friends? Gosh, no. And also," she added, with an innocent look, "I'm sort of curious as to what the limit of *your* metabolism is. What exactly is *in* a jello shot?"

"You've never had a jello shot?"

"Nope," Hope replied, "I just turned twenty-one a couple of weeks ago, and I was out of town. Before that, well, let's just say I had a bad childhood experience with liquor that turned me off drinking for a while. After—" She closed her mouth on whatever she'd been about to say and shrugged. "There didn't seem to be much point."

CeeCee nodded sagely, in the exceedingly smug way only a very drunk person can nod. "I've been there, girlfriend. One time, my bestie and I drank an entire bottle of Hypnotiq and decided to see if my sound waves could, like, make us fly."

I raised a judgmental eyebrow. "I've never heard this story."

She waved a hand airily. "Whatever, it was a long time ago, like, in the careless youth of high school."

"You're just a junior in college, CeeCee."

CeeCee waved her hands again, this time so flamboyantly, it looked like she was conducting an orchestra. "WHATEVER! The point is, the only way to get *over* an experience like that is to drink yourself *under* the table."

I sighed, my resolve slowly diminishing. Honestly, the longer I stayed out, the more likely the General and all his DSA minions would be the ones to drag Ollie in. I really wasn't that eager to go home and deal with my family.

I could probably tell my mother that I was obligated to take Astra out and entertain her, as part of my job. It's not like she could fuss at me in front of a couple of white girls without "losing face." My mother could never be what you called "taciturn," or "soft-spoken," but when it came to airing out family grievances in front of non-family, she tended to keep it on the DL.

"Fine," I sighed again, taking my cellphone out and sending a brief text to my mother. "But you only get ONE SONG tonight, CeeCee. Better make it count."

Five Hours Later

"WHAT'S CEECEE'S SONG COUNT?" Hope screamed in my ear over the drunken din inside the Salty Mermaid.

"I HAVE NO IDEA. SIX MAYBE?" I yelled back. "MORE JELLO SHOTS?" I offered her a fluorescent gelatin shooter that glowed highlighter yellow in the black lights of the bar.

She grimaced. "I GOTTA CONFESS—I'M REALLY NOT THAT MUCH OF A FAN OF JELLO."

I shrugged, slid a finger around the inside edge to dislodge the alcoholic gelatin, and downed the shot. "MORE FOR ME!"

"HOW MANY OF THOSE HAVE YOU HAD?" she yelled.

"WHY DOES IT MATTER?"

"BECAUSE I'M PRETTY SURE ANY OF THE LIMITS YOU SET ON THE NIGHT HAVE BEEN SMASHED."

"SMASHING LIMITS IS TOTALLY FEMINIST!" an oddly melodious shriek floated into our ears. I looked to my right. CeeCee had just exited the stage, still holding on to her microphone. "ALSO BY THE WAY," CeeCee continued, flicking a button on her wrist watch. The ambient noise of the bar was instantly muffled. "Cone of silence, much?"

My jaw dropped, which was unfortunate because I still had some yellow jello in it. CeeCee calmly closed my mouth for me. I swallowed gratefully, then stared some more. "What the hell, CeeCee?"

"Eh, the Verne-types at DSA headquarters who gave me my megaphone also gave me this thing, just in case my powers malfunction in some way? It'll contain my sound waves, you know? Just in case I, like, accidentally cause a sound apocalypse or whatever."

"Pause," Hope said, holding up a completely sober, steady hand (so, *so* unfair). "You could potentially cause a sound apocalypse?!"

CeeCee shrugged tipsily. "Eh, nobody really knows? I *totally* have this weird psychic ability with my voice where, like, everybody turns into my drooling minion. And also sometimes my higher notes give people totally hinky physical reactions? Like, sometimes people's ears bleed or whatever. It's hard to explain and PS: *I'm sort of drunk right now*. Nikki can explain better."

Hope slowly turned to me, an expectant look of horror on her face.

"Ummm..." Finding scientifically accurate words to describe CeeCee's weird power-set was *hard*....especially with this much alcoholic gelatin in my system. "Her voice vibrates at an as-yet-unknown frequency that seems to hypnotize people into doing whatever she says. But the frequency sometimes pyzo—physi—phi—it can cause ruptured blood vessels. But she has yet to target anybody unintentionally. Even when drunk."

Hope cocked her head to the side again, as if somebody was whispering into her ear. "My sources say CeeCee hasn't really been tested all that much in extreme circumstances, though?"

"Wait, what sources?" I asked, confused. "I mean sure, that's true, because it's not like CeeCee's been an official cape for all that long. She's had some sort of provisional internship with Camp Peary, but how would you even know that?"

"Ummm..." An awkward blush flooded her cheeks. "I got briefed...by...um...The General?"

"Wait, when?" I asked, suddenly suspicious. "I thought you just happened to be on the beach when Neptune hit. You didn't even know who the General was."

"Um, I was. On the beach, I mean. I talked to the General *after*. I just, um, got back from a trip...thing. Had to fly out to debrief in Washington."

"...What thing?" CeeCee asked, curiously. "Where'd you go?"

"Um...nowhere, really. Hope's blush deepened. "It was nothing."

"You just said it was a thing." I pointed out, drunkenly fixating on what she had just said. "How can it be *nothing* if it was *a thing?*"

"Jeez, you guys, you're literally being too *literary.*" CeeCee snarked. "If I wanted to experiment with a modern retelling of Odysseus versus the Cyclops, I wouldn't have dropped English 210. Bored bad, *singing better*. COME ON!" She yelped, bouncing like an extremely excited puppy. Switching off the cone of silence, she danced towards the stage.

"YES!" Hope exclaimed awkwardly, "KARAOKE SEEMS LIKE A GREAT IDEA."

"...Oooookay....?" I replied. "DIDN'T YOU JUST SAY—"

"THIS WILL BE SO MUCH FUN!" She yelled, dragging me across the bar and up the stage steps after CeeCee, a nervous, manic smile on her face. "I'VE NEVER DONE KARAOKE IN A BAR BEFORE."

"Cool story bro," CeeCee drawled sarcastically. The sound of the bar patrons diminished slightly as we got to center stage. "Just read the words on the screen and try not to sound super preppy, 'kay?"

"Wait, what?" Hope shrieked. "You picked a song already? What—"

"Oh, crap," I groaned, "CeeCee, you didn't—not—"

A thumping bass beat rumbled through the bar, syncopated sirens immediately following. "Oh *shit*," I glared up at the stage. "This is *so* not appro—"

"What song is this?" Hope whispered in a panic. "I don't listen to rap, I don't really—"

A high snare rhythm started to intersperse with the sirens. "Oh girl," I said, covering Hope's mic with my palm. "Pray to whatever god you worship that this doesn't end up on Viewtube."

"What do you mean?"

CeeCee pushed me away from Hope and shoved the mic in her face. "THAT'S YOUR CUE, SISTER-FRIEND!" she shouted, with admittedly, just a hint of her super-powered persuasion.

"Uhh...Uhh," Hope stared at the karaoke screen like a deer in the headlights. I cringed, steeling myself against embarrassment as she took a deep breath and belted out "*I don't wanna say/Fuck the authority—*"

and dropped her mic with a loud thud-crackle to clap her hands over her mouth, eyes wide with shock.

"Holy crap," I scream-whispered at Cee, over the thrumming beat of MC Shadez of Gray's villain rap track, *WillFully Blind*. "We just got Astra to drop the F-bomb. Suggestions?"

She snickered gleefully. "The show must go on." Gloriously unconcerned, she grabbed up Hope's mic and started to rap. "*—But What happens when/the big bad kills/And the Good Guys' skills/Include charging bills/Instead of cleaning up spills/And the media wants thrills/From Beverly Hills...*"

Hope stared at us, horrified. "I just cursed on stage!" she hissed at me through trembling fingers. "You just made me curse on stage!"

I squirmed. "Yeah, ummm...sorry about that," I whispered back. "This is sort of CeeCee's signature song."

"You *can't* be serious."

"Serious as a Catholic Auntie during Holy Week," I sighed. "But also, while she's rapping with that weird hypno-voice of hers, nobody's gonna notice us exiting the stage. C'mon." I grabbed her hand and slowly walked backwards, angling towards the shadowy steps at the left of the stage. Hope followed me stiffly, one hand still clapped over her mouth.

With CeeCee hypnotizing the whole bar, we managed to slide outside, unnoticed by any of the other patrons.

"I can't believe this," She moaned, slumping against the alley wall. "Quin is going to *kill* me."

"Wait, 'Quin'? You—you mean The Harlequin?" I sputtered.

"Yeah. She manages the PR for the Sentinels *and* the Young Sentinels," she explained. "And I've just performed the biggest Charlie Foxtrot *imaginable*."

"Oh, come on," I scoffed. "It can't be that bad."

"I'm *Astra*," Hope retorted, sounding like she was about to cry. She slid down the wall and sat on the sidewalk, hugging her legs. "My image is all about being the all-American, sweet innocent girl next door. I mean, people didn't even believe I was legally an *adult* until I got outed."

A guilty, sinking feeling flooded my stomach. "I'm sorry," I mumbled. "CeeCee probably just thought it was a harmless prank—"

A loud buzzing interrupted my apology. I grabbed my bag. "I'm sorry—I—"

She waved her hand at me graciously, yet somehow sarcastically, as if to say *No, no, please do stop your awkward yet completely necessary apology to answer a frivolous text instead of figuring out how to fix the nuclear bomb you just dropped on my career. I don't mind.*

I glared at her. "It's my *work* phone," I explained defensively. "It could be import—oh, *mother of pearl jam on FRENCH TOAST,* are you serious?"

"What?"

"Sorry, it's a long story, you see, my mom never let me curse when I was younger and—"

"No, no, not that," Hope interrupted impatiently. "I mean, sure, super interesting profanity substitute, but what does your text say?"

"Oh, um, well," I paused, unsure of how to explain. "You see, I have this annoying younger cousin Ollie, OK? And he's at the local creative arts governor's school as a Verne-Type performance art major and he's basically super horny and apparently super obsessed with proving society wrong and..."

"And...?"

"And earlier today he posted this video where he claimed "creator status" of the Neptune statue coming to life?"

"....and?"

I thought quickly. Well, relatively quickly. I was still pretty drunk. Better to leave out the part where I had actually found this out hours before the General had. "Aaaaand apparently that little 'performance art spectacle' was only the beginning of his 'campaign for enlightenment.'"

"What?!" Hope yelped, getting to her feet. "Way to bury the lead!"

"...How would you like to fix your PR snafu by stopping a mad, genius, hormonal, angsty pseudo-socialist teenager from recreating the battle of the Monitor and the Merrimac with automatons and laser cannons?" I asked.

She stared at me, dumbfounded. "Please tell me you're joking."

I smiled faintly. "He's just posted another video where he claims the reenactment will be 'a commentary on the futility of warfare as well as the mindless veneration of white historical patriarchy in the face of realism and oppression,'" I explained. "Honestly I think he just wants to see what happens when you give robot Confederate soldiers a shiny new metal boat and guns that go 'pew pew'."

"Why the heck can't the police just stop him if they're already aware of the performance?"

I grimaced. "They don't actually know where he's broadcasting from. He's posting these videos from some sort of secret bunker. He's a Verne-type, so he's got all sorts of software on his laptop to mask his IP address and make him untraceable. Not to mention, even if we did manage to track him down, we have no idea what sort of self-destruct booby traps he's rigged around his lair. I just got the message from the General—he thinks our best bet is to trap him at his performance tomorrow, and just hope things don't get nuclear."

"Nuclear?" Hope choked out.

"Not literally. I mean, I doubt he's gonna go for nuclear power *this* time, since the whole warfare-involving-futuristic-lasers thing means there's a huge risk of core breach and Ollie is generally really good at his technical designs. Even if his 'artistic vision' is somewhat misguided." Thinking back to Ollie's past *performative artistic engineering pieces*, I decided not to mention the fact that he focused more on the "artistic" part of creations, and not the "engineering" bits. The most consistent functional element he added to his creations was speakers, not an on/off switch.

She slowly started to bang the back of her head against the brick wall. "I feel like I should be used to weird situations by now," she mumbled, dropping her head into her arms. "But every time I think 'this can't possibly get more bizarre,' why yes, it does. With vengeance. And irony. And many, many hard to write incident reports."

Sliding down the brick wall, I crouched beside her and patted her back. "I'm sorry. This probably wasn't the vacation you signed up for."

She groaned and ran her fingers through her hair, leaning her head back against the wall. "Honestly? The vacation was an unexpected bonus. I finished my briefing with—I finished a couple days earlier than we thought I would. I haven't actually taken a real vacation since I got my powers three years ago."

"How long are you in town for?" I squelched my questions about her mysterious "briefing."

"The Sentinels lent me out to the DSA for two weeks. I've been here for ten days."

"Well that's alright then!" I said brightly. "Ollie's performance is scheduled for tomorrow. You'll still have three days of sunny beach time after that."

Hope stared at me. "Tomorrow? As in..." she paused, checking her watch, "...the day that started exactly one hour and seventeen minutes ago?"

I winced. "Guess Missy's running late with our ride then. You wanna be on drag-a-drunk-and-unwilling-siren-out-of-a-karaoke-bar duty, or do you want to attempt to find a cab right around last call?"

Hope grimaced. "Honestly? Neither sounds appealing." She started rummaging through her purse. "I was a little leery about trying this thing out, but your Verne-types assured me that it functioned well enough in beta tests...ah." She pulled out a black shiny metal brick.

I eyed it suspiciously. "What's that?"

"Hold on, let me just—" She fished out something that looked like a key chain remote. "Here we go." She placed the brick in the loading zone in front of the bar. "We should step back."

I stared at her. "Wait...you've got to be—"

She pressed a button on the keychain. With a series of metallic clicks, the brick slowly unfolded into a shiny, black SUV.

"SERIOUSLY?" I screeched. "They gave you a POCKET CAR?"

Hope looked at me innocently. "It's a loaner. They didn't give you one?"

"They won't even pay for my *parking!*" I hissed furiously. "You got a CAR THAT FITS IN YOUR PURSE?"

Hope grinned. "I'll just wait here then?"

I glared at her, turned, and stomped back into the club in a huff. *Celebrity capes.*

Chapter Three

"Operatives Typhoon and Nightingale later managed to subdue the suspect by utilizing available resources. Resources included a full bottle of vodka, a pair of novelty handcuffs, and the laces from a corset belonging to Nightingale's paramour. Agent Typhoon informs me that use of said laces was conditioned upon reimbursement for destruction of property, as well as dry cleaning bills for all civilian property requisitioned for the arrest."

After Action Report 5.12

7 AM, April 1, DSA Headquarters, Somewhere below Camp Peary
"So, are we clear on the plan, then?"
I looked up blearily from my fifth cup of coffee in two hours. "What?" I mumbled, half sarcastically, half confused from lack of sleep. "What plan?"
"Miss Aguilar, there is no need to be facetious. Your cousin's actions threatened the lives of many civilians and tourists today, and his encore performance has the potential to be even more dangerous."
This time, Special-Agent-In-Charge Hopper's crisp, no-nonsense schoolmarm tone instantly made me sit up straight and guiltily brush my hair back from my eyes. An iron-boned woman with icy blue eyes and steel-lined posture, SAC Ada Hopper was a military legend. Rumor was, back in her Army Ranger days, she assassinated a South American dictator by infiltrating his top-secret compound using only an Elizabeth Arden makeup compact, three steak knives, some dental floss, and the Spring Runway issue of Vogue. Hopper was also married to The General, but neither of them liked to talk about it much.
"Yes ma'am, I apologize. We are all clear on the plan."
I took a cautious look at the rest of my team. Cold Front rubbed his eyes and rotating his neck to crack it, probably as a by-product of sitting in the DSA War Room chairs since four AM. CeeCee's sobriety was still in question, especially considering that the only thing she had eaten since

her jello-shot-fueled karaoke performance was a plate of cheese fries and a diet cola (thoughtfully provided by the DSA cafeteria chefs upon hearing her rather impressive, word-perfect rendition of the entire third act of *Rent*).

Hope flashed me a chipper smile, looking annoyingly fresh— particularly because she had been in the War Room just as long as Cold Front had, after drinking twice as much as CeeCee. Despite our lightly chaotic night her uniform looked wrinkle-free, her hair non-greasy and immaculate, and her minimal good-girl eye makeup un-smudged. I, on the other hand, had sparkly black eyeliner smeared down my left cheek, my hair had died a limp and greasy death, and my fish scale-patterned uniform looked like an elephant's elbow.

In retrospect, Hopper probably wanted a helluva lot more affirmation from us than "clear on the plan." "We are one hundred percent alive and kicking and will not turn this into the final sequence of an '80s action flick" would probably have been more reassuring.

"Your team will deploy at precisely 1100 hours. I suggest you all get battle-ready." She sniffed, surveying our mostly disheveled status. "Please feel free to make yourselves presentable," she added crisply. "You may wish to visit the barracks' showers, Ms. Aguilar. And bring Ms. Tyler with you."

I grimaced and attempted to covertly swipe at the streak of black makeup on my face and look less like a KISS groupie. Hopper frowned at me as she left, but not before pointedly handing me a pocket comb from her jacket. I reached for it and sighed. "Whose turn is it for cowboy duty, Charles?"

Coldfront didn't even bother to lift his head from his crossed arms on the table. "Is that a serious question?" he mumbled sardonically.

"...Yeeeees?" I answered guiltily.

He raised his head a minimal inch from the table to fix me with a one-eyed death glare.

"Nicole Aguilar," he drawled, "are you the person responsible for the need to cowboy?"

"....Yes," I mumbled, even more guiltily.

"Did you have to leave two adorable six-year-old girls behind to report to DSA headquarters?"

"....Noooo...?"

"And, ultimately, whose cousin is responsible for this entire debacle in the first place?" he finished triumphantly.

"Mine," I admitted reluctantly. "Though, to be fair, he's more of a sec—"

"Don't make me freeze your swimsuit, girl," he threatened. "You think putting your tongue on a cold piece of metal is bad? I can make that happen with things that are *not* your tongue."

"Charles!" I winced. "I didn't say I *wouldn't*! You don't have to bring out the big guns!"

"Good," he said grimly. "Now go do your duty, cowboy."

"Fiiiiine," I grumbled. "CeeCee, come on."

"Come where?" CeeCee said, whirling around in her swivel chair. "Come why? Come how? *Comme ci comme ça*? Oops, not what I meant." She giggled.

"You know where we're going," I said through gritted teeth. I turned to Hope. "You wanna help?"

Hope looked at me, confused. "Help what? I have no idea what 'cowboy duty' means."

I waved towards CeeCee. "You know the phrase 'cowboy up'?" She nodded.

"You also heard the phrase 'fallen off the wagon'?"

Hope nodded again, comprehension slowly trickling across her face.

"We gotta get CeeCee off the Oregon Trail and up in her saddle. You know. Cowboy up, pardner!" I said, miming a whipping motion.

"Yeeeeeehawww!" CeeCee cackled, spinning in her chair. Her expression abruptly changing from gleefully schwasted to uncomfortably nauseated. "Ohh....I don't feel so good."

Hope sighed and gingerly took hold of CeeCee's chair. "Where do I roll her?"

I smiled. "First stop, the barracks' showers."

Two hours later, we sat in the DSA cafeteria. CeeCee was mumbling something rude (and Marxist) into her coffee cup, my face no longer resembled an avant-garde chimney sweep, and Hope was eyeing both of us in mildly impressed trepidation.

"So...I'm guessing cowboy duty is a regularly scheduled chore for you guys?" Hope asked cautiously, poking her scrambled eggs with her fork.

I shrugged, tearing into a warm biscuit smothered in apple butter. "Cold Front and the General seem to think that learning how to clean up after our own 'youthful recklessness' is part of our training."

"Seriously?"

"I mean, we're not exactly a high profile area, you know? Sure, we've got a ton of military bases, but the 757 is basically just a sleepy little group of cities that occasionally ends up in a travel brochure as a 'family friendly destination.'

She smiled wistfully. "My last real moment of 'youthful recklessness' turned into a nation-wide sex scandal—*so* unfair since it wasn't really. You're lucky you guys can party without paparazzi documenting every bad life decision."

I smiled in sympathy. "Yeah, I guess. I mean, I had my breakthrough when I was fifteen. CeeCee had hers even younger. We didn't really have a normal childhood, per se, but at least our awkward moments never got plastered all over the Internet."

"Yeah, except for the times when some desperate wannabe supervillain attempts to gain some notoriety," CeeCee pointed out, flicking through screens on her smartphone. "Speaking of which, have you seen Ollie's latest blog video?"

I raised an eyebrow. "Um...no? Since when do you follow Ollie's blog?"

CeeCee snorted. "Since I found out he posts all his devious plans ahead of time in order to get people to watch his 'protest art.' Duhh."

I moaned. "Why can't he just use Facebook like a normal person?"

CeeCee rolled her eyes. "He probably doesn't have enough friends in real life? Anyways, since the Neptune attack video went viral, people are actually starting to pay attention to him. Also, he's calling himself 'The Gepetto' now?"

I crinkled my nose. "Of course he is. How many potential spectators are we talking?"

"Well, his post has about 5,000 reblogs, and the local newspaper is linking to his announcement in its coverage of the whole Neptune thing. Oh hey!" she said, clicking on her screen, "There's a short video of all three of us at the karaoke bar! Cool...oh, no, oops. Not cool. Crap."

Hope's head whipped around. "What? What's wrong?"

"Um, well, ok, so, on a positive note, 'Astra drops the F-bomb' is only like five seconds long and SUPER crappy quality. Maybe people will think it's not really you?"

She turned bright red and mumbled something that sounded like "Shell" under her breath. "And the not-so-positive note?"

"...It has about 5 million views. Which, on the bright side, is WAY MORE than Ollie's video has, so at least we might be overshadowing him in the news!"

Hope made a sound somewhere between a teakettle and a forlorn kitten. "Oh my God," she whimpered, banging her head against the table. "I am so, so dead."

"Yo, chill!" I ordered, grabbing her plate before she splattered scrambled eggs all over the table. "I mean, like, I get you have an image and a brand to maintain or whatever, but what's one little curse word in the grand scheme of saving the world on a regular basis?"

She gave one last pathetic flop, her chin resting next to her orange juice. "You'd think it wouldn't matter at all. But it will. It always does. It's like having lettuce stuck in your teeth on picture day. Nobody ever forgets your awkward picture, even if you look fine all the other days. I'm gonna be a late night TV joke for *months*."

CeeCee scoffed. "It's an election year. I think you'll be fine."

"Yeah!" I chimed in, "And why would they care about grainy low quality footage of you possibly cussing when they could have high quality news helicopter footage of you fighting a hundred robot zombie Confederate soldiers with lasers? *On a boat!*"

She covered her eyes and whimpered.

"Did I just make it worse?" I whispered to CeeCee.

"Dude, you, like, are the worst pep talker ever," she whispered back. "And I say this as the girl who once drunkenly told Hopper that 'even if she had resting bitchy face, her figure was fly as hell.'"

Hope peeped through her fingers. "You didn't."

"Oh," CeeCee said drily, raising an eyebrow. "I assure you, I did. Or at least, Nikki assures me I did. Thankfully, I have very few memories of that banquet."

At least that made her smile, if somewhat reluctantly. "Well then, at least I have you guys to make sure the awkward moments are evenly distributed."

I clapped her on the shoulder, gathered my things, and stood up. "What else are teammates for?"

"Cowboy duty?"

"Now you're getting it!"

Chapter Four

"I'm a big fan of symbolism, but only, like, ironically. Symbolism is totes dead."

Cecelia, "CeeCee" Tyler, aka Nightingale, from her English 210 final paper, *Odysseus Sucks and Penelope Was a Lesbian: Queer Interpretation of Heteronormative Literary Canon.*

The Hampton Roads Bridge Tunnel, April 1, Noon
"Well this is the weirdest bait and trap assignment I think I've ever been on," Astra said, as she landed us on the roof of the Hampton Roads Bridge Tunnel control center. "Which, honestly? Is saying a lot."

I covertly attempted to pick at the wedgie caused by flying in a high-tech tankini. "Seriously? Didn't you save Chicago from like, a rampant Godzilla plague?"

Astra nodded. "Yeah, but that wasn't really a bait and trap. That was more a prevent-the-apocalypse sort of situation."

"Like that's LESS weird than 'catch the little arrogant prick of an evil genius' situation we have here today?" I casually made my fingers and toes erupt in tiny little octopus-like suckers and plopped down on the tilted roof, stretching my calf muscles. "We're just here to make sure nobody does anything stupid to provoke the zombie robots."

Astra looked slightly nauseated at my admittedly disturbing metamorphosis. "Zombie Civil War robo-sailors with lasers," she corrected after a moment. "And let's hope it doesn't get worse. Because as awful as a plague of gigantic plasma-breathing lizard monsters is, I can't even imagine what this will be like if things go...Charlie Foxtrot."

Grimacing, I nodded in agreement. "So when is this thing supposed to start anyways?"

"His video said 12:15," Nightingale answered, over comms. She was currently circling the area in a military helicopter equipped with a heavy-duty sound system. *"But it didn't say anything about what direction the ships would be coming from. Also, PS? There is a surprising*

amount of spectators here. I guess tourism really isn't dead in this town."

"Seriously. Aren't there any more historically accurate battle reenactments scheduled for today?" Cold Front replied from across the water, on top of the Chamberlin hotel. "Guess we'll all just have to keep our eyes peeled then. Knowing Ollie, those ships could be coming from anywhere."

Suddenly, Astra zoomed up and away from the bridge, angling her body almost completely horizontal. "Uhhhh, guys? Does the water look...oddly bubbly to you?"

Leaning out as far as I could, I gripped the concrete roof with my suckers and peered at the water below. "Um...maybe? I don't have your super-vision, though."

"Confirmed," The General barked into our earpieces. "Surveillance cameras show that the water is, indeed, bubbling. Be on high alert, team."

"Aye, aye, Captain." Nightingale replied, sarcastic, yet oddly upbeat.

Astra snorted, then pointed at a specific point about 500 feet from our spot on the bridge tunnel, where even I was could see a weird spread of white bubbly water. "I think I see something coming up in the center of that circle."

I squinted. "Are you serious?"

"Yep," Nightingale confirmed. "I got it through my binoculars. He's coming from down under."

"How does a seventeen-year-old kid even build a rig like that anyways?" I muttered, snapping on my battle goggles and stuffing my hair into a swim cap. "Like, seriously, what type of permit would you even need? A 'temporary underwater super villain lab slash laboratory form 12 b or something?"

"Probably available at the local DMV," Cold Front quipped. "Where IS Ollie, by the way?"

"He likes 'melting into the crowd' at his own events," I explained. "Something about the artist 'truly submerging himself into the experience of his audience, thus gaining complete understanding of his work through symbiosis.' Or something. I don't know, but it's really awkward when like nobody shows up."

Astra growled in frustration. "Well, he's not gonna have that problem here," she commented, scanning the crowd of what I guessed had to be about 300 tourists, drunk college students, and news teams. "What's the outdoor equivalent of a full house?"

"A headache," I replied grimly. "Anybody got eyes on the boats yet?"

"*You mean 'ships,'*" Cold Front corrected. "*I got several uncles in the navy who would be pissed that you would use the word 'boat' to describe the Monitor and the Merrimack.*"

"What are we even looking for anyway?" Astra asked.

I shrugged. "I'm not sure. I looked it up on Wikipedia—apparently the Monitor looked like a 'floating cheese box?' Whatever that means. Knowing Ollie, it'll probably look like something out of a steampunk wet dream."

"*More like 'The Terminator: But Wet',*" Nightingale said. "*Check it— they look like something my post-apocalyptic-death metal-cyberpunk ex-boyfriend would wear as a hat.*"

I stared at the two boats—no, ships—that had finally (and dramatically) risen to the surface of the bay. Nightingale's description was surprisingly accurate. Both ships looked oddly hat shaped, with double layer decks rising out of a flat base. Lines of zombie robot soldiers decorated the decks—dark blue ones on the Monitor, and silver ones on the Merrimack. You could tell that Ollie had at least gotten the army colors right, because both of the ships had their names emblazoned on the side in blinking, neon red fluorescent lighting. And every robo-soldier was armed with what looked like a laser blaster— because apparently, nothing says "war is hell" better than unnecessary futuristic guns.

"LADIES AND GENTLEMEN," Ollie's voice boomed across the water as he slowly ascended from the waves on a tiny platform off to the side of the ships. "...but especially the ladies!" He blew a couple of kisses into the crowd.

I almost vomited. Nothing is quite so nausea-inducing as your evil little cousin hornballing while possibly destroying an entire ocean front. With lasers.

"YOU ARE HERE TO WITNESS HISTORY. HISTORY IN THE SENSE OF RECREATION, BUT ALSO HISTORY IN THE SENSE OF PROCREATION. I DEMAND THE ATTENTION OF SOCIETY. I COMMAND THIS SYMPHONY OF WOE AND THE CRIES OF MY PROLETARIAT BRETHREN. LET THE BATTLE...REBEGIN!"

"Is that 'blending in with the audience?" Astra quipped.

"Guess he wanted his moment in the spotlight," I sighed, rising to my feet and stretching my arms, just as an enormous explosion echoed across the bay.

The first fifteen minutes were uneventful enough. Well, as uneventful as 100 robot zombie soldiers shooting red and green lasers at each other, all while floating on metal ships could ever be "uneventful." I sent a silent, hopeful prayer to St. Jude (the patron saint of lost causes) that we would just get out of here with nothing more serious than a couple of "boos" at Ollie's terrible attempt at socio-political commentary.

Then a group of drunk frat boys decided that the performance really needed some audience participation. Since they had already consumed the entirety of their beer stash, they decided to dispose of the cans...by throwing them directly at the battle.

"NO!" Ollie shouted. "DO NOT PROVOKE THE CYBORGS!"

An ominous *whirring* sound echoed across the water as 200 robo-sailors raised their laser cannon arms and fired a simultaneous blast at three airborne cans of Natty Light. A sonic *whoomph* hit my chest square on as the cans exploded in shower of red and green sparks. The crowd ooohed and ahhhed, because hey, who doesn't love free fireworks?

But the problem was that the cyborgs didn't stop right there and go back to their play, like human actors would. Instead, the ships started steaming towards the spectators, guns literally ablazing. The crowd erupted in shrieking chaos as everybody tried to get away from the onslaught of lasers.

"THAT'S OUR CUE!" Cold Front yelled over the comms. *"OPERATION BATTLEHYMN IS A GO!"*

"Cold Front, see if you can hit the decks with a big wave. Aim for the soldiers, knock 'em into the water. Make sure Ollie is out of the line of fire." The General barked calmly. *"We need him safe and able to advise. Nightingale, use the evacuation schematics I gave you to control the crowd. Astra, Typhoon, you're in charge of neutralizing the threat. Go. NOW."*

Astra sprang into action, grabbing me by the armpits and swooping towards the choppy water, where Cold Front had already managed to submerge several robots. "JUST DROP ME FIFTY YARDS BEHIND THE SHIPS," I screamed up at Astra.

"You sure?" She asked.

"Trust me!" Somewhere in the distance, I could hear Nightingale's calming voice directing the crowds to evacuate in an orderly, pre-planned pattern. Thank God for the General's obsession with detail.

Astra fell into an eye watering 60 degree dive and released me. I'd spent most of my training practicing high-speed aquatic drops exactly like this. I jack-knifed my body downwards, angling my arms in a streamlined point, gills forming over my ribs, my legs fusing together in a marlin tail. Hitting the cold water like a hot knife through snow, I sped through the waves doing my best to get a good visual of the boats' positions through my vision-enhancing goggles.

"Typhoon, you are directly under the Monitor," the General advised me. *"If these robots are anything like the King Neptune statue, your electric powers should be enough to neutralize them."* The General advised me.

Tapping the mini-microphone on my goggles twice—my underwater code for "affirmative"—I zoomed upwards, arms tingling with electricity. I hit the metal hull with as big of a charge as I dared, feeling the zap echo through my muscles. The underwater propeller instantly stopped. I quickly re-formed my legs, and turned my arms into tentacles, clambering my way on board, reabsorbing my gills.

Unfortunately, my creature-from-the-Black-Lagoon themed entrance must have tripped some sort of sensor in the cyborgs' system. As soon as my head cleared the deck, the five nearest robots turned on me. The first laser blast grazed my scalp, burning a nasty-smelling hole through my rubber swim cap. Ducking down, I hardened my skin into oyster shell armor, wrapped my tentacles around the railing of the ship, and *vaulted* up over the deck. Landing with a crash on top of some unlucky robo-sailors, I waded through the mess of Yankee automatons, my tentacles whipping through the crowd, shocking each robot I touched.

"Ollie says that there's a pilot's compartment near the cannon of each ship," Cold Front informed me through comms. *"He built it in case the autopilot function crashed. If you can get there without damaging the onboard controls, you can override the robot's programming with an emergency kill switch."*

I hissed as a laser blast hit the back of my neck, chipping away my oyster shell skin. The cannon was on the other end of the deck. "Seriously? Who puts the kill switch IN THE MIDDLE OF THE THING IT'S SUPPOSED TO KILL?"

"Ollie says that he had a remote kill switch, but dropped it in the Bay when he was 'gesturing dramatically.' Also, he wants me to remind you that as his Ate, *it is your job to protect him, not kill him."*

I growled in frustration. Ollie was right: As his *Ate*, my aunties would have *my* head if Ollie (or anybody else for that matter) got hurt in all of this. Totally unfair, but who was I to argue with an army of elderly Filipina ladies, armed with wagging fingers and guilt-inducing glares?

"Tell him that he owes me big time for his crappy design skills. I'm going in."

I risked a look to my left to see how Astra was handling the Merrimack. Ripping one of the cannons off of its mount, she cheerfully dropped it right over the ship. It punched an enormous hole in the deck, crushing several robots in the process.

Huh. Not bad.

Angling my path away from the edge of the ship, I cut a diagonal line through the onslaught of robo-sailors with my electric tentacle arms. I tried to conserve my energy with brief bursts instead of prolonged shocks—I had to move quickly and electricity took a lot out of me. Ducking and spinning away from suppressive fire, I managed to get to the control center—only to find that a stray laser blast had melted the door shut.

"ARE YOU FRICKIN KIDDING ME?!" I screamed in frustration, kicking at the door. "The DOOR is melted? Ollie didn't LASER-PROOF THE FRICKIN DOOR?"

"On it! Stay where you are!" Astra cried into my comms. I turned just in time to see her plow a mass of robots off the tilted deck of the sinking Merrimack, then launch herself into the air.

"Holy shit," I murmured as she landed on the deck next to me, laser blasts ricocheting off her skin like armor.

"Yeah, I get that a lot," she quipped, eyeing the door. "Hey Cold Front, did Ollie say where the controls are in relation to the door?"

"He says they are right across, about five feet off the deck."

"Excellent," she chirped, as she punched an on-rushing cyborg in the head. Grabbing his laser blaster as he fell, she carved a hole through the top of the door, floated up and *yanked*. The door groaned off its hinges and I dove through the doorway, looking for the switch. *And, of course*—there were about a hundred different switches, and at least as many buttons.

"OK, what type of kill switch isn't bright red and covered in a glass bubble?" I complained.

Nightingale giggled in our comms. *"Have you tried turning it on and off again?"*

"Ollie says to look for the big black toggle underneath the panel," Cold Front relayed helpfully.

I groaned and slid a tentacle cautiously underneath the control board, finding something that felt like an enormous pinball flipper. "Got it." I flicked it forward.

Nothing happened.

"Ollie says you have to do it five times in quick succession in order to kill everything—he made it that way in case he accidentally hit it with his foot."

I muttered a recipe for Ollie-flavored barbecue, and flicked the switch five times. In quick succession. With a beautiful sizzling crackle, all laser fire ceased. I clambered out of the pilothouse, my tentacles slowly turning back into normal arms. I breathed a laser-smoke filled sigh of relief as I was greeted by a tableau vivant of frozen cyborgs. Exhausted, I slid down to the deck, leaning against the wall, suddenly aware of the fact that I was naked from the waist down. *Son of a bitch.*

Hope landed beside me. "Want a towel?" she asked, politely averting her gaze.

"No. Give me a drink."

Epilogue

"Something, something, something, feminism, something, something, yay, whoo, bad robots dead. The end."

Nightingale's verbal after-action report, following Operation Battlehymn.

The next day, Hope, CeeCee and I lounged on the sandy goodness that is Virginia Beach, lazily sunning ourselves.

Cleanup had been relatively easy once the cyborgs had been deactivated. Cold Front had swept them up with some wind and waves. Then Astra and I had piled them onto a barge to get carted away to DSA headquarters. Officially speaking, DSA had been interested in the "ingenuity" and "creativity" of Ollie's designs, enough to grant him a "summer internship" at some secret headquarters down south. No word on *where* exactly that "internship" would be, and any of Ollie's questions about "credit for school" were met with icy, scary silence and tight-lipped military glares.

I wasn't too worried about the kid—he was still a minor, after all, and who knew what the DSA really wanted with his designs. Besides, "summer internship" was a magical phrase that got the Army of Aunties off my back.

I stretched out on my towel, happily sipping an iced tea. "So... you enjoying your first real vacation in three years?"

Hope gave a long, contented sigh. "This is bliss. A little boring...but bliss."

CeeCee grinned lazily, flipping through a fashion magazine. "Being bored is a luxury. Enjoy it."

"Oh, I am," she reassured her, flipping over on her stomach and grabbing her soda. "Believe me, this is me, enjoying boredom. My meager, two days of boredom."

A football sailed towards us, knocking over CeeCee's bottle of...something. I shrieked, my glowy, sunny reverie ruined by cold stickiness.

"Sorry, ladies!" A blond teenage boy came jogging towards us. "My buddy made a bad pass." He surveyed us, checking us out. "If you can manage it, would you pass that back? You don't have to throw it if you can't."

We all looked at each other and burst into giggles. *Seriously?*

Hope smiled innocently, reaching for the ball. "Yeah, I'll throw it. But I should tell you, I throw *like a girl.*"

CeeCee and I grinned wickedly at each other and sat back, drinks in hand, to enjoy the show. It was going to be a fun two days.

AFTERWORD

So here's where I get to talk about myself again. Life moves on, and it's been five years since I took a gamble and indie-published *Wearing the Cape*. It's been a wild ride that's introduced me to great people and allowed me to fulfill every wordsmith's dream of being able to actually support himself with his wordsmithery. (Actually that's not my *dream* dream—just a stepping stone on my way to it.) So I still live in Las Vegas, a fascinating town I have yet to write one word about. I still plan on finishing *Worst Contact*, my deeply unserious space epic. I continue to polish my craft, and look forward to expanding my experience with a few selected book/comic/game conventions in the coming year while picking up my writing speed. Oh, and I'm set to produce *Wearing the Cape: The Roleplaying Game* (watch for news on the Wearing the Cape Facebook page and in the WtC newsletter), fulfilling yet another dream. It really has been a great ride, and don't worry, I've got plenty more stories to tell of Astra and her friends. 2017 is going to be a great year; I hope you enjoy it with me.

Marion G. Harmon

Printed in Great Britain
by Amazon